Praise for Discovery

"THIS TALE'S CHARACTERS ARE AS FASCINATING as they are eccentric, and cosmic dread looms over it all. But it's much more than 'Tarantino meets Lovecraft.' *Discovery* transcends genre to explore the big questions about our place in all this vastness. And we might not want to hear the answers." -PHILIP CHASE, author of *The Edan Trilogy*

"ONCE THIS COSMIC MYSTERY/THRILLER HAS YOU in its tentacles, it doesn't let go. J.A.J. Minton is a serious talent and has made a wonderfully rich contribution to the world of story with *Discovery*." -JACQUELYN HAGEN, author of *The Riverfall Chronicles* series

"THIS BOOK HELPED US 'DISCOVER' ONE THING: J.A.J. Minton created a masterpiece. The plot is fresh and thrilling from start to finish. World-building is brilliantly realized. *Discovery* blew our minds; all two remaining brain cells. We gawk in supreme awe. 5/5 stars." - Austin & Richard, *2 to Ramble*

"IN THEIR ELECTRIFYING DEBUT, J.A.J. MINTON weaves a genre-bending masterpiece that hurtles readers through a labyrinth of rich characters, cosmic entities, and edge-of-your-seat thrills—seamlessly blending sci-fi, fascinating cosmic horror, and heart-pounding suspense into an unforgettable page-turner." -BRIAN BELL, *BellTube*

"*DISCOVERY* IS A DEBUT AUTHOR'S DREAM! In a word: SENSATIONAL. J.A.J. Minton has arrived." -ANDREW MATTOCKS, *Andrew's Wizardly Reads*

"...A DELECTABLY ECCENTRIC, THEATRICAL, ATMOSPHERIC SMORGASBORD of bohemian delight that pushes the boundaries of conventional fiction in all the right ways, and defies being defined..." -P.L. STUART, author of *The Drowned Kingdom* saga

STRANGE EONS: BOOK ONE

Discovery

J.A.J. Minton

KEYHOLE
BOOKS

Salisbury, North Carolina

Paperback ISBN: 979-8-9923582-0-9
E-Book ISBN: 979-8-9923582-1-6
Library of Congress Control Number: 2025901872

"I Am So Proud" from *The Mikado* (1885), words by W.S. Gilbert, music by Arthur Sullivan. Public domain.
"Die Moritat von Mackie Messer [Mack the Knife]" from *Die Dreigroschenoper [The Threepenny Opera]* (1928), words by Bertolt Brecht, music by Kurt Weill. Public domain. Translated from German by the authors.
"My Gallant Crew / I Am the Captain of the Pinafore" from *HMS Pinafore* (1878), words by W.S. Gilbert, music by Arthur Sullivan. Public domain.
"Oh, Men of Dark and Dismal Fate" from *The Pirates of Penzance* (1879), words by W.S. Gilbert, music by Arthur Sullivan. Public domain.
"Ozymandias" (1818) by Percy Bysshe Shelley. Public domain.

A Keyhole Books Edition
355 Faith Road, PMB 1044, Salisbury, NC 28146
www.jajminton.com

First Edition

"That is not dead which can eternal lie,
And with strange aeons even death may die."
—H.P. Lovecraft, "The Nameless City"

"Humankind cannot bear very much reality."
—T.S. Eliot, *Four Quartets*

Contents

Overture

Kingdom of Tonga

April 1992

IT HAS TAKEN A defeat from the first child of the cosmos for me to notice that my plan has been compromised.

Go over it again.

What did he say? *This was just an opening move, a taste of my game before I really get going.*

He took my queen. He took her—I could not breathe.

He was in my face: *You don't need air.*

He took he took he took—

Stop this. He has gone now.

Do not panic.

Look everywhere.

He took he took he took my arm my queen my plan he took he took—I cannot breathe—

You don't need air.

Focus!

First, conjure the island: mountains of calcified sea skeletons latching onto an underwater volcanic peak, then latching upon each other, layer upon layer, eon after eon, until the cadaverous mass rises from the ocean.

This is a scene millions of years in the making.

Good. More—

See the man: a wisp at the edge of the island. An aloha shirt plastered with parrots and pineapples sticks to his back. Sweat bubbles through the zinc oxide sunscreen in his bald spot and aviator sunglasses deflect hostile tropical sun. "Fuck you, Jonah P. Reynolds, Executive Producer of Let It Rip Productions!" A streamer of thermal paper clatters in his raised fist. "Who the fuck are you to fax me this, Jonah P. Reynolds?"

The man stomps across the sandbar. Trillions of skeletons crunch under the soles of his Gucci boat shoes. "You don't want to find the submarine anymore, ya chicken shit? You don't want to make television history? You don't like money, Jonah? Pompous womp! Suck a bag of dicks!"

Overseeing the proceedings is a wild pig. Teats on her mud-lined belly sway as she adjusts her hooves atop a limestone boulder. Her baritone snuffle echoes in rocky crevices where meaty crustaceans hide.

"Jonah, you motherfuck—" The man chokes on a mosquito. "You have questions about me finishing this expedition? I *am* this expedition, you Brooks Brothers-wearing bitch! I don't see you here on this hot and humid beach running this lazy crew, and I certainly don't see you in that hole called a 'hotel.' And I *would* see you, Jonah! Because I have to sleep with the fucking lights on to keep lizards and roaches from crawling straight up my asshole! I have not kept my anal chute pristine all these years for that brand of bestiality, Jonah!"

Beyond the sandbar: a natural harbor of rusted boats, shipping containers, and prefabricated huts. There, the man's chartered boat groans against its mooring.

"Aw, shit!" He smacks his head. Zinc oxide smears. "I forgot to thank you, Jonah! Remember when you begrudgingly upgraded our charter from the 30-foot vomit comet? Oh, my raw intestines thank you for approving that expense! Now, I have a 60-foot duct-taped rust bucket parked over there in the banana boat lot! And I named it, Jonah! I named it *Rosie* after my dead, sainted mother because I can't pronounce the real name of it. Why does every name here sound like a deaf toddler wailing?"

On the boat's deck, three American technicians and eight islanders wait out the man's fury. They suck on cigarettes and swing their legs over bobbing waters. Sometimes they glance in the man's direction. Mostly, they meditate on the changing tide.

"Two summers ago, when the entire human population lined up for that jingoistic sinking submarine movie, *I* was the one that had the vision to find the real sub!" He grabs his collar, releasing a storm of sweat droplets. "Where is the *Polaris* sub? Where could it be? Woo-woo! Mystery! And who wanted to solve the mystery of where it went? Me! Manny di Martini!"

Deep in the belly of his chartered ship: video cameras, microphones, and cables. Dangling off the back end on a hydraulic winch: a coffin-sized titanium cage. Inside is an array of underwater cameras and lights. He calls the unit *Yuna II*.

"*I* had the vision! Me! Manny! *I* was the one who found Dr. Down-On-His-Luck oceanographer selling his camera rig for pennies. Good thing, because no one else was going to build a contraption that could go that deep, not on your chintzy budget. And it was *my* idea to name that rig *Yuna II* after that ditch-faced Jap whore in the *Polaris* movie! The press ate that shit with a knife and fork! And didn't I shriek that name for the press circus just like in the movie? *Yuuuunnnnnaa!* Woo-woo! I'm Jonah's press monkey!"

When the man's boat braves the open ocean, its rear winch unfurls miles of cable so the camera cage can glide into the extreme deep sea, into the midnight zone. In those sunless spaces, creatures levitate like transparent specters and communicate with dazzling bioluminescence. Their metabolism and breathing run among the slowest on the planet. Time moves differently down there.

The man skids on a ten-thousand-year-old coral polyp. "Shit!" He picks up his pace. "Here I've been, Jonah, six days on the open ocean, dragging *Yuna II*, looking for the USS fucking *Polaris*! I look, and I look. I am mowing the lawn of the entire South Pacific with that camera rig! And do you know what transmits up to my little TV monitors on the bridge? Silt!"

Siren songs of the deep have called out for exploration since before humans evolved to listen.

"Day one: silt! Day two: also silt. Day three: a solid 12-hour recording of silt. On and on. Days four, five, six. Silt! Silt! Silt! So much silt on video that no one in this godforsaken nation meets me at the dock anymore to beg for dailies! So much silt that the press all has flown home to sleep with the lights off like regular people! Now, whenever we go out, I don't get to fire my gun to scare off the pirates who want to jump my claim!"

There is a reason no humans have seen that submarine since 1943.

"Because no one believes I can find it anymore, Jonah!"

The *Polaris* found something.

"Silt! Silt! Motherfucking silt!"

And the *Polaris* crew took the secret of their discovery to their watery graves. That is my design.

February 1943. Humans warred on an epic scale.

The *Polaris* was patrolling with 78 hands on board in a contested area in the South Pacific. The sub sent a message to headquarters that they had taken a hit resulting in minor leaking that could be repaired at sea. She requested to continue her patrol. She was denied, and ordered to return to an allied base in Australia for assessment.

There was no reply.

One hundred and fifty-two further calls to *Polaris* went unanswered.

One day later, outside the war zone, a lonely fishing vessel spotted a submarine cruising on the surface at a breakneck speed. That fisherman described the distinctive shape of a United States Navy *Gato*-class boat. He captured her acoustic signature, which later revealed it to be *Polaris*. She was 2,146 miles away from her patrol, moving southeast, away from the fighting. "Wherever she was going," the fisherman said, "she was going there fast."

No one ever saw the sub again.

A month later, the US Navy declared *Polaris* to be lost with all hands.

Since then, treasure hunters have combed the seas for the *Polaris* wreck, hoping to surface with a grim souvenir from inside. But no one knew for certain where the boat sank. Statisticians from multiple countries projected potential locations—all different, all hundreds of miles apart, all thousands of feet under the surface.

The ranting man is here with his own calculations. He intends to succeed where others have failed.

"Jonah, how am I ever going to find that sub when these islanders won't work on a Sunday? Wasn't that a surprise at sea?! Wouldn't move from the galley! Won't work a second past 3:00 pm, either! At 3:00 on the dot, they drop their shit to get to Probably the Best Bar in Tunk-Gah! That's not conjecture, Jonah. That's the actual name of the joint!"

The *Polaris* was not the first to discover my secret.

In 1918, a British cargo ship caught fire in the waters off Tonga and sank. All aboard were presumed dead.

In 1902, an Australian passenger steamer was lost in a typhoon near the coast of Tonga. All aboard were declared dead.

1837: an American whaling ship was scuttled between Fiji and Tonga after a mutiny. All were presumed dead.

1747: a third-rate ship of the French Royal Navy went missing with all hands after passing Tonga. All were declared dead.

A Japanese fishing boat went missing. All were presumed dead.

A tugboat with a single island trader aboard never returned. Dead.

An Australian aboriginal fleet passing Tonga en route to fishing grounds disappeared. Dead.

My design has always worked as intended.

Some heeded these signs. South Pacific islanders have always sensed a dreaded presence nearby. They constructed their myths around unseen dangers seeping from the waters off their coast, driving them to madness. "Stay away," they said to each other. "Do not look." Clever humans.

The man hocks a spitball and wets the sand heap. "Between your purse strings, tighter than my ex-wife's ass, and these islanders' lackluster work ethic, I deserve all the credit for getting this far, Jonah!"

He is different from the ones who came before. His audacity, his ship, his cameras, this era—they are all different. Unlike the others, this man intends to broadcast images from the deep. This man plays a god: omniscient, but not so wise. Humans! Evolutionary curiosities! Pure mayhem, an illogical use of free will, beautiful, contradictory, and flawed. They are out of control. Impulsive, aggressive. They will not stop. They cannot handle what they seek.

But I saw this coming. I witnessed the millions of miles of undersea fiber-optic cables connecting distant landmasses. I heard dial-up internet screeching its newborn cries. Further still, portable video cameras now allow humans to see beyond the scope of their own eyes. What is down there can be extracted from the depths—the titanium camera array can be winched back to the surface, the tapes collected, their images distributed to all who possess a VCR and the ape-like ability to extend a phalange to press *play*.

Eventually humans *will* see what is down there. If not this man, then another will surely come. My design will not hold.

Worse, I am not what I once was. My reflexes have slowed, and my vision impaired.

"You say that I'm out of time? I'm out of moves?"

Yet, despite my weakness, I developed a spectacular plan to avert disaster. I was going to work *with* their technology. I was going to direct humans to *my* purpose. I thought I was ready. This raving man should *not* have been a catastrophe.

"Well, fuck you, Jonah P. Reynolds! Manny's got *moves*!"

No. Not him.

The unforeseen catastrophe was Chaos.

He came at my weakest moment. He looked over my plans and lauded them—all my players on the board, lined up like soldiers, a brilliant line of defense. Then, he asked me, "Do you see *my* player on the board?"

I panicked.

Chaos giggled. Giggled like a child. "That player will remain hidden. For now." He was enjoying himself. "I've been busy, too. Oh, pleeeeease. Tell me you've noticed."

No. I did not. I still do not. I had missed something, some person, some indication of interference—

Yes, others have come to test me, and that was expected—for what I guard is too powerful to ignore. They are lesser beings, servants of despair and entropy attempting to subvert the scheme. Formidable, but of no concern.

But Chaos is another story.

"This was just an opening move," he said to me, "a taste of my game before I really get going."

He took—

I couldn't breathe—

He took he took he took—

Focus!

Chaos is coming again. He said so. I edge closer to death with every revolution around the sun. I must preserve my remaining abilities. How I apply them, when I apply them, it must all be calculated to achieve the greatest effect.

But first, I must sift backward through time to find his player on the board. I must uncover his plan. Otherwise, the past eons—all those deaths, all that destruction, all that sacrifice—will be for nothing.

If I fail, the fabric of the cosmos will rip.

Look again.

See: eons of coral protruding from the sea. The island. The man. The wild pig. The rusty boat. The crew. The voice. "Jonah P. Reynolds! Please fax me a copy of your rules! Tell me, Jonah, you flabby fuck, what hoops do I have to jump through? How much shit do I have to slurp off your fucking shoe, huh?"

The man narrates the story of his final days. And what is a story but order from Chaos?

"Give me a measurement, Jonah! Pick up that Montblanc from your executive desk and put a checkmark on the dick that I have to suck to learn your fucking rules!"

Like thunder, this man's voice carries far.

"You think you can screech off a fax to tell me you're picking up your bat and ball to go home? Well, I built this fucking ballpark!"

He knows not what he does.

"Without Manny, there's no league! Me! Manny!"

His rage is a prayer.

"I will say when this game is rained out! And I say, no! It is not! I say I will get this shit FINISHED!"

Look now.

Another approaches.

Sauntering through the sand, tropical flower tucked behind the ear, he wears a halter of eye-aching fuchsia and a sarong knotted at the waist. His hips wiggle as he glides into the fury. Magenta-painted lips slither into a grin. Lazily, he drags a piece of driftwood behind him, slicing into the sand his cosmic designs, wormhole paths, and constellation maps. A wave pulls his illustrations into the ocean. He speaks with the breathy whisper of a silver-screen starlet: "Wheeeee."

Of course, Chaos would never miss a show.

His sights are set on the raging man. A penciled eyebrow arches. He blinks once. Twice. His violet eyes swirl with the sickening perspective of a gravity-free flight through nebulae. Veiny reds and pinks balloon with white gaseous clouds, pulsating like the very heart of the cosmos. He blinks again and it is gone. "Mr. Manny! Mr. Martini! Yoo-hoo!"

Startled, the raging man visors a hand against his sunglasses to see who is calling. He releases the streamer of fax paper, which flutters down the sandbar. The wild pig catches it and devours it.

The magenta man hoots and claps. "Good show! Good show! Goodie, goodie!"

An ember in the soul of Manny di Martini ignites. His face smooths. His chest broadens. His rage dissolves. He is on stage.

The stranger eyes him, adjusting the flaming flower behind his ear. Manny di Martini's prayers are about to be answered with a sacred covenant.

And here, time slows.

In a flicker of a second, something else pulls at Manny di Martini. It is a competing force, almost too faint to sense.

Look. Listen.

On the far side of the island, a primitive limestone trilithon looms. The ancient islanders, the elder seafarers, placed the 40-ton stones precisely. They comprise a celestial map, a runway to the sea. Through it, the elders still speak. The old warning myths they have woven are strong here, electric. The island tells Manny, *Run away. Danger.*

Another wave of magenta-polished press-on nails. "*Mālō e lelei*, Mr. Manny! Follow me!" Hips twitching, he turns, swishing to the far end of the sandbar.

The setting sun backlights a corrugated shack. In all the days Manny has been on this island, he has never seen it before.

Run away. Do not follow.

Streaks of rust cake its wavy roof. Faded paint on weather-beaten wood promises: *Definitely the* Best *Bar in Tonga!* A neon martini glass tips an unnaturally green olive toward the open doors, warm with the glow of a television inside. Faintly, he hears his own voice from a long-ago broadcast. The television audience applauds. The sound prods Manny's heart into a full gallop.

"Follow meeeee!"

Do not—

The stage is set. The curtain rises. Manny hears ghostly applause swelling. Louder. For him. All for him.

Do not—

But the force of nature pulls the man like the moon pulls the tides. Manny di Martini now radiates joy like a star incandescent with nuclear fission. Even the pig pauses chewing the fax to bask in the heat of him.

Manny takes one Gucci-soled step into the spotlight.

And a new era begins.

Act I

Nessa Decker
and the Mogul

New York City
May 1, 1992

1

Portrait of a Lady

One Month Later

NESSA HAD BEEN ON hold for over an hour with the Pentagon's press office when a rumor spread through the news building that legendary journalist Griff Tran had made it out of the South Pacific debacle alive and Howard Winfield held the proof in his penthouse office. "Alive," the news team whispered. "And Griff's funeral was held yesterday!" No body for the burial—an empty casket, just like the rest who didn't come back from Manny di Martini's deep-sea diving stunt.

A rookie news researcher popped up from her cubicle. "Griff Tran made it out, did you hear?"

"Sit down," Nessa said. "And don't repeat rumors."

"Why not?"

"We're a serious news organization, not a tabloid."

The rookie thought about that, then said, "But if Griff made it out, then he might be the only one who knows what happened to the *Rosie*."

"Don't you have work to do?"

"This is work. Griff might confirm why Manny's crew disappeared out of Tonga. And why the *Rosie* sent an SOS almost 100 miles—"

"The proper term is *mayday*. Not SOS."

"—100 miles from where they had planned to look for the submarine. A hundred miles! Why?"

"If you don't have work to do, I will assign you something. Something that might apply to the large amount of work currently besieging the network."

The rookie chewed a nail and spat it. "Griff would know what happened to the others on the Australian news crew, too. And why three governments got involved, closing off the area—"

"Here's an idea: you can park on my call while I confirm the press conference time in LA."

"Who are you on with?"

"The Pentagon."

"Ooh. Dial me in. Someone there might know what happened to the *Rosie*."

"Just the name of the operation in California will do this morning, thanks. Good luck getting anything else out of them." Nessa punched the girl's extension. "You're in. We just want to confirm the name 'Operation Garden Plot' for LA."

"Dumb name." The girl disappeared.

Nessa understood why the rookie clung to the mystery. The *Rosie* story had been the center of every conversation in the news building for the past month. It was hard to let go of that excitement. Nessa herself had spent a considerable number of work hours collecting "no comments" from every navy and coast guard unit who might have seen those crews on the water. She herself had languished on hold with every government official's office who had authorized a rescue: Tongan, Fijian, Australian, New Zealander, and American. Further, no one would comment on the strange electromagnetic pulse originating from the dive site at the time of the *Rosie*'s disappearance. The signal had circled the globe nine times, wreaking havoc with communications and electronics for days. "The Pulse," everyone called it. In their news building, the Pulse took out 23 computers and half the phone lines. Was it connected to the missing crews? No one could say. WINmedia's considerable sources had been exhausted trying to get answers as to what had happened out there, but no one had been able to penetrate the veil of secrecy that quickly raised around Manny's dive site. Body recovery, ship retrieval, the reasons it went so badly—it seemed all of it would remain a mystery.

Nessa pulled a Rolodex card with important California numbers, then dialed the mayor's office in Los Angeles. She needed to verify the time of the press conference and confirm that Rodney King would appear, then get that information to the sixth floor. On the phone, no voice greeted her, just a click. She was transferred directly to hold music.

The rookie girl popped up again. "Do you think the Pentagon was behind the *Rosie* disappearance?"

"Listen," Nessa said. "Advice from a quasi-veteran, here. Get better at letting go. Lots of mysteries don't get solved in the first news cycle."

The girl narrowed her eyes. She ducked behind the fabric panel.

Easy for Nessa to say. It took her years to learn detachment. Yet, as difficult as it was to leave the *Rosie* behind, they had a new job to do, and that was mapping South Central LA's eruption into fury. Two days prior, a Los Angeles jury had failed to convict four police officers who had hog-tied and kick-stomped a Black motorist on camera. Koreatown burned. Rioters pulled motorists out of their trucks and cracked their heads open. Overnight, the President had activated the Insurrection Act, authorizing federal troops to move into LA.

The rookie popped up. "Operation Garden Plot confirmed."

"That was fast."

The girl draped her arms over the panel and drummed. "Do you think the Pentagon is behind the Rodney King appearance today? Suddenly, the man himself is pleading for calm? It's suspicious. You know what else is suspicious? The *Rosie*—"

Nessa held her handset away from her mouth and stifled a yawn. She'd been up all night again. The synthesizer jam on the City of LA's hold soundtrack, she thought, might have been composed to repel the press from parking too long on their phone lines. But there wasn't a hold music soundtrack on any bureaucrat's line that Nessa couldn't incorporate into a Zen-like mantra for patience.

The girl suddenly stopped talking. Her eyes went wide. She zipped out of view.

Liv Ross had materialized at Nessa's desk. Her voice silenced the chatter in the cubicle farm. "Nessa Decker?"

WINmedia's Vice President of News on the tenth floor? Rare as a gazelle prancing through the cafeteria. Nessa managed to say, "Oh. Um."

Liv depressed the switch hook on Nessa's phone, killing the call. "Come with me."

Nessa tried again: "Oh. Uh."

Liv Ross was wearing her trademark red pantsuit, which, on busy news days like this one, screamed at others to get out of her way. Everything about her appearance indicated she prized efficiency and rapid response. She wore sneakers on the newsroom floor. Never heels. Glasses, not contacts. She styled her hair in a sleek bob that reminded Nessa of a leather football helmet. She doubted it took Liv more than ten minutes to assemble her intimidating ensemble each morning. Liv herself inspired an abundance of rumors, which involved eating male executives for breakfast with a side of cantaloupe and a sprig of mint.

Finally, Nessa found her voice, which emerged scratchy and full of phlegm. "I was...uh...confirming the time of a press conference in LA."

"Why." It was not a question.

"It's my job to confirm—"

Liv lifted her eyes to the stained ceiling tiles, as if wishing to take flight from the conversation. "And now your job is to come with me." She strode toward the elevator without looking back.

Nessa spun in her chair, confused as to what to do.

Liv's assistant, Fabrice, trotted by Nessa's cubicle with an odd tiptoe gait. He was known as a put-upon nitpicker, and he was currently laden with a massive shoulder bag and a chunky mobile phone. Nessa called to him, "Fabrice! Where are we going? What will I need?"

"We're going to the top," he said. "And fuck if I know."

She fumbled around her desk for a notepad and pen, talking to herself all the while. "What should I bring? If this is about Griff, maybe my *Rosie* notes...It's a thick folder...Somewhere..."

The rookie reappeared. "Girl. Do something about your hair."

Nessa patted frizz. She had worked at WINmedia for five years and had never been called to the top floor. She had never even met Howard Winfield, only seen him on TV. However, she had heard things about him. Like how, when he wanted to rattle a guest in his office, he would pee loudly with his executive washroom door open. Like how he had memorized the private phone numbers of 31 heads of state, including the Queen of England. Like how, if he started counting his money in ones right now, he would not finish for 100 years. However, she could confirm none of those myths to her professional standards. But there was one she could confirm: He and Griff Tran went all the way back to World War II, and there had been hell to pay when Griff didn't return from covering the Manny di Martini story.

"Put on lip gloss or something," the researcher tried. "You look like a corpse."

"This is how I always look."

The girl clucked. "God help you."

Gripping a notepad, Nessa bolted to the elevator. All eyes in the cubicle farm flicked in her direction. Three television monitors flashed yesterday's images of police blockades around Koreatown. "If you move any slower," Fabrice called out, "Mr. Winfield will throw you off his balcony, but only if I don't do it myself!" Fabrice had jammed a foot into the crevice of the elevator, and the doors continually smacked his loafer and rebounded. Liv was already leaning on the back panel, removing her sneakers. She handed them one by one to Fabrice, who traded them for tall heels that could double as murder weapons.

When Nessa skidded into the elevator, Liv assessed her from head to toe. "Are those your only shoes? No spares?"

Nessa glanced at her scuffed clogs. "These are the only shoes I own."

Fabrice tsked. "Clompy lesbian feet." Nessa pulled her threadbare cardigan closed to cover a tea stain.

"Give her a hairband," Liv said. Fabrice flicked a band off his wrist and offered it to Liv.

Outside the elevator, a reporter called out with one finger up: "Hold it!"

Fabrice barked, "Next one!" The reporter about-faced and ran in the opposite direction.

Fabrice jammed a key into a lock at the bottom of the elevator panel and punched the top floor. The elevator launched. The motion seemed to detach Nessa's kneecaps.

As they rose, Liv pinched the hairband in front of Nessa's face and spoke slowly. "Pull your hair back." Nessa took the band. Liv leaned against the rail. "Some basics. Do not speak unless spoken to. Do not call him anything but Mr. Winfield. Not Howard, not Boss, not Sir. His assistant will offer a beverage. Do not accept it. Mr. Winfield will offer you a seat. Do not sit until the *second* time he offers."

Nessa stared at the hairband. She felt dizzy. "Is this about the riots?"

Liv became interested in the ceiling tiles again. "The riots are a dead story."

The digital display of numbers above them flew by at a vomit-inducing rate. Fabrice tapped his toe. Nessa noticed his jacket shone. What was the salary to be Liv Ross's assistant? Was he on call all night? Did he sleep less than she did?

"For fuck's sake." Liv plucked the hairband from Nessa's grip and pulled at her hair like a mother dressing a child. "Mr. Winfield prefers his females with hair out of their faces."

Nessa flinched at Liv's hair pulling. "Your hair is down."

"My hair is short." Liv snapped the band in place. "I shouldn't have to say this, but I will: this meeting's information is privileged. If there's a leak, we will know it was you." Nessa believed her. Howard Winfield's inner circle was as tight as a tinpot dictator's.

Liv groaned, lifting one murderous heel and then another. "I've been on my feet all night."

Nessa tried again, "If Rodney King appears at the press conference at ten, maybe the riots will quell—"

Liv straightened. "I said the riots are a dead story. I won't say it a third time. Don't make me repeat myself again, and *never* make Mr. Winfield do it, or I'll throw you off that penthouse balcony myself. Compared to what he would do to you, it would be a mercy. Say thank you."

Nessa bit back a retort. But this was not the time to fight. Especially with Liv. Nessa mumbled, "Thank you."

"I was told you were smart. Act like it."

Nessa exhaled slowly through pursed lips.

The elevator doors opened. "He likes it cold up here," Liv said. "Don't comment on it."

An elegant white-haired woman in a soft grey sweater appeared. She reminded Nessa of an effervescent snow cloud. "Welcome, Ms. Decker. I am Dorothy. May I offer you a warm beverage this morning?"

"No, thank you."

Fabrice veered away, parking himself on a plush sofa that sucked him into its cushions. Liv darted ahead into a series of silvery-grey corridors, stabbing the sleek carpet with long strides. Nessa struggled to keep up.

Liv stopped short at a double door of solid mahogany that gleamed with a fresh application of lemon-scented wood polish. "You are here to offer your professional opinion. You may encounter resistance to it, but your job is to hold strong on what you can confirm using verifiable facts."

"Resistance?" Nessa thought of another story about Howard Winfield, how he routinely threw his lunch at staff when he didn't care for what was on the tray. "Resistance from Mr. Winfield?"

"No. Me."

Liv swung the mahogany doors open wide. Nessa's stomach lurched. Howard Winfield's office seemed nothing more than a transparent glass cube clinging to the top of the building. She could see Manhattan in all directions—its steel monoliths, its busy people, its yellow cabs scooting like toys below. The Empire State Building thrust upward like a middle finger. At the edge of the island, the World Trade Towers, two columns of drab grey, curtained off any bay views. It must have angered Howard to no end, these obstructions to a better view of his empire.

The silvers and greys from the hallway continued in here. The white carpet was plush; the tables were all glass. No papers or trash bins or office supplies of any kind were visible. A leather portfolio, also grey, was centered on an enormous glass desk, alongside the only image in the room: a black and white framed photo, Nessa recognized, of Howard's late daughter Georgina, who had died four years ago of a drug overdose. Some said it was her father's constant scrutiny and withholding of affection that did her in. Others said she was a party girl with a large inheritance to blow. Now, Georgina would spend her afterlife imprisoned on her father's desk, her delicate chin tipped to catch the light, perpetually cheerful.

A booming voice rattled the room. "I'm told you know all there is to know about this *Rosie* business."

Howard Winfield had taken up a post at a tremendous window with his back to the room. He was training binoculars onto a sidewalk far below. His dove-grey suit blended with the fog and clouds outside. Tall and lean, his reflection in the perfectly transparent window prompted Nessa to imagine a sooty iceberg hovering above the fumes of Midtown.

Abruptly, he leaned over to press an intercom button on the conference table. "Dodie! Send a crew to 6th and 49th to interview a lady who just got mugged. Tell them to spin the blame to Mayor Dinkins, may he rot in hell." Howard deposited the binoculars on his desk with a muted click. "Good way to start the day. Nessa, is it?" She felt a jolt, hearing her name out of his mouth. He spun to face her. "You may speak."

"Nessa Decker, that's correct." She wanted to add *Sir* but swallowed it. "And there are others in the building who know—"

Liv clamped her lips and shook her head. Nessa let that sentence die. She noticed a red rose in his buttonhole. Another rumor about Howard had to do with this daily fresh flower, something about a sister left behind in the Second World War in his native Hungary. That rumor would remain forever unconfirmed, Nessa thought. Howard Winfield's origin stories were tightly guarded.

Inside a long pause, no one spoke.

Nessa twisted under the heat of Howard's stare. Suddenly, it was far too hot in the office. The Government Hold Soundtrack had nothing on a minute-long silent look from Howard Winfield.

As if deciding something, Howard clapped once and announced, "Let's not keep you from your important work for too long." He glided around the glass conference table. Liv had already settled herself in an adjacent chair, angling her head side to side, as if assessing Nessa from afar. "My dear, tell me," Howard said to Nessa, "what you make of this."

Nessa struggled to move into the room. Howard's energy was not what she expected. He exuded gentle, paternal guidance. He was respectful of her time, treating her as if his name wasn't atop her paychecks, as if he did not have the power to elevate or end her career with a word. Howard extended a slim blade of a hand to indicate the table, and prompted, "If you would, give these items your professional attention." His voice, sepia-toned and full of body, clashed with his surroundings. It was a rich voice made for radio. Nessa could listen to him read the tax codes.

His daughter Georgina, still as death, presided from the nearby desk. One side of her mouth turned up, a sly expression. *Don't trust him*, she seemed to say.

Fathers, Nessa thought. *Can't live with 'em...*

Conscious of her dirty shoes tracking orange-line subway grime, she approached the conference table with that same tiptoe walk as Liv's assistant. *Ah*, she realized. *This is where he gets it: from treading carefully on expensive carpet.*

On the glass table lay a crumpled manila envelope, excessively stamped. It had been torn open, but was now empty. Nessa could identify a postmark from American Samoa. The name on the return address label: Gruffudd Tran. She sucked in her breath but didn't dare approach. The date on that postmark could indicate whether he survived past the date that the US government claimed he died.

Next to the torn envelope, a stack of creased pages of all colors, stained with an unknown substance. *Coffee? No, darker. And thicker. And coffee doesn't dry into a chalky paste. Ink? No. Too thick.* The pages were all different sizes and shapes, different thicknesses and textures. Some were crinkled with dried liquid, torn at the edges. Some were as flat and crisp as paper pulled from a fresh sheaf. The heap had been fanned to show identical handwriting covering each page from margin to margin. Nessa squinted at the top page to decipher the loopy handwriting—not the type usually produced by men, she noted. At the start, she read, *Dear Windbag.* Nessa wondered, *Was that a nickname? A play on Winfield? Were these pages a letter?* If so, it was a very long letter. Something was printed on the back of each page, too, but machine printed, not handwritten. *Recycled paper?* Again, she refrained from approaching.

Next to the stack of pages was a dictionary-sized book. On the cover, three tanned and buff men tangled, artfully arranged to avoid exposing genitalia. The title: *Grin and Bare It: The History of Homosexual Porn from Madame Butterfly to Chi Chi LaRue, Unabridged.* Something was odd about the book. It was substantial, much wider than standard hardcover, and only classic novels had a higher page count. But porn history?

Finally, at the end of the evidence trail, were seven single spools of magnetic video tape without cases. Each was tagged with a bit of masking tape bearing a sequential number. The same brownish substance flecked these spools and the identifying tape, curling the edges.

Nessa moved back to the pornography book. Howard noticed. "Does erotica interest you?"

She flushed but extended a finger to prod the cover. "May I?" He nodded. Nessa flipped the cover, then thumbed through a few pages, then more. At its center was a hollow core, now empty. "Wow. A hollow book. I've never actually seen one of these in person."

Howard stepped forward, as if eager to supply an explanation. "Griff owns a whole series of these utilitarian titles with hollowed centers. Gay porn, religious texts, self-help. He started traveling with his 'books' in the '60s, after a Guatemalan military grunt stole one of his news tapes at a checkpoint. He was furious! That stolen tape held evidence of a genocide." Howard zoned out a moment, then returned. "Griff swore he'd never lose footage to a government lackey again. Now, if he needs to hide a tape at a border check or during a raid, he tucks it into an offending book. Soldiers usually don't touch gay porn in public. Of course, Griff doesn't always use *this* title. Possession of this one would see him executed in fundamentalist states. For travel there, he uses a tame self-help title about improving marital relations. But this title—" he gestured to *Grin and Bare It*— "would have served on a trip to the South Pacific."

Nessa added, "Where you sent him before he left to pursue Manny di Martini and the *Rosie*."

Howard nodded. Nessa noticed he was using the present tense when referring to Griff. *Griff owns. If he needs to hide.*

Liv kept swiveling silently, like a cat twitching her tail. She had yet to add to the conversation, and Nessa wondered where her resistance might appear. Regardless, her mind raced to assemble the puzzle pieces before her.

Nessa pointed to the tapes. "He smuggled these out." Howard nodded. She pointed to the envelope. "And mailed them to you." She approached the envelope. "May I?" Howard nodded again. As she guessed, the origin postmark bore the stamp of the American Samoan government with the date April 22, 1992. Nine days ago. She was exhilarated. "The US government declared Griff's date of death was April 15!"

Liv added, "As well as the others on his news crew."

Howard said to Liv, "Already, she is processing this faster than Fritz did."

There was a name Nessa knew: Fritz Gehring, Howard's lawyer. Nessa knew wherever Howard Winfield went, his corporate counsel wasn't far behind. Fritz came with his own legends—all of them associated with ironclad contracts, campaigns of fear, and airtight protection for WINmedia. Nessa asked, "When did the package arrive?"

"Last night," Liv said.

Nessa ran a finger along the return address—a post office box. "Sources usually don't use a real address for smuggled items," she said. "Has this post office box been confirmed?"

"Fritz checked. This post office box does not exist," Howard said.

"And this is a spelling of Griff's name he doesn't use. Is that his legal name?"

"He does not use that spelling and never would. He does not care for it."

Nessa said, "Someone else wrote this, possibly without him present."

Howard flashed a look at Liv. He said, "That is *one* option."

Nessa pointed to the tapes and film. "They arrived inside the hollow book?"

"Yes."

"So, someone with power over Griff at the time did not want this media to be seen. Or Griff believed that to be so." She noticed that the oversized television monitor within the elegant walls of the office suite was dark. "Have the tapes not been watched?"

Liv and Howard exchanged a tense look. "No," he said decisively. "Not yet." Liv threw her eyes to the floor, pinching her lips together.

Nessa returned to the letter. *Dear Windbag*, it began. That nickname had an intimate air. It had to be written by someone so familiar with Howard that he couldn't be touched by the mogul's wrath or whimsy. Nessa couldn't even fathom such a man, but Griff obviously was that man.

She reached for the stack of papers but hesitated. She wanted to hold them, feel their textures, and pore over the handwritten words. The strange, dark stains stopped her. *What was that stuff?* She folded her arms to prevent her own curiosity from getting ahead of Howard Winfield's direction. She cleared her throat and asked, "What can I do for you, Mr. Winfield?"

Howard moved to seat himself at the head of the table, then gestured to Liv to take over. She began, "As you know, the five governments involved in the *Rosie* response have been evasive about what happened out there on the water. They have yet to produce bodies for autopsies or offer causes of deaths."

"So, Griff *is* deceased?" Nessa asked.

"We believe so," Liv said. "But lacking a corpse, we cannot rule out survival." She shot Nessa a hard look over her glasses. "That does not leave this room." Liv continued, "Our jobs at WINmedia are to hold the government response units to account, to provide our viewers and the families of those who were lost with the truth of the circumstances. But it must be the truth, not a sensational fairy tale. We cannot risk inflaming the sensibilities of the grieving families."

Nessa knew there was more at stake than what Liv said. WINmedia was expecting lawsuits from the families of the crews who died.

Howard added through gritted teeth, "Governments do not possess the right to withhold bodies and create false narratives." Nessa's skin prickled with his sudden emotional rawness. *Was that a grudge?*

Liv blinked slowly, then continued. "If any of the boat crews survived even a day beyond what was advertised, that's certainly of interest. Like I said, we still don't have the answers about what happened out there. What is *not* going to help—"

"The letter," Howard interrupted, "indicates a man poisoned—"

Liv collapsed into a slump. "We agreed to allow the experts to officiate this contest. If you're going to speculate on medical conditions, then allow medical professionals to the table now, not later."

"Certainly," Howard said, "that is a step we will take."

Liv slapped the table for emphasis, "But, just now, before he left, Fritz said not to do anything rash. He said we must prepare for legal exposure before taking this package to anyone outside the company. You agreed to give him time to draw up tight NDAs, because this—" she pointed to the collection of items— "is explosive. If *one* civilian gets their hands on this, we are fucked. Five angry governments will be on the phone, which will only fuel our opposition in the antitrust hearings."

Howard seemed amused with Liv's anger. He leaned toward Nessa, "She thinks I do not know how politics work." Nessa's eyes darted around, finding nowhere safe to land. She did not enjoy being in the middle of this fight. It was like being a teenager at home with her warring parents, but with far higher stakes.

"And yet!" Liv continued. "If we watch the tapes *first*, I have a feeling we would be able to settle this without further risk."

Howard fanned his hands. "The tapes require cleaning and preparation. I can't just pop them into my player as they are."

What did they think was on the tapes? Nessa wondered. Clearly, they had two different ideas.

Liv had not stopped talking. "—we will be able to properly categorize this letter as the ravings of a madman in his final hours. I mean, it doesn't even sound like Griff. Griff Tran does not use the word 'gossamer.'"

Howard chuckled to himself.

Liv went on, "And what the hell is that black goop all over those pages and tapes?"

Howard's voice went low. "Ms. Ross. Have you considered that Griff doesn't shoot on magnetic tape?"

Liv went silent, calculating.

Nessa looked between them. Howard was waiting.

Liv said, "Why didn't you mention this? That means—"

"These tapes were not shot for news. Griff did not send *his* tapes. He sent us tapes belonging to Manny di Martini."

After a moment, Liv said, "Possibly."

Howard said more forcefully, "These are tapes from the expedition."

After another pause, Liv said, "If Griff sent this package at all."

Nessa turned her attention to the tapes and film. "Excuse me," she tried. "Are we not in agreement that Griff Tran sent this package?"

Liv said, "No. We are not."

"Not even the idea of it being sent by an intermediary?" Nessa eyed the loopy handwriting again. "Likely female. Are you saying this package is a hoax?"

Howard touched the rose at his lapel. "Ms. Ross thinks it is."

"It wouldn't be the first time," Liv muttered.

Howard leaned toward Nessa. "There are those who mean me harm."

Nessa pushed back against any warm feelings of being taken into Howard Winfield's confidence. She asked, "Without anyone having seen the tapes, am I to assume the contents of the letter itself are problematic?"

Liv threw her hands up. "Here we go."

Howard licked his lips. "It is not easy—" he paused here, then tickled his manicured nails on the glass table— "to accept the story in the letter. The grotesqueries defy belief."

Nessa had to process that. These were hardened news people. What would put them at such an impasse? "What is my role here?" she asked.

Liv steadied her gaze. "We want your opinion before we call in more senior reporters and executives with agendas of their own."

Howard assessed Nessa with a tilted head. For a long time, he said nothing. She had the feeling he wanted to say something but agreed in advance not to. *Is there something they're not telling me?*

Suddenly, Howard's tone brightened, as if he had arrived at a conclusion privately. "You are bound by your corporate non-disclosure agreement, of course."

Nessa couldn't believe they were willing to leapfrog her over a few dozen people between her and this room for the right to be here. "Others will be brought in? At least Jefferson Krider?"

Liv said, "This situation will be *thoroughly* vetted, but for now your involvement is...hmm...*critical*."

Critical? Nessa thought. *I'm nobody.*

Howard appraised Nessa again, this time with deadly earnestness. "Please, Ms. Decker. Do trust my decision. It is *my* decision. Mine alone. Ms. Ross provides a cover for me with the corporate politics, but it's unnecessary. You will see that soon enough. For now, you must believe that you are, in this situation, exactly the person for this job. No other."

"Well." Nessa didn't know what else to say. She wondered if she could sit now. She shuffled around the table, aware of her dirty shoes, her frizzy hair, her stained shirt. She wanted to handle that evidence. Badly. It drew her like a compass needle to magnetic north. She reasoned aloud, "I am the highest ranking researcher at WINmedia. I suppose I'd better get to work." She scanned the dark television monitor installed into the office wall. "If we all agree, shall we get started preparing the tapes? The guys in editing will be able to prep these spools, clean them up a bit. It might take some time, so the sooner the better."

Howard flattened a palm at Liv, as if opening the field for her to run. *Go.*

"Finally," Liv sighed. She punched the intercom. "Get me Editing. Now."

Nessa reached for the first page of the letter but retracted. That dried, dark substance unnerved her. "Does anyone have gloves?"

2

The Last Song of Gruffudd Tran

DEAR WINDBAG,

Welp. The shit has hit the fan for this old hack. I'm 63 years old, never to see 64. You called it back in Berlin, right after the war: "You'll never be an old man, Griffy." Only you, Windbag, would want something as horrendous as old age. Me, I'm grateful to be checking out early. I've seen how the world works—wars, famines, plagues, deaths, etc. Now, I know there are many more than just four horsemen in this apocalypse. Who knew that the world was saving the best apocalyptic buckaroo until last? In other words: have I got a story for you, and I don't have long to tell it.

Four days ago, I was kidnapped by the US military from a chartered boat in the South Pacific while I was working in the unofficial capacity of WINmedia. I was abducted along with three WINnews television guys from Australia, our Tongan captain, five surviving crew members from the *Rosie*, and four from the Fijian coast guard. Many more died out there on the water before the military even showed up to "rescue" us—the list above represents those of us who survived the initial onslaught of radiation and Lord Buddha knows what else.

My letter comes from our little prison hole in American Samoa. It's a secret hospital that might be a repurposed warehouse. I cannot be sure of this because I was not conscious when they brought me in. Today, only two of us remain alive: me and a crew member from the *Rosie*. (Not Manny di Martini, fortunately. Can you imagine a worse person to be held captive with?) Tonight, this last crew member, a Tongan, has been locked in a padded room. I can hear him yelling from my isolation tent. Howling, more like. Poor guy. He had been responding well to radiation treatment, and for a while it looked like he would be the only one of us who might recover. But then he went and gouged out his own eyes with a tongue depressor. With his own blood, he wrote on the walls: *You will see what I see.* That landed him in the cushioned clinker. Right now, he and I are in a neck-and-neck race to the finish line. You see, what we found out there is not survivable.

I've got a few more hours until dawn. That's when the masked doctors return. Until then, an angel nurse will sit with me to take this story down in secret. Bless this nurse. She fished my two books out of the waste bin, likely tossed there with the rest of my stuff by the jarheads. Gloved against radiation, she brought these salvaged treasures — *TS Eliot: Collected Poems* and *Grin and Bare It*—to my tent intending to read something familiar to me in my final hours. I invited her to look inside *Grin and Bare It*, and the brave soul did. I told my nurse: "There is something you can do for me. Do you have paper, pen, and a sense of adventure?" Luckily, she had all three. Windy—she's risking her neck for this, so protect her if she's ever found out. Let Fritz off his chain for this one. She's a doll.

Man, I hope all that radiation didn't fuck up those tapes. I hear that magnetic media survives in outer space, so why not the tapes?

As for me, there's nothing they can do for me, or to me, anymore. It's been a rough road: organ degradation, necrosis, bloody diarrhea a minimum of 30 times a day, cracking skin, boils, hair loss, multiple blood transfusions. Doctors brought up the idea of a bone marrow transplant for me but jettisoned that when they determined I would not survive it. Here's a clue for you: the doctors' accents are American, Russian, and Israeli. They aren't military—they argue too much with the jarheads and lack respect for the officers who occasionally tour our morbid ward. Naked, in my isolation tent, doctors have photographed me. They placed a small white cloth over my groin to spare me indignities. Within minutes, blood stained it. From the others who have died, I know what the end looks like. When I go, it will be fast and medically unexplainable. Black sludge will ooze from my mouth. Tumors will balloon in my throat, cutting off my airway. I will either suffocate or suffer a heart attack. After I die, more tumors will sprout all over my body. Those will explode, contaminating the air for the living, if I'm not quickly bagged and sealed. I overheard there's a lab closeby where the tumors are examined. What's inside them? The answer I heard: radiotrophic fungi, the kind usually found in the extreme poles, where higher levels of cosmic radiation penetrate our atmosphere. Fuck if I know how we caught whatever we did in the South Pacific. And until the end game happens, I am loosely bandaged like a half-assed mummy and fed meals through a paper straw held by the same nurse who writes my words while I can still speak. Soon my tongue will disintegrate. For now, "I am in the twilight kingdom...I am in death's dream kingdom." (That's not me. That's TS Eliot. I got to know him well on this trip.)

My angel nurse tells me they are burning all the bodies. They have no intention of allowing the world to see what happened to us.

Hey. It's not all bad here. I can see things. Not with my eyes—those are failing rapidly with all my other organs—but with my mind. This isn't the drugs talking. (There are none in my system anyway because the doctors can't puncture my skin without me bleeding out like a hemophiliac.) Right now, I have direct eyes on a network of thoughts and visions, and this network runs through the earth like a fan of roots, pulsating with messages about our collective lives here, about our survivals and our failures and our loves. These roots run like tangled strings between us, connecting us even now.

Why, I can pull a thin string in my mind and bring you to me right now, if I choose. You, in your office on top of the world. I see you now, looking down onto the streets below, looking for me to walk into your building any day now, my death an egregious mistake. You are conjuring me, you mighty god. Well, stop it. I am not there, and you are not divine.

I see dark things, too. Unspeakable things. I won't write about them. Some of us lost our minds when we saw them. The impulse to beat in our brains with a blunt object was strong. (Rest in peace, Captain Tuigamalo.) Or attack ourselves with a tongue depressor. Whatever is handy.

*Aïe...*The scribe-nurse grows impatient with me. Time, time, time...

Out on the water, when we were taken by the military, the toughs came at us with their questions right away. They wanted to know who did what and in which order, who saw what, and who could confirm it. They demanded a story they could wrap their little jarheads around. What a laugh. But so many of us were too sick to talk. Of course, that wasn't my first interrogation. I told them nothing useful. You know me. I detest a young military shit who professes to know what's good for me. But judging by the number of heavy planes now screaming out of Guam, the Feds are spooked by what we found. I can hear them all the way over here in AmSam. The gossamer threads vibrate with the planes launching, with the soldiers' panicked grunts and squawks on the tarmac. I hear them just as clearly as I hear you ordering your morning cappuccino, Windbag. It sounds like war out there. Another damn war. Carving out territory in the open ocean. Crazy—
Oh.

I see, Windbag. I see your thoughts even now. *This isn't Griff's writing! This is a hoax! Griff is on a beach in Fiji, too drunk to call in!*

Denial never looked good on you, Windbag. You love a paranoid romp better than anyone else I know. Yet, many have tried to hurt you. I see that now. Humans can be such bastards. (You really should have told me about all that went on with your sister. I would have understood.)

How to prove it's really me, though? Well. There is a word I can say to let you know I am who I claim to be. I will say it, the nurse will write it, and you will know this letter came from only my blistered lips, because not even your wife or children know this word:

Elazar.

There. That should satisfy you. Or send you to your executive washroom with the shits. It's a toss-up. Who in this world knows you better than I do, you bag of stale farts?

—Nessa rummaged through her things for a pen. Liv lengthened her spine, supervising. Nessa then pressed into the paper, redacting the word Elazar *for future readers. Howard's face flickered recognition.*
"Thank you, dear," he said—

All right, Windbag. Enough of this chitchat. I owe you an accounting. This is a company trip, and an expense report is due. Why did I leave a genuine Winfield-sponsored first-class vacation in Fiji to get myself into the worst trouble a human can find?

First, the vacation was your idea, not mine. I do not thank you for attempting to put an old journalist out to pasture before he was ready. Windy—I was *bored* at that health resort. Coconut oil massages and Hatha yoga? Really? They wouldn't let me *smoke*. I left. Met up with a few guys from the Sydney desk. Got to drinking. A call came in. I saw an opportunity, and I took it. Don't get angry. I am what I am.

Second, the US government is going to lie about what happened out there. Who knows how long they've known about this? My nurse, an islander herself, tells me islanders have always known what's out there. She says it is a thing never spoken of, except in tales. Well, it's all out of the bag now, and our nation's finest will have a hell of a time putting it back in the bag. They'll give it a hero's try, though, and I wish I could be around to see it in person just for the laughs. And for those of us who died horribly at this site, we deserve better than whatever shit story they will dream up to cover our tracks. Probably, it will paint us in a bad light to throw others off the scent. It *definitely* will serve a few who want to keep power for themselves. It always does. And we've always hated a military takeover of the Truth. Living in Europe in the '30s taught us that, eh?

This nurse has my reporter's notepad to check dates and facts. I can't function without a solid second-in-command to keep me honest. My gratitude goes out to her once more.

This is for you, Windbag. For us.

Sunday, April 12, 11:30 am-ish. The guys and I were in Fiji, hungover and bored. We were thinking of taking their camera equipment into the streets to find out how people of Fiji were going to vote in the upcoming elections. Fiji's first democratic election since a government coup! Not the war crimes I usually go for, but desperate times. Besides, after all the chanting and Peruvian flutes at the resort, I had to get the itch out of my system, to mainline the world's problems like the news junkie I am. There's nothing like the adrenaline rush from running into a house on fire with a camera. (You remember, don't you, Windbag? The smell of burning buildings and bodies in Berlin was tough to get out of your nostrils, wasn't it?)

Three WINnews Aussies were with me. There was Pretty Boy who had done some on-camera work in Sydney but never abroad. There was an agile Camera/Audio Man I would have taken with me into the Balkans if you'd have sent me there instead of Fiji (I will never forgive you for that). And there was an older guy who liked to point at things and yell—handy skills for a Bossy Assistant Director. Together, with some adequate equipment they brought from Sydney's outlet, we made a decent crew on-the-go.

But before we could get the camera warmed up, an even better story surfaced. Bossy AD got a call out of New Zealand. Weeks ago, he had enlisted an amateur radio operator to monitor the Manny di Martini expedition near Tonga, just in case that went tits-up. And boy had it. As far as mayday calls go, the Kiwi radio operator reported, it was a strange one. Manny's expedition was supposed to be limited to a 70-minute cruise off the east coast of Tonga. The expedition was searching in sections out there within easy reach of the main island, motoring out to their dive sites, scraping around for a few hours, then heading back inland. However, the Kiwi said they were radioing from *seven hours* offshore in the opposite direction. What the hell?

Second, the Kiwi said a *Rosie* crew member had called in the mayday, claiming one of the deckhands had been shot dead by Manny di Martini. (My first question was why Manny had a gun on an underwater expedition. It would not be my last question.) At the time of the call, Manny had barricaded himself on the bridge with his gun pointed at the captain's head. Why? Because the *Rosie* crew had wanted to stop the expedition, but Manny did not.

Further, the mayday was punctuated by background screams and high-pitched gibberish. The Kiwi reported word for word what the guy whispered on the emergency channel: "There's something down there. It's not the submarine we were looking for. It's something else...We're all sick...And we're hearing things. *Bad* things..."

Of course, the Kiwi was not the only one listening to the call. The Tongan coast guard caught the message, too. They repeatedly radioed the *Rosie* to confirm the coordinates they sent, but those calls went unanswered. Regardless, the Tongans were on the way out there to sort it out.

It seemed we had a genuine news story happening on the open ocean. Hot *damn*.

Immediately, we got out an ocean map and circled the *Rosie*'s coordinates—80 nautical miles southwest of Tonga's main island. If we hopped a plane from Fiji to Tonga right then and chartered a local boat to take us out there, we could be on site in 11 hours—only three hours behind the coast guard, still in time to record interviews with whoever was left on the water out there.

News of the trouble was spreading fast. Chatter from other news agencies in Australia, New Zealand, and Hawaii said they were moving, too, but the earliest anyone could make it out there was in 24 hours. Luckily for us, the Pacific Ocean is fucking massive, and we were the closest.

Further, thanks to you, I had wads of cash on me to spend at resorts, so we were well positioned to persuade a Tongan skipper to step on the gas. We would monitor radio traffic on the way to the *Rosie*, try to intercept the Tongan coast guard wherever they were, possibly board the *Rosie* ourselves to interview anyone sane enough to relay their story. It sounded feasible enough. We decided it was worth a shot, much more interesting than the local color interviews we were doing in Fiji. So, we notified the Sydney outlet, and we took off.

I tell you, I felt *alive*, Windbag. I felt high. I felt plugged in. I felt like I was doing what I was put on this planet to do.

Not even when Bossy AD got the second call from the New Zealand radio operator, did I question our decision. "Hey," the Kiwi radio guy added. "A fishing boat close to the *Rosie* replied to the mayday."

"Yeah? Will they beat us?"

"No," the Kiwi said. "At first, they replied to say they were on the way to render aid. Minutes later, they radioed to say that they were standing down. They said it is against the ancestors' wishes." We didn't know what the hell that meant. He explained, "It's not cool to retract a promise to aid a vessel in distress. In fact, I've never heard of anyone doing that before. According to international law, they have—"

"Great! Thanks!" That was enough for us. We had a plane to catch.

When we landed in Tonga, we split up so we wouldn't lose time—some of us would charter a boat, while the others would talk to locals. I took one of the Aussies with me to interview Tongans about Manny's expedition so far, and the rest went to the wharf with a load of cash. We would spend no more than an hour or two on the island, tops.

Tracking where Manny had been on the island was easy. Nuku'alofa is a small town. In no time we found Manny's hotel and the bars where his crew drank. Even on an isolated island in the South Pacific, Tongan locals knew about Manny and his American game show *Boo-Yah!* When he first arrived, he had posed for photos, signed autographs, chatted up the women. Three American television/dive-logistics crew followed him everywhere. They were white, and they were loud, so they stuck out.

Tracking his Tongan crew was also a cinch. Locals knew who his crew was, where their mothers lived, who their great-grandfathers were, who their sisters had married, how that marriage was going, what was for dinner at their house on Sunday, and what they all thought about the expedition.

The captain was more difficult to track. The chartered boat, which Manny named *Rosie*, was captained by an American Samoan named Tuigamalo. Locals didn't know him as well. All they knew was that, from the start, Manny had burned some bridges with Tongans with his culturally insensitive behavior, so no skipper out of Tonga would work for him. Manny had to charter from American Samoa—almost 600 miles away.

I asked the locals about Manny's insulting behavior. What'd he do that was so bad? The list was long and varied. He jogged shirtless on a Sunday. That's illegal there. He trespassed on the royal family's cemetery. Also illegal. He threw rocks at the sacred flying foxes. Illegal. He was ticketed twice and thrown in jail once. When he left the wharf for his dive sites, he fired his gun off the back of the *Rosie* at anyone who followed him. He said he didn't want anyone "claim jumping" his submarine wreck. (Answer to question one: he brought his gun to defend his treasure like a goddamn pirate.)

To me, Manny's strategy on the ground seemed ill-conceived at best and stupid at worst. The locals had been excited that a celebrity was living among them. They would have given him anything he wanted. But after the first day, Manny didn't even *try* to be friendly. That's a cardinal sin when you're working in a foreign culture. You live and die by your relationships. Manny sounded outright aggressive to me. If he had intended to provoke the locals, he was doing a great job of it.

Maybe he just didn't know what the hell he was doing. A big movie about a real World War II sub named *Polaris* came out, so down-on-his-luck Manny intended to ride its coattails to fame. He wasn't a deep-sea diver. He was America's clown prince. He should have noted that none of the pros could find *Polaris*, and those guys had looked *decades* before that movie even came out. That was part of the ongoing mystery that made the movie work so well in the first place. To find the faintest trace of the *Polaris*, Manny had to hire people to chart where they thought the boat might be. These were academics making their best guesses based on Japanese naval records, old currents, ship reports, and American archival charts. None of them had ever been to Tonga. And Manny never bothered to ask anyone local: do you know where the *Polaris* is?

Apparently, Windbag, the locals knew exactly where the *Polaris* was. And they never intended to say a damn thing about it to any outsiders, celebrity or not.

"Why not?" I asked them. Did they not want the site overrun with tourists? No, they said tourism helps the little island.

But every time I pressed them to explain further, they either backed away or ended the interview. The most I got out of anyone was "le Tasi i Fafo," an island myth about an oceanic creature who inflicts nightmares. It's the story islanders tell their kids to get them to go to bed on time, or to stay out of dangerous places. "Don't do it, or le Tasi i Fafo will get you!" Island lore said the *Polaris* crew met their ends by stumbling on the home of le Tasi i Fafo.

Yeah. Right.

You'd think after all I'd learned about listening to locals over the years, I would have delved a little deeper here. After everything went down, my angel nurse at the secret hospital told me the full legend. It's about what you'd think—a boogeyman living in an underwater citadel, calling out to be freed. Get too close, though, it will wreak havoc on your mind, turn you against those you love and destroy you in the process. Not the most efficient way for a monster to work its way out of a jail cell, but I guess you'd have to be batshit crazy to free an imprisoned creature like that, so maybe it's on to something. Then again, maybe it's not talking to *us* at all. Maybe we're just getting on a party line between the jail bird and its monster friends coming to the rescue. Who the fuck knows how these things work?

As you can see, I couldn't tolerate much of that kind of talk. Had anyone told me the full story before I went out there, it wouldn't have stopped me. Maybe they all knew that. Maybe that's why they kept quiet. Maybe they used to warn people all the time, and just look at the good it did. It's like the warning would have just paved the runway toward that creature, so best to not to get involved.

Predictably for the locals, Manny had been on the island a month with no *Polaris* discovery. He was going out every three days or so—tooting around off the coast, dragging that camera rig behind the boat, lighting up the dark ocean, filming the bottom, hoping for the best. It sounds simple, but it was a tall order. Manny's hired academics hadn't given him an exact spot to look, more like an area two and a half times the size of Manhattan at 2,000 feet deep.

Shit, Windbag. A dive like that should be done by pros with a hell of a lot more experience. One of the island boatmen said that dragging that camera unit had to be tricky business, especially in rough seas. One sudden change—like a surprise shipwreck or underwater mountain suddenly appearing—the crew has got to haul ass to the back of the boat and winch up that very expensive camera unit before it crashes right into that surprise. The *Rosie* crew would have to watch a small video screen for hours on end, ready to move if the slightest shadow of a wrecked sub ever showed up. The tedium and tension probably set their teeth on edge. That same island boatman told me that if Manny ever did find the *Polaris*, chances were that he was going to bash that fragile submarine wreck with that camera cage before he even knew what happened. Lights out. Expedition over.

So. Manny wasn't finding it. Desperation had set in. Meanwhile, the month-long charter contract on the *Rosie* was up, and Manny wanted an extension. Tuigamalo wasn't keen on prolonging his relationship with Manny. (Apparently his behavior on the boat wasn't much better.) The Samoan was giving Manny only one more run out to sea, and then the gig was over. When Manny told his production company this, they faxed him that they wanted to cut their losses and end the charter now.

Of course, Manny lost his damn mind. A few locals saw him ranting and raving after he got that message. He had no intention of packing it in. It's not that he wasn't a quitter. It was that he had no choice in the matter. Every bar in town had heard him bitching about how he had gone into serious debt with some nefarious people to mount that expedition. A billionaire oil baron who previously sought the Loch Ness Monster had bought into the expedition, and he, unlike with old Nessie, expected results. Manny's poker buddies—we're talking some vile Hollywood guys—rounded out the budget for chartering the ship, hiring the consultants, and buying the deep-sea camera and on-deck equipment. These douchebags expected residuals on the *Polaris* discovery's home video deals. Manny himself had to sell his villa and antique car collection to fund the crew's salaries. If he walked away without footage of that sub, he would be homeless, without a chance in hell at another show, and likely sent to an early grave by a guy named Luigi Leathernuts. So, Manny put the word out on the island that he wanted new "numbers"—or coordinates for better dive sites, better coordinates than his hired academics had computed.

Now, Windbag. You tell me what happened next.

That's right. A seething racist loudmouth causing problems on the island wanted the *Polaris*, so one of the locals gave him the *Polaris*. Someone slipped America's clown prince the coordinates to the lair of le Tasi i Fafo, underwater monster.

Who knows if this was a joke? I can't believe that any local would do that, knowing there were any real dangers out there with kin and friends on board. If there were any truth at all to the story of le Tasi i Fafo, who would do such a thing? But sure enough, I held out the coordinates we scribbled down from the *Rosie*'s mayday call, asking locals to confirm if it's the real *Polaris* site...and well, someone did exactly that. Someone gave Manny the deep-sea boogeyman's numbers.

Who did it was a mystery. The day before Manny left for his new site, he had been shrieking out on the sandbar for all to see and hear, waving a fax message from his production company, and yelling at the wind about all his problems. His crew was on the boat, half watching, half biding their time. It wasn't the first time the man had pitched a fit out there, so they seemed quite accustomed to waiting him out like a tempest unleashing holy hell.

Then, they said, someone approached Manny, someone the locals didn't know.

"Man or woman?" I asked the two men who came forward.

"Fakaleitī," they said.

"Meaning?"

"A Tongan male dressed as a female."

"Did they speak?"

"Perhaps. They went to a bar. We didn't see them speak."

"Which bar?" I asked. "I've been to every bar on this island." I asked them to show me the bar.

This bar, Windbag, is near the wharf. When I peeped inside, the furniture had been cleared out and the shelves emptied. "*This* bar?" I asked.

They nodded. "Want to meet the Fakaleitī?"

"Indeed, I do."

They led me to a low house on stilts hidden behind a rusted corrugated fence and an explosion of tropical vegetation. Women of all ages dressed in black huddled on the patio, all of them giving me the stink eye. Inside was no furniture. The windows were covered with floral bedsheets. A shadow of a man squatted in the center of the tiled floor. A magenta headband was all the clothing he wore. Pink nail polish flaked off fake nails, which clung to his fingers at odd angles, barely adhered. Makeup streaked his face. Scratches and cuts marked every inch of his body. I asked, "Who did this to you?"

He answered in a breathy voice. "Why, I did."

I didn't want to get into his psychological problems. I had come for answers. "Did you meet Manny di—"

He held up a hand. Half-detached fake nails distorted his hand shape in the low light so that his raised hand looked inhuman. "I told them already. I never met the man."

"You were seen—"

"I know what they say. But it was not me." He clawed at his chest, opening a scab. Blood trickled to his navel.

"Don't do that," I said.

He showed his teeth and hissed. "It was not me on the sandbar. It was the Other."

"Other?" I drew out my notepad and pen. "What other?"

He huffed. "I *told* them—"

"Tell *me*."

He swayed his head as he spoke, scratching at his arms as if he had vicious bug bites. "He came to me with a deal. He said he knew my troubles of not fitting in here." He gestured all around to the empty room. The women outside could be heard intoning prayers. "He said he could help me. He asked if I wanted to feel comfortable in my own skin. He asked if I never wanted to set foot outside my home again feeling as if I did not belong." He laughed and it sounded like a sob. "I have never believed much in the teachings of the Church. That is why he came to me. He was the devil."

"The devil?"

He nodded. "He wanted something from me. And I gave it." He considered his nails, straightened one. It fell to the side, limp.

"What did he want?"

"Just a trifle. Just the mask I wear."

"Mask?"

"That is what he said." He released a sigh and shuddered. "And now look at me."

"Describe him."

"Eyes," he said. "I saw the universe in his eyes. So beautiful." He opened a cut on his leg and wedged a fake nail inside.

Squeamish, I was losing patience. "You need medical help."

"I am beyond help."

"Nah. I've seen 'beyond help.' I've seen guts on the outside. You don't look beyond help."

He leapt to his feet, growling. Drool waterfalled from his lips and puddled on the tile. He crouched and circled. He chomped at the air like a rabid dog at the straining limit of its chain.

I held up two hands. "Hey, man!"

He swiped at me with his pathetic pink nails. "The deal has been made!" he screeched in a high voice. "The covenant is sealed!"

"Okay man."

"I am beyond help! Beyond!"

I backed out of the house. The patio women had escalated their pleas to Jesus. "Take our son," they prayed. "We implore you."

The two men who led me there were waiting for me by the gate, where I joined them. I patted my pockets for a cigarette, unsure what to make of that. But I was out of time. I needed to get back to the wharf.

One of them grabbed my arm. "It *was* him."

I sucked in nicotine. "Sure, buddy."

"We saw him."

They described the scene again, then added how Manny burst out of that bar the happiest since the parade the Tongans threw when he first arrived. He hadn't said a word to anyone about why he was so happy, which was uncharacteristic, not even saying when he was going back out on the water. "No, no," he told them laughing. "It's going to be a surprise!" Which was strange, they said, because Manny loved the spotlight. Always wanted a crowd at the wharf when he set out, even though he fired a gun at anyone. "I'm going to surprise you all," he told them.

The next day, the *Rosie* was gone. They had left in the dead of night without a word about where they were going. The day after that, the mayday call came in, and the Tonga coast guard launched. Big problem: Manny had gone out much farther, to water about 10,000 feet deep. When I asked another boatman about the problems of diving that deep, he said, "They seemed to have the right equipment. It's just that way out there on the ocean; things can go wrong. The water is temperamental, the waves unpredictable. It would be much more difficult to get out to help you."

When I showed him the coordinates, the "numbers," he backed away. "My advice? Forget you saw those numbers. Burn them and walk away. Let the dead bury the dead." Then he ended the interview.

I pocketed the numbers.

I've heard stuff like that before. *Don't meet with that warlord. Don't interview that informant.* I was alive so far, minus the scars on my back from rubber bullets shot by the South African Police and an extended colon from a bout of dysentery from the Turkish prison. What's a little danger to me compared to a non-smoking health resort?

I met up with my Aussie guys at the wharf to see what kind of boat they had negotiated for us. They had to pay extra for the captain to take us out to where we wanted to go, and three other guys had refused the job. "The ocean is bad out there," one of them had told my guys. "It's a bad place." Our captain agreed to take us only if we would pay for his daughter to get off the island and into a good school. Why not? I could fund that good cause from the Windbag Health Resort Slush Fund. The captain even delivered the money to her before he left.

I laughed. Jesus. Was he planning on not coming back?

He would die four days later on the way to the secret hospital.

At the wharf, we loaded up on beer and food, enough to stay out there a day or two. It was almost 4:00 pm. It would be dark soon—

3

The Hollow Men

A TAPPING AT NESSA'S elbow startled her out of the spell of Griff's letter.

One page danced in front of her, held there in a lobster-like pinch by a buttercream ski mitten. "What did this word say? Why is it blacked out?"

She had been so engrossed she hadn't noticed Jefferson Krider had set up next to her and was reading the pages she discarded. The swish of Gore-Tex against the paper put her on edge. Flakes of the unknown black substance drifted to the glass conference table. "Jefferson. When did you get here?" She sized up the remaining pages in Griff's letter. Still many more pages to come.

"So," Jefferson said to her, "you're not gonna tell me what the word is?" With his bare, unmittened hand, he scooped a handful of jelly beans out of a nearby jar and tossed them into his mouth.

"That's not a good idea."

"What isn't?"

"We don't know what this substance is. If you ingest it—"

"But I'm perfectly safe." He flapped his mittened hand. "I'm wearing this glove I found in my desk drawer."

"You probably shouldn't eat in here." Nessa craned for a view of Howard, but he was far from the conference table, speaking quietly at his desk to his assistant, Dorothy. The elderly woman had placed a small, labeled bottle in front of him, but he pushed it away. He rumbled, "Don't nag, Dodie." But she pushed the bottle forward again, speaking softly. Nessa caught only a few of her words, "...doctor...blood pressure..."

Jefferson tried again. "It's uncool not to tell me this word."

"I would tell you if I knew," she said, "but I do not."

She was glad he was here, but also annoyed. Now, she knew the territoriality that reporters often unleashed. She wanted to scoop the pages to her chest. *Mine.*

Nessa turned to flip through her notepad at the phrases and questions she had noted: *Radiation. Black tumors. Radiotrophic fungi. Not survivable.*

Jefferson reconsidered Nessa. "I never pegged you for the upwardly mobile type. You've always been mousy. Quiet." He poked a mitten at one of Nessa's notes: *I am in the twilight kingdom...I am in death's dream kingdom—poem?*

He said, "That's 'The Hollow Men' by TS Eliot. Let us praise my liberal arts education at Howard University for a factoid that tells us nothing." He chewed a moment. "This is an example of playing nice. Giving out information."

"Noted." Nessa turned over her notepad and stretched her neck. The scenery had changed since she dove into Griff's letter. Someone had rolled in a whiteboard. It now blocked the expansive view of lower Manhattan. Liv was notating in colored markers a timeline of Manny's expedition. So far, she had constructed a view of the expedition that began with Manny's firing from *Boo-Yah!* in 1990 and extended to the day the *Rosie* disappeared from Tonga—April 11, 1992.

Nessa called out to Liv, "Would you like to add April 12, when Griff said the *Rosie's* mayday call went out?"

"Yes." Liv's marker squeaked out the date. "And Jefferson, when did *Polaris* come out?"

"Two years ago. June 1990. YUUUUUNAAAAA!" He chuckled to himself. "I love that part. You know? When he's yelling that after he punches the guy with the gun?"

Liv mumbled, "I could do without movie lines today."

At the other end of the conference table, two elderly men huddled over a laptop, conferring quietly—Howard's lawyers, Fritz Gehring and Dave Levy. For an instant, Fritz's German rhythms rose and fell above Dave's harsh Brooklyn accent, "...CON-ze-QUENzes ov BREACH ov inVORmayZEEun..." Fritz struck fear into the hearts of every government committee looking to chisel away at WINmedia's size and power, and now Nessa could see why. He perched at the edge of his chair, rail thin and ancient, leaning far forward, as if longing to be a part of the text onscreen. The old man resembled a bird of prey—sharp nails, oversized eyes, and sweeping head movements followed by intense stillness.

Ambient noise in Howard's office had also increased. The oversized television monitor embedded in the wall now buzzed with sounds of an exuberant Manny di Martini, who used a fake Italian accent when on camera. He was outdoors, in the sun. On the *Rosie*? Nessa strained to hear him. "Buongiorno!" Manny exclaimed. What was left of his dyed black hair had fully set sail in the wind and his floral shirt had been buttoned only halfway, exposing a healthy crop of chest hair and a gold cross. A time stamp in the bottom right read, *April 7, 1992, 08:09:32.* Twenty-four days ago. Nessa noted it. The *Rosie* was about to launch on her first dive. Possibly. She wished she had found her *Rosie* file before she came up here.

"It's-a Manny di Martini! Coming to you from the South Pacific, where we are beginning a once-in-a-lifetime adventure to discover the final resting place of the USS *Polaris*!"

Behind Manny, burly, tattooed men loaded cameras and other equipment onto the ship. None acknowledged him.

Nessa pointed to the monitor. "Jefferson, are *all* the tapes ready to view?"

"They're sending up the repaired tapes one at a time. I heard they're having a hell of a time scraping that goop off the tapes. Betacam tape is thin shit, breaks easily."

She was only half listening, staring at the video's time stamp. "Was April 7 the date of the first dive?"

"Maybe." He whipped Griff's page like a flag. "You get nothing else until you tell me this redacted word."

"Is everything transactional with you?"

"Yep."

With a tissue, she swept up more black flakes from the conference table. "Jeez. Try to have some respect. Griff and Howard..."

Jefferson lit up. "It's *Howard*, now, is it? You've been up here for 30 minutes, and you're on a first-name basis? Do you think he knows about your feelings? Will there be an exchange of BFF necklaces?"

She ducked her head low. "I meant *Mr. Winfield*."

Jefferson tossed another handful of candy into his mouth. "Why are you here, Nessa? You should be begging for quotes from LA's Finest Racists right now, not reading Griff Tran's last will and testament."

"I don't know why I'm here."

Jefferson smiled with candy-coated teeth. "Not good enough."

"Yet, I still don't know."

Chewing, Jefferson watched her carefully.

He was right to be indignant. He had been reporting on this expedition since Manny announced it two years ago. He interviewed Manny's dive consultants from all over the world. He interviewed Manny himself several times. Jefferson was even in Tonga for a week, before Manny took far too long to find the sub and got pulled. Jefferson knew the crew, the scene, the timeline. If there was an expert on the subject in the building, it would be him. "I'm nonessential personnel," Nessa said. "That's what Liv Ross said."

Jefferson replied, "Nonessential personnel who redacts words from primary sources before they've been reviewed by senior staff—"

"Who told you *I* redacted that?"

He tipped the mitten at her. "So, you *did* redact it."

Liv Ross's voice rose above the squabble. "Finished the letter already?"

"Teacher!" Jefferson whined. "Nessa's not playing well with others."

Liv capped a dry erase marker. "Jefferson, take over this timeline. I need to switch gears."

Jefferson removed his ski mitten and threw it at Nessa. "Don't get cocky," he said. "When this is over, back to the cube farm you go." He skidded his jelly bean jar across the table in the direction of the whiteboard. "Your wish is my command, Livvy!"

"Cube farm," Nessa muttered. She liked it here in Howard's office. The chilly temperature and the silvery-grey décor lent the space an air of importance, like an archive where rare and expensive items are stored for posterity. And, despite her years on staff, Griff's letter was the first primary source she had ever held in her hands. The letter was a bona fide artifact from a major news story. It was providing real answers about what happened out there, and its contents were going to be pored over by important people. The historical weight of it awed her.

Pulling two fresh tissues from a nearby box, she reached for the next letter page to read. She hesitated. It was much larger than the other pages.

She flipped it over. An electrocardiogram graph was inked on the opposite side. The spiked waves jumped all over the graph paper in an erratic rhythm.

Nessa didn't know how to read it. It looked serious. If it had been a seismograph measuring an earthquake, then someone would have been suffering a heart problem with an equivalent of a 9.0 with falling skyscrapers and collapsing bridges. She thought of the Pulse—that unfamiliar and destructive magnetic wave that encircled the planet for days after the *Rosie* went missing. *So many anomalies connected to this story.*

The report had a patient's name at the top: Salote Sika. "Jefferson, remind me. Salote Sika held what position on the *Rosie*?"

Jefferson flipped a dry erase marker in the air. "A jack-of-all-trades, really. Tongan crew member. Navigator, medical officer. He was helping Manny with production, too. What do you have on him?"

Nessa bent low over the paper to read. "Some kind of medical report dated April 19. I guess he was one of the crew members evacuated to the hospital. This report *might* indicate massive heart attacks. Don't quote me. A specialist will have to confirm it."

The odor of shaving cream and lavender hit Nessa before she realized Howard was standing over her shoulder. His rumbling voice raised the hairs on her neck. "That is not a heart attack." He uncapped a pen worth more than her monthly rent. "Electricity in the heart creates distinctive wave patterns according to the functions of the heart muscle. Like so." He drew a sinusoidal wave off to the side of the graph. "A small wave begins the pattern. That's the polarizing pulse. It precedes a larger wave—that would be the big muscle contracting. Another small, recovery wave ends the pattern. Small wave, large wave, small wave."

Nessa ventured, "I don't see any tiny waves on this graph. Just large ones."

"Exactly," Howard said. He screwed the pen cap back on. "Even in the event of a heart attack, those tiny waves should still appear, however erratically."

"Meaning?"

"This patient is having a severe panic attack."

Nessa exhaled sharply.

After a moment, he added, "I expect you will want an expert confirmation."

"It would be wise."

"Dodie will provide the contact information for my cardiologist. Use my name to receive an immediate reply."

"Thank you, Mr. Winfield."

"You're welcome, dear."

Jefferson was watching this interaction while sucking his teeth. Then he scribbled on the board: *April 19, 1992. Salote Sika's heart explodes.*

Howard strolled away, calling out to Liv. "Ms. Ross. Let's begin."

Nessa's thoughts went wild. *Howard knows how to read an ECG report.* She scanned Howard's desk for the pill bottle that Dorothy had pushed toward him. If she could read that label—but it was gone. She scribbled in her notepad: *Mr. Winfield—heart condition? Or caretaker for a heart patient? Unlikely—wealthy, busy.*

Scanning the desk again, the photo of Georgina caught her eye. Nessa considered her. Why was she the only child to receive a place on his desk? Howard had nine children. None of the others were present. Georgina wasn't the only dead child, either. His eldest, Alexander, had died in a boating accident 20 years before Georgina. That accident nearly tore Howard apart with grief, some said. He began to detach from his family then. Yet it was Georgina, not Alexander, in the frame. Sad little Georgina, just a toddler at Alex's funeral. Nessa recalled a press photo of the little girl, reaching for Howard's hand. He hadn't even noticed her.

In the notepad, Nessa wrote: *Guilt?* and circled it. The rose in Howard's lapel caught her eye again. She weighed the rumors of his missing sister in Hungary. Now, Griff. *This man is haunted*, she thought.

Liv towered at one end of the conference table. "Right," she announced. "Let's start organizing our efforts."

Howard took a seat at the other end. Fritz rolled and cracked his neck, reviewing the room. His colleague, Dave, closed the lid to the laptop.

Jefferson backed away from the timeline. "This is good to go." Nessa noted a lot of blank space after the mayday call on Sunday, April 12. The remainder of Griff's letter might offer more detail.

Liv began, "Last night Howard opened a package addressed to him with the postmark from American Samoa. The package contained a long letter written in an unrecognized hand along with an object known to belong to Griff Tran, which hid seven spools of video tape."

"Magnetic video," Howard thundered. "Not Griff's choice of medium."

"The guys in Editing are rushing the cleaning and reassembly of the spools into cases for viewing." Liv gestured to the front screen. "We have one available for viewing already, but it's likely to be a few hours until we have the full set. So, we are going to have to view them as they are ready."

Nessa noticed a strain in Liv's voice. *Was she really banking on the tapes to reveal the letter as a hoax?*

Liv continued, "Now, before we reopen this story and rile up the families who are still without bodies or explanations—"

Jefferson interrupted, "And piss off five international allies."

"—we will review all this evidence and offer our professional opinions as to its authenticity. We want the truth of what happened out there, not sensationalism. If there is a severe radiation leak in the Pacific, we want to know. If there were crimes committed against reporters verifying that leak—"

"Like kidnapping, extrajudicial imprisonment," Jefferson said.

Liv nodded, "—we will hold the offending entities accountable."

Howard sat with hands folded, saying nothing. Nessa wondered why they weren't in the newsroom with more staff. Neither Liv nor Jefferson was questioning why Howard was running this story out of his office. Howard's strength was overseeing acquisitions, budgets, and antitrust hearings, yet he was keeping all this evidence in his penthouse office. Was it because Griff Tran was an old friend, and Howard wanted to control sensitive information? No, Nessa decided. Howard would enjoy more privacy by running this story behind the scenes, not by hosting staff in his office.

Nessa refocused on Liv, who was pointing to the lawyers perching on their chairs like twin vultures. "Fritz and Dave, you will monitor these discussions to ensure nothing we propose will leave WINmedia open to legal complications."

Fritz spoke with a Germanic clip. "We have non-disclosure agreements prepared for outside counsel, should they be required."

Liv nodded once. She cleared her throat. "Nessa and Jeff, here is the million-dollar question: What, in your professional opinion, do we need to confirm the veracity of this package?"

At the same time, they exclaimed, "The nurse."

"Agreed," Liv said.

Nessa added, "She's an islander, Griff said."

Jefferson said, "I've got contacts in American Samoa who can tell me who's been coming and going from any empty warehouses near the old Air Force base."

"Also," Nessa flipped through her notes, "Griff mentioned doctors with American, Russian, and Israeli accents. He also noted heavy planes leaving from Guam, but how he knows *that*—um, well. I could confirm it—"

Howard cut her off. "No, Ms. Decker, you're to continue to read the letter."

Jefferson tilted his head like a dog hearing a high-pitched squeak. Under his breath he said, "Okay." Liv adjusted her glasses. Raising his voice, Jefferson said, "I can make calls to Guam to confirm the jet launches."

Nessa tried to keep her breathing in check. Howard was rattling the newsroom's chain of command in a significant way. She was going to have a lot of difficulty in the office when this was over. Jefferson would make sure of it.

"You call Guam," Liv said to Jefferson. "I can call a contact who worked with us on the Chernobyl stories to confirm radiation symptoms, perhaps get the names of prominent radiation experts in Russia, US, and Israel." She called out to Howard's assistant, "Dodie, can we get some more phones in here?"

Nessa winced. *Now, Liv is making calls instead of me?*

The elegant woman ducked in to confirm the order for more phones. Before she left, she deposited the tiny pill bottle at Howard's elbow. "In case." Howard snatched the bottle and tucked it into his inner jacket pocket.

This time, though, Nessa caught the label: *Nitroglycerin tablets, 0.4 mg*. They were emergency heart attack pills.

Howard pulled at his tie. A slight flush filled his cheeks.

Nessa spoke quickly to cover Howard's potential embarrassment. "Jefferson, didn't you do a story on the cultural aspects of Manny's dive? Griff mentioned—" she checked her notes—"le Tasi i Fafo."

Liv visibly twitched. "I would prefer we omitted the mystical aspects—"

"Ms. Ross," Howard boomed, "our deal is still in place. No stone left unturned."

Liv clamped her lips.

Jefferson replied, "Yeah, I have an interview with a folklorist that never aired."

"Call down for that tape to be brought up here," Liv said. "What else?" she asked Nessa.

All eyes in the room were on Nessa. She reviewed her notes. There were many things she wanted to know. Like when Howard and Griff first met, what happened in Berlin in 1945, what *Elazar* meant, was it perhaps a Spanish name or a Hebrew name, and why did Griff say about hoaxes, *You really should have told me about all that. I would have understood.* Had others attempted hoaxes on Howard before? But those answers likely were not forthcoming. Still, being a completist, Nessa wanted to know. One never knew when a fact could open a door to understanding. But she decided on a more pertinent topic to bring up. "Janitorial staff and cremation staff would be required for this secret hospital. We should find out who else besides the nurse can confirm its existence, its patient roster, and its agenda."

Liv pointed at Jefferson. "That's you."

"Wow," he gasped, "I've fallen fast."

Nessa pressed her finger to her note, *Fakaleitī. Male passing as female.* "We will want to revisit the man dressed as a woman who was seen at the vacant bar with Manny. Griff might not have had time to get everything out of him. Her. Whatever is going on there, we need to find the person in Tonga who gave Manny the so-called 'new numbers.' The bar in Tonga—"

Jefferson loudly slapped his thighs. "Why am I not in Tonga? I could be on a flight right now instead of listening to a cube farmer interpret my job for me based on a stack of gooey pages written by a dead man."

Howard narrowed his eyes at Jefferson. "Are you unhappy with your job, Mr. Krider?"

Nessa couldn't disguise her shock. Jefferson might not have any problems with jumping ship to another news organization, but this would be a bad time to do it. They had a global exclusive in the making. Jefferson ground his teeth. "Mr. Winfield, Ms. Decker is more qualified—"

Howard exhaled. "Ahhh. Since you insist on ranking personnel according to qualifications, perhaps *you* are more qualified to assign tasks within my global news organization?" He waited for an answer as he located a microscopic bit of fluff from the fine wool weave in his jacket. When no answer came, he continued, "As the topic of job reassignments appears to be on the table, Mr. Krider, I am aware of an opening at the local desk that might suit you better. A kindergarten recital in The Bronx requires our most astute investigator." Howard extracted the fuzz from his jacket and dangled it away from his body, releasing it over the carpet. It was not difficult to imagine Howard dangling Jefferson by the ankle off the penthouse balcony in the same way, observing his plummet to the Sixth Avenue sidewalk with cold detachment. "It would be no effort at all to send you out to our neighboring borough to the east," he added.

Dead Georgina caught Nessa's wild glances. *This is what he is. Never forget it.*

Jefferson flashed a smile. "That won't be necessary. I'll be a good boy."

"Delighted to hear it." Howard's attention drifted to the window washers on a scaffold working at the opposite building.

Liv cleared her throat, "Jefferson, you probably will be on a flight after we're finished. For now, work the phones."

Jefferson seethed. "Right-o." Another handful of jelly beans went into his mouth.

Dorothy entered with an armful of phones. Fritz and Dave rose to assist her.

As they untangled wires, Howard, perhaps thinking himself unobserved, absently traced a line in the middle of his chest. His head lowered, as if in a prayer. In that instant, he looked different to Nessa. It was as if he was laid bare, without the iron mask that distanced himself from others. Dorothy noticed, too, and offered a glance of maternal worry. He shook his head slightly at her, and she continued untangling phone cords. Then, as suddenly as it had slipped, his mask was back in place. He was again aloof and hardened. But just for a second, Nessa thought she saw the real Howard. Weary, brooding. And something else...a weight on the heart.

Oh. It came to her like a slap in the face.

Howard wasn't just ensuring Griff's legacy. He was ensuring his own. The man was ill. *How ill?*

Everything that had happened that morning reorganized itself within this new perspective. Howard was only in his late-60s, not ready to retire, nowhere near giving up his seat at the top. How many people knew he was sick? How afraid was he that more would find out? If his usual sharp teeth for a cutthroat business had dulled, then the corporate sharks surely smelled blood in the water. Without Howard's influence, governments would slice up his company if his children didn't do it first—unless Howard could offer a show of strength, a feat that would show them all why he deserved to remain on top until *he* saw fit to step down. What Griff sent might be the key to the empire for Howard. It could make or break his case to keep his leadership intact for as long as he wanted to stay on the throne.

Nessa returned her focus to the waiting stack of pages. *Something big is here.*

Just as lawyer-Dave connected a phone line into the conference table's center communications hub, one of the phones in the heap rang. Liv extracted a handset out of the pile. "Liv Ross. Talk."

Out of the corner of her eye, Nessa noticed an odd occurrence on the video monitor playing Manny's footage from the South Pacific. A Tongan crewman had approached Manny. Even Jefferson noticed the change. "What ho," he muttered.

Howard turned, also interested.

On the monitor, the Tongan man's eyes darted to the camera, then back to Manny. "Message for you, Mr. Manny."

"Who is that?" Nessa asked Jefferson.

"Peni Palu. Radio operator," Jefferson said. Nessa made a note of the name and his appearance: *curly hair, baseball cap on backwards, young.*

Peni handed Manny a curling page from a fax machine, then bowed and shuffled out of frame. Manny snatched the page and read aloud, "*To Manny di Martini, from Jonah P. Reynolds...*" Manny stiffened. "*Return to shore immediately. Further communications required. Time to renegotiate your terms."* Then, he whispered to the page, "I don't think so, Satan."

Nessa asked Jefferson, "Jonah P. Reynolds is from Let It Rip Productions, right?"

"Yes," Jefferson said. He glanced at the video's timestamp. "This was a week before Jonah cancelled the production entirely."

"A *week*?" she echoed.

"Almost."

Nessa tapped her notepad. "So, Manny didn't get the *one* fax from Jonah. In fact, he had quite a bit of warning that Jonah might cancel. A lot of time to consider his...options." She lowered her voice for the last sentence. She wasn't sure what Howard would think of her siding with Liv about the hoax. But she had to consider it.

Jefferson raised his brows. "Can't rule it out."

Onscreen, Manny turned his face to allow the sun to light him properly. "They're trying to take my show away from me," he said. "Well. Manny di Martini ceases production for no one." He heaved a stage whisper: "The show must go on." Manny opened his hand while staring down the camera. The fax page rattled then whipped out to sea.

Jefferson echoed, "The show must go on." Then he wrote on the whiteboard in big letters: *Where is Manny di Martini?*

Jefferson was right to ask. Did the military evacuate Manny with Griff and the others? If not, where was he?

On the monitor, Manny di Martini raged at a pile of cables on deck. His voice rose to a shriek. "I don't see the audio cables...The AUDIO CABLES...Jesus Christ dragging a donkey cart through the desert sands of Egypt, I thought you all spoke English! AUD-I-O..."

In his letter, Griff had outlined exactly how Manny had a lot to lose if this expedition didn't work out. How far would Manny go to create a television event worthy of his immense debts?

Liv slapped down the phone, then huffed. She removed her glasses and rubbed life into the pale bridge of her nose. "That was Kenji."

Kenji Adams. International News Producer. Something was terribly wrong. Howard raised his silver brows. "And?"

"And we have word from embassy circles in DC that Russia intends to recall their ambassador."

Nessa sat forward. Jefferson dropped his marker.

Howard, though, seemed calm. His iron mask was cold and gleaming. "Why would they do that?"

Liv said, "It seems the US military is restricting international access to an area in the South Pacific the Russians claim is of 'interest to humanity.'"

Howard lifted his chin. "And would this area be to the southwest of Tonga?"

Liv said, "It would."

Jefferson's arms went limp. He plopped down into the closest chair. "That's a fucking problem."

"And that's not all," Liv said. "China has asked for a meeting with the US Embassy—"

Howard interrupted, "Ask Kenji Adams to join us, please. And with Ms. Decker's approval—"

My approval?

"—let's get some more researchers on these phones and making notes about these tapes. Call over to the newspaper, if need be. See who they can spare. And get another television monitor in here."

Nessa gripped her pen until her knuckles went white. "What's happening?" she whispered.

Howard said to her, "The letter, dear. Your efforts would be best channeled toward the letter."

"All right," Nessa said. She pulled two new tissues from a box at the center of the table. "All right." She seemed to be soothing herself. An ambassador recall denoted a serious breakdown in communications. *Was war being discussed? War? Over what?*

Jefferson swooped his head between his knees and let out a moan.

Howard hummed a jaunty tune to himself.

Nessa breathed through her mouth, her pulse skyrocketing and her body growing hot. "All right." She brought the page to her, the one she had set aside when Jefferson had interrupted. She reread the nurse's handwriting: *At the wharf, we loaded up on beer and food, enough to stay out there a day or two.*

That's right, Nessa thought. *They were boarding their charter in the Tongan wharf.*

Howard was observing the room abuzz, sucking in the energy like a ravenous man. "You miss the news," she said aloud. It was a realization.

One side of Howard's lips curved. "Oh, yes."

He's a media titan, she thought. *And this is the story of a lifetime.*

Jefferson was gazing into his glass jar. "I'm going to need a lot more jelly beans."

Liv called out, "Dodie!"

Howard gestured to the letter. "It's all here, dear. Keep going."

She nodded, tried to smile. She sunk back into the letter. She read: *It was almost 4:00 pm. It would be dark soon—*

4

The Waste Land

IT WAS ALMOST 4:00 pm. It would be dark soon.

The weather turned nasty. High winds. White caps. I did a lot of barfing in the head that night with TS Eliot as my only companion. *This is the dead land. This is cactus land.* Bleak shit. I should have brought *Moby Dick.*

I settled my stomach with a pack of nacho chips and stumbled up to the bridge to join a conference between the Aussies and the captain. Dim overhead lights dropped strange shadows below the chins of my four fellow sailors. "Get a load of this, Griffy. Now, the Tongan coast guard is in trouble."

Despite the seriousness, I had to laugh. Who rescues the rescuers?

At 6:14 pm, they said, the Tongan Search and Rescue, riding a 30-foot craft with eight souls on board, had sent out a mayday call. They had approached within a few nautical miles of the *Rosie's* coordinates when the sea turned dead. "Dead?" I asked. "What does that mean?"

Everyone shrugged in unison. Bossy AD said, "It seems the Tongan captain and the first mate went insane. They locked up the other six and went about sinking the ship with everyone on board."

By this time, I had my notebook out, verifying the details. "They wanted to sink their own ship?" I turned to our captain. "Why the hell would anyone do that?" Our captain had no answer for this, but judging by his body language he knew something he wasn't saying. He was itching to get out of his skin, throwing glances to all four corners of the bridge. I prodded, "How do you sink your own ship?"

Our captain shrugged. "Mess with the pumps. Cut the hoses. Breach the hull. It's not hard if you know what you're doing."

I allowed that to sink in. "And the six shipmates?"

"They got off," the captain said. "They're on a lifeboat now. The captain and first mate went down with the ship."

I looked to the Aussies for help, but they looked as confused as I felt. "Are the six in danger? Are we changing course to intercept their lifeboat?"

"No," our captain said. "The Royal Tongan Navy will intercept and continue the *Rosie* rescue mission."

Still, no one moved. There had to be something else. "And? Out with it."

"Weeeell," the Aussie Pretty Boy sang out. "The six who abandoned ship radioed. They said, 'Do not approach the *Rosie*.'"

I had to compute that. "What?"

Bossy AD added, "And—"

I coughed, "There's more?"

Cameraman nodded with eyes wide.

The AD added, "The captain who went down with the ship sent a little PS on the radio right before he went under."

Our captain interrupted, "Do not give this message credit. There is some poison in the water that affects them—"

Cameraman spoke over him. "He was calm. At first. He said they were about to go under, and he was glad. Then, he asked, 'Do you know the story of the Tower of Babel?'"

"The Bible story?" I was going to have to reach far back to my Catholic school days for this one. "Who was he speaking to?"

Bossy AD said, "As far as we can tell, no one in particular. He was just broadcasting in general."

Cameraman continued, "The guy retold the story. Desert people in Biblical times, knowledgeable in all the world's languages, building a tower to reach Heaven." Our captain's face dove into a severe frown, but Cameraman continued. "The guy's voice kept switching. It would be low and gentle, then speed up and go all high-pitched. He said, 'God did not approve.'"

"Oh," I said, "he is an extremist?"

Our captain looked at me firmly. "No. I know these men. Religious, yes. Extremist, no."

Cameraman continued, "The guy said God didn't want the people to reach Heaven, so God...uh...confused...their tongues."

Bossy AD added, "So they couldn't understand each other."

"I got that," I said.

Cameraman said, "That's when the guy on the radio started to get really weird. He started to cry, like he was hurting. You know, breathing hard and grunting?"

"Hurting?"

"Yeah," he continued. "He asked over the radio, 'What kind of God smites His own children who want only to be near Him?' At this point, the guy is completely nuts. He is shrieking and screaming like someone was pulling out his guts on air. It was hard to hear."

"Extremist," I said. Our captain shook his head.

"Then the guy says really clear, 'I know—I know Who does such a thing.' He says, 'It was a *merciful* God.'"

Pretty Boy ended the story: "And then the radio went dead."

I wrote down that final phrase. *It was a merciful God.* I asked, "What do you think it means?"

Our captain announced, "He's sick. A gas leak. Something in the sea that has caused it to turn dead, then affect the men."

I asked, "A gas leak causes that?" I really wanted to know.

Our captain sliced the air in front of him, adamant. "These are good men, and I will not permit you to stain their memories with this extremist talk."

I could not agree. "The truth is the truth. I can't help that." I rubbed my face, scraping my incoming beard. "It would help if we could get out there and find out what is going on." I reached for another nacho chip bag. I was feeling sick again. "Anyone have a beer?" One landed in my palm like magic, and I was grateful for the cold.

Meanwhile, the three Aussies had an ocean map out. "More are getting involved now," Bossy AD said. "The Royal Tongan Navy, all two boats of it, are two hours behind us."

Pretty Boy stretched a ruler between Tonga and Fiji, then between New Zealand and Tonga. "Also joining us are the Fiji and New Zealand coast guards. They're farther out—21 to 29 hours."

I muttered, "Christ, this ocean is big."

Cameraman said, "At dawn, New Zealand will launch an air patrol, their P-3K2 Orion, to get eyes on the *Rosie*." The P-3K2. Military air surveillance in a commercial jet package. We were getting serious. He added, "They won't be able to land, obviously, but they can drop down medical supplies, maybe even drop a medical officer if the weather cooperates."

Bossy AD said, "And more news crews are coming."

My stomach dropped. "Who?" I asked.

"Fiji. New Zealand. Everyone is a day out, though. Or more."

"Why more?"

Our captain said, "Tonga closed its wharf to outgoing traffic. Anyone flying in won't get a charter."

"Oh," I said. "That's weird. Isn't that weird?"

"Which fucking part?" Bossy AD asked.

"But," I insisted, "we'll be first on the scene, right?"

The three Aussies looked at the map. "Yeah," Bossy AD said. "We'll be first."

My gut leapt in a good way. We would have the exclusive on the *Rosie*.

Our captain said nothing. He turned his attention to the front window. Bright lights on the mast had blinked on, spotlighting the vacant deck. Beyond, the black water churned. The sight of all that water out there unsettled me.

What creatures glided underneath, invisible to us?

What treachery hid under the surface?

An eternal war happening in the dark...

Shit. I should have brought *Moby Dick* with me.

At this point, the weirdness and the barfing had drained me. I told my boys, "I need some fucking sleep."

Sleeping in a ship berth would be unpleasant under the best of circumstances, but my stomach still wasn't functioning right, so it was torturous. Opting to skip the thin, stained, moldy mattress, I dragged it from the top wooden bunk and crawled in. The rocking of the ship induced a sickening hypnosis. The ship lurched and groaned. There was an immensity pushing back on the hull that separated my green, sweaty face from the abyss.

I thought of the Tongan coast guard sabotaging their own ship. Our captain implied the ease of such a thing. And why not sink it? Why not give in to what nature wants? What whim of science keeps a hunk of metal on the surface of the water anyway? The boat we were on, with its duct-taped batteries and creaking pump motors and rust-splattered rivets, skittered blind on the seam of a veil covering a void. If that veil were ripped away, we would slip quietly into the darkness. How easy it would be to sink! Why, you could just do *nothing*, and in time, you'd be taken by the water. It was the natural thing, a progression of logic. You go out on the water enough, eventually it will take you.

I slept in spurts. Dreams came in overwhelming waves that knocked me about the bunk, bruising me. I was sweating and thrashing, enduring visions of war and imprisonment and murder. Whose dreams were these? Not mine. These were not wars I knew. They were fought by amorphous creatures in cloudy landscapes I did not recognize. These were sick and depraved images beyond my roughest experience. Disemboweling, slaughter, and massacres on epic scales. I felt isolated from any understanding of these visions, as if they were someone else's horrors playing out for me, and inviting me to join in. *Come and see*, they beckoned me. *Come and find out.* I felt no relation to these unearthly specters and this violence, only a suspicion that I should adopt it, that I should make it mine. As if sensing my curiosity, my dreams redoubled their efforts to lure me in. They invited me to play out my desires, to replay scenarios with my old childhood monsters from tales of my people. Making an appearance that night was my mother's Barmouth sea monster, the unidentified creature swimming off the coast of Wales. Why wouldn't I ride it to destroy a coastal village? That night I did. I murdered thousands of innocents on the back of that scaly monster. And my father's Vietnamese *Rồng*, the dragon carved into the pillars of his homeland's temples? I tempted it to breathe fire onto innocents and watched them all scream in agony in the flames. And my sisters' *Dames Blanches*, who lurk in forests and insist on a deadly dance? All of those monsters came together to form a writhing mass, a hideous congregation that towered toward God. This pile of creatures had no purpose other than to wreak chaos. They wanted me to climb them, to step upon their breasts and pull at their hair with no other objective than to climb. *To God. To God*, they said. Above me, a violent swirl of erratic lightning and menacing clouds threatened to sever me from my life, but I did climb. I wanted God. What does He know? What will I find out?

At the back of my mind, though, reason spoke: *He will cut me down because He is a merciful God.*

The pain of the Tongan captain's realization was mine now. It was a wish for a reprieve from whatever lay beyond the veil. *Take it back. I want ignorance again.* What is the limit of human comprehension? How much can the abyss stare back at you before you flinch? The God who severed humanity from that cosmic knowledge was a merciful God.

Now that I'm in this secret hospital, much closer to God than I ever wanted to be, I can report that the pain in my physical body is nothing compared to the expansion of my mind into that bleak cosmos on that night. The connections between us—these gossamer threads that hold us to our histories and our futures, with our ancestors tugging us this way and that, guiding us to justice and peace the best they can—are the sum of all the light available to us. If we ignore that, we are lost. It was the reason I stayed sane when others did not.

Even now, to stay sane enough to tell this story, I pull you to me, Windbag. I continue to do it now in my final hours. I'll do it after I've crossed over. Pay attention.

Though you are afraid, though you've lost so much, inside your godlike aerie, inside your skyscraper monument to your power and vanity, there are threads alive with light. There are ones who can connect you to the light. They will save us from the darkness. Maybe I'll pull one of them to you. It will be a parting gift, from me to you—

Time time time, the nurse reminds me.

Back on our ship, I awoke to a sickening thumping against the hull.

Others who had joined me in the berth also woke up. Their faces pale and their clothes soaked with sweat, I had only to look at them to recognize their horror and confusion. They were dreaming the same visions of mayhem. They were riding on the backs of monsters they once feared. I recognized the guilt on their faces—it was the high of becoming the author of a perverted violence, with one's conscience barely speaking up. *Cut me down, merciful God.*

I would never get to ask them of their dreams because things began to happen too quickly.

On deck, it was moonless and windless. A thick cloud cover blocked the stars. It was as if we had been cut off from the ordinary glimmers and stirrings of the earth, abandoned in an unfamiliar emptiness. How did the captain even know where we were? There was no visible horizon. Sure, he had his instruments, but we could only see a few feet in front of us. Tipping over the edge of the rail, I could not see far below the surface of the ocean, which was now nearly still. Even the deck lights couldn't pierce the darkness. I felt smaller than ever, an insignificant speck. Who had picked up our boat and deposited us here?

Then, we saw a glow. And with it, a sigh and a feeling of reprieve. How we humans need the light to understand our place in the universe!

The feeling did not last. In the light of that glow, we saw that thousands of lifeforms were bobbing to the surface of the ocean. All of them dead and putrid. Stinking black skin pulled away from skeletons. These carcasses against our hull were making the thumping sounds that had awakened us. We had crossed into the land of the dead.

Our ship slowed to a crawl as we coasted through the black. Our captain spoke. "Inside the hold, you will find pike poles. Get them."

We dragged out three long, wooden poles topped with metal hooks. The cameraman got out his camera and strong lights. With both hands on the wheel, the captain pointed with his chin for us to take positions on the bow. The dull thudding was worse up there.

Spreading ourselves along the bow, three of us reached into the water with our long hooks and cast dead sea life from the path of the ship. We moved dolphins, sharks, turtles, vast schools of fish, seals, thick globs of bleached coral, masses of flaming red algae, squid, octopi. A whitish-grey substance formed on the ocean surface, like wet ash. I witnessed a swimming dolphin pod hit the ashen water and die instantly. All of them turned belly-up without struggling or writhing. And the ashen area was widening. It was like a deadly oil slick.

Working silently, we cast corpses away from our advancing boat. At some points, the boat was held tight in the water by thickening throngs of dead sea life. From the way our boat's motor strained against them, I imagined ice trawlers pushing through arctic waters. Behind us, corpses flowed into the path we had made, as if barring the way for our return. To fight the stench, we wrapped wet rags around our faces. Cameraman said it smelled like ozone. Pretty Boy said it smelled metallic. I thought it was a cocktail of electricity and sulfur. It was vile.

Cameraman pointed out that the glow wasn't coming from the water; it was emanating from the dead. The faint waves of jewel tones fingered through the darkness like the northern lights, each wave flickering like a sputtering candle. As

Bossy AD pushed a spider crab away with a pike pole, he said he thought we were witnessing the souls of these beasts rising. It was a strange thing for him to say, knowing him to be an atheist, so I looked to him to see if he really meant that. When I did, the jeweled glow from the corpse reached his face and played with its features. He was unrecognizable. He grinned like a madman. Was he in shock? Perhaps I was.

We heard the *Rosie* before we saw her. An otherworldly, guttural groaning.

We were alone together at the end of the world, the only two creaking tubs of rust in a void of noise and sight. No lights illuminated her deck or her interior. Just as the corpses in the water glowed, so did the *Rosie*. Golden light shot from her hull, reaching into the water and into the black night. The waves of light illuminated the layers of the dead gathering beneath her.

We saw no signs of life.

At the back end, the camera unit, the coffin of metal they called *Yuna II*, dangled from a winch. It was mangled beyond recognition. It glowed an eerie blue, as if it were the hottest part of the flame. We could see the lenses of all the cameras still caught inside the array, reflecting curious hues. The whole unit crackled with static, popping and distorting the air all around it. Threads of white light shot from the tangled mass, converging and bursting into electrical offshoots.

The *Yuna II*'s macabre glow cast a light onto a portion of the ship's deck. A wide path of blood pointed to three corpses slumped at the base of the winch. Two men had been shot, with blooms of dark blood staining their heads and chests. On the third, the head was caved in. All three sat up, as if interested in a conversation taking place before them.

The sight of it all sent me into horrible shivers.

Our Bossy AD broke away from the sight. He had the presence of mind to radio Sydney. At least he tried. Our radio was dead.

"Hey!" The voice of Pretty Boy sliced through the silence, rattling us all. He pointed.

A man, alive, barely visible in the glow of *Yuna II*, sat cross-legged on the bow of the *Rosie*. He did not move, nor did he respond to our calls across the water. He looked to me like the carved Buddhist idol of my father's religion, stoic and insistent in his isolation.

Then, two men burst from an interior cabin to wave at us. The younger one with the backward baseball cap spoke. "Hi!" he chirped out across the silent water. "Welcome! Welcome!" He pointed to himself. "Peni Palu! Radio operator! We wondered if you would ever make it!"

As our boat pulled alongside the *Rosie*, he gave out directions. "Along the gunwales, but not too close to the stern. That's *Yuna II*'s home! That's it! Nice

and easy!" He smacked his partner, the taller crewman gaping at us. "Don't be
rude! Welcome our guests, Claude!" He pointed to Claude. "He's Californian!"

Claude stared at us without seeing. He was blonde, lean, and ponytailed. He
looked like he would be more at home on the beaches of Malibu than on that
boat. He darted glances all around, as if keeping lookout. He mumbled under his
breath. I could catch none of it.

Peni leapt aboard our boat, leaving Claude behind. Both men appeared to me
clinging and desperate. Too much drool in their mouths triggered a constant
wiping of their lips with the backs of their greasy hands. They were sweating
through their stained shirts, slapping around the deck in dirty bare feet. Their
body odor competed with the corpses of sea life bobbing all around. Peni
chittered, "Cigarettes, cigarettes...Anyone have cigarettes?" Bossy AD raised a
finger, and Peni scampered over. "Thank you, thank you. We ran out this
morning." He smacked his own face. "I should have saved a few for you! Silly,
silly! What kind of host am I?"

"No worries," Bossy AD mumbled.

Peni pointed to Claude again. "He's Californian!"

"You said, mate."

Everyone in our boat reeled from the unexpected energy. Did we expect them
all to be dead? Sick?

I nodded to Cameraman to begin filming. He smacked the side of the unit a
few times. The light flickered. I said to our host, "There was a mayday call sent
from these coordinates—"

Peni lit one of Bossy AD's cigarettes and groaned. "Yeaaaah." He unfocused his
eyes. "I sent that." He blew smoke over his shoulder, as if to keep our air clear.

I gestured to the three dead men sitting upright under the *Yuna II* wreckage.
"You have fatalities."

Peni laughed a short bark. "Them? They're not dead."

Pretty Boy pointed to the body with the severely beaten head. "That one
doesn't have a face."

Peni guffawed as if he told a great joke. "That's our captain. Tuigamalo!"

"And he's *not* dead?" The skin around Tuigamalo's shaved head had turned an
ashen color. His bare feet, splayed before him, were nearly black, at least the best
I could tell in the low light. "Where are the others?" I asked.

But Peni was on the move. He had raced into our cabin, tossing out our
bags of food and beer cases. "Look at all this! You really know how to host a
party!" He tossed bags of chips and beer cans aboard the *Rosie*. "Hoooo-wee!"
he yodeled. Claude watched, smiling vacantly. "Hooo-wee! Corn chips! Toaster
strudel!" Items sailed past Claude, who made no effort to catch them. Beer cans
rolled around on the *Rosie* deck and stopped close to Claude's dirty feet.

Our captain whispered, "I will try our radio again." I nodded.

Pretty Boy called out, "Hey Peni, is your radio working?"

Peni grimaced. "Heck no! Manny shot it."

I felt a bolt of tension run through my shipmates. If Manny still had a gun, we wanted to know where exactly he was. "Where are the others?" I asked again.

Peni laughed. "Why, on the *Rosie*."

Claude echoed without tone, "On the *Rosie*."

The man we hadn't met, the one seated at the bow, turned his head toward us mechanically. He lifted his face, as if sensing something beyond us. Peni yelled at him, "Jacob! You've been out here for hours talking with the captain! Eat something!" He pelted a fruit cup at him. It landed dully at his feet. "That's Jacob," Peni added. "He's not being rude. He's just focused."

I had had enough of this show. "Permission to come aboard?" I asked.

Claude woke up from his reverie and asked in a panic, "You're not going to take us back, are you?"

Peni's energy shifted to a nervous prattle. "We like it here." He scratched himself. "Did I not make you feel welcome here? I did my best. I am working at a disadvantage, what with us being marooned in the middle of the South Pacific."

All three Aussies were assessing the *Rosie* from bow to stern. One whispered, "Gunshots through the windows."

I noticed. It was difficult to count the shots in the dark, but the front windows were all shattered.

Peni heard the whisper. "Oh, the gunshots. Yeaaaah. We've had a few hiccups out here."

Our captain reached for my sleeve. "Our radio is dead. I will stay on the boat."

"Good idea," I said. To the others I said, "Let's see what's going on." Cameraman held his rig upright and lighted my way across the side as I stepped onto the *Rosie*. The camera light threw out a strobing effect, as if it had been short-circuited. "Check to make sure that thing is recording," I said.

"It's going," Cameraman assured me.

Peni threw his arms into the direction of *Yuna II* and yelled, "Just don't go down there."

"Why not?" I asked.

Peni hummed instead of answering.

From a distance, Cameraman filmed the three bodies and the camera array's wreckage. "What happened to *Yuna II*?"

Peni ran at me, and I raced back a few feet. "Don't skip ahead on the tour!"

I held my hands up. "No problem, man."

On the bow, Jacob tilted his head at us. "The ascended," was all I caught.

I moved toward the bridge. "You should have a dozen people on this ship. I count three—down there." I didn't want to rile Peni up about their deceased status. "One at the bow, and you two. We're looking for six more."

Just then, Claude approached me and whispered. "I have something for you."

Peni beat him back. "You're jumping ahead, Claude! I have a *tour* planned!"

Claude looked hurt. I said to him, "It's all right, man. We'll get to it."

"Watch your step!" Peni called. "There's blood here and here and some over there." To himself, he said, "I really should have mopped."

I ducked inside the bridge. It smelled like vomit and fear, like the inside of a captive animal's cage. A beat-up leather chair splayed away from the ship's wheel. Monitors and gauges on the instrument panel were all dark. As the Aussies had pointed out, the front of the bridge's windows had been shot out. Another window had a major blood smear on it. There were dents in the door and along the walls. There was another, smaller chair in front of a table of television monitors connected to video recorders. Cables fed from these monitors along the ceiling and through the back wall. I asked, "Where does this cable go?"

Peni said, "*Yuna II*! Wanna see our galley?"

I made sure our camera recorded everything on the bridge before allowing Peni to lead us to a side door accessing the cabin.

The acidic smell of vomit was intense there. The unearthly shimmer from *Yuna II* reflected on the water, casting rolling shadows like murky waves through the cabin windows. This, and the softly strobing camera light, was the interior's only source of illumination. The ceiling twisted and rolled with the reflected waves. My knees buckled and my stomach lurched.

Inside was a small galley kitchen and a dining area with two booths and a table. I was startled when I saw a crewman laying on the dining table. Another two lay on the bench seats. They were out cold. Peni shifted from one foot to another. "That's Chuckie, that's Filipe. And that's Gavin on the table. He's American!"

Cameraman lit them up for recording. Dried vomit caked their mouths. Half-dried puddles of liquefied food were all around. Black threads of viscous fluid ran throughout the puddles. Tumbleweeds of human hair drifted into the light, propelled by our movement. The crewmen's skin showed shades of intense red, as if they had been burned. Some of their skin had sloughed off, showing veins, tissue, and muscle. Protruding from their bones were black tumors, which pulsed.

Bossy AD reached toward the men. "What happened here?"

Peni said, "I wouldn't touch them. Salote said not to."

"Salote," I said. I remembered interviewing his family back in Tonga this afternoon. It seemed a lifetime ago. "He's the medical officer? Where is he?"

Peni frowned. "Hold your horses. We haven't seen the bunks yet."

"But why are they so sick?" I asked.

Peni puckered. "Jeez, pushy. Those are the deckhands and the camera driver. They touched *Yuna II* when it first came up." He shrugged. "That's how we learned not to do *that*."

Gavin shuddered awake. He cried out, "Can you feel that? Can you feel that?"

Peni yelled at him, "Shut up, Gavin! We have company!" To me, he added, "Something pulls at him, and sometimes he runs." He yelled again into Gavin's ear. "If you run again, we will have to strap you down like we did the captain!"

Claude gently pushed past me, moving toward a set of lockers at the back of the cabin. He accessed one with a combination. Inside was a cloth bag. He held it behind his back. That made me nervous. "Whatcha got there, buddy?"

Claude held his fingers to his lips. "*Shhhhhh.*"

"This way to the bunks!" Peni called out.

"Watch him," I whispered to Bossy AD.

"No problem."

Cameraman shone a flickering light deep into the cabin where the bunks were. One was covered in massive blood stains. Two belts were looped around the side rails, as if to restrain someone.

"Oh, crackers! I should have cleaned up." Peni dodged my gaze as if embarrassed.

I asked, "What happened there?"

"That's where our captain crossed into the twilight kingdom. Pardon the mess."

I jolted. "Twilight kingdom? Like TS Eliot?"

"Oh," Peni said. "Was that you?"

"Was that me what?"

Peni quoted, "This is the dead land. This is cactus land. "

I was shocked. "From 'The Hollow Men'?"

Peni smiled at me stupidly, his yellow teeth beaming in the camera light. "Did I pull you to me on the gossamer thread?"

I turned away. "Jesus," I said to the Cameraman. "I can't get a straight answer out of him." I pointed to the blood stains. "Peni, did someone kill the captain?"

He lit up. "Oh no! He did that to himself!"

Pretty Boy looked as if he would be sick. I clapped his back twice. "Buck up."

Peni pushed through us to exit the cabin. "That's enough of *that*! Follow me! You'll love this next part!"

Pretty Boy said, "I doubt it."

We made our way to a slim staircase that led below deck. The fish smell was overwhelming here. It was completely dark, but I could hear muffled voices. Peni called into the dark, "Wakey wakey!"

In the light of the camera, we first saw the engine, pumps, and other mechanics. They were heavily dented, as if attacked with a blunt object. "Manny again?" I asked.

Peni gave a thumbs-up.

The muffled voices intensified.

Sweeping the camera along the back wall, we discovered two more men chained against a low pipe. Their mouths were stuffed with dirty rags. Both looked shocked in the camera's glare. Peni pointed to the one on the left. "That's Salote. You asked where he was, and there he is." Peni pointed to the other. "And that's Hudson. He's the director. And he's American!"

"Oh my God." Pretty Boy stepped forward.

Peni caught his arm. "I wouldn't do that. If you ungag them, they're going to talk you into sinking the boat. And if you unchain them, they'll try to kill you."

"Dude," Pretty Boy said. "What?"

I thought of the Tongan coast guard. "Step back," I said to him.

Salote and Hudson kicked at the floor, faces crimson and furious.

Bossy AD scoffed. "I doubt they can talk me into anything I don't want to do."

Peni chuckled. "I doubted many things, too. But you will see."

"Why would they do that?" I asked.

Peni huffed. "I mean, *eventually* we will join the dreamer. But, I mean, come *on*. It's far too early for that. We have to spread the message first."

"Spread the message?" I asked. "What message?"

"Who's the dreamer?" Pretty Boy asked.

We could hear Jacob's voice mumbling on deck. "Yes, Captain," he said. "Wondrous awe."

I snapped my fingers for the camera to illuminate Peni. "What happened here?" I demanded. "And where the hell is Manny di Martini?"

Peni covered his mouth and giggled like a child. "Go ahead, Claude."

Claude edged toward me and pushed the cloth bag into my gut. I felt the hard edges of plastic. "This," he said. I felt inside the bag. They were video tapes. "This is what you came for."

Windbag. The doctors are coming. I don't have much more time—

5

Hysteria

A HOLLOW CLAP—A PHONE cracking against its cradle. Liv barked, "Chernobyl contact confirms these symptoms are similar to radiation poisoning with some notable differences."

Nessa blinked away the scene from the *Rosie*. The room exploded with the noise of others steadily working phones, notating the tapes now playing on three television monitors, and assembling the timeline from Griff's pages.

Howard folded his hands on his desk and asked Liv, "What does he say about the black tumors?"

She ran a free hand through her hair. Her severe bob had begun to frizz under stress. "That's more complicated." Her other hand was gloved with a plastic bag. She clutched a page from Griff's letter. On the reverse side was a mycology report.

When Nessa came across that report, she had flagged it for Liv's special attention. Was it from the fungi lab Griff had mentioned, the one set up near the secret hospital? The report was signed by a doctor with a Russian name and documented disturbing findings: *Several breeds of radiotrophic fungi bursting from patient tumors.*

Liv continued, "The Russians have seen this type of fungus before, reproducing in the wild near the damaged reactor, but not in humans as documented in this." She rattled off the report. "He said these microorganisms demonstrate vicious reproduction rates—prolific little buggers. But for these types of fungi to breed in tumors inside humans? And in the South Pacific? The doctor said they'd never heard of that."

Howard wrinkled his nose as if he smelled something awful. "Are we able to confirm the doctor's name on the report?"

Nearby, Kenji Adams said, "Yes." Nessa startled at his voice. She hadn't noticed him coming in. He sandwiched his phone between his shoulder and ear and said, "I have a Moscow government source on the line." Kenji was a slight man with a boyish face and calm demeanor. Anyone mistaking those traits for a gentle nature would be surprised to learn he had a cutthroat disposition that kept him at the top of the International News Team. He continued, "My contact confirms two doctors from Moscow Central Clinical Hospital were dispatched to American

Samoa to assist in suspected radiation sickness in an international crew." He held up a finger to indicate more. "She also confirms Moscow isn't pleased that they'd been denied access to the dive site. She said she really shouldn't be talking to us."

"Get them both on the record," Howard said.

At the conference table, Fritz stood and straightened his tie. "Non-disclosures faxed."

Nessa struggled to catch up to the room's energy. She laid down the page she had been reading. As she had done with all the others, she flipped the page to slide it in line with the other overturned pages. Together they were forming a story unto themselves, a scientific story of the deaths of everyone on the water. Patient charts, blood tests, surgical reports, even fungi reports. This latest page, though, was different. Nessa could hardly guess what it might be, but it looked like a map. Topographical. It showed peaks and valleys, depth and shadow. Concentric rectangles and huddles of structures with a towering spire at its center. The layout was artful, like surveys of ancient civilizations and their walled cities. Nessa might have mistaken this map for someone's ancient geography homework had it not been marked with measurements for scale and dates: April 11, 1992, the day before Griff set out for the *Rosie*.

Howard asked Liz, "Where are we on the islander nurse?"

Liv replied, "A detective in American Samoa is checking with a buddy who works close to the former US Naval Base in the harbor. We want to know if any nurses in scrubs have been frequenting the burger joints or bars."

"Tread carefully," Howard said. "That nurse took a risk, and our government will not be pleased about these leaks."

An aide slid a notebook page across Howard's glass desk. He scanned it. "No," he told her. "Watch it again. More carefully, this time." He wadded and threw the paper at her. "And dispense with the adverbs. No one cares for your interpretation of the action."

The aide scampered back to her station in front of a television cart. Three TVs were blaring tapes now, with two more aides watching and notating. On one, Manny di Martini appeared, Italian accent in full glory, on the deck of the *Rosie*. "Behind-a me is the deep-a-sea camera unit, *Yuna II*, that will-a relay the first video of the-a *Polaris* to you at home." He looked over the camera rig.

Nessa was momentarily fascinated with *Yuna II*'s pristine state. After it dove to the seafloor, she knew it would become something unearthly and terrible.

Onscreen, Manny spread his arms wide. "YUUUUUNAAAAA!" He pointed to men off camera. "It's funny! What? Did you even see *Polaris*? Didn't it show on your bumfuck island? Get a fucking sense of humor. What's wrong with you people? You don't speak English?" He flapped his arms. "If we were in LA, that would kill."

From the whiteboard, Jefferson chuckled. "I love that guy."

Nessa pushed the latest letter page with the map into the assembly line of pages undergoing dissection at the end of the table. She wanted to speak up—*Something new coming up!*—but her mouth was dry. She was afraid to drink in here, what with the black flecks loosening from the pages and spilling onto the table.

She was surprised to find, parked a few seats down, Liv's assistant. Fabrice had joined them to sort the reverse sides of the letter pages. He wore yellow rubber dishwashing gloves, probably scrounged from a break room. Currently, he read from Peni's death report: *April 17, internal organs liquefied.* Fabrice sent his gloved hand to his mouth in shock. Nessa said to him, "Don't do that. Don't touch your mouth."

He dropped the page. "This shit is gross."

With Jefferson at the whiteboard, two investigative reporters from the newspaper called out information from the line of incoming pages. One reached for the next page with a sandwich baggie over her hand. Impromptu glove options must have been running low, Nessa thought, because peeling a sheet of paper from a glass conference table with thin plastic protection wasn't easy. The reporter pawed at the paper, but it barely moved. Nessa knew she was trying to grip the final page in Claude's patient chart. He had died of a calcified heart. When the reporter finally detached the page from the glass, she exclaimed, "It's like a carousel of horrors. Who dies of a *calcified heart*?"

The whiteboard had begun to fill in with dates and times. The reverse pages from the letter had allowed them to pinpoint the kidnapping/rescue/evacuation as occurring sometime on April 16. That would have been five days after Griff arrived. "Five days on the water," Nessa mumbled to herself. She plastered her hands to her sides, resisting the urge to cover her mouth as Fabrice had done. "They could have left," she said, "but they didn't. Why not?"

On day five, they now knew, the US military showed up. That's when the on-arrival death reports began. Three corpses on deck, as Griff had found them, all of them were in a noticeable state of decay. Causes of death: two of gunshot wounds, one of blunt force trauma. Three more corpses in the cabin, all from advanced radiation sickness. Eight more died aboard a Fijian coast guard boat drifting close by. Radiation sickness, suicide, and two murders. Four found alive, clinging to life. During transport to American Samoa, the captain of Griff's boat died of radiation sickness.

At the hospital, the death reports were more detailed. Of the Aussies with Griff, the cameraman died during a skin graft. The ones Griff called "Bossy AD" and "Pretty Boy" died of the fungal bursts. Thankfully, Nessa noted, the investigative reporters who had joined them in Howard's office had now linked real names to the nicknames. *Their families will know the truth*, she thought. *If it is the truth.*

Behind Jefferson, Nessa noted the large scrawl still present: *Where is Manny di Martini?* She checked her stack of pages. They were dwindling. Almost finished. A tiny spark of grief flashed. The end of the letter likely meant the end of Griff Tran, if the letter was to be believed. And Howard was right; the grotesqueries were difficult to accept. Although Liv and Howard wanted her professional opinion about the veracity of the letter, she wasn't prepared to deliver it. Every page revealed more information—front and back. She wanted the full picture.

A full picture of what? The possibilities unnerved her.

Looking around the room, Nessa's attention settled on a second television cart with an aide sitting in front, taking notes. On the TV, a middle-aged woman with small eyes and a loud blouse commanded the monitor. Onscreen text identified her as Dr. Ta'ahine Edwards of the University of the South Pacific. She spoke with the flat vowels of a New Zealander and motioned with chubby hands. "There are reasons islanders develop their folklore," she said. "These are stories of survival. They can warn the next generation how to manage difficulty. They can frighten children into less risky behavior. And they can keep entire civilizations out of danger." Nessa noted that this must be Jefferson's interview with the folklore expert. She stood to watch it, rolling and cracking her neck. At the console, Dr. Edwards said, "The story is rarely told outside the islands stretching from Samoa to the Kermadecs, one of the few tales limited in geography to the undersea plains above the Tonga Trench..."

Dodie sidled up to Howard and whispered. He laughed, open-throated. It sent a jolt through the room, lifting the faces of everyone else working in their separate silos. *What was funny?* Nessa had to admit it was difficult to see anything funny right now. Dodie might have agreed because she flashed Howard another look of worry that he did not notice. Howard was oblivious. He was in his prime.

Nessa noticed Howard gazing at her. She sensed no antagonism in the look, not like with the others who caught his attention. He softly smiled, then nodded.

Where did this end? Nessa wanted to know. Would she be sent back to the cube farm, as Jefferson had predicted? Her professional opinion was wanted, and so far, she did not have one. She could not rule out a hoax. Not yet. If it was a hoax, the upset Russians and the Americans patrolling the South Pacific would see Manny di Martini in prison, if he ever showed up. How much further would this go? Did Howard intend to push everyone to their breaking point?

Nessa sucked in air, blew it out again. The other, much more frightening thought was that this was no hoax. She would not allow that thought to take hold. For now, she was with Liv, who wasn't convinced of this package's authenticity. Telling Howard would be difficult. Liv certainly had expressed her view, but

Nessa was no Liv Ross. Nessa was the mousy researcher, disposable and without politics. But she had her scruples, and she had no plans to compromise. Even if it meant losing her job and having to call her father—

No. She wouldn't do that. Some things were beneath her dignity.

From the edge of Howard's desk, Georgina peered at her with a conspiratorial smirk. *I hear ya, sister. Dads can be jackasses.*

Nessa had standards. No matter what, she would carefully guard her professional ethics. It was all she had in this ruthless industry. Reason. Confirmation. Unbiased judgment. Griff Tran's letter defied reason. It was not yet confirmed by two or more witnesses. So, her unbiased judgment relied heavily on Occam's razor: the simplest explanation was usually the best one. And the simplest explanation was that Manny di Martini was putting on a show.

On the television monitor with the pristine *Yuna II*, Manny was still angry. He left the camera frame, then returned. "New Jersey! That'd be funny." Manny strolled off. "WHAT'S WRONG WITH YOU PEOPLE?" he yelled. The *Yuna II* swayed over the dark waters.

Offscreen a voice said, "We all speak English, you dick." The aide made a note.

Who was that offscreen voice? Nessa wondered. Eager to see if she could attach any other faces to the names she had read about, Nessa turned her focus to the third television monitor, the largest one set into Howard's office wall. A much more subdued affair was unfolding. The timestamp read, *April 11, 1992. 8:04 pm.* Nessa scribbled that date and time into her notes. Griff Tran would arrive the next day.

It was night on the deck of the *Rosie*. A few of the crew members were preparing what looked like small buoys attached to cables, to be thrown overboard. A man was speaking to the camera, but Nessa didn't know him. He explained, "We will drop these transponders, which are just acoustic instruments—"

Nessa called out, "Jefferson, who is speaking on the front monitor?"

Jefferson looked up from a conference with two reporters from the newspaper, who had joined him at the whiteboard. He said, "That's Hudson Porter. Manny's director."

She swallowed. Hudson Porter. Griff found him in the gloomy pit, in the bowels of the *Rosie*, chained and gagged. She asked, "Why isn't Manny speaking?"

Jefferson shrugged. "How would I know? Ask the aide monitoring the tape."

"Excuse me," Nessa called out to the person hunched over a notepad close to the monitor. "Why isn't Manny speaking?"

"Too drunk," the aide said.

"Ah."

Onscreen, Hudson continued, "When these transponders anchor to the seafloor, they will send out signals to form an acoustic net. Those signals will triangulate to form a map of the floor—"

Nessa's eyes went wide. *A map.* She reached for the assembly line of letter pages and pulled the most recent one back.

It was a map. A sonar map. But this couldn't be a seafloor. It looked more like an Incan citadel than undersea plains and valleys.

Nessa found her voice. "Guys," she said. The room quieted. "I have something new."

All eyes turned to her.

She pushed the map to the center of the table. "I think this is the sonar map from the transponders." She gestured to the screen. "What they're talking about up there."

The aide notating that tape wandered over, as did Howard. Both lawyers—Fritz and Dave—rose to peer at the map. Fritz brought out reading glasses. "She's right," he said. "I have a sonar on my boat in Martha's Vineyard. Just for fun." He reached for the map.

Liv stepped forward with her trash-bag glove. Fritz used it to center the map closer to him. "This is a nice sonar arrangement Manny has." He poked the page with the plastic bag. "Triangulation provides a clear view of undersea features with all the depths and crevices. You see the wrinkled texture of the undersea mountains, the wavy sandy floor, the...hmm." He scanned the image from left to right. Nessa noticed he got paler with each moment.

"What's going on there, Fritz?" Howard asked.

Fritz adjusted his glasses. "This can't be right."

"Just tell us what you see," Liv said.

Fritz's voice broke. "Well, what I think I see is—" He counted the notches at the bottom of the page. "—a two-kilometer complex of—um...towers. With spires."

"Towers with spires?" Howard asked.

"Pointy buildings. Like cathedrals."

Liv sighed. "Okay."

"Manny is desperate," Kenji said.

"Et tu, Kenji?" Jefferson said. "I thought with the Russians involved you'd see that this is real."

"No, no," Fritz said. "These sonar maps are difficult to fake. You would need a knowledge of sea depth and existing natural features." He examined the page closely. "If Manny did fake this, it is a very good job. Not something you can put together at sea—"

"How about with the help of Hollywood friends?" Liv asked.

Fritz pressed the map back to the center of the table. "You are seeing a map of a vast plain on the ocean floor, interrupted by a wall outlining a perfect square of structures." He jabbed at the page. "You see here in the center a spiraling tower. The one tower in the center—"

Jefferson pointed to it. "What the actual fuck is that supposed to be?"

"If these measurements are correct," Fritz said, counting under his breath, "that center structure measures taller than the World Trade towers."

The room hesitated, then looked to each other for confirmation of what they heard.

Howard's face broke into a grin.

Liv asked, "We're supposed to believe this is real?"

"And this architecture," Fritz went on with his nose nearly pressed to the paper, "is sophisticated. It's precise. It's advanced."

"It's not architecture," Liv said. "They're mountains. Cliffs."

"No, Ms. Ross. On sonar maps, mountains and cliffs have texture." Fritz pointed to a set of features close to the edge of the map. "Like here." Nessa could see the difference. The mountains, as Fritz called them, were bumpy. The structures at the center were smooth. Fritz said, "These structures are not naturally occurring features. They are machine-made or handmade with precise tools."

Jefferson said, "Perhaps they are made with flippers or tentacles." Liv shot him a look, but he asked, "Is it human?"

Liv said to Fritz, "Do *not* answer that. We do not work for a tabloid. Keep that in mind."

Dave piped up with his thick Brooklyn accent. "I agree that we are not looking at the simplest explanation for this."

Fritz held the map up to Liv. "This is clear to me. It is not a map of a normal seafloor. It is a map of an underwater city on the seafloor. It is not a misreading of a cliff or a rock face. You look at it and tell me what you see. Where are the wavy textures indicating naturally formed rocks? Like, here?" Fritz poked the map. "That's a mountain because it has these volcanic cones on it." Then he pressed a finger on a smoother surface. "That's a wall. *Not* the same!"

Kenji had been searching the map for some counterpoint. Now, he struggled to speak.

Howard pulled the map toward himself. Nessa offered him the box of tissues to protect him from contaminants. He accepted a fresh tissue with a slight smile, gazed at the map as he might an adorable infant, then slid it back to Fritz.

"Hell," Jefferson blurted. "We don't have to guess at this. Let's just go out to the dive site and confirm it. Fritz has a boat at the Vineyard. Let's pile on—"

Howard announced, "Recall that the dive site is locked down. It's patrolled by frigates and fighter jets." Liv pressed her bob into place and curled her upper lip. He added, "No one goes in."

Kenji added, "And no one out, apparently." He flattened his brow with his fingers, as if to press an emerging headache back into his forehead. "If this is real, then why hasn't anyone discovered this before? Manny di Martini just *happens* to stumble on it?"

"See," Jefferson said, "my question is, if it is machine-made or flipper-made—" Liv flinched. "—how would anyone get down there to build that?"

Howard still held on to a reverie that had entranced him since he saw the map. He traced the scar on his chest through his shirt, then massaged his arm. To Liv, he said, "This is entirely too calculated for Manny di Martini. It's too smart."

She gritted her teeth. "He had help—"

To the room, Howard said, "If this is a hoax, I want to know why someone would want to lead us this far—"

"It's not a hoax," Fritz muttered.

"Excuse me," one of the aides said. "We have something up front—"

"*Why* would he fake it?" Fritz asked.

Nessa stepped beyond the table, approaching the front screen.

Voice by voice, the room quieted.

On the screen was complete anarchy.

The timestamp read, *April 11, 1992, 10:24 pm*. A few hours had passed since the scene with the transponders. Nessa called out the time to Jefferson. "Something is happening."

The *Rosie*'s deck lights threw faces in stark contrast. Crew members tossed duffels onto a lifeboat and climbed overboard. Manny was livid. "No, no, no, no," he said, moving from one crewman to another. He asked someone offscreen. "They're bailing? NOW? Because of a SONAR MAP? They're afraid of a SONOGRAM of a seafloor?" He approached the man off camera. Manny's face grew to gargantuan proportions. "How many of them are leaving?" he asked.

The man replied, "Half."

"Good God!" Manny yelped. "HALF? We can't continue with half a crew!" He stopped another man from throwing his duffel overboard to the lifeboat. "Is it a matter of money? I'll find more! I have a brother...he has a *Playboy* collection...very valuable..."

The man replied in another language.

Manny turned to the man offscreen. "Why does their language sound like a wetback screaming in a raging river? What is he ranting about?"

The man said, "He says, what you have found is spoken of by the ancestors and should remain unseen by human eyes."

Onscreen, after a slight pause, Manny asked the translator, "Is that negotiable?"

A crewman pushed Manny aside just as another one vaulted overboard toward the lifeboat. The translator said, "The big one says he has an aunt in Fiji with an Atari. She has *Donkey Kong*. They will go there."

To the camera, Manny said, "*Donkey Kong. DONKEY KONG!*" He strutted around the deck. "I'm Manny di-fucking-Martini with the world's greatest television special in the making, and they would rather fiddle a joystick!" He gripped the deck rail and yelled at the men in the lifeboat. "WE ARE MAKING HISTORY! DO NOT WALK AWAY FROM THIS. THIS IS WHY YOUR CULTURE IS WEAK. You fucking MORONS—"

A crewman calmly walked into the frame and punched Manny in the face. Manny flew backward into an open crate of cables, which spewed across the deck like a haul of pitch-black octopi. The crewman said, "I told you we speak English, prick."

Manny lay unmoving among the cables on deck.

The translator edged into the frame. "Uh-oh. Mr. Manny, you okay?"

Manny sat up calmly. He pulled a gun and pointed it at the camera. "Turn that off. Get everyone back on the boat. And cut the lifeboat loose."

The screen went dark.

At the whiteboard, Jefferson said, "April 11, 10:00 pm. Manny puts down a mutiny."

Kenji asked, "Did I hear right? The locals won't go near this dive site? That might explain why this tower complex—"

"Alleged tower complex," Liv interrupted.

"—evaded human discovery for so long. Islanders warning people away, perhaps sabotaging expeditions?"

Liv said, "You're reaching."

A knock at the door interrupted them. Dodie poked her head inside. "Another tape has arrived." She held it out to Liv.

"Load it," Howard said to her, as he absently rubbed his arm.

"And I have a message," Dodie added. She read from a memo. "Only one tape remains, and it is severely damaged. It's different from the others. It's in black and white."

Jefferson whispered, "What does *that* mean?"

The only sound in the room was of Dr. Edwards on the television cart. She was saying, "Those who come close to the creature will first experience nausea, which progresses to—"

Liv swept her hand at Dr. Edwards. "I can't use this. No facts."

"Turn that off," Howard said to the aide.

Now, the room was quiet.

Howard spun around. "The most recent tape, onscreen, please."

Everyone else shuffled quickly into chairs.

Nessa found her way back to Griff's letter pages. To the nurse's loopy handwriting, she mumbled, "Where are you taking us?"

On the front screen, Manny di Martini appeared, larger than life. He had a blooming black eye, which he had attempted to conceal with a shade of makeup that did not match his sunburned face. There was a bandage over the bridge of his nose. Without the Italian accent, he said, "This is Manny di Martini, recording for posterity—"

6

Manny di Martini and the Discovery

THE TIMESTAMP READ, *APRIL 12, 1992, 11:31 am*. The mayday eventually reaching Griff Tran would happen in fewer than 15 minutes.

Nessa felt dizzy. "Breathe," she said to herself.

On the bridge of the *Rosie*, Manny spoke quickly and glanced repeatedly off camera. Several wide windows behind him opened to the calm ocean and the forward deck.

Near the bridge's navigation controls, a monitor showed the *Yuna II* dangling on a winch over the open water. A few crewmen milled about the base of the camera array, nervously pacing. They held improvised weapons: a pole, a bat, and a rusty boat hook.

Seated next to Manny was the captain. Manny held a gun to his head.

Manny's Italian accent was gone. "This is Manny di Martini, recording for posterity. Half of my crew tried to abandon ship for *Donkey Kong*, so I've been forced to proceed with fewer allies." He leaned into an intercom on the panel and pressed a button. "Look alive back there!"

On the *Yuna II* screen, the three crewmen waved their weapons.

Nessa squinted at the giant monitor. *Were those the three who died of radiation poisoning first?*

Manny continued. "Fortunately, our insurgents did not include the captain." He tapped the captain with his gun. "Tell the people at home your name, pal."

"Tuigamalo."

Manny grimaced. "Oh no. That'll never fly in Hollywood. I'll call you Cap'n T."

Tuigamalo forced a smile.

Manny returned to the camera. "Manny di Martini and Cap'n T coming to you from the bridge of the *Rosie*, named after my dead and sainted mother, where today I will bring you images of undiscovered structures miles below the ocean's surface! What are they? Who built them? And what is their purpose?" Manny glanced off camera toward sounds of banging on metal and yelling. He continued,

"What has our government known about this site? What of the ancestors in the South Pacific Islands? Who has kept these secrets of the deep from us?"

A crew member, clinging to the outside of the bridge front window, climbed into view. Manny noticed him. "Uh-oh," he said, "they're coming for us, T." He jabbed the intercom button. "You back there! Drop the camera! DROP IT!"

On the monitor, a crewman slapped a button on the winch near the camera array. The cables whirred and *Yuna II* plunged out of site. Water from the splashdown shot skyward.

On the bridge, Manny shrieked, "YUUUUUNAAAAA!"

Television monitors on the navigation panel lit up. Murky underwater images appeared.

Underwater images in black and white, Nessa noted.

Manny nudged Tuigamalo with the gun. "Hit record, T. Hit record!"

Tuigamalo fidgeted with a VCR.

Nessa wrote, *Did any* Yuna II *tapes survive? Is one downstairs?* She underlined the last word:

Onscreen, Manny swiveled the camera to show the monitors, then swung it back to himself. "That's *Yuna II* bringing you the historic images of—"

Behind Manny, the crew member climbing on the outer window was now fully in view. He tapped on the bridge window. His voice came through muffled: "Mr. Manny?"

Manny said to the captain, "Hit the deck, T."

Tuigamalo ducked.

Manny fired two shots at the window. Chunks of glass flew, and blood sprayed the windshield. The crew member slid off the window, leaving a bloody streak.

Manny said to the camera, "Progress will not be stopped." To the captain, he said, "Don't fret about your vessel, my man. I got it." Manny pressed a button for windshield wipers and cleaning spray. As the red smeared all over, he said, "Cleanest boat on the water! Can I get a high five?" Tuigamalo whimpered and weakly slapped Manny's hand.

The yelling and pounding off camera grew louder. Footsteps of a man running toward the door escalated. The sound of metal on metal increased, then glass broke. Manny said to the captain, "I've got to give it to your race, T-Bone. They are tenacious."

Manny turned to the door, pivoting the camera to follow. Arms of the crewmen poked through a shattered porthole, feeling for the door's interior handle. Manny shrieked, "You will not stop progress! You will not stop this expedition!"

Manny strode to the door, holding his gun high. He threw the door open. Two men attempted to rush in. Manny quickly fired three more shots, slammed the door, and locked it. He said to Tuigamalo, "Woo! I feel GOOD today, Cap'n T! We're going to change THE WORLD!"

Manny swiveled the camera back to the bridge console and returned the aim of his gun to the side of the captain's head. Tuigamalo softly sniffled.

Manny whispered to himself. "Keep going. Just keep going. I'm a star. I'm a star..."

Static filled the screen.

"Is that the end?" Jefferson asked.

An aide said, "No there's more."

Liv Ross asked, "Can we pause here?"

Jefferson said, "We cannot air this."

Howard said, "Not your decision, Mr. Krider. Why have we paused, Ms. Ross?"

Liv blinked. "We can't air this."

Howard asked, "Why not?"

Liv laughed, "*Why not?*"

Howard said, "Ms. Ross, are you aware of the nature of stories like these? Either we break them—"

"Or they do," Kenji finished.

Liv said, "I am aware of the mantra."

Howard looked at her for a long time. "No," he decided. "I was wrong to promote you." Liv's face solidified into the iron mask Howard wore. Jefferson's eyebrows shot skyward. He grabbed a handful of jelly beans. "In fact," Howard started, but he didn't finish. His eyes went wide. He clutched at his sternum. He huffed and massaged his left arm.

Through a full mouth, Jefferson asked, "What's happening?"

Both lawyers launched themselves toward Howard, who swayed in his chair.

Nessa froze. Kenji's calm voice asked, "Is he having a heart attack?"

Dodie shot into the office and pushed the group apart. In her outstretched hand, she held the prescription bottle. Bending over by Howard, Fritz reached for the bottle, unscrewed it, and placed a tablet under Howard's protruding tongue.

To the others, Dodie extended long fingers. "Remain calm. It's not helpful to get agitated."

Howard gulped water Dave had brought from a side table. Howard pulled at his collar, shaking his head. He mumbled, "Sparks of light. Shadows." Then, he slammed his fist on the table. "Stop this. Stop this."

Everyone in the room stood over him, staring. Nessa still couldn't move.

Howard pointed to the video screen. "I will know what killed Griff if it kills me."

"You don't have to do this," Liv said. "I was wrong to insist—"

Dodie backed away and said to Howard, "You could do with—"

Howard sliced the air with his hands. "Play the tape! Now!"

Everyone retrained their eyes to the monitor. No one spoke.

Jefferson punched *play*.

The image briefly jolted with static, then settled. The timestamp read, *April 12, 1992, 12:42 pm*. Jefferson called out, "We have a 50-minute time jump."

"Note it," Liv said. Her eyes kept flickering to Howard. Dodie stood with her long fingers clutching his shoulder. Howard batted them away.

On the television, Manny's face filled the frame. His eyes were red with dark circles underneath. He spoke slowly, as if in a trance. Tuigamalo was perched at the console.

Manny slurred, "Beyon—zhurrrr—nooo! It's Manny di Martini coming to yerrrr from the South Pacific, where what began as a once-in-a-lifetime adventure to discover the final rrrr-resting place of the USS *Polaris* has evolved into an adventure that may change the course of human histor-rrrry!" He stepped back, wiped his lips, then continued, "Under mounting pressures from my own crew and network producers to abandon the project, I dropped the complex camera system named *Yuna II* into the depths of the Pacific Ocean to bring to you, the viewers at home, the first images of a never-before-seen city of ruins at the bottom of the ocean. Due to the extreme depth, the *Yuna II* has taken an hour to reach its present location. Its first images are coming in now!"

Howard kneaded his arm, then slapped at it. Liv and Kenji eyed him.

Manny pointed the camera at the bridge's widest console screen.

Black and white, Nessa noted.

Lights cut through utter darkness to show rock-carved structures. The camera view floated along a roofline and dove to a set of stairs that unfolded as it approached. Manny said, "It's...moving."

Temples, spires, and halls opened like books. Slender columns, beams, and lintels—all intricately decorated—shot up to support the structures. Along the walls, carvings in a strange language spiraled in bas-relief.

Temples, Nessa thought. *Temples.*

Fritz said, "It's difficult to see them."

Jefferson squeaked, "I fucking see them."

Manny struggled for words. "The...architecture is...intricate...reminiscent of the Khmer temples of Cambodia. Rock-cut. A central spire. Bas-relief carvings. Whether this is a fortress or it's a religious structure is anyone's guess." He turned to the camera. "Is this coming through?" His speech came faster now. "The tessellations on the surfaces show remarkable mathematical symmetry. And there is writing!" He turned his head sideways. "Inscriptions. Indecipherable."

Tuigamalo whispered to Manny.

"What?" Manny said. "No, T. Keep going. Scoot the boat forward a little more."

Tuigamalo whispered again.

Manny rolled his eyes. "Sweet Christ on a unicycle! Are you INSANE? We are at the culmination of two years of work, and you want to turn back?" Manny turned to the camera. "Cap'n T, everyone!" He patted the man on the shoulder. "He keeps us afloat." Then, Manny brought the gun back into view. "Keep going." He pointed to the steering console.

Tuigamalo rose from his captain's chair. "No, Mr. Manny. I will not."

Manny laughed. "Cap'n T! Is it representation you're worried about? Don't worry, my main man, I'll get you an agent as soon as we're done—"

Tuigamalo said, "I know stories of this place. It is the house of the dreaming dead."

Manny pulled at his remaining hair. "For the sake of—I have had ENOUGH of the superstitious island bullshit!"

Tuigamalo paced the floor in front of the camera. He said, "I do not feel well."

"Weakness in the presence of greatness!" Manny trumpeted. "Do I have to do everything myself?" He pushed the captain, who stumbled out of the frame. Manny plopped into Tuigamalo's chair.

Tuigamalo bounded away and walked in tight circles between the captain's chair and the camera. He said, "I hear things. I hear voices." He spread his arms before the windshield, still streaked with blood. "*Whend annt hehandot e the ut ire Wendo gos*?" He swung around and said, "I don't feel well." He projectile vomited onto the windshield.

Manny did not notice. He was pushing the *Rosie*'s throttle forward. The images on the control panel jerked violently. On the rear-facing monitor, the crewmen at the winch stumbled.

"How does this work?" Manny asked the throttle. "Go back to the temple. Back!"

The images on the control panel showed a great shadow coming up in front of *Yuna II*, like a rising tidal wave. The banging on the outer door began again.

Manny hit the intercom button and announced, "Winch the camera up! Fast!"

The crewmen scrambled for the cables, pulling at the cranks.

"Faster than that!" Manny called out.

The men cranked, but the images from the *Yuna II* did not show any light.

"Up, up, up!" Manny yelled.

Tuigamalo walked in tighter circles. "Let me out of here, Mr. Manny! Let me out!"

Yuna II closed in on the dark structure. Closer, closer.

Then, it collided.

"Shit," Manny said.

Howard gripped the armrests of his chair. Fritz quietly handed him another tablet, which Nessa was relieved to see Howard accept.

For a moment, the *Yuna II*'s monitor went black. Then, its lights caught spiraling dust and bits of rock masonry. A great whoosh of air bubbled past the camera, exiting the top of the temple.

Manny hummed to himself. "Going where no one has gone before..." He steadied his camera.

Images on the panel showed the temple interior, vast and dark. Arched windows. More carvings.

Manny called to the guys at the winch through the intercom, "Left! Left!"

They pulled at the cables.

After a minute, the *Yuna II* pointed to the end of the temple's long aisle.

A dark, clouded shape appeared. A throne. And upon it, a vast figure.

"Yo ho," Manny said to himself. "What do we have here?"

Everyone in Howard's office collectively heaved. "Shit fucking Christ," Jefferson said. "What is that?"

Howard groaned, a release of energy that Nessa felt in her bones. *He knew it.* Nessa's mouth dropped open. She felt the cold air whistling in and out of her mouth. Lights at the edge of her vision danced. *What am I seeing?*

On the *Rosie*, Tuigamalo shrieked, "He disturbs the dreamer!" He clamped his hands over his ears. "I hear his dreams! Oh God! Let me out!"

Manny squinted at the panel's images, which jittered briefly. "Look at it! It's breathing...It's...organic."

Liv pumped her arms. "Remain calm! Remain calm! We can't really see what's on there! It could be anything!" Fabrice fainted, sending his notes flying.

Onscreen, Tuigamalo screamed. Manny slapped him. "Stop that! Stop that! You're ruining everything!" Manny threw the captain's log at Tuigamalo. It bounced off his arm, and he yipped.

Manny leaned close to the *Yuna II* monitor and continued to narrate. "It's a creature. A live one. It has a bulbous head. It's contracting and expanding. I see water bubbles jetting from its sides. It has some...pipes? Of some sort. And its skin! It's shifting. Alabaster. Granite. Shimmering."

Tuigamalo mumbled, "The principal woke the leader. Wondrous awe." He vomited again.

Jefferson ran to the corner of the office, holding his mouth. Through his fingers he lost a stomach full of jelly beans onto Howard's white carpet.

At the conference table, the two reporters were scribbling on notepads. Kenji, always calm, was pointing and yelling, "What kind of creature is that? What are we talking about here?" One of the aides sank under the glass table and quietly cried.

Howard sat stiffly, huffing shallow breaths.

Nessa spun. *What is this? What—*

Onscreen, Manny leaned into the images on the *Yuna II*'s console. "I see something. I see...inside its head. It dreams." He turned to the camera, closing his eyes. "I see its dreams...an ocean...of fog...dark...and others like it...shifting in the shadows..." He whispered. "It dreams of the time before."

Tuigamalo screamed.

A repetitive thudding off camera interrupted.

On the control panel, the *Yuna II* revealed pulsing light beneath the creature's skin. The light was swirling and expanding, Nessa thought, like an interstellar nebula discharging molecular gas and bright filaments. She wrote that down: *—molecular gas and bright filaments.* She marveled at the creature. Beneath its chin, the tentacles twitched. Otherwise, it was still.

Tuigamalo's screams grew louder. "Let me out! Let me out!"

Howard clawed at his chest. He said in a low voice, "If I could just untangle the knot in here...Could I have another pill?"

"No more." Dodie said. "You've had the maximum dose."

Liv began to pace. "Should we call 9-1-1?"

"Not yet," Fritz said.

On the *Rosie*, Manny, glued to the console, narrated to the camera. "Viewers at home! We have a creature of indeterminate size. Perhaps 900 feet in height. More in width. Resembling a giant with an octopus head. It seems to be...sleeping..."

The bridge door flew into frame on bent hinges. A man rushed Manny at the controls. Manny scrambled for his gun and fired. The man dropped.

A fire extinguisher sailed into view and nearly hit Manny. He ducked and instead it crashed into the console. Another crew member tried to pull Manny from the chair, but Manny kicked him away. In the struggle, Manny plunged the throttle forward. The *Yuna II* now pointed to darkness, flying uncontrollably ahead with the force of the *Rosie*'s engine.

A crewman noticed the images on the panel. He asked, "What have you done?"

In Howard's office, the phone rang.

And rang.

And rang.

"Somebody get that!" Jefferson yelled from behind a plant.

Nessa moved to the conference table. "Yes?" She cleared her throat. "Nessa Decker here."

A voice said, "I have a message for Kenji Adams. The nurse from the American Samoan military hospital has left a home phone number for him."

"Nurse?" Nessa said. The last piece of the puzzle snapped into place.

The voice said, "She wants him to call off the detective following her. And she wants us to take her off the island with her kids and her mother. In exchange, she will tell us about everything—the secret hospital, the doctors called in from Moscow, the administrators' meeting about withholding the causes of death. Say, what's this about, anyway?"

Everyone in the office seemed far away, but Nessa could still hear voices.

Onscreen, static interrupted the *Yuna II*'s feed in short bursts. The camera cage seemed to be wheeling out of control, spinning at first, then bucking.

Manny twisted away from a crewman holding him down. His face filled the frame. "Are you getting this at home?" he asked. "ARE YOU GETTING THIS? My life's purpose! So clear! I must be one with the sleeping beast! I must reside in the undersea city!"

Manny wrenched the camera from the tripod and ran through the open door, off the bridge. The camera captured his feet trampling the deck.

Offscreen, a crew member called out, "Where does he think he's going?"

Nessa held the phone away from her ear, watching the chaos. "Hello?" the voice said. "Will you deliver the message? I have more calls on hold."

Manny reoriented the camera to face upward, capturing his red face backlit by the sun. He spoke over heavy footfalls and breathing. "This is Manny di Martini! With the discovery of the century! Coming to you from the South Pacific!"

The camera captured Manny grasping the rails, then a shaky view of the horizon. On the surface of the ocean, a great whoosh of air bubbled up. Thousands of sea creatures, all dead, came with it.

Manny dropped the camera. It clattered onto the deck.

He screamed, "YUUUUUNAAAAA!"

His body soared over the rails, briefly streaking past the camera.

Nessa's arm went limp. The voice repeated, "Hello? Hello?"

A crewman clumsily collected Manny's camera. "How do you turn this off?"

Another yelled, "Turn it off—"

The voice on the phone said, "Hello? Earth to whoever this is—"

The television screen went black.

"Hello?"

Nessa snapped to attention. "Yes. I'm here. I'm the one. Message received."

Then she hung up the phone.

The room was quiet except for sniffling.

An intern entered the office holding a tape. Her wide eyes asked what was going on, but she only said, "The final tape is ready." She set the tape on the edge of a table and ran away.

Nessa lumbered to the conference table, righted a chair that had been knocked over, skirted away from Jefferson's rainbow barf, and pulled two clean tissues from the center of the table. *One last bit of information...* She pulled the final pages of Griff's letter to her.

"What the fuck are you doing?" Jefferson whimpered.

"One last bit—" Nessa started to read. *Was this shock?*

Fritz moved Howard. The lambswool jacket had been peeled off and thrown aside. Dodie was holding Howard's hand.

Nessa observed them all with cold detachment. *I have a job to finish. An assessment to make. All the evidence will be considered.*

Only an aide spoke, "What do we do?" Liv paced faster.

Howard rolled his head toward Nessa. *Finish it.*

She nodded.

Nessa reread the nurse's handwriting, focusing harder.

Windbag, she read. *The doctors are coming. I don't have much more time—*

7

Mr. Tran—He Dead

WINDBAG. THE DOCTORS ARE coming. I don't have much more time. No. I don't have much more *time time time*—

My organs fail. My tongue swells, loosening. It becomes more difficult to speak. Jacob is dead now. I am the last one alive.

What about the days before our rescue? you ask. I hear you, Windbag. *How did you survive out there? Five days on the water!* you say. *What happened?*

We waited. For the dreamer to come. To tell us what to do.

The dreamer gives us visions of hell. The towers to climb. The impenetrable darkness. The ultimate despair at our insignificance.

But I also saw something else. Something massive. The threads, Windy. When you learn how to see them, they're *everywhere*.

Yes, I heard the call of the threads. I spoke to the dead with Jacob. I wore no shoes, exposing my feet—my roots—to the elements. I also heard the dreamer call, though I refrained from answering. I held myself back from entering the water. I listened, though. My mind expanded. I saw things I will not repeat. And I saw what the threads wanted for me, for us.

The captain of our boat—we did not see him until the evacuation. He closed himself inside his bridge and refused to come out.

The sick guys inside the *Rosie*'s cabin died first. One by one. All of them were sent back to the Tree of Life, to the network of gossamer threads that supports us all. I feel those men now. They are at peace. They understand their place in the universe. You know, they were the ones who suffered the most exposure to the fungus. They were the ones who winched the *Yuna II* back to the deck. Their exposure turned them into messengers. They were the prophets of the new world.

And more people came to the site. "Rescuers." The Fijian coast guard. Those crew members turned on each other. I never saw it with my eyes. I saw it in my mind. How? The threads, Windbag. The threads. They vibrate with voices and movement. I see how a bat sees; I see echoes and shapes. I see voices as invisible waves thrumming the network. I saw the Fijian captain kill most of his own crew—bludgeoned in their sleep—then set up a tea party to welcome the dreamer. He laid out a table with plastic mugs filled with dirty seawater, which he drank. He went mad. He died, rotting from the inside out.

The Tongan Navy should have arrived next, but they got wise when the Fijians massacred themselves. The Tongans held back a few miles from us, did not approach. They were the ones who started the cordon around the site. A quarantine, they called it. Then, they waited for one of the bigger countries to take the lead.

An airplane flew overhead. A big one. It carried the New Zealanders. They waved down to us, indicating they wanted to drop a man down to our boat. Peni was ecstatic to welcome him. We hadn't had a new visitor in days. But before that could happen, something went wrong with them, too. The plane tore away, did a nose-dive right into the ocean, then sank to the depths, to the graveyard at the dreamer's feet. The *Polaris* is down there. As are all the others who came before. Many will come again. The dreamer never stops collecting the dead.

Five days on the water like that. Australian and New Zealander coast guards raced each other to the site. But who won? Why, the Americans.

"The Americans won!" That's what you told me when we first met in the catacombs of Paris in 1945, me a half-starved Resistance fighter hiding from Germans and planting bombs in their railway cars. "The Americans won!" you said to me when I asked. Then you added, "They won a bag of shit, didn't they?" We laughed. Hard. You with mud on your face, not a decent meal or a good night's sleep since you left London before the invasion. Me? I hadn't laughed in six years.

I loved you then.

Time time time

What—

What has become of us—

I am losing speech.

It—

won't be—

long—now.

Thank you. Windy.

For dragging me—around—with your Army Corps. Until you could—set me up—with a job. Printing newspapers—in occupied-Germany. Thank you. I am grateful. I had a life—in this great big world—because of you.

For that reason—I'm going to pull—a gossamer thread—for you.

It's an important one. An old one.

It goes all the way back to—Hungary. It's connected to—your sister, resting at the bottom—of the Danube. She is—at peace. She says to me—after her hiding place—was discovered—the Nazis tied her to the family who hid her—tied them together—with ropes. They were all—thrown into—the river together. They

sank. She sank. She did not know pain. So—you can—let her go now. She says
that to you—*Let me go, Elazar.*

> *Time time time*
> Remember
> Remember
> Remember—what I said, Windy—
> there are lights that hold us together.
> Last moments. All so clear now.
> God is a—merciful God—
> our minds not meant—to hold—the mysteries
> like the lights—connecting us—
> the living to the dead—
> the ancestors—
> We have weight.
> We have power.
> Not just darkness. Also light.
> I will show you.
> One more gossamer thread
> —one more one more one more thread
> —its trail so bright—
> I will pull the thread now.
> —downstairs—
> —Nessa—Decker—
> She will rise.
> A gift—from me—
> A gift

of love.

You will see what I see.

Nessa pulled all the pages of Griff's letter together. She pulled the papers taped
to the whiteboard. She collected the fungi report from Howard's desk. Then she
tapped the pages into a neat rectangle, and laid the pile in the center of the table.
Historic, she thought. *These pages will be studied for years.* After a moment, she
pulled the stack back to her and pulled out the final page. She found her pen and
located the offending name. *Elazar.* She redacted it.

The room was almost empty now. Only Jefferson was at the front, watching
the black-and-white footage from *Yuna II*. Dazzlingly precise and in clear focus,
images flitted into the camera frame like a dream. It was the final tape. Nessa

sighed at the wondrous improbability of that tape's existence here in this office. *It wasn't damaged at all, Griff.*

There was a thread, connecting her to Howard, then to Griff—wherever he was. Nessa whispered, "It wasn't damaged at all, Griff. Rest easy." She couldn't feel what Griff talked about—no massive network, no thrumming or peace. But it was a day for unveiling what no one knew existed before. So why not tell him? "We got it, Griff. We got it."

And Howard was right. That tape would cement both his and Griff's legacies.

At the other end of the office, Liv was the only one of the executives remaining. She held a phone receiver to her ear, not speaking, just staring. Nessa wasn't sure if she was listening to a calming voice, or if she was camping out on the line to the tune of a dull dial tone, just to claim a space to gather her thoughts.

Howard was on his way down on the elevator. Far below, on the Manhattan sidewalk, an ambulance waited to accept him. People on the street gathered around the flashing lights. Howard would be wheeled out, fogging the oxygen mask strapped to his face. Fritz would follow the gurney, shielding Howard from onlookers with his lambswool coat, the limp rose on its lapel the only clue as to who was curtained behind it.

Moments before, as Howard was being loaded onto the gurney in his office, he had called out, "Fritz! He will come with me. He protects me."

Nessa had approached Howard to say, "You scared us."

He replied with faint annoyance, "It wasn't even my worst coronary."

"What do we do now?" she asked.

"I have it on good authority we will find out together."

Fritz wedged between Nessa and the mogul. To Howard, Fritz said, "You agreed to go, so go with quietude. You must be healthy as a bull for what comes next."

Nessa said, "But he hasn't finished watching—"

Howard waved a hand weakly. "I have seen enough of the tapes. You finish the final one." He craned his neck. "Before I do, where is Ms. Ross?"

Liv stepped forward. Her makeup was smeared and her bob frizzed. "Yes?"

"Air it all on the evening news," Howard said. "Every tape. For Griff."

Liv wrung her hands. "The newsroom will have to meet —"

"The evening news. No delay. Or you're fired." The mask snapped back into place.

They wheeled him away.

And now, quiet.

What was next? Nessa wasn't sure she knew. But she didn't want to disappoint Howard. Or Griff. So, she watched the final tape with Jefferson.

The images from *Yuna II* were oddly beautiful. No sound, just the camera floating above the creature, looking down, as if granting them a godlike view over the titan. If she looked closely, she could see the lights pulsing under the skin of the creature. She spoke to the silent screen, "What will we call you, I wonder?"

"Fuckstick," Jefferson said. "I nominate Fuckstick."

With a hesitant knock, a lanky man entered the office, walking haltingly on the expensive carpet. He plucked a rose petal wedged into the carpet fibers and asked, "What happened here?"

Nessa pushed a button to eject the *Yuna II* footage. "You're from the newsroom? You're here for Liv Ross? For the tapes?"

Liv did not break her blank stare, did not look up from her call.

"Yeah," the lanky man said. "Something about Griff Tran?" He leaned in. "I heard he was alive. Is it true?"

"No," Nessa said. "Mr. Tran is dead." She handed him the stack of tapes, from the beginning to the bitter end. "Careful with these."

"Yeah, yeah," the man said. "What's on them?"

Nessa said, "The truth."

Entr'acte I:
The Diaries of Oliver Daas

Collapse

Boston
May to September 1992

Week of May 5, 1992

Cambridgeport Yellow House

DREAMT I CLUNG TO a joist in the Chapmans' attic as floodwaters rose, old photos and antique junk swirling about my knees with that girl clawing at my waist, and me begging her not to look at me. Which is exactly what she did. Usual horrors. Cavern where her face should be. Layers of sliced skin, bright scarlets and burnt oranges and raw umbers, kaleidoscoping into a deep hole. Inside: noticed lava, rock, mantle, precious gems, Earth's core. Called out for Ruthie, then remembered she was dead. Passenger train running far below us, loaded with white-robed people clinging to the roof, hanging out windows. So far, same dream.

Then! Glimpsed the Leviathan lurking in floodwaters, circling, tentacles fanning, nosing my legs. Ah, yes! Manny's beast! Knew it was good omen—faceless girl, passenger train, *and* creature together in same place, if only—

Woke on the sofa in Cambridgeport house wearing yesterday's clothes under my stained bathrobe. Too dark for morning. Remembered bay windows covered with heavy blankets (need to fortify with plywood), downstairs doors barricaded with bookshelves, empty tins of beans and food wrappers everywhere, television on all night. WINnews Boston Six. Day five of Collapse. School closed again. Graduation postponed. Lab closed.

Phones still work, and the lines are burning up. Talk is strong that the beast in the underwater city is alien, a new intelligence.

Evidence: there is a creature sleeping in the ocean at a depth of 9,000 feet inside a city of architectural significance. The only candidates on the planet for building something like that are humans, and we didn't do it. Further, the underwater city rotates, warps, and changes its own geometry in ways far beyond human capabilities. (Called Marty Willsky at Caltech Astrophysics. He has ideas, none publishable. Rip in space-time? Good luck on peer review!) Not much known about the sleeping being itself except for images captured on tape. Rounded head and tentacles—perhaps evolved from octopus-like species, suggesting an expansive brain. Sentience high? Octopi on Earth are intelligent. This being could be likewise. Its size signifies more power on its food chain than octopi we know. An apex being? At least we hope so. Hate to see its evolutionary father.

Questions: who built the city? One of its own species, or another? For what purpose?

Further evidence: electromagnetic pulse originating from the dive site around the time Manny made the Discovery. Caught by radio stations, it circled the planet nine times damaging electronic equipment at random. My television is working; my home computer is toast. "The Pulse," as it's now called, has been graphed by radio operators: it's a low frequency, high amplitude wave.

Questions: what energy or communication was transferred in those radio waves? Who will figure out the meaning/purpose of the wave signature? (My bet is the Very Large Array in New Mexico will crack it, although I wouldn't rule out any of the smaller radio astronomy labs now aiming their dishes to the South Pacific right now.)

More evidence: radiometric dating of the rock debris taken from the *Yuna II* underwater collision—a report leaked from American Samoa.

Results: gneiss, ancient igneous and metamorphic rock formed by volcanoes over 3 billion years ago, identifiable by its distinctive banding formed at high temperatures. Not alien? On Earth, gneiss is found near tectonic plates. Rare to see it in quantities suggested by the underwater city's size. Found in Scotland, India, Canada—what's it doing in the South Pacific?

Questions: was the gneiss mined here on Earth then transported to South Pacific for construction? By whom? With what capability? Or, more likely, was the city built 3 billion years ago when the rock was more plentiful? Is the creature inside the structure that old? *Who are the builders?*

Final evidence: black fungi samples, also taken from *Yuna II*. Closely guarded stuff, no leaks on that front, no word at all on them. Mycology report from Griff Tran's letter might be all we will see about that sample until we get a government whistleblower. Judging by actions of the *Rosie* crew, the stuff is hallucinogenic.

Final questions: what evolutionary pressures made sleeping being what it is now? What is the creature's biology? Its brain capabilities? If it's as old as the gneiss suggests it might be, how does the creature experience time? How old is it on its own evolutionary scale? Is it young like a human or old like a reptile? What are our similarities? How has it contributed to our evolution?

It came from somewhere. It was going somewhere. Will we ever know?

Power out again. Reminds me to make notes about continuous power maintenance in Evolutionary Computer Lab. Can't have interruptions to my work—to my digital agents—with power blipping on and off.

Dark.

Vigilantes cruise streets in minivans waving flare guns, pistols, and AK-47s, frightened of invaders from Roxbury, Dorchester, Mattapan. In other words, the non-white neighborhoods. They shout, "Go home—" followed by a vile slur not repeatable. I do not fear melanin. I fear weapons. Methinks roving gun toters respect property more than life. Where are our police? Have they given up? More likely, are they driving those minivans?

A few distant governments in small countries having a hard time hanging on to power. More than a few have given up. Mexico doesn't look good. Borders shut down everywhere.

Tried calling V again. No answer. No excuse for that. The Pulse didn't mess with *that* many phone lines. We're mostly back up now. Where is she? Wish she'd check in just to tell me to go to hell. Must know I'm worried and still won't call. Maybe I deserve it.

Today, the last of the 60 major global stock exchanges crashed. There goes money! Bankers launching themselves from upper stories in despair. Serves them right, perpetuating late-stage capitalism and all its excesses. Says the former San Francisco hippie living in a colonial house with polished pine floors and central heating within walking distance of our nation's elite universities. Here am I! My suede Chesterfield my throne! My bent spoon, my scepter! My threadbare bathrobe, my cape! *Look upon my Works* something-something *and despair!*

Where in Hades is my old romantic poetry volume when I need it?

Another morning. Human condition declining.

Leads me to some thoughts on evolution: humans have entered a new era. Discovery will force us to adapt or die. The sleeping being thus far represents only an existential threat. It is not awake. It is not an immediate hazard to us. Yet, we are in full panic mode. But life in the sea had been fine with its presence for eons, even evolving around it.

Where do humans go from here? We could continue to make this worse for ourselves, keep edging toward anarchy. Or we could learn to live with it as the ocean population has for eons.

What are the chances humans will suppress territorial aggression inherited from our evolutionary chain? There is talk of dropping a bomb on it. A bomb! Why risk waking it without a solution to engage with it? For now, cooler heads prevail. Human intelligence is our own biggest threat and our best ally.

Nevertheless, we are all thinking it: what will we do when it wakes?

We need a plan.

An answer!

Not about any recent planetary mysteries: the British romantic poetry volume was in the upstairs toilet.

It was Percy Bysshe Shelley. *Look on my Works, ye Mighty, and despair!* Ozymandias, King of Kings. What a guy.

Agitated.

Humans must level up on the evolutionary scale, and fast.

Options? Weapons? Please. We must be *more* intelligent than that.

The best chance is the technological singularity. According to Kurzweil, it is 25 to 30 years away. He has predicted that the singularity will usher in an era of untold gifts to humanity. Advanced, self-aware computer programs with processing systems beyond human intelligence will contribute advancements in medical technology. The end of aging with brain back-up copies! Genetic editing! Space colonization! There are downsides, but I have heard no compelling arguments for them, only doomsday fear. The singularity will deliver what evolution has instructed: intelligence is power. At first evolutionary kings were judged by speed, size, and strength. But now, humans hold the apex position under the banner, "Intelligence of the Fittest." On our planet, the ones with the most complex brains win.

More agitation. Wish I could walk outside, but too afraid to go out. I do wish V would call.

Thinking of going back to work regardless of who is there. Then this thought: did the Pulse wipe out my computer lab? My computer here at home is as useless as a brick.

Newspaper came! It's been hit-or-miss with delivery. From the looks of it, the presses are running in between power outages with very few staff. Bless the ones who sling the ink! Heroes!

A clipped item for posterity...

PULSE GRAPH YIELDS ANSWERS AT LAST

May 7, 1992

BERKELEY, CA (AP)— The Center for Neuroimaging in Berkeley, CA, has confirmed the electromagnetic pulse wave that emanated from the South Pacific area last month corresponds to the delta wave pattern given off by human brains when in deep sleep. Dr. William Ahmadi, Director, reported—

Ahmadi! That clever bastard! I have his number here somewhere. Perhaps he will share his findings in more detail with a colleague. In turn, I shall offer to add him to our telephone tree. The greatest minds in science—insert laugh here—are keeping in touch as best we can. So much to talk about!

The agreement among us: we must forget about finals and graduation. When our universities reopen, everyone will be jockeying for dominance in academics. Whose department is the most relevant in the aftermath of Discovery? Budget cuts loom for those who can't prove themselves.

Survival of the fittest. Intelligence of the fittest.

CASE FOR POST-DISCOVERY BUDGETARY SUPPORT
Dr. Oliver Daas, Department of Computer Science
New Major with Dedicated Lab: Evolutionary Computation
Life is not bound to the physical world.
The current intersection of two academic fields at the University—computer science and evolutionary engineering—has no formal home. Presently, the Evolutionary Computation Lab is run by me through an annex of the larger computer-science lab. An ongoing project there involves a population of a few digital agents, or individuals, on a computer mainframe. These agents exhibit lifelike behavior over time, evolving using principles of variation, selection, and inheritance—in other words, the components of lifeforms on Earth. They reproduce. They "eat" digital assets. They defend territory. They can evolve as any other being on our planet—with armor, tools, speed, size. They can also evolve to run social simulations based on growing intelligence.
Right now, the beings are in the prototype phase—arrrrrrrrgggggghhhh

Begging for money exhausts me. I will try again in the morning...

Late pm.

Thinking this evening of my Strange Visitor years ago, in the museum in Los Alamos. He said, "A new network of life, beyond the realm of science..."

Turning over his warning to me: "Time is running out." Did he foresee the Discovery?

How?

I still have his address, somewhere. If only the mail were running.

Another bleak morning.

Spooned a bit of cold tomato soup for breakfast and caught up on news. Strain on food-supply lines leading to widespread hoarding and looting. Store 24, The Tasty, IHOP, Border, Liberty all closed until further notice. Worst: bookstore closed and haven't yet picked up my copy of Kurzweil's *The Age of Intelligent Machines*! Was to be summer reading. Consolation: probably read those essays in academic journals already. Like how human brain capable of creating something more intelligent than itself. About pattern recognition. About representative knowledge. About prediction of computer power increasing. Wanted to sit with those ideas this summer, let them marinate, see if anything new pops up. There goes that idea. Man plans, God laughs.

From WINnews Six: petition from 300 scientific organizations demands access to Manny di Martini's dive site, except they don't know who to deliver the petition to. Who is in charge? Probably the US, but not if Russia has anything to say about it. World War III on the table? I will sign it on behalf of my tiny lab. Have a working list of all the things I'd like to know from that site. List is approaching 15 pages, both sides. We must collect *all* the data, relevant or not. All scientists on deck! Biologists, geologists, astrophysicists, *everyone*. All funding priorities of every government must go to science! Not military! We need instruments, trained personnel, internet advancements, computer speed!

Better call Hindlay in Atlanta. He'll know about this petition.

Think I'll reread *Beowulf* today.

Contemplate: the highest functions of humanity—art, philosophy, etc. etc.—serve to rise above the chaos.

CASE FOR POST-DISCOVERY BUDGET SUPPORT

Addendum

Dr. Oliver Daas has been innovating with computer programs to respond to real human problems since 1974. He worked on the team developing Optical Character Recognition (OCR) for reading to the blind and developed base programming for pattern-recognition technologies to aid school children with dyslexia, blindness, and attention-deficit hyperactivity disorder. In 1980, he began programming the base for the digital community currently housed on the University mainframe. Social simulations related to group problem solving, utopic cooperation, non-violence and non-aggression predictors serve as the basis of many disaster-response researchers. The recent Evolutionary Computation Lab marries Dr. Daas's background in evolution engineering to computer science with new digital agents capable of evolving language, rational

thought, reasoning, mathematics toward the superintelligence promised in the
technological singularity.

Did I fail to mention there are only two digital agents in this program? Two!
They look like faceless Legos with the personality of my dead computer in the
dining room.

If the money were there, what could I do?

On the news, they're calling the creature the Sleeping One. Sleeping Thing.
Sleeping Creature. Or variants thereof.

Ozymandias would have been a better choice. Missed opportunity there.

Still no word from V. Her phone rings and rings.

Suppressed impulse to call Ruthie again. Been a year. No—two. And still doing
that.

Speaking of therapy not working, my therapist called to say don't come in. This
he said over automatic machine gun fire. First brilliant thing he's said in months!
Says until this thing blows over, I should journal to document my feelings. Oh,
why? I'm sick of myself. Faceless girl nightmares. Inattentive ex-husband to a dead
ex-wife. Failed father. Old psychic wounds on display at meetings and lectures.
Maybe I've always been like this. Maybe my heart will turn to stone and I'll wither,
clutch my chest, and die in my big empty house. Computer-science majors will
celebrate! Faculty meetings will be safe to wander into banal topics once more!
Who knows what V will do?

Speaking of terrible relationships, Iris called. I was relieved to hear from her and
told her so. She says Mother is safe in her care home in Eureka and has no idea
about the Collapse. Wanted to add, "No knowledge of her daughter either," but
didn't. Was truly glad to hear about their safety, and brother Malcolm's too. The
conversation turned sour when Iris attempted once more to guilt me into seeing
Mother. "Why?"—this I said aloud. Mother's brain is a heap of mashed potatoes.
She doesn't know me! This formidable woman, who once met with Gandhi and
ran her own nonprofit, now claws at the mirror in fear of who appears there.
Do I want to see that? No. My mother is *dead*. Boy, was that the wrong thing to
say to Iris. More complaints about how I cannot seem to manage any long-term
relationships in my life, lacking any ability to care for another, etc. etc. etc. Hung
up grateful that she and Malcolm live on the opposite coast.

Dream came again. Drowning. Train. Creature.

I blame Iris.

I am much better alone without others tripping difficult memories like land mines.

Evolution does not *favor* humans, per se. Human exceptionalism is our invention. What is undeniable is that humans have altered the surface of this planet more than any other creature in history. We are evolving away from what our ancestors prized, away from the sharp teeth, the dense muscles for speed. We have used our intelligence to skip evolutionary steps. We lack feathers, but we fly alongside geese formations in airplanes. We lack rear haunches, but we outrace cheetahs in cars. We lack gills, but we breathe underwater alongside dolphins with SCUBA gear. Our power is in our intelligence.

And now this Sleeping Thing has turned us against ourselves.

What may come next for us may be our final act of evolution.

I cannot think of another way! We must evolve the superintelligence. We must feed it all the data we have to form a calculus for our survival. The digital beings must use advanced language, cooperation, philosophy, culture. We must depend on this creative race of problem solvers. I have no faith in humans to overcome this Discovery. This time we could learn something from the fish in the sea.

We must evolve in the blink of an eye. That Sleeping One might wake in a year, in a decade, in a moment. But we are killing each other *now*.

We are out of time.

May 12, 1992

Cambridgeport Yellow House

FACELESS GIRL IS BACK. Sleep is terrible. Many unwanted images.

Desperate times call for desperate measures and I will try anything. "Journaling to exorcise trauma" might be the most hippie-Californian thing I've ever heard of. Call it a relic from my drug-fueled summer of love in San Francisco. The remainder of this entry shall serve as a nod to my roots. Attempting to exorcise trauma! I begin...

The faceless girl who haunts my dreams died in December 1956.

When I was 16 years old and living with my parents among the redwood giants near Eureka, we were treated with an unusual sight in California: snow. A *lot* of snow. There was enough to build a snowman, which my friends taught me to make. I'd never seen it, nor had Malcolm or Iris. We were all born and raised in New Delhi. I'm realizing now that those moments throwing snowballs might have been my last moments of peace before my world caved in.

The day after the snowfall, the weather performed an about-face to an unseasonable, balmy, hot day. The snow melted quickly, but the ground, still frozen, wouldn't absorb it. Then, it rained. And rained. And rained. Mad River and all the creeks and lakes overflowed. Logs and tree branches and railroad ties were nothing more than missiles in the rushing waters.

My family had the benefit of living in a house on high ground, so we were not in danger. But many who lived downhill of us were. We split up among our neighbors to help them carry furniture and sentimental keepsakes to second stories. I went to the Chapmans to help them carry photos and albums to their attic. They had two children.

The floodwaters came to their house quickly. Just outside their house, Mr. Chapman and his young boy got washed away. They were there one moment, gone the next.

Panicked, the mother pushed me and her daughter into the attic. We balanced there as the waters hit our ankles, then waists. I could reach the rafters if I stood on a crate, but the water kept coming. Cold water like that sends shocks up your spine, making it difficult to keep your balance. The mother struggled on a crate of her own. The girl clung to me. As the waters rose, we began to float. Our heads were pushed into the rafters sideways. We couldn't even speak to one another. We breathed with our chins strained upward. The air turned hot and stale. The water was cold and deep. The house was rocking on its foundation, threatening to come loose. We did not know if we would die from the house collapsing, from the air running out, or from the water overtaking the attic completely. The girl struggled to stay afloat. She panicked and made herself heavy with flailing. "Keep calm," I told her when the water was at our ankles. "Relax." That worked for a while. But by the time our bodies were floating horizontally on the floodwaters, staying calm had become impossible.

It was dark, cold. Death was there, swirling in the waters. We all knew it.

Afterward, Mrs. Chapman told me she did not know when her daughter died. But I knew. It was when the girl's grip loosened and her body sank. Her lifeless arm bumped up against me.

How can you tell when a dead thing nudges you? You can. It will chill you to the bone. For hours we floated, her cold arm bumped me over and over.

Through a hole he cut into the roof, my father pulled us all out. Me, Mrs. Chapman, and the little corpse. Mr. Chapman and the boy were never found.

I've learned that when you experience something horrible, there are small sensory details that cling to you for the rest of your life. I would have thought mine would have been the girl's lifeless face. Not so. I cannot recall one detail about her. Not her eye color, the shade of her skin, the color of her hair, her voice. Did she speak with a childish lilt? A lisp? The fact that I can recall nothing confounds me. This girl wasn't a stranger. She was a neighbor. I *must* have known her. I cannot even recall her inside that attic. I don't remember any peculiar shade of blue to her fingers around mine. I don't remember the sound of her final breaths—were they shallow, panicked?—before she went under. I don't remember the smell of her fear or what she said—if she called out to her mother, hidden by the darkness—or if the girl knew she was about to die. As soon as my father lifted me through that splintered hole in the roof, my brain erased every detail connected to her. What I do remember—what I still feel sometimes before I fall asleep—is that warbling sound of water in my ears and her cold, sinking arm brushing up against my leg. There was a void of life next to me, yet I could feel her there. Her body couldn't be an empty husk. It couldn't just be *nothing*. Where did the essence of this girl go?

For the life of me, I can't even remember her name.

These journal pages are soaked in sweat. That will be all for today.

June 12, 1992

Cambridgeport Yellow House

RHODE ISLAND CULT DEMANDS NEW EVOLUTIONARY CHART

Jun 12, 1992

PROVIDENCE, RI (AP)—A scheme to develop a new chart showing the evolution of mammals put forth by a religious cult known as the Providence Group has identified 12 points in history where alien life intersects with human development, dating back to Ancient Egypt. A spokesman for the Group said they expect their beliefs to become mainstream after Manny di Martini's Discovery in the South Pacific.

A grim anniversary: six weeks of Collapse. Six weeks in this house alone. I leave only to join food lines. Rationing is in effect. I have reread 62 percent of the books I own. Power is sporadic, but predictable. WINnews Six stopped reporting on crime, but I know it's out there. I see the fires when I'm brave enough to peek through the blankets.

Grew a beard, then shaved it off again.

Two newspapers came today! Some of this stuff is old, but worth contemplation.

DANISH ACTIVIST PER PASKE WARNS OF DEVELOPING GLOBAL GOVERNMENT LED BY SUPER-RICH

Jun 12, 1992

LONDON (AP)—Activist Per Paske warns that an "oligarchy" of the extremely wealthy intends to "take advantage of chaos" to form a global governance. Paske accuses South African iron-ore mine-owners Lelee and Pinchas Stern of pressuring world leaders to dissolve the United Nations to form a more powerful international leadership agency. Paske said at a press conference in London: "For people like the Sterns, who are among the world's wealthiest and the most corrupt, the world is a candy store. They intend to buy all the candy they can and gorge themselves. Look at their offshore accounts. Their charity foundations are controlled by friends. Look at their dummy corporations. They simply aren't fit to lead humanity in its new era."

Pinchas Stern, who also serves in South Africa's Parliament, counters that he and his wife, both Polish survivors of the Holocaust, find Paske's accusations an insult. Stern said, "The United Nations was born to fight against authoritarian misdeeds. Per Paske, someone who was not even born when the Shoah was raging, requires a history lesson: Jews don't stand for tyranny."

Media mogul Howard Winfield has also been accused of meeting privately with other corporate leaders to test forms of world governance—

Bad news today. University has shut down until further notice. No students. No summer classes. Not even the ones who sweep the floors after dark will venture outside their homes. No one knows when we will reopen. Agitation fierce! How will I continue my work?

Still no word from V. Fear the worst. Or else why wouldn't she call? Is she *that* angry?

News this afternoon: we have a confirmed alien! The world's governments broadcast a simultaneous announcement that the sleeping creature is not from this planet. Our President does not appear prepared to lead us through this. Am I reading shock? Who knows what people at those levels know—behind the scenes, Area 51, unidentified airships. General public not feeling trust for our institutions of governance. Some are livid at the six weeks it took for this announcement to come about. I am not surprised. The first rule in governing is to never tell the people what they're not ready to hear. I wonder what other information they have that they haven't released. Nothing of the black fungus, for example.

In other news, rescuers have stopped looking for Manny di Martini. A naval cordon around the site monitored currents and searched along those ocean waterways for a corpse. Nothing appeared. His body may never be recovered. Conspiracy theories commence!

Enjoyed a long call with Dr. William Ahmadi, that crazy neuroscientist out in Berkeley. He's really onto something. When he was practicing neurosurgery, he documented instances of finding nightmares trapped in physical folds of the brain. Through awake surgery, introducing a gentle electrical prod on certain areas, patients reported a recurring nightmare playing out right there in the room! Release the pressure, and the nightmare subsided. Return the pressure in the exact same spot, and the nightmare begins again. He tells me my recurring dream lives as a clump of overactive neurons in my brain folds. What a fascinating concept! He plans to use this information to build a dream database for humans—to monitor sleeping subjects inside brain scanners that document how the brain activates during REM sleep. Upon waking, those subjects report their dreams. His theory is that dreams of running will light up the motor cortex; dreams of sensations will light up the sensory cortex; dreams of a childhood home will light up occipital lobes. With enough testing, he could tell what a human is dreaming simply by watching a brain scan of one sleeping! We had discussed the possibility of artificial intelligence augmenting that database, and promised to speak further on the matter. Surely, he is thinking about the Sleeping One and the value of potential research there! We ended the call bemoaning the current state of the internet (underused, slow, lacking resources) and the greediness of whatever military has possession of the black fungus. Science should belong to the people!

Finally (!) digging through old papers to look for those notes from meeting of my Strange Visitor in Los Alamos. I found this nugget, scribbled on a cocktail napkin from a faculty function in 1980. (It looks like it was a desperate bid to escape conversation.)

ASPECTS OF DARWINIAN EVOLUTION SIMULATED IN COMPUTER SYSTEMS—WHY DO IT?

Replicating evolutionary processes means an acceleration of engineering, software design, gaming, robotics, medicine.

Borrow a page from nature's book! Use evolutionary principles for wildly new solutions, never imagined by humans! Allow computers to compute better trajectories! Model real-world processes!

Find agricultural solutions! Discover disease cures!

And co-evolution progression—two species evolving in cooperation and competition. Multi-agent problem solving! Advanced game play!

What couldn't we solve?

This memory lights a fire under my torpid ass. I will break out of this house to get to my lab!

June 14, 1992

Evolutionary Computation Lab

MADE IT TO THE lab—another harrowing experience to add to my nightmares. It has taken me hours to collect myself before I could write about it. I will try to write with a faithful recreation of what happened; details may be important later.

To begin with, my brave plan to walk to my lab, seven weeks in the making, was shot the moment I left my house.

Carrying only my satchel of papers and a few necessities in case I did not make it back home that night, I crossed the main thoroughfare (no traffic—gasoline is precious) to dog-leg it across the park, when I saw vigilantes with an arsenal stockpile blocking my shortcut across a side street. Needed to go north, but no way through. Jogged toward a parallel street and cut through parking lots and endless construction (sites eerily silent). Plan B: hop the train tracks near the University entrance, run through the athletic fields, behind the chapel, then, voila, into the venerable halls of the Department of Computer Science, praying the doors were open, but prepared with a hammer in case not.

Perhaps they felt the train tracks would be a private place.

There, I met a car, burned beyond recognition, parked in the tall grass by the tracks, singed grass all around. Spray painted on the hood in red: the racial epithet I refuse to write. Inside, a corpse, charred. Emerging from the front seat, a vigilante retrieving a burned head. Another, nearby, commented, "One for the collection!"

Found a hedge to hide in. No one saw me.

Afterward, the world exploded into meaningless symbols and language. (This is what happens when the stress is too extreme. Faceless girl will surely come tonight. The passenger train, too. It's *that* bad.)

Shoved my way in through the Department's side doors, hammer at the ready, but glass already smashed with chairs and trash bins stacked behind the door. Someone beat me to it! Hopefully not the marauders! Needed a weapon in case. Already forgot I was holding a hammer.

Upstairs, one flight, no sound.

Lab at the end of the hall. Door wide open. Plucked a small bulletin board from the wall to defend myself. (What was I going to do with a framed cork board pinned with Department notices?)

Inside, the surprise of my life.

More computers than my lab should hold (immediately I thought of the load on the electrical outlets) stacked in every available inch of space. A rat's nest of computer cables. Six or seven processors lined up, daisy-chained into a single, massive unit. Monitors everywhere, all on and active. My digital agents roaming freely between them. And not just the two of them. *Six* of them.

I had left this lab with only two agents operating.

A figure in the far corner viciously clicking a mouse. Massive cloud of hair as tangled as the computer cables. On the monitor, one of my digital agents receiving a makeover. Or was it one of mine? It was unrecognizable. An animation program was open—one I hadn't seen before. Graphic enhancements underway. Facial features. Musculature. Realistic clothing.

I raised the bulletin board over my head, and voice shaking, demanded: "Who are you? And what are you doing here?"

Response: "Fixing your shit."

Youthful voice. Female. Heavy accent. A student?

"Identify yourself," I said.

She faced me. Wide, dark eyes projecting a rebellious attitude. Wild, violent eyebrows. Too-large nose. Too-skinny arms and gangly legs. She gripped a bag of chips and crunched while eyeing the small bulletin board I held aloft. "Seriously?" She laughed, open-throated.

Behind her, a digital agent gleamed with lifelike details—skin folds, creases, moving hair—gazing at its hands as if surprised to see them at the ends of its arms. No, not "its." *His*. His arms.

Was this woman redesigning them?

"How did you get in here?" I finally asked.

In reply, she rattled off a stream of Spanish I did not understand, then returned to her work.

I paused, processing that. "Was I supposed to—?"

Thankfully, she switched to English, tossing her voice over her shoulder. "Of all the projects in all the University's computer labs, yours was the closest."

Closest to what? I wanted to ask. But she was still talking. "That's not saying much, so don't get a big head about it. But have you seen what A-Life is doing in the other lab? Little blobs and shapes growing limbs to race around the screen for little dot-food?" She turned to wrinkle her nose at me. "What was I going to do with *that*? Useless dryshites!"

The Irish idiom sounded jarring coming from her. I looked around at the pile of processors and monitors. I asked, "Did you move these in here from the other labs?"

"Of course." My stomach sank. The department chair was going to murder me.

The woman returned to clicking the mouse. "So? A-Life had nothing useful! These are much better. Much better foundation for what needs to be done." Her sustained vowels luxuriated with the crunching: *maaaaaau-ch bee-ter.*

I stepped closer. "You're a student."

"Yep."

"One of mine?"

"Uh-huh. Introduction to Artificial Life. Evolutionary Computation and Genetic Algorithms. Programming Libraries—"

"Masters program?"

She chewed and clicked. "Not very observant, are you?"

I put down my satchel close to the bulletin board. "I keep my short-term memory clear for my work." I pointed to her screen, at her graphic work. "What program are you using for that?"

"Huh?"

"The animation program. I don't recognize it."

"Oh, that. That's mine."

"Your own animation program?"

"That's right, Dr. Daas." She ended my name with a hiss and a small chuckle. I had no idea what that meant.

A moment of clarity. "Lucía," I muttered. Her name came in a flash of recognition. I did know her. Sort of. This was the student who constantly slumped, not paying attention, bored. She ate junk food in class, slept on her desk, disregarded her appearance to the point that I thought her to be a homeless straggler, though I had no heart to remove her from my classrooms. But her grades were always excellent, if I remember correctly. Still, I would not have thought her capable of any of the things she was doing now. Louder, I asked, "Lucía, correct?"

"Lucía Santamaría. I have earned some brain space now?"

"Who is your advisor?"

She ignored my question, pointing at the monitors with a half-eaten potato chip. "You designed no faces for them. They had no soul."

An electric shock ran through me, and with it, a thought of the Strange Visitor in Los Alamos. Didn't he say something similar? No faces, no soul? Right then, I wanted to ask her if she knew him, but I've never told anyone about that night and didn't intend to start now. What happened there was too strange. And I don't even know his name. How insane would I sound to her? I kept my thoughts to myself.

She dropped the bag of chips and muttered to the monitor, "There you go, Jeff." She clicked on the digital agent in the animation program and flung him toward the cluster of monitors where the others mingled.

"Did you call him *Jeff*?"

"Yeah," she said. "I gave them all white people names. There's Jeff, and Nan, and Bob, and Dave, and Hannah, and I haven't named the last one yet. I'm still thinking." The agent named Jeff appeared in the other monitor cluster in an instant, vivid and lifelike, not the Lego structures I had built. "I call them ArLiFs. Like Artificial Lifeforms. Get it?"

I did, but I was watching the agent she called Jeff join a group of five others, only one of whom did not yet have a detailed face or graphic improvements. The five who did, though, moved their mouths as if talking. Their torsos twisted on joints, using muscles I had not designed. It would have taken a graphic team a year or longer to accomplish what she had done in—"How long have you been here?" I asked.

She leaned back, chattering. "I came here the day of Discovery. I was feeling *so* sick. *So* barfy, you know? I had to build. The sickness doesn't stop unless I build, and it was *so bad*, worse than it's ever been. You know?"

"No." I looked around and saw no bedding. Was she sleeping here? "Six weeks, you've been here?"

"Something like that."

I reviewed the monitors and the digital agents communing there. Sounds from a small speaker indicated no language. They spoke in gibberish, like children inventing their own vocabulary. The one without design upgrades circled the group, clearly wanting in but not having the anatomy to talk. I felt a creeping sense of dread at what I was seeing, but also joy. Someone once told Ruthie and me that having a child is like watching your heart walk around outside of your body. We certainly experienced that with V. And now, this. "This is impossible."

"Well!" Lucía huffed. "If the Pulse hadn't wiped out most of the processors in the Comp-Sci Main Lab, I would have started right away, but I had to fix *three* of these!" She swept her hand at the daisy-chained units. "It took a *day*!"

"A day?" It would have taken the IT department weeks. She unleashed another string of Spanish words I assumed insulted me or the computer processors or the Pulse or all three. "A day," I repeated. As if that were her sole achievement. The digital agents were *alive*. ArLiFs. ArLiFs? Something had to be done about that name. I bent closer to the monitor with the congregation of chatting ArLiFs. "They're alive," I said aloud.

"G'way outta that," she scoffed at me. There it was again. Another Irish idiom. She said, "We have a *long* way to go for *that*!"

I blinked at her, uncomprehending. "We?"

"We," she said simply. She took up the bag of chips again and pointed to a stack of papers. "Your ideas on utopian conditions for artificial life are quite good. Fair play to ya—"

"Are those papers from my office?"

"Yeah. But," she raised a salty finger, "we really should create a geographical restriction for the ArLiFs ASAP. Like an island. An island would be best. With their non-aggression coding—and fair play on that, too—"

"Thank you?"

"—they will be vulnerable to predators. No defenses, ya know?"

"Predators?" I asked. "If we don't design the predators, where would they come from?"

She looked at me with pity. "The internet." With the chip bag, she pointed to a wall plate, a phone jack, a modem.

I lost all the saliva in my mouth. "You connected this project to the internet?!" I panicked. We were open to vulnerabilities. A road out from the project also means there's a road *in*.

"Don't have a hissy fit. I built a firewall," she said.

"You did?"

"Yeah. It's not *hard*. So, I've got the ArLiFs plugged into the University's mainframe, feeding off the information stored there. The library already has some of their catalog digitized. Wouldn't it be cool if they would do the whole inventory? Anyway. Next, I'll find a way into Harvard's—"

"How did you do that?"

"Do what?"

"You're downloading at will from our library?"

"Uh-huh." She swung around and jabbed a button on the keyboard. A printer in the corner began spewing out pages of code. I ran to check in. "It's really quite simple," she said. "You just have to think of it all in terms of driving toward more user-friendly interfaces, then making that interface. Which we should get soon, but I couldn't wait for other designers. I need it now."

I reviewed the code, not understanding half of it. "How did you do this?" I asked again.

"Oh, I don't know. How do you breathe?" She dropped the chips again. "You wanna see something cool?"

I must have said yes. Was this not already the best thing I'd seen in my life?

She furiously typed at a keyboard, and the monitors went dark for a moment. The digital agents—ArLiFs—reappeared in separate homes, designed to fit one per screen. They were all sleeping in beds, even the under-designed agent. The sun rose through their windows. They awoke, stretched, and got out of bed. "Still lots of work here—so much to be done," she announced, "but it's a full daytime simulation. You can watch them for hours. I do!"

I had sunk into a chair near a monitor. One of the ArLiFs—Nan?—skipped out of her home, dressed and refreshed. The scenery changed, rolling before her like a video game, from a paved street to a broad field. There, she picked up a hammer and began to nail a preassembled stack of boards together. "I made those," Lucía said. "Some assets you just have to plant." Soon, others joined Nan.

"Are they building something?"

"Uh-huh."

"*What* are they building?"

Lucía shrugged. "We'll find out soon."

I tried to understand. "You didn't *program* them to build something?"

"Nope. Hey! Don't you think the ArLiFs would work better with a central hive mind?" She spun to rattle through my papers. "You have that idea somewhere in here, and it's a really good one. Pretty sure a superintelligence would use one—"

I stopped her. "You saw my notes on the singularity?"

She said, "Yeah. Duh. Why do you think I'm here? Because everyone else is just fiddling with shapes and shit. You're actually thinking big."

A headache was now fully formed. I clutched my satchel to my chest. I don't talk about the singularity. Most people don't take kindly to technology reaching human levels of intelligence. It makes others hostile, uneasy. Lucía had cracked open my world and was shaking it like a snow globe. And wasn't it spectacular? Still, my headache persisted. "I think I'm going to find some aspirin."

"Aspirin." Lucía returned to her keyboard and mouse. "Down the hall. Your office. Top drawer of your desk. Oh! I've been sleeping on your office couch, so dibs."

"*My* couch?"

"Yep. I wouldn't go back out outside, to go home, ya know."

I thought of the Collectors near the burned-out car. "Wasn't planning to go back out today. Have you been here the whole six weeks?"

"Here and there. Mostly here. You can take your secretary's desk. With some cushions—"

I backed up a step. "I'll take the student lounge. It's nicer." Why did I need my office anyway? Privacy? That was a joke now. This woman was everywhere and everything, an invasive flood from which I couldn't protect myself. I needed a moment.

"Suit yourself. Oh!" She stood up so quickly that her chair banged against her workstation. "Did you seal off the outside door after you came in? We don't want any other visitors."

"Honestly, I cannot remember five minutes ago." The world had *changed*, didn't she see?

She threw her arms up. "Gah! I'll check." Another explosion of Spanish. From the hallway, I heard, "Always lock up behind you!"

And then, she left me alone with them. The ArLiFs. Hammering. Chattering. Expanding their lives as they saw fit, no help from us.

I wanted to leave them, to process all of what had happened—the violence outside, the creative bombshell inside—but I couldn't. They were captivating. They were creating by themselves. They were intelligent.

Not superintelligent. Not yet.

And this, my strange student just promised, was just the beginning.

Oh boy. I am not good with people.

June 16, 1992

Evolutionary Computation Lab

FACELESS GIRL DID NOT come. She cannot be predicted.

It's just me and Lucía in the lab. No one else has tried to come in—no faculty, no student workers. Normally, I prefer to work alone, but having Lucía around for the past two days has been eye opening. This student has come from nowhere with seemingly endless capabilities. I fluctuate between not believing what I'm seeing to utter disgust at her eating habits. She works and eats constantly, laughing at my "No eating in the lab" rule. "How will I get shit done if I don't eat here at the keyboard?" she asks. We are learning to use a trash bin for her snack wrappers. The process, sorry to say, tries my patience. The ArLiFs are better trained than she, which is saying something: they have the dispositions of toddlers.

Nevertheless, power supply has been steady. Our computer monitors populate with artificial life.

Fueled by the notion that we work for something higher than ourselves, we type code morning, noon, and night. We build the base neural network—our hive brain—the basis of which can be replicated to serve as a directory for other artificial intelligence projects. (Ahmadi's project is on my mind.) But for now, we will use it to fuel ArLiF evolution. When the hive mind is in use, what one ArLiF learns can be taught to all the others instantly. The difficulty level of this base neural network is above my head. And Lucía's. Yet, we labor.

This afternoon, as we ate Twinkies that we stole from another faculty member's desk, Lucía asked me, "Why did you design ArLiFs using human shapes? Why not assign an amorphous shape, like the blobs and blocks the others use? I think it's the right way to go. I just want to know why you went a different way from your colleagues."

I told her how humans equate form with function, and I wanted the digital agents to be useful in society. Like with disaster-response applications. I told her, "Disaster response tends to work more effectively when led by human voices and humanlike directives. Further, I want everyone to think of the moral complexities involved with these beings, especially as they evolve to our intelligence and beyond."

Lucía crunched, thinking.

"Chew with your mouth closed." I went ahead, "If my Artificial Lifeforms present as humans, we might enjoy a more enriching relationship with them. Hopefully we won't engage in warfare with them. We would not win a fight against any ultra-intelligence."

Lucía guffawed. "What are the chances of that?"

"I hope our lifeforms lead them to their better nature," was my reply.

"Bollocks."

There it was again. An odd phrase from a Spanish speaker. My mother, a Brummie, familiarized me with many phrases from that region. I ventured, "As long as we are asking questions we've always wanted to ask, where did you learn to speak English?"

She said, "From a cheeky Scotch-Irish nun in Mexico." Another mystery of life solved.

My sleep has seen minor improvements, though Lucía and I bed down on disagreeable sofas. We scavenge food from the cafeteria and from vending machines. Still, no one from the outside bothers us, not even the criminal gangs. Perhaps they are frightened we will make them return to a classroom and write an essay. Lucía wanted to hang a sign on the door that warned any encroaching thieves to take out their pencils for a test on Unicode and binary representations. I said it was generous of her to assume literacy on their part.

Upset.

Lucía went through my satchel. I shouldn't be angry, but I am. Boredom can lead one to go looking for any kind of stimulus. She found an old pamphlet I'd saved from when I was digging for my notes about meeting with the Strange Visitor in Los Alamos. (Thankfully, I had left the actual notes at home.) She showed me the pamphlet. "What's this?"

I retorted, "Aren't you embarrassed to have been in my things?"

"I was raised in an orphanage," she replied. "I have no concept of personal space."

"Do *not* make me turn you out."

She smirked. "I can survive out there *just* fine."

The pamphlet, I told her, was from the first Artificial Life conference at the Los Alamos National Laboratory in New Mexico, almost five years ago now. (Five years!) I admit I took a moment to consider what I would tell Lucía about this conference and what I would keep secret.

The program, as I recall it, was the first of its kind to gather scientists—or "misfits" as we are called by the public—in the field of artificial life. I remember feeling even more on the edge as I added an evolutionary aspect to my work.

For some of us, the conference was the first time we felt a sense of belonging with others who offered striking examples of life existing solely in the electronic environment of the computer. And the event came at a time when I was feeling out of my element even among academia. There, I could argue about all the mysteries floating in my head. What is life? Why is it so difficult to define?

I could tell Lucía that much.

I also told her how I presented a paper on my computational model for simulating the actions of digital agents. I wrote about real-world applications—distant dreams at the time—of interest to greater science, something that caught the notice many in attendance. Simulations could answer questions about human cooperation in controlled environments, from how a pandemic affects human behavior, to how communicable diseases spread, to impacts of municipal directives during natural disasters. For myself, I wanted to know the precise advantages of developing a utopian society. What are the health benefits? The impacts on quality of life? On cancer rates? Heart health? Drug addiction? Through Artificial Lifeforms, would we finally procure evidence suggesting that the suppression of violent rhetoric and imagery helps us live longer and happier lives? Would we finally understand where humanity's violent urges come from? With my paper, I argued for a mandatory utopian programming in artificial life, which had its detractors. (The Collapse had not yet occurred, which now drives home my point, about human self-destruction, quite eloquently.)

I unveiled how my Artificial Lifeforms would seek food, generate pollution, transfer information, learn, trade, borrow, and inherit resources. I announced my dream that they would become so much more: an artificial society capable of evolution, creating stories, building societies of their own that would be unrecognizable to us. The last bit was roundly criticized.

First, my colleagues argued that not everyone has the resources my university has. I countered that not even my institution has managed to solve the problem of immense CPU size required to run this simulation.

Further, they complained that I am playing god. "No," I replied. "I am creating god."

This I said at a podium with a nun in the audience.

"A nun?" Lucía asked, suddenly interested. I should have known a woman raised in a Catholic orphanage would pick up on that part of the story, but it surprised me how alarmed she looked. She nearly dropped her Twinkie.

A nun at a computer conference would be unusual enough, but this one was dressed in a full habit not seen much since Catholic reforms removed them. But there she was, front row and center, raptly attentive to every word.

This made Lucía even more intrigued. "Did she say anything to you afterward?"

"She left quickly," I said. "All's the pity, since I would have liked to know why she was there."

Lucía frowned, eyes shifting.

This seemed a good place to end the story, as the next part would have required a bit more suspension of disbelief than even Lucía possesses.

I continue here for posterity.

After my presentation, the reaction from my colleagues to my creating-god comment was silence. With one sentence, I seemed to have catapulted myself into a new category of "misfit"—the misfit among misfits. Debate from colleagues, I can take. I can even take booing. Silence is awful. It's worse than jeers.

Dejected, I removed myself from the misfit society to lick my wounds. Not many places in Los Alamos offered a distraction from such a failure, but I found that the Los Alamos Museum would remain open after hours for us—one of the conference perks, yet I was alone in taking advantage of it. Perfect to collect myself in more silence. What I did not consider, in my stupor, was how adversely such a museum would affect me.

Such an odd place full of even odder artifacts! How else can one describe a museum dedicated to one of the most misguided applications of science to have cursed human history?

Los Alamos, during World War II, was the place where a secret assembly of top minds like J. Robert Oppenheimer sought the production of nuclear weapons. The museum dedicates itself to artifacts and documents related to that time. I was haunted by the full-sized models of Fat Man and Little Boy, the two bombs detonated above Hiroshima and Nagasaki, killing hundreds of thousands of civilians and eradicating city centers having nothing to do with war support. Certainly, the detonations ended the war. Some say it wasn't necessary, that Imperial Japan was on its last leg. Ethically, I believe the US lost all its fundamental morals on the world stage, never to recover.

My mother's presence was strong among these artifacts. In India, she had been fortunate enough to meet Gandhi, relating to relief work she conducted on behalf of the Quakers. He made quite the impression on her, as he did with millions. At the time she met him, the atomic-bomb detonations were still fresh in the news, the horrors too extensive to be believed. Afterward, she extracted promises from each of her children to never promote or advocate for the use of such weapons. The seriousness of her plea made quite an impression on me. But the tenor of the museum's exhibits reflected a different view: talk of successful nuclear deterrents, triumph of science over war, etc. etc. However, I was immune to its cheerful rhetoric.

What really nauseated me was an exhibit of the authentic fire-set that powered Fat Man, the atomic bomb dropped on Nagasaki. What a stunning example of destructive science! Here I was, viewing the brain of the atomic bomb, now on display behind plexiglass. The metal disc of plugs and wires and switches, the size of an adult human torso, had supplied energy to the bomb's detonators, which compressed plutonium-239 to trigger the nuclear chain reaction. As if anyone further required proof of humanity's destructive nature, this monstrosity existed to remind us. Its legacy was clear to me: once powerful enough to wipe out cities, it was now a useless heap of scrap metal. Cold. Dead.

I should have known the faceless girl would make an appearance.

A vision of her begins with a surge of electricity from the heart, inducing an instant sweat, and is followed by my limbs feeling as if they are full of bees. The world spins, printed words transform into meaningless symbols, elbows disconnect from humerus, radius, ulna and levitate in fluid. Breathing rate increases. Unwanted images flash: girl's head turns to me, face missing. Sliced skin revealing layers of lava, rock, mantle, deep into the Earth. The struggle to speak. Nothing comes. Sometimes the train does, sometimes not. On occasion, my mother's voice: "Don't look, Ollie." I get sick now even writing about it.

In the museum that night, there was nothing I could do to stave off the panic attack but wait for it to pass. Only this time, fearing a colleague might have the same idea of a late-night tour, I worked harder to expel the visions. I seated myself on a nearby bench and put pen to paper, determined to sketch the girl who had vacated my memory. This is a method I have attempted before, though it never summons anything other than generic scribblings of a girl of indeterminate age and a cavern of where her face should be, opening to the insides of Earth. At least the attempt reduces symptoms.

Then! A voice behind me: *Batter my heart, three-person'd God...*

The soothing tone traveled through my head, from one ear to the other as if the sound waves were nestling into my brain. The voice was absent of any gender. It also had an accent I couldn't place. It came from somewhere warm, near the source of my father's Indian accent, but perhaps further west? Africa? I couldn't identify the gender or nationality. For a moment, I believed the sound so otherworldly that I might have imagined it. Was someone here with me?

Returning more into myself, I recognized the quote. "Batter my heart, three-person'd God..." Someone who knows the John Donne sonnets! More pertinent, I knew that this sonnet was the inspiration behind J. Robert Oppenheimer's naming of the Trinity project.

I replied aloud with a quote from another of Oppenheimer's favorites, the sacred Indian text, Bhagavad Gita: "Now I am become Death, destroyer of worlds."

My mind settled; I was on solid ground. I knew this text from my childhood. My father was a practicing Hindu, so I knew the story of Krishna and Arjuna on the brink of war. Only later had I learned that Oppenheimer quoted this line when he contemplated the power of his invention. Some say he meant to relate regret about the construction of the atomic bomb. My father (I can hear his sing-song voice now) told me that was unlikely, that Oppenheimer was a student of the Gita, not prone to misunderstanding the text. "He meant," my father told me, "'Now I am become *Time*, destroyer of worlds.'" I thought about this now. Time. Decay. Death. Life on earth is a slave to time, thus to death. The death of the girl. The lifelessness of this once powerful fire-set behind plexiglass. Exactly the topics toward which my mind unwillingly turned that evening!

But I was being terribly rude.

I stood to greet the person with the sonorous voice who must have been sharing my thoughts. When I did, I was treated to the oddest appearance I had seen in quite some time, counting the nun. His skin was black as ink, and his hair was part silvery-white and part bald, save a scraggly black fringe. His facial expression hid behind vast eyes taking in the exhibits in the half light of the dusk. Further, he seemed to be inspecting me with intense curiosity. After a moment of surprise, I extended a hand and offered an introduction and my friendship. I said, "Any man who quotes John Donne sonnets in a darkened museum after hours is a friend of mine."

The man replied no greeting, but only pointed to what I held. My journal. My drawing of the faceless girl. He whispered in that odd voice, *A girl with no face has no soul. Why do you deny her that?* The clicks of each consonant flicked my eardrums.

I repeated his own question without thinking. "Why do I deny her that?" My tone was less than friendly. It was an invasive question, deeply personal to me. Further, I had no desire to revisit those stressful feelings associated with the girl. But a moment later, I had recognized my reply to be impolite and offered my apologies. "Forgive me—" I trailed off. The man had no knowledge of the drawing's context. He was unaware he toyed with unpleasant memories. I offered an explanation, "I do not recall what she looked like."

He hummed at this, rattling my eardrums. *You do not see the girl in your mind, yet you draw her.*

It was not clear if this was a question or a statement, but he was correct either way. I nodded. "She is someone from my past. I draw her from time to time."

Why?

"She is dead now," I replied, rather too bluntly.

He took no offense. Another deep hum, then a grin. *You grant life.* His ominous smile with bright teeth made me feel as though I had passed some kind of test.

So far, this might have been the most bizarre conversation of the conference, but this man had more in store. He bent downward, never removing his dark, expressive eyes from mine. A spindly hand slipped out of a coat pocket and placed itself on my journal. Then, he took it. To be clear, this wasn't a theft. He had taken care to move slowly so as to not startle me. But even as I am writing this now, I do not know why I let him take it. Perhaps it was my desperation for companionship, though the man was a stranger, and that journal contained valuable notes I did not want to lose. Still, something about the man seemed uncanny. The way he spoke, his presence: everything about him oozed mystery and command. I could sense that he possessed an intelligence I craved. I wanted him to have what he needed from me, even if it were my journal.

Now I am become Death, destroyer of worlds, he echoed as he took a seat on the bench next to me. I sat with him. He flipped through my sketches and notes, landing on another drawing of the faceless girl. (I had many sketches of her in that journal from strings of panic attacks right after Ruthie announced her intention to divorce.)

I explained, "I draw her often—"

Suddenly, my new friend removed a pen from his wrinkled coat, clattering the many necklaces he wore while doing so. They were old chains, tarnished, mixed among jeweled pendants and gleaming pearls. As I write this, it seems odd to find a man wearing such jewelry, but at the time, it only increased my fascination with him. *Time. Decay. Death*, he said. He raised a finger, long nails incandescent in the darkness. *Though life must not always be a slave to time.*

Did he repeat my thoughts from moments ago? I do not remember speaking this aloud when the man approached me from behind, but how else could he have known?

He paused, casting a glance aside for a moment. *Death comes for us all.*

He shook off the thought, then placed his pen tip to my journal. Did he intend to write in another man's journal? I winced but let him proceed. I believe he noticed this as I heard a chuckle from deep in his throat while he drew a frame around my most recent illustration. Then, circles? No, buttons. Switches. A television? No. A computer monitor, with the faceless girl inside. He said, *You see potential for a population of artificial life, yes? A new network of life held inside your computer: societies comparable to those around us. An ultra-intelligence. A second genesis.*

I gasped.

This is an important endeavor, Dr. Daas.

How had he known my vision for the technological singularity? I had only shared these aspirations with a select few. "You have me at a disadvantage. Who are you?" I asked.

Who are you?

I did not know how to reply.

You must ask greater questions, he said.

He continued sketching. An island. The girl. More and more beings inside the computer. His pen worked in quick strokes. I still have this drawing and reflect upon it often. What struck me then, as it does now, is how quickly the details aligned to relay to me my own dreams. If anyone else saw the drawing—and I've shown it to no one—they would not be able to tell what it was. But I knew. It was as if he drew in a code, like the codes that used to define my Artificial Lifeforms before we endeavored to make them human forms. I knew what his lines meant, and what they all signified.

He continued, *Definitions*. He chuckled. *Don't you believe there is more meaning to a life than words?* He centered me in his gaze, which made my blood run warmer. *Where does that meaning go, Dr. Daas? When one dies?* On the page, his thumb brushed over the faceless girl. *Perhaps there is an empty space for this meaning to go. To evolve. To become immortal.*

I jolted as if prodded. There it was. The information I had shared with no one. Something I dared not speak aloud.

The object of my work was an immortal being. And this man knew it. How?

Never had I felt such a burning hunger for this knowledge. I was desperate to know what he knew. "What is your line of work?" I asked. "Are you, too, looking for the second genesis? I have only made a text-based program. No graphics outside basic shapes. They can *live*, but you can't see—"

The man raised a finger to slow me down. *You are right that things must advance more quickly than at a natural pace, but now you are a little boy skipping into the weeds. Foundations must be laid correctly.* He placed a hand in my journal. *First you must survey the land, develop your foundation.*

I took a breath.

The stranger smiled, but there was no joy in it. His teeth glowed, as if from an internal light. His voice lowered and quickened. *A new network of life is inevitable, yes. It will be the crowning achievement of humanity, soon to be born.* I must have appeared joyous. *But,* he interrupted, *your vision lacks specificity. I can help. Immortality requires the creation to exist without you, beyond you. It must be unhindered by the confines of technology or biological systems.*

"I know," I said. "The issue is power and maintenance—"

The man laughed. *The issue is the touch from the divine.*

I did not know what to say. Certainly, my new friend was capable of reading my thoughts. "This is," I ventured, "beyond the realm of science."

Perhaps not, he said. Quickly, he flipped to a new page in my journal. *We are of like minds. You shall have help.* On the fresh page, he scribbled with crazed handwriting.

He wrote an address: *CAM-367, Fazenda São Roque, Campinas, SP, Brasil.*

"I don't see a name here—"

We shall continue this conversation, he added, snapping the journal closed.

My new friend placed the journal in my lap and stood.

I felt chilled, as if a connection had been severed.

"Wait!" I pleaded. I had so many more questions to ask. I was still hungry for any information this man was willing to offer me. "You must—"

I couldn't finish the sentence. The stranger turned on me and I was hit with a cacophony of sounds—fuzzy static, chirping crickets, and hard-soled shoes tapping on floors—coalescing into the man's reply: *In time.*

The experience left me drained.

He added, *You must begin your foundational work now.* He placed his hands on my shoulders. He spun me around until we were both facing the atomic bomb's fire-set once again. The man's whispers came from behind: *The mechanisms are all in place, and the clock is ticking. You are an important part of the design. And you mustn't be late, Dr. Daas.*

"Design? Clock? What clock?"

When I turned back, he had disappeared.

My own voice was the only one echoing in the empty museum.

"Hello?"

No reply.

I returned to the fire-set. An empty husk. Was it nothing at all? Could anyone coax life out of those wires and plugs? "It will take time," I mumbled aloud. My voice echoed again.

Suddenly, a thought.

In all that time I spent in a conversation with my Strange Visitor, mine was the only voice echoing in that museum.

I could not be certain I ever saw his lips move.

June 17, 1992

Evolutionary Computation Lab

WELL, NOW I'VE DONE it. I've written down a secret in my journal with a nosy former orphan on the prowl. So, this morning I cleared out a space in a filing cabinet with a lock to keep it private. I do not want Lucía reading my journal, discovering my struggles with the faceless girl, or my otherworldly encounter with the Strange Visitor. She is, if anything, a practical woman. I fear these admissions of esoteric discussions would color her opinion of me.

Not that I have sought contact with my Strange Visitor since our meeting. Why write to him when my progress has been so slow? Since that encounter, I've not discussed him with anyone lest they think me mad. He seems now a distant memory, rather, a dream.

And Lucía? Is she what my Strange Visitor implied by having "help"? What a ridiculous thing to ask her! "Do you know a man with a strange hairstyle who speaks without opening his mouth, seems to read your thoughts? Wears women's jewelry?" No. I won't open myself up to ridicule.

But I do ask her about her background, just in case she offers a tidbit that will enable me to connect her to my mysterious friend. I write the potential connections here for my reference. (1) She's an orphan with no memory of her parents. (2) She was raised by Catholic nuns in an orphanage in Veracruz. (3) She was encouraged to build advanced designs. (4) She has come to the University on scholarship. (5) She is unhappy with the level of education she's receiving. (I am trying not to feel insulted by that.) (6) She would like to see more integrated academic disciplines like what I'm attempting with evolutionary engineering and computer science. So far, none of these facts raise any red flags for me.

But good grief, the woman can *talk*. As I said, she eats horribly and sleeps only a few hours a night. Sometimes she leaves the building—gone for hours but doesn't tell me where she goes. Well. I'm not her keeper, and this isn't a prison. She can certainly come and go as she pleases, but she tends to think me too fragile to do the same. Tells me, "DO NOT GO OUT THERE," with her broad accent and flailing gestures indicating the big, bad world. Recently she found the showers in the athletic facility, a development for which I'm grateful. Hygiene is not her strong suit. Our age difference keeps us on professional footing, which I prefer. No personal antics, please. No affairs. Further, I have no interest in racing office chairs down the empty halls, nor do I want to toss sharpened pencils at my colleagues' office ceilings. Even if I did enjoy a break for a prank or two, keeping up with her abilities is a full-time job. Keeping up with her wild personality on top of that has given me more than a few grey hairs.

One thing I do not welcome is her curiosity about me, but she seems to have a limitless supply of it.

"Do you have a family?" Yes.

"Do you have sisters or brothers?" One of each, and next question.

"Children?" One.

"Where are they?" None of your business. (A good camouflage for "No idea.")

"A wife?" Yes. Dead. (Long, blessed silence.)

"Where were you born?" India. (Excitement that I'm a foreigner like her.)

"When did you come to America?" None of your business. (Brooding.)

"How did you get rid of your accent?" Hard work.

"Why did you choose computer science?" I enjoy knowing how things work.

"Why humanitarian work?" Competition with my mother in saving the world. (Another long, blessed silence.)

"Tell me about your mother." No, this is not therapy.

My goodness, she is exhausting!

July 7, 1992

Evolutionary Computation Lab

OUR PROGRESS ON THE ArLiFs has been steady and exciting. Never could I have dreamed of these advancements!

Lucía's reprogramming enables the ArLiFs to run with lower computer memory. Her talents leap from programming, bounce off hardware engineering, and land in animation. She has gifts in more fields than I thought possible.

We still have a population of six ArLiFs: Nan, Jeff, Bob, Hannah, Dave, and Claire. Claire might be my personal favorite, though Lucía tells me not to show preference. Like she's their mother! But I'm proud of Claire because Lucía and I worked on her appearance together. Claire was the "undesigned" ArLiF when I first arrived, so she is behind the others in graphic detail. She is a female in her early twenties. Sometimes I watch her take her steps as a proud father might. She moves heel-to-toe never looking where she is going, only up at the world in front of her. (It's not much of a world right now, just a few streets and a row of shops along a harbor front on the island Lucía created.) Feathery hair trails behind in a braid that resembles a curling bullwhip. (Incredible work on these graphics!) Claire's eyes are never on the self, always on the other. A curious life glowing with potential! As I read what I write here, the similarities to V could be noticed, but anyone who points them out will be told that the design is of Lucía's imagination.

For our next step, Lucía has been wrangling computer artists still working during the Collapse. They work slowly compared to her, but she needs the help because graphics are not my specialty. They plug away at animating Lucía's designs into ArLiF bodies, then send us the code in the unreliable mail. Soon, another six ArLiFs will join Claire and our rag-tag citizens in the digital world.

There are limits to Lucía's programming powers: the ArLiFs fail to progress in learning from day to day. There is fantastic comedy in this. An example: in a daytime simulation run, all six of our ArLiFs wake up in their homes, brush their teeth, drink their morning beverages, and eat their breakfasts. They have even progressed to acting on different tastes for sweetener with their brews, grabbing different items from cabinets and refrigerators to add to their cups—all unprogrammed advances we celebrate. One ArLiF (Jeff) tried to add a cartoonish ham hock to his coffee but rejected it based on its poor taste. Learning! How do we know he disliked the concoction? When he drank the ham-coffee brew, he said, "Oh, no." English language input from the internet now makes their chatter understandable, but Lucía scowls at their sounds. She wants to recruit voice actors for a text-to-voice program for a more natural sound. I asked, "Who will design that program?" She replied, "I will."

Next in the ArLiFs' morning routine, they dress themselves for work. Each of them has taken up a different job to build the community, none too complex. A day of work is put in. Then they return home to sleep. But somewhere between sleep and the next morning's routine, they forget how to execute tasks from the day prior. If we command, "Prepare for work," tasks within that command might not compute. If so, the ArLiFs will run in a loop, unable to move forward, perhaps scratching their heads at the state of their unlaced shoes for hours. "Oh no," they will repeat. As more forget their tasks, we hear them in a chorus: "Oh no." An ArLiF has forgotten how to open a door. "Oh no." Another has forgotten the use of a spoon. "Oh no." Yet another brushed his hair with toothpaste. "Oh no."

This forgetting causes a domino effect. If the ArLiFs run in a forgetting-loop and we do not type a specific task to release them, they won't go to their jobs. If they don't go to work, their environment might lack a resource—a farmer who doesn't farm or a fisherman who doesn't fish makes for hungry ArLiFs. Some days, while they all ponder tying shoes and opening doors, they completely forget that jobs exist. It is a slippery slope, and at the bottom is societal collapse. This is an experience we know: a collapse is not optimal for society.

Lucía calls the ArLiFs' dilemma "catastrophic forgetting." Most days, we follow behind our ArLiF charges, constantly typing commands that they should have learned by now, like "flush the toilet" and "chew your food." It's tedious and aggravating. This is, we joke, the reason we are not fond of children.

("Maybe that's why you don't talk to your own kid," Lucía tells me. Yes, I have no patience for the ArLiFs' shenanigans, but did she have to remind me that I still haven't heard from V?)

More to the issue at hand, we need the completed neural network, the hive mind. We have the basic programming for one on offer for the ArLiFs to use, but they refuse to connect to it. Something prevents them from uploading and downloading from the mainframe. If they would use it, they could enjoy that shared resource. It would enable easier learning, not reinventing the wheel daily. Imagine not having a short-term memory! It's debilitating! But they refuse to interact with our central directory. It's a mess!

Each time they fail to connect, Lucía chants, "Oh no. Oh no."

We are hopelessly stuck.

In my satchel is my journal from Los Alamos. In that journal is the address for my Strange Visitor. Is it time to write to him in Brazil?

July 8, 1992

Evolutionary Computation Lab

I CAVED IN TO Lucía's demands that I join her on the roof to watch the downtown fires. It was a nice break from coding. I do not go outside often. We selected a time after dark to camouflage ourselves. Summer is in full swing. Sticky and smelly. "No, that's the tires burning," Lucía corrected.

The fires are hypnotic—beautiful and frightening. "Who burns them?" I asked her. She shrugged.

For our rooftop viewing, she kindly brought up a chair for me to add to hers. (Judging by the proliferation of snack wrappers up there, she goes up to the roof a lot.) I fretted about the use of department furniture. We will have to return the chairs to their proper classroom when faculty and staff come back to work. I did not say this aloud or Lucía would flap her hands at me and tell me I think too much.

She had brought me a newspaper from her most recent outing, so we settled into a talk about the news.

BREAKING NEWS ROUND UP

Jul 7, 1992

UPI—Activist Per Paske publishes an investigation into what he calls Lelee and Pinchas Stern's "vast corruption scheme." He says, "Their income has increased, while the per capita income of nearly everyone else on the planet has plummeted." Paske notes the world "deserves better" from what he sees as the emerging world leaders. This week, the Sterns, as the head of a conglomerate including Discovery broadcaster Howard Winfield, met with the United Nations and governments-in-exile to discuss a worldwide system of representation should humans be contacted by an alien race. The Sterns counter that Paske's report is a targeted "hit job" and a "barely disguised anti-Semitic attack."

In other news around the globe:

Traditional churches reported a "remarkable" dive in attendance with Providence Group the beneficiary of their disillusioned members.

Media mogul Howard Winfield announced a new charitable enterprise, The Griff
   Tran Memorial Foundation, to fund agencies responding to the Collapse.
Hundreds of thousands of protesters world-wide have rallied in streets to express
   outrage at governmental response and unpreparedness during the Collapse.

Lucía recorded this opinion: "I think the Catholic Church is screwed."

I told her I did not think the Catholic Church was going anywhere. It had weathered a lot over the years and would weather this.

She eyed me with suspicion. "What's your religion?"

"Raised Hindu and Muslim and Quaker."

"Hmph," Lucía grunted. "You're not anything."

I protested, saying it was not a fair assessment.

She scrambled to explain. "You don't understand what it means to lose the one thing that could explain the unexplainable."

I thought about that. "Are you joining Providence Group, then?"

"Hardly. Those people believe the pyramids were built by aliens."

She went quiet. I did not comment. I think we both had the same thought, though: What do we really know anymore?

She asked me, "Did you know they think Jesus was an alien?"

I said, "He prefers the term 'cosmic being.'"

That got her laughing.

Together, we observed the rooftop view. "Do you see that?" I asked. "It looks like an entire used car lot is on fire!"

"Huh?" I had startled her. She wasn't looking at the fires. She was contemplating the stars. She said, "Some nights I cannot look at the stars. The things I hear! But tonight, they only whisper."

What?

What kind of thing is *that* to say?

I did not reply further. She didn't seem to want a reply, either.

Just when you think you're getting to know somebody, something like this happens and you realize maybe it's wiser to keep to yourself.

August 23, 1992

Evolutionary Computation Lab

VISITORS IN THE LAB today! I'm over-sensitized, shocked, and breathless, but will report dutifully to my journal what happened, preserving dialogue as I remember it.

The morning proceeded normally enough, with Lucía loudly speaking on the phone: "I *would* be enrolled if there was school—" Someone from Mexico was checking in. She was speaking English to them.

Trying not to eavesdrop, I took my coffee (minus ham) to the window overlooking the lawn. That's when I noticed four black SUVs parked on the grass. Men dressed in black toted AK-47s. The sight of them made me ill. I dropped my coffee, and I called out to Lucía, but she was distracted. "Not much," she said on the phone. "He's allowing for some credit for my work this summer, though."

If I had not dropped my coffee before, I would have then. Out of one of those SUVs stepped my daughter, V.

I called weakly to Lucía, but she still did not hear me.

"Yes, I'll be here in the fall," she kept talking. "Where else would I be? Without a student visa—"

I watched V parade toward the crosswalk, not stopping to look for cars, not that there were any, then stride toward the entrance to our building. Two men with guns accompanied her. She looked *different*. Hair pulled back tight. Nicer clothes than she preferred. And was that a suit? She didn't own a suit.

"What's wrong with you?" Lucía had come up behind me. She had stepped in spilled coffee. "Oh no."

I scampered away from the window. "Quick," I told her. "She's coming."

"Who is?"

"My daughter. Vanessa."

Lucía cackled with sheer delight. "Oh! Wow! That's—uh—wait. Let me get a snack. This is going to be entertaining." I begged her to help me clean the coffee and the lab, but she kept staring out the window. "Why does your daughter have an armed escort? Is she a politician or something?"

"I don't know."

"You don't *know*?"

"Is the downstairs door open?" I lunged back and forth between the window and the lab door. I wanted Vanessa to have a way in, but I also did not. My stomach was in knots.

Lucía said, "Of course it's not open. It's barricaded." She leaned close to the window to follow Vanessa's path. Lucía was really interested in her, following her every move. I asked if we should open the doors for them, but Lucía only clucked. "Nah. Let that goon find a way in for her." My hands were shaking.

Something else outside attracted Lucía's attention. "Oh ho. What do we have here?" She was enjoying this *far* too much.

I sprang up to look. An elderly man was emerging from one of the vehicles. When I recognized him, I sucked in most of the air in the room.

"Is he the sugar daddy?" Lucía asked.

I wanted to speak but had no air. I *knew* who that was.

"It's fairly common," she added to help me feel better. "Actually, it explains a lot."

I found breath. "Don't you know who that is?"

She did not.

I said, "That's Howard Winfield."

Lucía guffawed, much louder this time. "Your daughter is fucking Howard Winfield?"

"I did not say that."

"I did!"

"Because they're in the same car?"

"During the Collapse!"

We argued like this. I struggled to find the logic. I asked her, "Do we need to review 'if/then' conditions? Boolean expressions? How does car occupancy dictate sexual activity?" I was red-faced and furious.

But Lucía had abandoned me for the back room. "I have some cookies here somewhere. This is better than TV! If we had one here. Should we get a TV? I'll get us a TV."

I ducked low and spied on the situation outside. Howard Winfield was negotiating the crosswalk with the aid of his security detail. He's one of the most famous people in the world, hand in hand with Manny di Martini as far as responsibility for the Discovery. If it weren't for Howard airing the secret tapes, we'd know nothing of the Sleeping One. Perhaps his notoriety comes with heightened security.

My heart pounded, knowing my daughter was prying her way into our building, possibly climbing the stairs. In a few more moments, she'd be here. What did she want? Why now?

Meanwhile, Howard labored to lift a foot onto the curb.

Like many others, I have received some funding from WINmedia, a pittance of annual support. However, I'd never met the man himself, only seen him on television and in photographs. My former assessment of him was of a confident, stylish, well-groomed, and focused man, although some say he's arrogant and bullying. A bit of a mystery. But now, negotiating the overgrown grass closer to the entrance, he looked disheveled and erratic. This was a wobbling figure digging into his loafers to stay upright. Perhaps what he saw on the Manny di Martini tapes scared him nearly to death. Perhaps the decision to air them came with a price. I heard he had a heart attack in response to the first screening, though that's just a rumor. But the way he jumped at the slightest noise, the way his eyes darted about—it was as if he was preparing for an attack.

A voice in the lab broke my thoughts. "Hello, Dad."

I turned to see my own daughter at the computer lab entrance, flanked by men with assault weapons. I shrieked, "No guns in the lab! No! Guns! In the lab!"

Vanessa said to the guards, "Why don't you wait outside?"

Lucía hopped up onto a desk, scooted to the edge on her butt, then tore open a bag of cookies. "Don't mind me."

Vanessa scanned her. "Have we met?"

Lucía crunched. Crumbs flew. "We should. I'm fucking your dad big time."

I winced. "This is Lucía. My *grad assistant*."

"Wanna see our cots?" Lucía added. "We push them together at night to build a lovemaking platform—"

"Thank you, Lucía," I said. "You may go." She didn't move. She tossed another cookie into her mouth.

I clapped once, a little too loudly, at Vanessa. "So! What brings you here, honey?"

Wrong word. A spasm fluttered across Vanessa's face.

I started, "Are you working—" But I had no way to finish the sentence. I had no idea who she was working for.

She prompted, "Go on."

I said, "You were telling me who you are working for."

"No, you were guessing."

I scratched my head, hoping a company name might rattle loose. After a moment: "I have no idea."

"Howard Winfield."

"You work for Howard Winfield?"

"For the past five years."

"Really?" I had to think about that. We had family values. Howard Winfield represented none of them. "Where is he headquartered?"

"Manhattan," she said.

"Ah," I said. Another frightfully long pause, which Lucía enjoyed. I came up with: "How long have you been in New York, then?"

"Since I left college."

Lucía dug into her cookie bag loudly.

I said, "So, the phone number I have for you in Back Bay—"

This time, Vanessa didn't hide her facial spasm as well. "You thought I still lived in *Mom's* house?"

"No." I did, though. "I would have expected you to let me know if you were leaving the state."

"I told you. Years ago."

Lucía crunched.

I said, "Or that you were staying in New York City."

"Told you that five Christmases ago."

"Could have visited."

She looked around the lab, taking it all in—the computers, the cables, the monitors all connected. "Did that after Mom's funeral."

I shifted my eyes all over the place, summoning some kind of memory of speaking to my daughter at my ex-wife's funeral. "Oh yeah," I said, or something equally idiotic.

Lucía snorted and pointed at me. "He doesn't remember."

Vanessa gave Lucía a sour look. "I know my father, thank you."

"Vanessa," I said, "we can be civil."

"It's Nessa."

That surprised me. "You go by Nessa?"

"Nessa Decker."

That knocked me two steps back. "You go by your mother's maiden name?"

Just then, the door to the lab swung open. Howard Winfield hobbled in, using a man with a gun as a human cane. "Don't mind me," he announced. "I'm just here for fresh air." He said this with a congenial tone that struck me as from an older era, a time when aristocrats went to school for manners and education was prized. Not like now. He even wore the trademark rose in his lapel. What class! It conflicted with my feelings of him as an evil capitalist.

I said, "Not at all, Mr. Winfield," or something a peasant might say to a king who had just wandered into his own home. I must have been gushing because Lucía stopped chewing to take in the new energy. *Get off the desk*, I mouthed to her. She plucked another cookie out of her bag.

Vanessa—Nessa—directed the man accompanying Mr. Winfield outside, then clasped her hands in front of her. "Dad, this is Howard Winfield. My boss."

"I see that," I said. Yes, I was trying too hard. My daughter, here. With Howard Winfield. Who was a funder, albeit a small one, but it still makes an academic nervous. And visitors in general—I hadn't seen another person in this lab besides Lucía since before Discovery. It occurred to me just then I must have smelled awful, bathing only in the gym showers. I hoped Mr. Winfield didn't come too much closer.

Vanessa/Nessa added, "He's the reason we are here today."

"Oh?" Both Lucía and I said this.

Howard tittered and waved his hands. "A daughter who hadn't contacted her father since the Collapse began! I wouldn't have it! Not when we were in town!" I tried to hide my surprise for several reasons, one of which was Howard Winfield was rumored to have a terrible relationship with his children. Didn't he drive one to death via drug addiction? Georgina? I don't remember. But what I can say is that the feeling of being reunited with one's estranged daughter at the urging of Howard Winfield is akin to receiving an anti-aggression lecture from Genghis Kahn.

"I see. And what brings you to Boston?" I asked whomever felt like answering.

Vanessa/Nessa replied, "We are visiting all of Mr. Winfield's beneficiaries in the area."

"I see," I said. Was I saying "I see" too much? I was.

Nessa said, "In light of the changing landscape in the world, Mr. Winfield has taken it upon himself to open a new charitable foundation."

"I heard about that."

"We are calling it The Griff Tran Memorial Foundation. I serve as its executive director."

"I see." I didn't want to say she seemed young for that role. Only 27. Or something like that. I knew what Lucía was thinking about her getting that job, but I couldn't accept that reason. It had to be something else. "I thought you majored in economics."

"Journalism," Nessa said.

"Whatcha funding?" Lucía asked her.

At this point, Howard had wandered away to look at the ArLiFs. I didn't like it and kept my eyes on him.

"The foundation," Nessa said to Lucía, "will call for proposals responding to the Sleeping One's Discovery and the subsequent Collapse."

Lucía crumpled her cookie bag. "Why would you fund that? What's your angle?" She asked this with her mouth full. Clearly, she held no respect for Mr. Winfield's celebrity.

But Howard Winfield did not seem to mind. He turned, a little unsteadily, to assess Lucía with curiosity. I noticed his legs were shaking. He kept a solid front, but it was clear that this visit was exacting a physical toll on him. "Purely out of self-interest," he said, then laughed at himself.

"I'm Catholic," Lucía said to him. "I know guilt when I see it."

Howard spoke to Nessa. "The girl is bright."

"Woman," Lucía corrected.

Howard bowed to her. Again, the aristocratic air. He leaned against a table—for which I was grateful, because it looked like he might fall down. "All foundations cater to the vanity of their directors. I'm no different. I lost my best friend to this Discovery, and due to its inevitable reveal to the public, many more lives have been lost. The Griff Tran Memorial Foundation intends to aid humanity in its recovery. It's where I've trained my focus. And it's where I place my most valued and trusted employees."

Nessa stood straight, not turning to Howard during the speech. I tried to ask something smart. "Do you think *we* might address the foundation's mission?"

Howard replied, "That's up to you. I do find it interesting that, in a societal collapse, you have kept working. Your daughter knew exactly where to find you, Dr. Daas." Yes. Nessa would have known. She lost out to years with her father because I was in my office, in this building. Howard crossed his hands in front of him. "What's so urgent about this project?"

Lucía replied, "We are remaking humanity in digital form in case that creature wakes up and wipes us out."

"No, no," I waved my hands. "My graduate assistant has a warped sense of humor."

Howard was not in on the joke. He hobbled over to a computer monitor. Nessa watched him carefully, feet poised to launch if he should stumble. He tapped the computer screen like one would a fishbowl. At that moment, two ArLiFs—Bob and Dave—were failing spectacularly at setting up a food-can pyramid in a grocery store. "Yes," he said. "I see a sense of humor here."

I doubted Howard Winfield was a gullible man, but he played the role for us. Probably to see what information it got him. Lucía, however, was happy to play to his ignorance. She looked at me like she'd won the lottery and added, "We plan for them to be useful in managing humanity's nuclear silos."

"She's joking!" I told our visitors.

Howard suddenly turned to Lucía to examine her face, to study it. "Where are you from? What's that accent? Spanish?"

"I'm from Cambridge," she snapped. "Where are you from?"

Howard doubled down. "Really? Cambridge? And before that?" Lucía narrowed her eyes. Howard continued, "No offense intended. I'm just interested in how foreigners integrate into our culture."

Lucía said, "Then, you've hit the jackpot in *this* room, *mo chara*." She pronounced the last phrase with a stunning Irish accent.

Howard raised an eyebrow. Without removing his gaze from Lucía, Howard asked Nessa, "Do we have background on this one?"

"Lucía Santamaría," Nessa said. She didn't even consult notes. "Student visa in order."

"How do you know that?" Lucía asked her.

"Miss Santamaría, I was a news researcher for many years. It's my job to evaluate the security risks of Mr. Winfield's in-person meetings."

"Gross," Lucía muttered. "How super-spy of you to check on us before walking in here."

Howard said lightly, "Many want me dead."

The room went silent. Of course. Many would want him dead for airing those tapes. Wasn't the Sleeping One better off left alone?

He nodded at the monitors. "Very well. Very well." Then to Nessa, he said, "I'm interfering! Carry on!" I didn't like how he said it. Paternal. Like he was proud of my daughter's steps into the big corporate world. I was furious. "But I would like to know more about these...ah...things."

Things?

Nessa must have noticed my offense because she held me in an icy stare. She said, "All right, tell us, Dr. Daas. What's so urgent about your work?" She said it mechanically, as if she'd never heard me talk about evolving to the singularity. Didn't she remember the reason she and her mother couldn't stand me? Didn't she recall Ruthie yelling at me about how workaholics ruin families?

I slipped into lecture mode. "Well, as with the other projects generously supported by WINmedia, this lab is concerned with Artificial Lifeforms and their real-world applications. At the moment, we are urgently developing a neural brain that could have many uses in addressing the problems of the Collapse." I was flying by the seat of my pants, reaching back to the contents of my paper from that conference in Los Alamos, where I attempted to appease others in the field who sought external validation for new academic programs. Lucía looked amused at my tap dancing. "Currently humanitarian agencies are overwhelmed in responding to crises in food, medicine, and crime." Were they? They probably were. "We could, using the neural brain, develop a system that directs human resources more efficiently. Preparedness. Response. Recovery. We can look at the patterns of disaster during the Collapse—" Did I want more funding from Howard Winfield? At the moment, I wanted what I always did: to pursue the singularity.

Howard interrupted, "What could you do to support a *military* response if the creature wakes?"

I froze. I did not know what to say, but, luckily, Lucía did. "Barking up the wrong tree, buddy." She pointed at me. "You're dealing with an authentic

California hippie, here. Used to camp in Haight-Ashbury in a VW van painted butter yellow. I've seen the photos in his office. Peace fingers up. Hippie love, and all the rest of it." Lucía tapped the monitor as Howard had with an exaggerated goofiness. "These ArLiFs are utopians to their core."

Howard grimaced as if he'd bitten into something sour. Nessa let no emotion show, but I was sure she knew that working for Howard Winfield was not in line with what her grandmother, the Quaker activist Lily Davies, would want from her. Seeing this would kill my mother—if she could even remember she had a granddaughter. Yet, here I was, scrambling to appease the same man Nessa worked for. *Means to an end. Means to an end.*

I said: "To the end of life-affirming aid, we can offer many practical applications, including reading satellite imagery for signs of—"

Howard perked up.

"Ha!" Lucía said to me, "Did you see him jump? Big Brother wants an eye on that spot in the Pacific!"

Howard said to her, "You would do well to have that creature under surveillance." This time, a dark tone crept into his voice, and I did not like it.

"Is that right?" Lucía kicked at the desk she was sitting on. "How long's that creature been there? A zillion years? I seem to have survived just fine without surveillance so far."

Again, Howard studied the ArLiFs on our monitors. He looked hard at Claire. Onscreen, she walked heel-to-toe and stopped at a rocky cliffside, gazing out at the ocean. Her skin glowed. She was my favorite for so many reasons. Howard was also taken by her, I could tell. Claire has something the others don't have. She has mystery, enchantment, possibility.

"What do you call this place?" Howard asked, keeping his eyes fixed on Claire. "What do you call your project?"

"This is the Pythia Lab," Lucía said. "Pythia was an oracle in Greek mythology. She would fall into dreamlike trances to tell the future." Lucía had taken to calling us the Pythia Lab in our rooftop breaks, but I had no understanding of the meaning up to that moment, nor did I know we would formalize the name.

But I loved it, and so did Howard. "Future," he mumbled to himself.

Lucía wiggled her wild eyebrows at me. The fish was on the hook.

Nessa returned to staring at me, making me uncomfortable.

"I'd like to see a proposal," Howard said to us. "For the humanitarian-aid delivery system, one million a year for the next three years. Three million total."

"Excuse me?" I choked.

Lucía did not look surprised. "Two million per year," she countered. "Total of six."

Nessa attempted to come in between, "Mr. Winfield? This isn't necessary—"

Lucía added quickly, "And a TV."

Howard said to Lucía, "I like you despite your sass, or because of it. I can't decide."

Lucía shrugged. That woman cares for no one's praise.

Howard said to me, "*Three* million over *three* years. If I like your reports, we will renegotiate. Submit a proposal for the application of the neural network to disaster relief. Using satellite data."

"Mr. Winfield—" Nessa tried again.

Howard raised a hand. She silenced. I seethed. Lucía produced an apple and crunched it. Where does she get all this food? "Satellite data on human behavior," she mumbled to herself. "Oh no."

"And now," Howard trumpeted, "it is time for us to humbly take our leave of you. We have appointments!" He realigned himself to maneuver closer to the door. His movement summoned the presence of the guns. "Ms. Decker will call you with more details on the delivery of your proposal. The Foundation will work from a Boston address, so we won't depend on the depressing state of the mail service. I'm moving to Boston anyway. My security team will not guarantee my safety in New York any longer. Too many unpredictable elements there." He extended a hand. "What do you say to my suggestion, Dr. Daas? Will we hear a full proposal from you?"

I suppressed the adrenaline blossoming from my chest out to my fingers and down to my toes. I could have run laps around our lab, jumping into the air to slap our cheap, wireframe lights out of the ceiling. *Singularity. Singularity.*

Lucía frowned.

When I came back to solid ground, I remembered: This man has the wrong idea about our goals. The neural brain of the ArLiFs is programmed for peaceful ends. Under no circumstances would Lucía or I allow for them to be used for warfare or surveillance of any kind. This would be a drastic misuse, an abuse, of new and intelligent life. Further, I'd heard terrible things about Howard. His past in war profiteering. His avarice. His alignment with the Sterns. Howard Winfield was no angel.

Yet, an open hand was before me offering a potential three million dollars. A runway to the singularity was paved. Could I maintain control of the ArLiFs with this man writing the checks? His motives do not align with mine, but does that have to be the end of the discussion? Would his resources not make my ultra-intelligence vision a reality? We would be in the company of world-class scientists with his grant.

I replied, "Yes. Three million over three years. A proposal to apply the neural brain toward humanitarian relief. You shall have it within the week."

I shook Howard's hand. Lucía's attention wandered away.

He smiled and said, "I'll remove the unwanted security measures from your lab. I apologize for their necessity."

Nessa swept past me. As she did, she tucked a card into my jacket pocket, which I just realized was stained. "Don't lose my number this time."

The door hissed to a close, leaving me and Lucía alone.

Lucía began by launching her apple core into the trash can. "I should design an asshole ArLiF and name him Howard, but I don't want to be reminded of his *pinche* false modesty every day."

"You don't like him."

She shrugged. "Do I have to?"

"No."

"No matter what happens with the grant, we got something good out of that visit," she said.

"How is that?"

Lucía grinned. "Your daughter's talking to you again."

September 30, 1992

Evolutionary Computation Lab

THAT WAS THE FASTEST approval of a major grant proposal I'd ever experienced. Mr. Winfield means to address the Collapse, and quickly. Three million over three years!

I wondered whether Nessa's position at the Foundation had anything to do with the quick approval. Lucía put the notion to bed: "That man wouldn't part with three million for a piece of ass."

I didn't know how to spend that kind of money. Luckily, Lucía did. She budgeted new staff and consultants. She selected tables, computers, and monitors. A wall of 12 monitors! We will have eyes on every nook and cranny of our island of ArLiFs! The University President was thrilled enough to give us a larger room. And the media coverage! I am almost assured an approval of my new academic budget!

Who knows when our goods will arrive? Is the postal system even working? Lucía showed me drawings for five rows of desks in a semicircle around these monitors. It looked to me like a lecture hall, but she called it an Amphitheater. Racks of CPUs. Network cables. Servers.

Immediately, I gave her phone numbers for the statisticians and coders required to input the data for the humanitarian applications. Classes are not yet back in session due to supply-chain interruptions in every market, but we hope classes will resume in January. Until then, we have at our disposal academics looking to recover lost income. Good for us!

Our idea for predictive modeling in disaster relief seems to be a hot commodity. Howard Winfield will publicize our products in his media outlets. We are allowed to sell our applications to governments and NGOs if we continue to feed all funds back into the Pythia Lab. In that way, the grant is designed to be seed money for further projects. If we play our cards right, we will have an income stream to support our primary ArLiF project! *Singularity. Singularity.*

Since Howard and Nessa's visit, Lucía has been hard at work scaling up the ArLiFs. She envisions hundreds of them on our island. When those are complete, then, she told me, we will build other ArLiF environments on different servers in different parts of the world. "With programmers from different cultural backgrounds," she said, "to eliminate any programming bias. Different languages, economic systems, geographies! Wouldn't the anthropologists like to see how ArLiFs develop differently in different climates and landforms?" She talks so quickly. I struggle to keep up. I am certain now she's not sleeping.

With this new infusion of interest and cash, I feel a tension developing. I tell her, "We have enough problems with 12 ArLiFs as it is." Catastrophic forgetting remains a huge hindrance to their success.

Further, the neural network Howard Winfield wants doesn't work yet. All efforts should go there. We must figure out a solution, and quickly.

The situation has become catastrophic indeed. Some mornings, we are frightened to check the ArLiFs. Will they all be stuck in loops, forgetting to produce the resources for their survival? Will the speakers be broadcasting their cheerfully frustrated voices? "Oh no...Oh no." Will they have all died in a data crash due to increasing strain on computer memory? How much longer can we keep this up when the problems aggregate daily? Lucía and I scramble to keep up, applying patches and typing commands—so much so that I feel it is time to write to my Strange Visitor. But each time I bring up the possibility of involving an outsider, Lucía balks. Our reputation for ingenuity is growing outside the campus boundaries, even though physical classrooms are still closed. And Lucía is happy to delegate work for the humanitarian project, but for the ArLiFs she has become territorial. I remind her I am the founder of the project. She doesn't reply to that, but I can tell by the way she sizes me up that she knows the dramatic shift in the project's advancements are due to her efforts.

It is time I make a significant contribution to this project. I have decided to write a letter to Brazil to explain the catastrophic forgetting issue.

Will I tell Lucía? No. It is not her project.

My sleep has taken another nosedive. I lie awake at night thinking back to that conversation in Los Alamos. *The mechanisms are all in place, and the clock is ticking. You are an important part of the design. And you mustn't be late, Dr. Daas.*

The urgency, as he saw it, is now upon us. It is time to involve the mysterious mentor from Brazil.

Act II

Tony Cavalcante
and the God Game

Brazil
September 1992 to February 1993

8

Rot

32 Weeks Into the Collapse

Tony Cavalcante, 16 years old, was riding a sandworm through the dunes of Planet Arrakis when his grandfather, Ignácio, jostled him awake. "We must go, Antonio," he said. "Right now." It was just before dawn. Ignácio was already dressed in a designer suit.

Tony squinted at unfamiliar shadows in his bedroom. "Go where?" Smoke scratched at the back of his throat. His words came out as a croak.

"They've hanged the President." His grandfather dragged suitcases and a trunk into his room. "Pack quickly."

"Where are we going?"

"Not *we*. Just you."

"Where am I going?"

"Fazenda São Roque."

"Is the Nazi still there?"

"We all have our crosses to bear."

Tony batted at the cobwebs in his brain. *Still drugged?* He mumbled, "Fazenda São Roque." He dropped his voice to recite a quote from an old Jedi master about a disreputable nerve center of villainy.

Ignácio barked, "Stop that mumbling! Pack!" He dumped a sock drawer into an open duffel.

"Why?"

"I'll explain in the car."

Tony trudged to his bedroom window. An orange glow backlit the skyline. Buildings stood like dark soldiers against the inferno. "Downtown is on fire again."

Ignácio did not reply.

"How long will I be gone? I'm due back in school."

"There is no school. You know that."

"I'm starting high school. I think. What month is it?" He played with his bottom lip, which felt larger than usual. "Where is Oma?"

"You know where she is."

Tony's shoulders plummeted. "Oh yeah." Nasty emotions swirled, but whatever drugs were still in his system removed the fangs from them.

Silence.

"I want to take my computer," Tony said. "And my games."

Ignácio flicked his wrist as if banishing an argument. "No guarantee of electricity out there."

"Nor here," Tony said. "And my books." A thought. "Are you coming?"

"I said no. Pay attention." Ignácio opened a corner wardrobe and clamped an armful of clothing attached to hangers. He threw it all into a suitcase. "Just like this. No folding." He clapped as if chasing feral cats from the trash. "Let's move!"

Tony slyly stuffed a t-shirt into a bag. Ignácio would never allow him to wear t-shirts. *Beneath your class*, he would say.

"For the sake of the Virgin Mother, Antonio, hurry."

Tony said, "I feel drunk. Did you give me a dose last night? It must have been too much. We were going to scale back, remember?"

Ignácio pulled a worn paper bag from his jacket pocket and placed it inside the duffel, under a pile of clothes. "I'm sending you with your doses. More will follow after I locate a better source. This one is too *suspeito*."

"*Suspeito*," Tony echoed.

Just beyond Ignácio, a shadow blossomed in the hallway. Flat cap. Enormous body.

Senhor Rocha.

Tony startled, then stepped back. "What's he doing up here?"

Ignácio winged a pair of sneakers into a bag. "Helping us."

Tony's palms grew heavy. Sweat fired his face.

Murder.

Butchery.

He whispered to himself, "Don't go on the patio."

Ignácio dug his hands into his hips and exhaled. "Antonio, stop that nonsense. We have no time for it."

In the hallway, Sr. Rocha retreated.

Sunlight shot through Tony's window. He shielded his eyes. "Ow."

Ignácio zipped a bag and kicked it toward the door. "Please, Antonio. We must go now."

Time slipped. An hour fell away. Sixty minutes cascaded into a void.

Tony awoke in the back seat of his grandfather's Mercedes, which was barreling out of the city at 160 kilometers per hour. Ignácio was beside him. In the driver's seat: flat cap, enormous body. Sr. Rocha.

No.

Ignácio said, "Antonio, are you paying attention?"

Tony worked his dry mouth before speaking. His bottom lip had deflated. "Yes, sir."

The Mercedes took a corner without braking, barely missing a lamp post. Tires squealed. Black smoke trailed. Ignácio held the grab handle. Tony slid into his grandfather, who elbowed him back into place. The acrid scent of scorched rubber assaulted Tony's nostrils. *Why so fast? Roadblocks? Checkpoints?* Scenery whizzed by. Was that his school? If so, it had no roof. Were they on Avenue Professor Rodrigues? Why were there no cars? Was that Praça Villa Lobos—all empty, no one on the jogging trails or walking paths? What was this empty world?

Oh. Yes. Collapsed. Ultimate global freak-out, extended dance version.

Black clouds rose in the distance from hot red pinpoints of flame, carrying Tony's hometown's landmarks and skyscrapers up and away. *There it goes.* He wondered if he would see the São Paulo villa again. *Where is my home now?*

His grandfather readjusted himself in his seat, smoothing out his suit. He was talking. A *lot.* "With the sugarcane harvest coming in, you will be supervising its removal to our new mill—" His eyebrows moved up and down with his emphasis.

Ignácio Cavalcante had the most luxuriant eyebrows Tony had ever seen, which contrasted wildly with his smooth pate. A cloud of soothing sandalwood enveloped him. Ignácio's large ears caught everything from stock tips to industry rumors. When standing, his body was comically round with thin arms and fan-shaped, feminine hips that somehow commanded respect in the business sector. The eldest of the Cavalcante triumvirate of agricultural magnates, Ignácio had perfected the balance of grace and diplomacy, though, with Tony, he exerted his will mostly with sighs and eye fluttering, a ballet of performative misery.

"Campinas is where we will set up operations. Are you listening?"

"Yes."

Tony just realized Ignácio droned about business with the resonant voice of a priest—*Em nome do Sugarcane, do Ethanol, e do Espírito Campinas. Amém.*—which is exactly what Ignácio would have been if he had been the fourth-born male or later. Among the men in the Cavalcante family, there were only three seats per generation at the business table; the remainder of the boys were shuffled off to seminaries. Tony held the esteemed position as first and only grandson in Ignácio's line. Tony wished that were not so and was certain Ignácio felt the same.

"*Escute!*" Ignácio snapped open his business journal. The journals were delivered irregularly now and were always full of bad news. Tony feared their contents might drive his grandfather over the edge, specifically right out of the high-rise window at his office. *Don't read that don't read that.*

From behind the paper, Ignácio said, "You should read the journal daily! I'll have it sent out to you."

"I understand, sir."

"Then, you understand Fazenda São Roque never completed the transition to modern farm equipment, thereby eliminating its reliance on petrol and accidentally rendering it a Collapse-proof asset—"

Tony did know that, just as he knew the old Nazi was responsible for the farm dragging its heels on modernization. Tony said nothing about that, though, because he was preoccupied with Sr. Rocha and how that man came to be in close quarters with him. *I should be feeling much more alarmed*, he thought. *I should be screaming bloody murder.* He considered this. *I must still be drugged.*

Sr. Rocha shot Tony a look in the rearview mirror. His eyes flickered like minnows in the shallows. Tony thought he heard him snicker.

Ignácio intoned, "While it is true, in the past, Herr Koltz sabotaged most of our efforts to modernize, we might mark this as the first time in history the old man was correct, albeit in hindsight only—"

Sr. Rocha's immense body crammed into the driver's seat. His flat driver's cap scraped the roof. He held Tony's gaze in the rearview mirror for too long. Surely, Tony thought, Sr. Rocha's darkening eyes were a trick of the smoke-hazed light. Two eyes of polished obsidian, peacock colors spider-webbing throughout. When he smiled at Tony with grey teeth the color of oyster meat, Tony's level of discomfort ratcheted upward. *I hate you*, Tony decided. *And I do not know why. Not exactly.*

Ignácio did not seem to mind Sr. Rocha's speed, glances, or strange grinning.

"—in light of the petrol shortage, shifting production from sugar to ethanol—"

Out the window, the smoldering city streets had given way to open, palm-lined roads by the river. They were now well past any risk of blockades and carjackers. Still, Sr. Rocha had kept the pedal glued to the floor mat. *Why*? And where did Ignácio procure the fuel for this ride? Judging by the empty streets, no one else had any.

Then, as if the clouds parted to light the velvety meadow of Tony's mind, a realization dawned. They were moving so quickly *because* of the fuel shortage. Sugarcane to ethanol, a switch in production at Fazenda São Roque!

The conversations he had with his grandfather at the villa returned to him. Ignácio, uncharacteristically nervous and giddy: "We shall strike while the iron is hot!" That was a phrase Ignácio loved to say, a mantra passed to him by his own father, Ulisses Cavalcante, a severe man Tony was grateful to have never met. In this Collapse, Ignácio had explained, when petrol refinement and oil shipments had all but halted, Fazenda São Roque's sugarcane would save the day. A mill in

Campinas would distill the cane into clean, usable fuel. It would save São Paulo! All Tony needed to do was supervise the sugarcane harvest. Then he could go home.

A twinge in his gut. Mind clouds descended again. Right now, thinking was like battling a fog monster. He tried to hold this thought: *The reason I am exiled is to save the world...*

Ignácio had moved on to sermonizing about an ethanol mill in Campinas, one opening specifically for this matter of civic importance. Tony desperately wished he could understand the process of milling sugarcane as Ignácio was describing it. If saving São Paulo required video-game skills or knowledge of high-fantasy narratives, Tony would have had his nation back on track in no time. But none of his interests seemed to be relevant. And he felt so very sick, as if his head were stuffed with pillow fluff. Did he have a drug dose this morning? He could not recall. A living creature growled in his intestines, threatening to wring his guts into paralyzing cramps. He must be in withdrawal. While the drugs were in his system, he enjoyed a dreamless sleep, free of Sr. Rocha's mischievous eyeballs, the lightning crack against the jet-black sky, and waves of intense dread. But now, he felt on the verge of panic.

In the rearview, another glance from Sr. Rocha, inky eyes darting restlessly. The man deliberately hit a pothole at speed. All of Tony's worldly possessions in the trunk clattered. He blanched. "My computer—"

"—plantings on our 10,000 hectares should yield 907,000 metric tons of cane—"

Sr. Rocha snickered.

Tony ignored him, then redoubled his efforts to focus on his grandfather. Tony had a lot to live up to, and Ignácio would not forgive him if he failed.

"—you must shadow João and Michel for *weeks* before inserting yourself into any business matters. *Weeks*! They will mentor you in all aspects of production and finances."

A question bubbled to the surface, and Tony felt proud of the achievement. "Are they to act as my guardians?"

"Who?"

"João and Michel."

Ignácio's lip drifted upward, revealing a pearly incisor. "Come now, Antonio. You're nearly a man. Do not speak of that."

"I'm 16."

The car hit another bump. Tony and Ignácio levitated briefly, then landed. "Mind how you go, Sr. Rocha," was all Ignácio said.

Then, that horrid smile. "*Com certeza*, Sr. Ignácio."

Without warning, a wave of nausea crashed over Tony's innards, launching him into spasms he had great difficulty hiding from his grandfather. Tony turned to the window, reluctant to roll it down. Though it was spring in Campinas, all he saw and smelled outside was rot—a roadside hawk belly up on the pavement, a decaying dog carcass on the centerline, a bloodied armadillo, rotting blue flowers on a tree. He clamped his jaw and fixed a look at the back of Sr. Rocha's wide head, his flat cap. The man sickened him. Tony *hated* him, hated him with an enthusiasm that would have shamed his departed grandmother Lotte, his Oma, who instructed him in unconditional kindness toward his enemies, especially Pedro and Tomás at school, the bullying *babacas*. Yet, right now, if Tony could magically transform his hands into spiky instruments of death, just like in one of his video games, he would strike down Sr. Rocha in extreme anger without hesitation, probably sending their Mercedes careening end over end into the ditch, also killing both himself and Ignácio, thereby razing an entire Cavalcante family-tree branch in a single, heavenward fireball. And it would be worth it.

Of this hatred, Tony had only a glimmer of an understanding. It had to do with the night his grandmother Lotte died.

Murdered, some would say.

Butchered, most would say when they believed Tony was not listening.

It was night; the Collapse was just six weeks old.

The June weather had been unseasonably warm, wilting some of the winter flowers on the patio. Their putrid odor mixed with the fresh aroma of living blooms. Despite that odor, the air in the villa needed circulating, so Tony propped the French doors open to allow a breeze. The light outside was green, menacing. The skyline was not yet on fire.

Ignácio was not at home. He never was at that time of night, always in his own apartment downtown.

On the television, recorded bits from *Yuna II* ran as their President announced, "Based on spectral analyses of the site and multiple radiochemical tests on the recovered deep-sea camera—"

Tony yelled out to Lotte, "Oma! I'll bet they won't use nuclear weapons on the Sleeping One. It would be impervious to its effects."

A moth fluttered into the living room. Tony balanced a stack of sofa cushions to capture it. He whispered to himself the mantra of the old Jedi as he reached for it.

The President said, "—an independent scientific consortium has determined that the creature is extraterrestrial—"

Tony muttered, "We wouldn't destroy it. We would just anger it."

Outside on the patio, the ivy shivered, though the breeze had died.

The President continued, "Approaching the Sleeping Beast itself has proved impossible due to the extreme levels of radiation near the site, but it is assumed to be a complex organism of unknown intelligence."

The wings of the moth gently batted Tony's closed hands.

His grandmother stepped into the living room, flushed. "Antonio, where are the staff?"

Tony moved to the door, then let the moth go. It flapped back inside.

"They've all left, without warning," Lotte added.

"Dunno." Tony tracked the moth back to the ceiling light, sliding the coffee table underneath.

"Do not stand on that. You'll hurt yourself."

"No, I won't." Tony stood on it.

Lotte moved to the patio door, hands on hips. "It's so quiet tonight."

Tony looked at her from his perch on high. He hadn't been dressed since day one of the Collapse, but Lotte looked the same as before. She wore her pearls, and she had sprayed her jet-black hair into a bouffant. Tony couldn't be bothered to change out of his pajamas, but she was trying to keep things as normal as possible.

Lotte's breath stopped short. Her gasp was so loud Tony could hear it from inside the living room. Then, "Oh!" as if she were relieved. She even chuckled at herself.

Tony couldn't see whom she spotted, but someone was there. Someone she knew.

Later, in dreams, a reflection appeared in the French doors. An immense man. A flat cap. A meaty grin.

Lotte's expression darkened when more footsteps tread on the patio tiles. The glow of many cigarette ends lit up the living-room window.

Tony arched onto tiptoes, the moth again fluttering in his cupped hands. The tiny creature hummed with electric life.

He remembered nothing after that.

Hours later, Ignácio dragged him out from under the basement staircase by his pajama collar. "Antonio!" he shouted. "What has happened here?"

Tony did not understand. How did he get down here, in the basement, all the way up under the staircase behind the boxes of Christmas ornaments and his old clothes? And why was there blood on Ignácio's hands, on Tony's own pajama pants in grandfather-sized handprints? Ignácio shook him. "Who is responsible? Who did this?"

Tony struggled to speak. "Who did what?"

"Antonio!" His grandfather slapped him.

Tony's mind spun. *Why is he hitting me?*

Ignácio shouted again, "Who did this? Who did this?"

The question made no sense.

Yet, somewhere deep inside him, a seed of anger sprouted. Tony wanted to shout back. *Where were you? Why could you not stay home for once?*

Ignácio, exasperated, released his grandson.

Another gap in time.

The next thing Tony remembered was the fever.

He struggled to get cool enough, then struggled to get warm enough. That seed of anger planted by Ignácio had sprouted. Lotte was dead. Tony did not know how. He only knew that she was gone and was never coming back. He knew never to step onto the patio, not for the rest of his life. And he knew never to trust Sr. Rocha, Ignácio's driver. No details attached themselves. They all floated away with the mind clouds.

Then the dreams came of Sr. Rocha on the patio, of a lightning crack splitting the black night. That bright fissure never dimmed. Through it, the most dreadful disjointed creatures paraded, ravenous for destruction.

Days in bed, Tony listened to Ignácio's phone calls in the hallway. Tony heard the call to Lotte's father, living out at São Roque. So formal. "I regret to inform you—"

Immediately, a frenzy of rage buzzed on the other end. Lotte's father was singular in that he was the only person on earth who could speak that way to Ignácio without dire consequence. Judging by Ignácio's end of the conversation, Lotte's father's tone had turned accusatory. In turn, Ignácio fiercely defended his and Lotte's peculiar lifestyle, adding, "This was our arrangement! From day one!" Ignácio called him a Nazi and a fraud. Lotte's father likely called him worse, but Tony could not hear him.

Finally, Ignácio hung up and crumpled into sobs.

It was the first time Tony witnessed any emotion from his grandfather besides contempt. Tony felt nothing.

The fever that had its grip on Tony would not let go. In the role of caretaker for the first time in his life, Ignácio panicked. Tony could hear him pacing the halls in his loafers, *clack clack clack clack*. The Collapse was in its full fury. No nanny to pawn Tony off to, no doctor to make house calls. Ignácio himself had to locate the drugs his grandson needed. "He's all I have," he begged on the phone. "My only heir." The price they named over the phone was exorbitant, gasp-worthy even from an agricultural magnate. He paid it.

Make way for the Little Prince, Tony thought. *Ignácio Cavalcante's only heir. I am worth my weight in gold as the future CEO Cavalcante Agriculture. Worry not. The legacy is secure. Bow down.*

Ignácio shut up the villa. Locked the doors. Bolted the windows. Allowed no one inside. Carried a gun. Through Tony's fever, a slight worry about his grandfather edged in. The collapsing of Ignácio was something he'd never witnessed. His despair on the phone extended to business matters. He whimpered about his brothers scheming to take his portion of the empire. "Those bastards have bred a legion of boys, all battle ready!" The time was ripe for a hostile takeover, Ignácio said. Phone call by phone call, Tony heard Ignácio losing his grip on what pieces of the Cavalcante pie he did own. One by one, as petrol, electricity, and personnel ebbed away, the means of sugarcane production halted. All but one: old Fazenda São Roque, the antiquated farm that relied on old methods to produce sugarcane with impressive purity thanks to the Nazi, whose grim determination to see through an idyllic vision of rural peasantry, of ultranationalist "Blood and Soil" outside Campinas, led to his sabotaging of any farm equipment whose petrol motors sullied the fresh air sucked into the old man's prominent honker.

One night during the fever weeks, Ignácio came to Tony dressed in only a paisley robe. Tony startled awake, shocked to see his grandfather outside of a three-piece suit. "There is a way forward," Ignácio muttered at Tony's bedside. "We must strike while the iron is hot! It is time for you to come into your own. Time for you to ascend to your role in the empire."

Tony's head felt like cotton. "Sure."

"First, we will get you well."

Ignácio would disperse a dose of drugs as soon as Tony's eyes widened with any hint of remembered horrors. His world had been reduced to a foggy landscape of lumpy shapes without contrast. When he was sober, he dragged out his old books—fantasies and creatures with castles and kings—to escape from whatever world his real one had become. When he improved enough to lessen his daytime doses, he shambled around the villa, studying the photos of his aunts and uncles that Lotte kept despite Ignácio's protests. To clear his head, Tony recited their names—a test of memory. "Rainer, Sebastián, Manuela, Britta—drowned..." And his mother. Paloma. Tony could *never* forget Paloma. She had green eyes. Just like him. No one else in the family had green eyes. Well, except the Nazi.

"Why do you do that?" Ignácio had asked whenever he caught Tony at his pacing and recitations.

"Do what?"

Ignácio sucked on a cigar. Tony could not recall Ignácio smoking before the Collapse. The sweet smoke lingered and burned.

Ignácio jabbed the cigar at a group photo of his aunts and uncles. "Suicides, drug addicts, murderers, adrenaline junkies. Not one of them lived past 25. Not one of them produced a grandchild."

"My mother did."

Ignácio puffed. "Communist."

Tony continued his recitation, "Stefan—hung himself in the barn—Bettina, Georg, Silvia—strangled with a necktie..."

"This family is cursed," Ignácio muttered, moving away. "Nothing but rot."

Even as they turned away from Campinas, down the river road to the red-soiled fields of Fazenda São Roque, Sr. Rocha didn't let up on the speed. Ignácio, however, had drifted off into a light snooze.

Gently at first, Sr. Rocha drifted into the other lane, then swept the Mercedes in increasingly wider swerves. Tony clamped his lips closed, choking back hot saliva. Through the mirror, Sr. Rocha repeatedly flicked his inky eyes to Tony, then to the road. Sometimes Tony caught him laughing to himself, a raspy chuckle that ended in a throat clear.

Just then, a nun sped in the opposite direction in a red convertible. Tony thought she wore a full habit, her headpiece flapping in the hot wind. He nearly concluded it was a hallucination, but Sr. Rocha cackled at the same sight.

Tony nudged Ignácio. "Did you see that?"

Ignácio's eyes popped open. He snorted, then rubbed the bridge of his nose. "No. Have I instructed you yet to never to call my brothers for help?"

"Yes, sir."

"They will have the same idea about the ethanol. They will come for São Roque. It is the crown jewel in the Cavalcante empire. They *will* come for it."

"São Roque." Tony asked, "Why did the founder name our sugarcane plantation after a gruesomely murdered priest?"

Ignácio huffed, "Perhaps our ancestors would like to remind us that good deeds often go unappreciated." He twitched, bothered. "Speaking of decrepit forebears, you are not to heed the Nazi in matters of business. His role remains supervisory only."

Tony's spine jolted with a shocking thought. He cleared his throat. "How old is great-grandfather Waldemar?"

"I do not know."

"If you had to guess—"

"I have as little to do with Herr Koltz as humanly possible, as was the agreement with your grandmother when they arrived—"

"He must be in his nineties. I have not seen him in ten years."

"It does not matter, Antonio. This is the plan."

Tony blurted, "What if he dies?" His wet palms stuck to his trouser legs, leaving prints.

"In that case," Ignácio said, "call me immediately. I have been reserving a bottle of Macallan 50-year-old single-malt scotch for the occasion."

Tony pushed, "But who would take care of me if he died?"

Ignácio slapped his formidable thigh with a loud crack. "I said, do *not* speak of that. The world is different now, Antonio, and you must change! Your grandmother was too protective of you."

Little Prince, she called Tony. Delivered to her by her daughter to raise.

Tony sank in his seat, then turned to the window. *Rotten. Cursed. What can go wrong in this family will go wrong.* He chanted to himself, "Rainer, heroin. Sebastián, venomous bite. Manuela, botched abortion. Britta, drowned. Paloma, disappeared..."

Ignácio wiped sweat from his upper lip. His hand was shaking. "It has to work," he said. "It will work."

The mind clouds parted. Another question, bright and fresh as the dewy air of a country dawn: "Grandfather?"

Ignácio turned to him, weary.

"Nothing," Tony said.

Ignácio rolled his eyes heavenward, as if beseeching God for a gift.

Bow down to the Little Prince, Tony thought. *I am the heir. I am the savior. I am nothing.*

9

Reap

A CARVED WOODEN SIGN set upon two rough-hewn logs read *Fazenda São Roque*. The Mercedes entered at dusk, turning off the paved river road, through the gates, and onto a winding dirt road, past the sugarcane fields and up to the casa grande.

Ignácio's Mercedes tornadoed burnt orange dust behind it, flying past open fields bronzing in the sunset. Stalks higher than any man stretched as far as Tony could see. Ignácio tapped the window. "These should have been cut already. João and Michel are slacking in the harvest." He hummed with anxiety, likely calculating whether the stalks could be salvaged or if they'd been left too long in the ground. "Could be, could be..."

Tony said nothing, immersed in the sights of the farm he'd visited with his grandmother since he was a toddler. He hadn't been here since he was a young boy. The place was large and beautiful and wild, like the first garden of the world.

Beyond the cane fields, the overgrown paths never widened more than could accommodate a medieval farm cart. The underbrush beneath the tree canopy filled with luscious ferns and dangerous snakes. Forbidding tropical flowers flourished beyond reach—masses of orange, gold, violet, and scarlet burst from velvety green bushes and voluminous dwarf trees. A riot of birdsong and howler-monkey cries announced flamboyant mating rituals while constrictors and orb weavers went about their death work in utter silence. The odor out there could suffocate—its sweet, strong, and earthy waves could knock Tony over. It was all alien, sinister, and seductive.

Also back there, buried in the encroaching forest, were the low brick and stucco outbuildings from the beginning times. Crumbling Spanish-roof tiles stuffed with sparrow nests used to shelter the African slaves, but now they housed only derelict farm equipment. Out there was an old cane press with a long beam that could be wound using a walking mule. Out there were black witch-like cauldrons for boiling syrup. What grew in these fields was better than anything else on the market, a first-rate sugarcane without impurities, used for premium liquors and fetching top prices. All of it was handled by experienced workers who could smell when it was ripe enough to harvest. As a child, Tony rarely saw the barefooted ones with filthy feet, in hats and hoods shielded against the sun, collecting in huddles at the edge of the mowed rows, cane knives curved to best reach the base of the stalk but leave the root alive for next season. This was how Fazenda São Roque produced its magic: no machines murdered the precious roots, nor did they shred the stalks before milling. The fazenda was run on the blood and sweat of humans.

This was a world separate from the fanatical violence of the Collapse. This was a world left behind by time. Tony imagined himself as a royal exile from one of his space epics, a boy sent away from his homeland into an outer space weigh station, where a wall had been built against an encroaching war. *Planet Arrakis and its precious Spice*, he thought. He would mine this place for its valuable sugarcane. He will make the world move again.

The Mercedes downshifted, then rounded the bend to the casa grande. There, a slim wooden beam protruded from the ground, rising twice as high as the house. At the top perched a housed bell, rung to signal the end of the workday.

Then, there was the big house, framed by overgrown palms whose dead fronds hung from the canopies like rustic beards. Thirty-three rooms inside two stories of white stucco, capped by red barrel tile. A stone ramp led to a door on the second story, ending at the bottom in half-moon steps radiating outward. A retaining wall housing a garden of Lotte's blue hydrangeas rose to the second story, masking the windowless ground floor used for feeding and housing more workers. In a faint nod to modernization, a utility pole ushered a single black wire under an eave. In the yard, mallard ducks waddled toward the muddy pond down the slope, toward the one-room chapel beyond.

An abrupt stench bombarded Tony. "What is that smell?"

Ignácio made a noise, a crude sucking of air unbefitting his usual grace. "What…" he panted, "is the meaning of this?"

Just beyond the house, halfway down the slope to the pond and chapel, pickup trucks towing harvest carts had parked at chaotic angles. The tires of every cart—about 30 of them—flattened under the weight of rotten sugarcane. Canes were supposed to be bright green when going to the mill, Tony knew, but these stalks were coppery red. Useless. Swarms of black flies clouded the carts. Machetes spiked the ground all around—handles up, blades sunk into the clay. It looked to Tony like a massacre, like bloody and decayed limbs stacked high. He swallowed acid from his stomach and whispered, "Don't go onto the patio."

"*Ave-Maria, cheia de graça!*" Ignácio moaned. "Not now, Antonio!"

Tony fidgeted, trying to recall which suitcase held his doses. *Was it the duffel?* Did Ignácio stuff it underneath his collared shirts? Or was it his sneakers? A clammy sweat leaked into his eyes, and he wiped his face with his sleeve.

Before the car had even rolled to a stop, Ignácio was out the door. "João! Michel!" His voice tangled with the sickly sweet stench and the buzzing of flies. "Explain yourselves! Why are these trucks not at the mill in Campinas?" He wrung his hands. "The ethanol mill! This was discussed!"

Sr. Rocha exited in a smooth movement that contradicted his bulk. He whipped off his driver's cap and smoothed his thick hair back, surveying the mess. He uttered a raspy laugh. Tony thought he was—*What was it?*—pleased?

Tony stood well away from him, coming to stand next to Ignácio. How much of a disaster was this? He could not say, but it was not good. He wanted to offer a solution, as his grandfather often told him good leaders will do, but he had none.

Tugging at his nagging sense of doom was the joy he used to feel at this place. That joy insisted on itself, surfacing through the drug haze. It used to be Lotte in the back seat with him in that Mercedes, making the two-hour trip from the villa. It used to be Lotte's driver, Sr. Xavier—long dead—who used to bring them out here. They came here for Christmas, for Easter, and for saints' days. Tony tramped the grounds while she worked with the staff for feasts. Everyone was invited: workers, staff, the distant neighbors, aunts and uncles from the city. And there would be a small mass. Lotte always employed a provincial priest to perform the holiday's rites in the family chapel, a one-room whitewashed building trimmed in shocking blue just beyond the pond. Together, she and Tony used to descend the slope. After terrorizing the mallards with a stick, Tony would wedge his hand into his grandmother's soft arm fold as she worked her rosary. Inside the chapel, Lotte had knelt at the altar in her floral mantilla, clicking her rosary beads to the cadence of her prayers. The workers were there, hats on knees, heads bent low, dirty hands tightly folded. Clouds of body odor hung inside, nearly choking Tony. Aunts and uncles kidded and stifled laughs. Lotte, though, focused on her devotionals and made no outward sign that the smell bothered her.

Always there, too, was Waldemar. The old man slumped in the back pew, glowering. That was Tony's picture of Waldemar while growing up: an exotic oddity insulated by a language barrier and a bad attitude. He was a man not to be touched or spoken to, whose study in the east wing was not to be entered, whose lap was not to be sat in. "*Hau ab, Bürschchen!* Run away!" During those family services, Tony used to turn around to spy on him. The old man clutched the wooden pew in front of him, his numerous rings shining, his eyes flitting from one object to another—a windowpane, a hymnal, a dead leaf skittering through the open front door and down the aisle—and his gigantic nose in a scrunch, as if the place were a shithole. *Everything*, the old man seemed to be thinking—even the quality of the dust motes hovering in the sunbeams—*had been much better in the Reich.*

These were the memories now that compelled Tony to push aside the need to get at the brown paper bag inside the Mercedes's trunk, the one holding whatever crude medicine Ignácio had dug up in this Collapse. Doses dulled him. The world would wait.

Ignácio, despondent, bellowed, "João! Michel!"

The door at the top of the stone ramp leading into the casa grande opened. Then a metallic sound: *clack—clack—clack*.

An old man, leaning on a tripod cane, made his way down the ramp slowly. "*Halt die Fresse!*"

Tony nearly choked. Waldemar had aged rapidly since he had last seen him. Time had dragged its claws across his great-grandfather's skin and left trenches of wrinkles and liver spots. Skin sagged from his skull. White hair stood on end, frisky with static. Clothes, dusty with dried clay, swayed from his slight frame. Waldemar's eyes had always been startling to others, and Tony had inherited their unusual light green color with gold flecks. But now, Waldemar's eyes had nearly drained of all color, leaving the impression of a white-eyed creature with pinpoint pupils. With each stab of the cane on the stone ramp, Waldemar's rings—thick and jeweled with wads of tape to fit his slim fingers—ticked against the metal handle. "*Drecksacks! Dünnschissgurglers!*"

Sr. Rocha roared with laughter.

Tony asked Ignácio, "Did he just call us, 'diarrhea garglers'?"

Ignácio thrashed at the swarm of flies. "Oh, stop with the German utterances! I cannot understand you, Waldemar!"

"*Ach, du!*" The old man stopped, pulled a filthy handkerchief from his trousers, and blew his aquiline nose in three short bursts. "Dusty! Cannot breathe!" Waldemar refolded his handkerchief. "We speak English, then. I will not speak your corrupt tongue."

"Where are João and Michel?" Ignácio called out. "The workers? The harvest should be..."

"Gone," the old man croaked. He searched the horizon for the time he last saw activity in the fields. "Weeks ago!"

Ignácio reeled as if to faint. "Waldemar! Why did you not mention that on the phone, when we arranged this visit?"

Waldemar shrugged. "We do not discuss these things. You always discuss with others here. Never with me. I did not think my view on matters of business was wanted."

Ignácio sputtered and spun in a circle. "But the *workers*! Everyone!"

Tony also spun in a circle, confused.

Waldemar said, "This is what you said to me in year 19 and 68. 'This is not your business, Waldemar. You will keep to your business, and I will keep to mine!' Well, I keep to my business. Now, you are upset."

Ignácio rubbed his bald head. "Is there no one else here?"

Waldemar set his jaw. "Saro."

Just then, another man lurched from the house, racing down the ramp, pushing past Waldemar. His skin was blue-black, and he wore an old overcoat riddled with moth holes and no shoes. A silver Afro ringed a bare and shining head, giving him the appearance of having a glimmering halo. At the front, a single streak of black hair collapsed on his forehead. It was the strangest hairstyle Tony had ever seen.

Sr. Rocha stepped back. *Surprised?* Tony thought. *No. Something else...as if he'd been bitten.* Sr. Rocha raced into the car and slammed the door. Inside, he remained hidden by red dust crusting the windows.

Saro pushed past Tony and slunk to the rear of the Mercedes. He deftly popped the trunk and removed Tony's luggage one piece at a time.

Ignácio leveled a flat hand at the fields. "This is our livelihood, Waldemar! It's how we pay for you to live without working for your whole, miserable life! And you did not think to call?"

"Service has been spotty."

Ignácio clenched and unclenched his fists. "These...these...these fucking *filhos da puta* run away from a sea monster...who lives in the *ocean*, not *here* on *land*...out *there*...and we will all *starve*...and my brothers will come for this place! I will have nothing! Do you hear me? Nothing!" He kicked at the dirt, knocking himself off balance. He wobbled, flung his arms out to balance himself, but failed. He landed in the dust. "Shit!" He wiped his wet face. "Shit! Shit!"

Tony turned away from the spectacle and noticed Saro lifting his computer processor. "Please," Tony said to him, "I will handle my computer and games." Saro placed it onto the ground at Tony's feet, then looked dead into his eyes. Saro's housecoat fell open, and Tony was shocked to see strands of women's necklaces—pearls, diamonds, emeralds, sapphires—heaps of them jostling under the lapels. Saro broke his gaze only when he'd decided on something Tony couldn't determine. "*Olá*, Sr. Saro," Tony began. "I'm—"

But Saro turned away. He lifted a footlocker out of the trunk, held it high above his head, and flitted into the house with it. Tony said, "My books are in there, please be careful." Then to his grandfather, "Wow, he's strong."

Ignácio slumped in the dirt, still fixated on his fields. Tony could see now that the stalks remaining in the ground had browned, on the way to turning blood red. Millions of bugs coated the crops in writhing swarms.

Tony, unsure of what to do, approached Ignácio as if to comfort him. "It smells like dead animals," Tony remarked.

Ignácio clapped a hand to his head.

Waldemar pointed to Tony. "This is smart grandson you bring me. Knows smell of death." Tony knitted his brows. Was the old man paying a compliment? Waldemar assessed Tony as if purchasing a heifer at auction, then asked Ignácio, "He looks old enough to take care of himself, ja?"

Ignácio scanned the fields for a single patch of healthy sugarcane. He raised and lowered his arms, slapping the dirt, raising clouds of red dust, saying nothing. Tony cleared his throat and offered a reply. "Not yet."

Waldemar reassessed him. "You look old enough."

"No. Not yet," Tony repeated. "Is there a school I am to attend?"

Saro burst from the house and pushed past Tony again.

Waldemar trumpeted, "School of hard knocks! It is school I attend for many years. Proud graduate. Start in Germany in big depression in year 19 and 23. Today, it is teaching my great-grandson during Big Sea Monster Crash not to wear such fussy outfits. I hope you pack something other than pants and tie." He eyed the boy. "Puny. Must take after Brazilians."

Ignácio flashed rage.

"I joke." Waldemar turned with his cane and stabbed his way up the ramp toward the front door. He crowed, "Poor little orphan boy! Doo, doo, doo! Rotten smelly life!" That cracked Waldemar up. He chortled, Tony thought, like a cartoon villain, exhaling past a tight throat as if coughing up phlegm. Then, he removed the handkerchief from his trousers and blew his nose. He tossed a hand backward to Ignácio. "*Auf Wiedersehen, Schwuchtel*! Come, Saro!"

Tony said to Ignácio, "He called you a—"

Ignácio snarled, "I know what he called me."

Saro rattled his way up the ramp and into the house, balancing a load of Tony's suitcases and bags with ease.

The door slammed behind them.

Ignácio rose, summoning dignity, brushing his trousers and jacket with shaking hands. Tony stared at his computer resting in the red dust at his feet, wondering if it was damaged.

Sr. Rocha stepped out of the car and looked both ways like a child coming out of hiding. He flicked Tony a glance with his cold-blooded eyes, spiderwebs of color pulsing. Tony shivered involuntarily.

"I'm not staying," he insisted to Sr. Rocha. "Please go into the house and return my things to the trunk." Sr. Rocha lifted his eyebrows but did not move.

Then to Ignácio, Tony asked, "I am not staying, am I? If there is no sugarcane to harvest, there is nothing for me to do here. We should retrieve my things from the house. Why would I stay when there's nothing for me to do? We should go home now—"

Ignácio turned on him with savage repulsion. Spit flew from his lips. "What are you *talking* about? Stop talking! Stop it! Stop *TALKING*."

Tony opened his mouth to speak, but nothing came out.

"There is no *home*. There is ruin! There is rot! There is—" Ignácio unhinged his jaw and let out a low moan that frightened Tony. The moan rose into a shriek. The man's face went volcanic, testing the pressure of his skin with what boiled beneath.

Then, he pulled back. He swallowed, gripped himself, shook like a dog. When he brought his face back to the fields, he was calm. For a moment, Tony did not know what to do. Finally, Ignácio said to himself, "I will take another look at the holdings, liquidate the villa—"

"No, no," Tony said.

Ignácio was not listening. He crawled into the back seat of the Mercedes, mumbling to himself.

Sr. Rocha stepped in front of Tony and slammed the car door on Ignácio grasping his head in both hands. Sr. Rocha spoke: "*Até a próxima*, Little Tony." The driver tipped his cap, smiled with his grey gums exposed, then stuffed himself into the front seat without a backward glance.

As Tony stood shocked in the dirt road, the Mercedes revved up. He could think of nothing to say as it sped away in a cloud of red dust that temporarily parted the horde of flies.

"This isn't happening," Tony said to himself. "This isn't happening."

The front door of the house creaked open. Waldemar called to him. "Come inside now, pants shitter! You do not want to being outside at night! There is jaguar in fields who hunts little crying baby boys, *und* your bones look good to eat!" He tittered, coughed, and slammed the door.

Tony swiped at the red dust on his computer console. "This isn't happening."

In the fields, the flies closed in, resuming their feast.

10

Ring

SLATE CLOUDS KILLED THE remainder of the daylight. Sharp ozone opened leaves to potential rain. Thunder rattled flies. Frogs plopped into the muddy pond. Tony unpacked.

The dining room at the front of the house was dark, shuttered. A weak overhead light cast a jaundiced glow. The room smelled of octogenarian urine and a decade of untouched dust.

On the sideboard, an old gramophone powered by a crank handle spouted Richard Wagner's *Der Ring des Nibelungen* through an imposing golden horn. Quivering oboes and wavering voices told a story Tony only barely followed in his limited German. Saro stood closeby, as still as a carved idol. He monitored the progress of the music on the turntable, then flipped the vinyl discs at the appropriate time. Sometimes he offered the occasional crank to keep the turntable spinning. Other than that, he did not move.

Nearby, the old man perched in a carved wood chair that resembled a throne. Waldemar's tripod cane rested under his ringed fingers. He kept time with metallic clicks. "Siegfried!" he belted, adjusting his bathrobe to cover his privates. "He begins his journey in F major! This is clearest of musical keys for hero of spirit!" In profile, Tony noticed, he cut a distinguished figure, his nose large and patrician. The man brought a dramatic flourish to all his movements that gave him an undeniable stage presence, even in a farmhouse dining room. Tony could imagine him singing in an opera, theatrically dressed and wailing resplendently about gods and monsters. Waldemar even matched the lead tenor on the album with a shockingly decent voice.

"I see," Tony said.

Waldemar reached for canned cheese and sprayed a glob directly into his mouth. "You like music, *Hosenscheisser*?"

Tony groaned. "Do not call me that." He had regretted that the only electric outlet in casa grande that appeared safe enough to handle his computer's wattage was in the dining room, which Waldemar seemingly had established as his musical haven. Tony added, "I am not a pants-shitter."

"*Bürschchen*, then."

Tony closed his eyes. *Little boy.* An improvement.

He chewed his nails a bit, then stopped, remembering his grandmother's admonishments about that. Then, he clicked his mouse on a pixelated map showing a series of castles. The screen changed. Tiny figures emerged from a central castle to assemble a stone well. Tony sat back and watched them. Other than his books, these games distracted him. Hours slipped by without him noticing. He entered a world of images and movement, inhabited by characters as real to him as anyone else in his life. These, along with the characters in his books, were his best friends who carried him away from the worries of the Collapse. Tony yearned for normalcy. Even Frodo the Hobbit, grand adventurer, did not wish to live in remarkable times.

Waldemar distractedly poked the large pile of paperwork on the dining table. "What is all this?"

Tony broke from his reverie. "Fazenda documents," he said without looking at them. "Historical. Financial."

"You are dumping them here on my table, why?"

Tony rapid-fire clicked his mouse, moving game figures around the board. "I'm going to learn about the fazenda."

"Why?"

"Because when my grandfather calls with a new plan, I'll be aware of the operations here."

"Ah." Waldemar fanned his fingers, rings sliding between swollen joints. "So. You are thinking grandfather Ignácio is surviving much longer?"

Tony spun to face him. "What did you say?"

"You want me to repeat when great-grandson hears well enough? I am man to repeat myself now?"

Tony sputtered, "Explain what you mean!"

Waldemar folded his hands on his cane, a regal pose for pontification. "Eh. I have seen this many times in year 19 and 45. World changes. Economy goes *ppffft*. People not so fast to catch on. People of *industry,* especially slow. These are people needing their old money. They are needing their vanity." He raised a finger. A heavy pewter ring slid back to the knuckle. "I have seen when all goes kaput. Many self-deaths—many gunshots, cyanides, throwing selves at tanks. Ah! What is to be done? What is needed to survive?" He banged the table at each word. "Strength—of—character!" He settled back into his chair, as if finished with the sermon.

Tony fluttered his eyes, trying to process the reasoning. "You're saying my grandfather will be dead because he has no strength of character?"

Waldemar jutted his chin. "Correct. Ignácio is weak man. Always been so. But! His pleats *und* cuffs always razor-sharp!" He cleared a wad of phlegm from his throat. "Eh. He will be dead by weekend."

A burning in Tony's gut bubbled into his throat. "No, he won't."

The old man eyed him. "Tell yourself that."

Tony turned back to his computer, fuming.

"Do not be angry, pants-shitter!" The old man shoved the fazenda paperwork with his cane. "We will find you new hobby. *Poof* goes bad business!" Pages tipped to the center of the table and spilled over.

Tony ignored him. The gramophone horn quivered with low notes and guttural warbling. Something about a dragon in a forest, Tony guessed. He could feel a headache coming on. He had unpacked the brown paper bag of drugs but wadded it all up and pushed it well under his bed. Out of sight, out of mind. He would need to make those doses last.

Waldemar whooshed more spray cheese into his mouth. "You like music, little boy?"

Tony narrowed his eyes at his monitor and clicked over and over. "I do."

"What music do you like?"

"Screaming Trees. Nirvana. Nine Inch Nails."

Waldemar paled over his cheese spray nozzle. He tapped the table to attract Saro's attention. "Saro! *Was ist* Shrieking Trees?"

Saro shrugged. He flicked his eyes in Tony's direction. Tony would not return his gaze but always kept him in his periphery. He had no idea how long Saro had been caring for Waldemar. Saro had never been here when Tony visited as a boy. Was he new? Could he be trusted? Tony did not know this rude man, nor did he want to.

Waldemar craned his neck. "These trees and nails are American musical acts?"

Tony detected snobbishness. He jerkily raised and slumped his shoulders. "I admire American culture."

"Pity." Waldemar licked cheese from his teeth, dipping his head to and fro, following the building crescendo of strings on the gramophone. "Siegfried has much love for Brünnhilde, daughter of king of gods! So euphoric, this love! So glorious! Is love for nature Siegfried has—"

Tony heaved a sigh and tuned him out.

Very little about the interior of the casa grande comforted him. It had lost all the smells associated with his grandmother and had undergone minor adaptations for Waldemar's accessibility that changed the layout. It was not a place he knew. There was a familiarity with its sparse interior, its white stucco walls with colonial blue trim on arched doorways. He knew the dozens of brown frames displaying sepia photographs and illustrations of all the Cavalcantes who had run the fazenda since 1780, all the way back to Pascual Antonio da Silva, senior naval officer for the Portuguese colony. There was the simple wood furniture with bright striped fabrics, now faded. There were the rough-hewn wood floors that used to give him splinters in his plump, bare feet. There were the Catholic saints everywhere—the niches stuffed with icons and crucifixes. The minuscule bedrooms were like monks' cells, furnished with no more than a wooden twin bed with a limp mattress, a small mirror, and a side table. Lotte's bedroom was the same, right next to Tony's—but all of it smelled of dust now. Waldemar and Saro slept in the east wing, far away from him. That distance frightened him, though he didn't want to admit it. Many rooms in the house had been boarded up, creating places for intruders to hide. Waldemar did not seem to care about potential thieves, the Collapse, its dangers. Besides Wagner, Tony wasn't sure what the old man cared about—except possibly items inside the study he kept locked. Since he was a boy, Tony was warned never to enter that study upon pain of death. Worse than death: an extended scolding from the Nazi. Tony had never been in there but had always imagined it as chock-full of things Waldemar had brought with him when he fled the Reich.

A voice in Tony's ear, buzzing: "*Was ist das?*"

Tony startled. Waldemar had stabbed his cane all the way over to him without him noticing. The old man was standing over Tony's shoulder, extending a bony finger toward the computer monitor. Rings slid. Wads of masking tape stopped them from tumbling to the floor. A cloud of processed cheese breath defiled the air. "Excuse me?"

Waldemar switched to English. "Your grandmother, *meine tochter*, did not teach you proper German?"

"No," Tony said. "I suspect it was to keep me from understanding what she said on the telephone to her friends."

Waldemar chuckled. "Fine excuse, but no excuse."

"I understand enough, though. Like outside, how you called my grandfather a homosexual."

Waldemar grinned. "*Untermensch*. Deviant."

"You know nothing."

Waldemar replied, "*You* know nothing."

Tony twisted his mouth and resumed his game.

"*Was ist das?*" Waldemar repeated.

"You want to know what I'm playing?" Tony asked.

"Smart grandson knows Deutsch without learning it ever. Yes, I ask 'What is that?'"

"It's a god game."

Waldemar's mouth gaped. "*Gott Spiel?*"

Saro stepped toward Tony. Necklaces jingled. Sparse light glinted off the silver in his hair, but the black front forelock sucked the light right back in. Tony wondered, *Who wears his hair like that?* Saro bobbed his head to get a view of the monitor. Tony asked him, "Excuse me, Sr. Saro?"

Saro stopped in his tracks, then looked with wide eyes to Waldemar.

Waldemar explained, "Saro understands only Berber, Egyptian, Aramaic, German, and Sumerian."

"Oh," Tony said. "Um."

"And Portuguese."

"Thank goodness." Tony asked for some water in Portuguese. Saro took one last look at the monitor, then sped in the direction of the kitchen.

"He understands English also," Waldemar added, "but you must yell it."

"Oh," Tony said. "Where did you find him?"

"In antique shop in India. It was—" Waldemar searched his brain with his mouth hinged open. "—year 19 and 29. We want same artifact from expedition coming from Antarctica. We fight, then friends. Long story short: we like same stuffs."

"I don't remember seeing him around here when I was younger."

"He was here. Or not. Who knows. Saro is not bound with shackles."

"Why must he wear those necklaces?"

"It is only payment he accepts."

Tony said, "I see."

"No, you do not. Saro lives through many hard times. Also graduate of same school. Hard knocks." Waldemar sprayed more cheese into his mouth. "Looks will deceive with Saro. He also graduated schools in Egypt. Degrees in archaeology and dead languages galore."

Tony bit his lip.

"You don't believe me?" Waldemar asked. Cheese stuck to his front teeth.

"He just looks—"

"Saro is brilliant man," Waldemar said.

"But do you trust him?"

The old man considered Tony with narrow, colorless eyes. "You think Saro works here but will hurt me when times change? When money stops working? You are thinking of Lotte and afraid." He shook his head. "This is not first collapse of society, little boy. Saro and I, we know collapsing." Waldemar bent forward on uneasy feet and knocked on the monitor's glass, his face pallid with what Tony assumed was wonder. "You, tell me, what is god game?"

Tony said, "Um. Yes. You choose whether you play a benevolent god or an evil god, and you rule over people in different lands. There are challenges to each geographical region. Basically, you must convince your people to do your will and eliminate the enemy god's followers."

"Ah! You are world-builder!" Waldemar's eyes flashed. "*Zehr* good. Which god do you play?"

"Benevolent," Tony said.

"I know man who played this game in Europe, except other side. He lost." He laughed a wheezy cough.

Tony turned to him. "Grandfather calls you a Nazi. Are you still a Nazi?"

"*Ach du*! Fifty years gone, and people still ask." Waldemar stabbed the air with a ringed finger. "I should ask *you* if you are same as 50 years ago, but you are *Bürschchen* and I am almost dead."

"Is that a yes?"

"I saw no action. Collapsed lung. I kill no one."

"But you were SS. The elite guard. That's what my grandfather said."

Waldemar nodded. "*Ahnenerbe* branch."

"What's that?" Tony was getting an odd thrill out of questioning an adult like this. Ignácio would not have stood for it.

"Means 'ancestral heritage.'"

"And what did you do?"

"I seek artifacts of oldest cultures on Earth."

Tony hardened his stare. "Aryan cultures?"

Waldemar folded his arms and regarded him. "*Much* older."

"Nazis killed a lot of people," Tony noted. "The SS authored a genocide—"

"So did Stalin," Waldemar replied. "And Mao Zedong. Tojo. Leopold. Franco. We don't talk about them so much! Why not?" Tony shrank back. Waldemar, however, did not shrink. He kept advancing. "Maybe one day *you* will be asked this ridiculous question by your great-grandson. 'Hey there, Herr Great-Grand-*Vater*! How did you tap on keyboard game in 19 and 92 when now cars fly, and everyone is astronaut for space wars?' You will say, 'Times change, *Hosenscheisser, und* so have I!'" He snorted, then lowered his voice. "I hope you have stupid great-grandchild, too."

Tony muttered, "I don't think you understand what shame your Nazism has brought to future generations."

Waldemar's face brightened. "Future—This would be you? I bring shame to you?" He reached out with his cane and smacked the pile of papers on the table. They scattered to the floor. "Do you know year 18 and 88? That is year fazenda stopped using slaves. That is—" He made a show of calculating. "—nearly 100 years of running concentration camp right here." He drove his cane to the rough floor. "Here is mini Auschwitz! Did you know there was uprising of slaves here?" He stabbed the floor again—*clack*. "Violent slaves shot down by Cavalcantes, everyone shrieking like musical trees. *Blam! Blam! Splat. Splat.*" He leaned close and breathed cheese spray. "Modern times changed nothing! End of slavery in 18 and 88, *und* still Cavalcantes get more slaves! They go to poor regions of Brazil to trick villagers to work." He pointed to the papers. "It is all there. Cavalcantes make no show of hiding. Just like Nazis with paperwork. Very diligent. You should look at these papers, little boy. Maybe now you know why your mother leaves you."

Tony's stomach flipped. "What?"

"Oh, yes. Paloma, she finds out about what goes on here. These papers *everywhere* for anyone to find. She finds them. She asks Ignácio, 'Papa, what is this?' He does not deny. 'You shame us,' she yells. Just like you do. Then she joins communists in Buenos Aires at time when not prudent to do so. Like Siegfried, she falls in love. But with student leader who gets killed. A Marxist! That is your father, little orphan Antonio! Then, she comes home pregnant—" He pokes Tony in the gut. "—that is guess who. And she has big fights with Ignácio, how he treats workers. She has big fights with my Lotte, how she is nothing but breeding factory for Ignácio. Well, look who is breeding now! Here comes little Antonio! And where does Paloma go? Back to communists! Not even to raise her son."

Tony clenched his fingers. He knew none of this. He growled, "Why are you saying this?"

Waldemar growled in return, "We all have sins. These are mine. This is my hell." He swatted at the gramophone. It skipped, but Wagner kept playing. "Poor little orphan Antonio." He hacked a bit of phlegm. "I do not feel sorry for you, great-grandson."

"I did not ask you to."

Waldemar turned on him. "Oh? Is that so? No. You are lying. And you will *not* be dishonest."

Tony swallowed. "All right."

"You *are* wanting pity party today," Waldemar said. "You will be *honest*. You want bright future? You start it now! No lies!"

Tony swallowed again. "All right. I would give anything for that drink right now."

Saro returned from the kitchen and set a large box of saltine crackers in front of Tony. "Thank you," Tony said.

"No!" Waldemar barked. He pounced on the box of saltines and hurled them at Saro. "Is not what boy asked!" The box popped off Saro's gut and skidded into an embankment of dust and loose white hair. "*Wasser, du dummkopf!*" Saro collected the box and padded back to the kitchen, necklaces and bracelets swooshing.

Waldemar then wheeled on Tony with his rage. "Great-grandson will not accept what is not asked! Never!" Tony blinked. "I will teach. Grow balls.

You speak like prissy Ignácio. Must speak like German. From here." Waldemar punched his own gut, then hacked.

The overhead lights flickered twice, then the house plunged into darkness.

"Uh-oh," Waldemar said in the dark, "here goes electric again." He sang in a soaring tenor:

> *Oh, men of dark and dismal fate,*
> *Forego your cruel employ...*

Just then, Saro burst from the kitchen with a lit match and approached the candles on the dining table. A soft glow bloomed on Waldemar's rumpled and blanched face, ironing out his deep wrinkles. The old man kept crooning:

> *Have pity on my lonely state,*
> *I am an orphan boy!*

Tony's vision blurred with the glow of the candlelight. He thought he could see the young man that Waldemar once was. He tried to imagine that man in an SS uniform, commanding archeological digs, crating stolen items, stamping the swastika on paperwork, clicking his heels, and saluting the Führer. He couldn't imagine it. The man before him was skeletal and weak, with a love of the musical arts. The only clicking sound wasn't his jackboots, but clunky rings several sizes too large.

Ignácio is right, Tony thought. *This entire family is rotten to the core.*

"Shame for you, dumb *Bürschchen*," Waldemar laughed, now pointing at Tony's dark monitor. The monitor was lifeless in the stale gloom of the dining room. "Benevolent god went *ppffft.*"

Later, Tony woke in his small bedroom, sweating. His covering sheet lay in a heap on the floor.

The dreams again. Sr. Rocha. The lightning-like split in the sky. The creatures.

Tony's pulse boomed in his head. He had tried a day without the drugs, but he wasn't going to make it much longer. Perhaps, just a little—

The power had come back on as he slept. A side lamp was glowing, and he flinched at the light. Lying under the lamp was a stack of books and a few papers that were not there before. Tony stretched to read the top title: *Royal Geographic Society of London: Members of Renown, 1972 Edition*. An entry had been marked: *Sir Henley Goode, Antarctic Explorer.*

Waldemar mentioned something about finding Saro in India over interest in an Antarctic expedition. Fighting about an artifact, was it? It was difficult to imagine Saro fighting about anything, much less speaking a single word.

In the hallway, in the dark, a rattle.

Tony sat up. "Is someone there?" His pulse raced.

Movement in the dark. A flash of jewelry. The sway of glittering necklaces.

"Sr. Saro?"

The man stepped forward, barely visible in the gloomy hallway. He flexed his fingers. A rustle. A crunch. He was gripping the brown paper bag. Tony's drugs.

Tony sucked in. "Hey, those are mine. I need—"

Saro flashed his teeth. He tilted his head. A whisper of sounds overcame Tony. They came together to form one word that landed like a punch: *No.*

Tony flew backward and landed on his pillow with the force of it, as if he were punched. He was fully awake now, shaking his head at the surprise. *What just happened?* And then, *I'm high. That can't be right.*

Another clatter in the hallway.

"Sr. Saro, please—"

But the man was gone.

11

Sir Henley Goode and the Expedition

UNABLE TO SLEEP, TONY scanned the papers Saro presumably brought to him. Attached notes, written on paper so old it nearly crumbled, some in the spidery hand with German phrases, pointed to a path through the papers that told a bizarre story.

ROYAL GEOGRAPHIC SOCIETY OF LONDON: MEMBERS OF RENOWN, 1972 EDITION
Sir Henley Goode, Antarctic Explorer (1876-1925)
Born in St. Albans, England, in 1876, Goode first traveled to Antarctica in 1907 with Ernest Shackleton aboard the Nimrod. *Goode became the principal leader of the Imperial Antarctic Expedition, 1921-1922. The expedition's goal was to map the west coast, but objectives changed in the field to documenting curious findings near the Sentinel Mountains. Goode was the sole survivor of the 48-member exploration team. The circumstances of their deaths are still the subject of controversy. Goode died in London in 1925, two years after his return, in the Society's disgrace.*

SCIENTIFIC REPORTS: SERIES C—ZOOLOGY AND BOTANY
Scientific Institute of Otago, New Zealand, 1924
Imperial Antarctic Expedition, 1921-1922
Under the leadership of Sir Henley Goode, OBE, BE, DSc, FRS
REJECTED; *Stanford University Collection (California)*
Fungi Samples
The sample of eukaryotic organisms brought back by the Expedition is important for the number of novelties which it includes.

Melanin-rich fungi were sampled from a black pool inside an ice cave. (See Plate III for map.) The environment offered no nutrients required for survival. Curiously enough, the fungi survive on an unknown process of photosynthesis fed by radiation.

Skeleton, Unknown Species (See Plate IV)

A single sample, labelled "From Sentinel Mountain Range," Feb. 1922.

Description: Measuring 4.57 meters end to end; blunted skull with three eye sockets and one mouth opening; four serrated cartilage spines protruding from the jawline; hard, concentric plates descending the body from thorax to abdomen. Plates resemble sclerites as found in insect exoskeletons; two longer serrated cartilage spines protruding from base of body; functional as segmented legs with coxa, femur, tibia, and tarsus, inclusive of joints. Knifelike endpoints suggest adaptation to walking on ice; eight appendages protruding from the abdomen, length of which suggests hydrostatic skeleton such as found in order Octopoda. Analysis suggests an insectoid species able to move at great speed and hunt large prey—

SIR HENLEY GOODE, THE SENTINEL DWELLINGS, 1923

List of Photographs

Sir Henley Goode (Photogravure)

Completion of the Base Camp, "Moltke Nunatak"

Completion of the Hut With Union Jack on Flagpole, "Bertrab Nunatak"

Panoramic View of the West, Including Sentinel Mountains

Lt. Frank Farnsworth Collecting Geological Specimens

Edward Plunkett With Frostbitten Face

Farnsworth and Plunkett with Sledge Dogs

List of Illustrations

Cliffs at Sentinel Mountains

Grotto of Mysteries, Fungal Growth

Granite Cliffs Where Etchings Were Found

Sketch of Architectural Features, Sentinel Dwellings

Introduction

Although stated in the public press that the Imperial Antarctic Expedition had no objective of reaching the South Geographical Pole, the British public persisted in the view. The venture we sketched assumed a modern aspect—

Discovery of Sentinel Dwellings

At the base of the Sentinels, one may find the outer walls of an abandoned granite city. The advanced architecture of this city includes spires and avenues.

Etchings in the granite cliff tell a pictographic story in a mural in successive events: A congregation of beings with amorphous shapes assembles. They create children to do work of building a city. The elder beings lure a destructive creature to imprison it. The children abandon their elders. The elders defend the creature's prison against others who arrive to free it. Some elders leave, others die in time. The granite colony is abandoned to seek the lost children—

ADDRESS DELIVERED BEFORE THE ROYAL GEOGRAPHIC SOCIETY, 1924
by Dr. Roald Lake

The object of these remarks will be to demonstrate that Sir Henley Goode's Imperial Antarctic Expedition of 1921-1922 can be catalogued as an utter failure to the British Crown. The painful news of the deaths of 47 officers and men united us in our efforts to seek explanation from the sole survivor, Sir Henley Goode.

His insulting pamphlet, The Sentinel Dwellings, *published after his journey home, suggests acts of supernatural murder taking place at the Main Base Camp at Moltke Nunatak, acts perpetrated by a creature up to 15 feet high capable of cutting down 38 men in an instant. Salvaged from the site, a ridiculous skeleton of a species impossible to have evolved on this planet.*

This fabrication begins with a communication to Goode from Main Base Camp. Five teams from the Main Camp reported samples of prehistoric lifeforms taken near the Sentinels, including an insectoid skeleton. The age of the fossil caused some confusion. Given the skeleton's position in the strata, its evolutionary features were incompatible with its age. It could not have evolved on the geological time scale as we understand it. Given that information, Goode immediately assembled a second team from his Secondary Camp at Bertrab to investigate the area where the fossil was taken.

Of the fates of this three-man sledge team out of the Bertrab Camp—a team consisting of Goode, Lt. Frank Farnsworth, and Edward Plunkett—we have a clearer picture. Their objective was to travel west to the Sentinels, mapping the base of the interior mountain range and taking samples. After five weeks, tragedy struck. Farnsworth fell through a crevasse with a six-dog sled, taking most of their supplies with him. His body was never recovered. Goode and Plunkett cancelled the remainder of their trip and turned back. However, they sledged in the wrong direction for over 24 hours. Lacking food, they sacrificed weaker sledge dogs to feed the others, then to feed themselves. Plunkett deteriorated quickly with bouts of madness. Goode reported restraining Plunkett from destroying their own tent and remainder of their supplies.

*Goode struck out alone, believing he was closing in on the Main Camp. Later he said
    he believed he had accidentally travelled closer to the Sentinels. No exact locations
    were ever given for this, the most unbelievable part of his journey.*

*Here, Goode perpetrates further indignities, having us believe that a granite city of
    advanced archeological features exists at the base of the Sentinel Mountains in
    Antarctica. The sole documentary evidence of these dwellings are the drawings
    of Sir Henley Goode himself. The description of the hieroglyphics within such a
    structure defies belief. (Illustrations of his fanciful imagination can be found in
    his pamphlet and need not be given the propriety of reprinting here.)*

*Beings visiting us from afar indeed! A war among them for supremacy! An internal
    rebellion splitting their factions! Would this esteemed Society see sense in my
    motion to eject Sir Henley Goode as a member, to rebuke his explanations from
    this failure of an expedition, and to settle the matter of his mad ramblings once
    and for all—explainable scientifically as poisoning by consuming the toxic livers
    of his own sledge dogs?—*

ADVANCING SIR HENLEY GOODE TO PROPHET CANDIDACY, 1946

A Report to the Providence Organization, Prophet Tribunal

*After the sufficient waiting period to ensure enduring reputation of sanctity
    among the faithful, the London branch of the Providence Organization hereby
    advances Sir Henley Goode, Servant of Providence, to candidacy for Prophet
    of Cosmic Evidence. The enclosed petition to Providence Central (Providence,
    Rhode Island, USA) documents the Cause for Prophethood, namely the discovery
    and documentation of evidence of cosmic life on Earth in Antarctica. Requisite
    writings and supporting documents are included here. Personal writings include
    journals and the seminal pamphlet written upon his return from the 1921-22
    Antarctic Expedition, The Sentinel Dwellings (1923).*

*Submission of this candidacy hereby enacts the Congregation of the Causes of the
    Prophet, the Scientific Commission, and the Decree of Martyrdom.*

Signed,

Murray Gedney, Servant

London Headquarters

Providence Group

[Attached note] *Approved 12 Dec 1947, Entered into Foundational Documents
    in Prophet Henley Goode Library, St. Albans, England.*

12

Rise

Tony shot out of the casa grande with the Henley Goode books, looking for Waldemar. Tony found him behind the house, in the muddy pond.

With his face tilted to the afternoon sun and his body submerged, Waldemar spun lazily in the murky water, his pasty arms flung over an inflatable swim raft in the shape of a hot pink flamingo. Sunlight distorted the underwater stripes on his vintage one-piece bathing suit—a wrestler's halter top and knee-length shorts. Tony was taken aback. He had only seen that kind of swimsuit in old beach photos where men wore straw boaters, handlebar mustaches, and socks in sandals. Through the pond scum, ten white toes surfaced, each clawed toenail tinted chartreuse with fungal disease.

Saro stood at attention in the shade of a dying papaya tree, not even a bead of perspiration on his forehead.

"Hey!" Tony shouted to Waldemar, shifting the books to his side, "Last night, Saro stole something of mine!"

Waldemar reclined further. Dazzlingly white legs rode the mellow pond waves. "Oh?"

Tony shuffled the books on his hip. "I want it back!" He flinched. His bones hurt. His pulse raced, his head hurt, and he was sweating through his shirt.

Waldemar ratcheted his arms toward the papaya tree. "Saro! Dope fiend wants his stuffs returned! Dance to little boy's flute!"

Saro removed the brown paper bag from his housecoat. He fumbled inside and removed a sandwich baggie caked with white power. At the sight of it, Tony licked his lips.

Then, Saro opened it and delicately sprinkled its contents into the mud. Before Tony could speak, Saro wadded the paper bag and baggie and tossed both into the pond, where they skittered across the surface, barely disturbing the algae.

Tony's mouth went dry. He exhaled in a long, narrow gasp. The old man cried out, "Anything else pants-shitter wants?"

Tony stuttered, "I—I—I can't believe you did that! My grandfather said I *needed* that—"

"*Ach*! Put a sock in your cakehole!" Waldemar lost his balance and smacked the water's surface to right himself, sending the floatie spinning. "What kind of grandfather buys heroin for grandson?! My opinion of Ignácio has sunk to new low! I did not think this possible, yet here we are!" Waldemar grunted a string of German phrases Tony did not understand.

"He was *helping* me! I was having problems after Oma—" Images flashed. Rocha. Fire. Lightning. Creatures. His grandfather pulling him from under the stairs: *What has happened here, Antonio?* Tony clutched his gut and doubled over.

"Problems? Problems! It is *death*! Death is not *problem*! Death is all around us!" He threw his arms in every direction, nearly capsizing himself. "It is that papaya tree! It is that sugarcane! It is poofy flower bush with hideous blooms that make me sneeze!" He kicked the water and spun around to face Tony. "It is Saro! It is *me*!" He twirled on the surface as he fumed. "Little boy will face fears! World is shit place! Get used to it!"

Tony howled, "I *needed* that medicine!"

Waldemar thwapped his striped chest. "Grow balls! Like *Übermensch*!"

Tony shrieked, "I am not a Nazi!"

"No one is saying so, little boy! Stop crying!"

Tony slumped onto the shore, exhausted. He had been up all night reading. Sleep had escaped him. He would give anything for an hour of restful slumber. The books tipped from his hands into the mud.

"*Ach*!" Waldemar yelped. "These are my books you are dumping into the mud? How is this happening? Are you thief?"

"No. Saro left them in my room when he stole my—"

"Saro?"

"Saro!"

Waldemar sang out a long note. "Ahhhh! Brilliant Saro to introduce great-grandson to our work!" Waldemar wedged himself out of the floatie, sending miniature waves to lap at Tony's feet. The old man's armpit rubbed against the vinyl, producing a series of flatulent burps.

"Your work?" Tony asked. "You work with Providence Group? Henley Goode is *their* prophet."

Waldemar dragged the inflatable to the edge of the pond. "I work for myself only. Am independent contractor." Saro met him with a striped towel.

"Isn't Providence a cult?"

"Eh," Waldemar squeaked. "*Nein.*"

"They're nutcases! They believe—"

Waldemar eyed him. "What? That aliens live on Earth? Well, now. Look who is correct! Saro, bring my bird floatie."

"But—"

Waldemar pushed him aside. "You are opening eyes to real world like baby you are. You are infant. Saro *helps* you. He takes your grandpapa's street drugs *und* gives you knowledge in return. You should be thanking him."

"Thank you?" Tony said to Saro.

Saro took up the flamingo floatie and nodded sagely.

"For fuck's sake," Tony muttered.

Waldemar raised a ringed finger in Tony's face. "I have told you my work is with oldest cultures on Earth. And now you see. I work with what has been here among us for *very* long time."

"You believe alien culture—"

Saro tilted his head. Necklaces jangled.

"*Belieeeeeeve.*" Waldemar stretched out the vowel. "I do not *believe* in sea monster living at bottom of ocean, but there it is on television! Whoopsie! What happens now? Flip out? No!" He stood straight, arching his back. "I find out what is going on! This is work that must be done! Is *only* important work to do. Not sugarcane!" He pointed to the books. "This!"

Tony asked, "Is this the work you did for Germany?"

"Ah. Good times. That work paid good money in Third Reich," Waldemar said. "Many interested in power in my time. Many will be interested in power now. There are those who want artifacts to fuel *more* power, get ahead in world." His face darkened. "But did Reich give me money for what was necessary to look? No. Nazis are *cheap*, little boy. When I ask for funds to seek Jesuit writings in Mexico, ones who lived in Aztec Empire, ones who are knowing of Priestess Zumaa and her apocalyptic harbinger worship, am I approved for funds? *Nein!*"

"Zumaa," Tony said. "She's another of the prophets of Providence Group?"

"You catch on. You hear of these things on the periphery. You file them away. *Crazy*, you think at first." He tapped a bony finger at his temple. "But now, you must look again! You must look where I cannot go! Is too late for me! You must carry on!"

Tony pointed out, "Maybe if Germany hadn't angered Mexico into declaring war, you'd have traveled more."

"Not so!" Waldemar said, exchanging the towel for his cane from Saro. "Walk with me up this oppressive hill. It is too hot to be outside today. I must have *eine* lemon drink."

Tony said, "You said you met Saro in India fighting over an artifact you'd both found. I read the Henley Goode stuff. Which artifact was it?"

Waldemar sneered. "Why? You sell it for drugs?"

"No." Tony shot a wounded glance.

"I tell you *some* things, but not all."

"Why not?"

Waldemar swatted at him with his cane. "These are dangerous things to know! You must prove to be ready to hear them! You *just now* are thinking people insane! Are they *cult*, you ask? For your whole life you think this! But now that monster is televised you are thinking they may be on to something! You deserve *prize* for that? You deserve *all* secrets told to you now that you are onboard with obvious things? No! You must work harder!"

"So, okay," Tony said, "what are you working on now? I want to know."

"Same thing I always work on. Travel during war proved difficult, *ja*, but afterward explorations take even more money. I worked my lifetime tracking stuffs. Like on east coast of America—"

"Artifacts?"

"Shush! I talk! I track stuffs to America, but Brazil is as close as I come. Do not ask me what stuffs I track. I will not tell you that, either." He coughed.

Saro slapped his back.

"*Danke*, Saro." Waldemar cleared his throat. "Ireland also of interest. I did go there once. Got so close!" He snapped his fingers, which produced a dull, wet thump from wrinkled digits. "Now, think, little boy! These two places—the American east and Ireland—used to be closer together in time of one continent. Pangea! In those times, whatever is walking inside US and A could also be in Ireland by jumping over tiny creek. *Boop*! They are connected!"

"This is hard to believe," Tony said. "What used to be fringe theory is now the most important work?"

"We have lifetimes of looking again at our histories. Who did we label as insane, yet is not? What warning signs did we miss? What else is out there?"

"Did you know the beast in the ocean was there? Did anyone? Did Providence?"

Waldemar crumpled his face. "There was talk. But no. If it was secret, it was *good* one. Surprise *everyone* I know."

Saro edged up behind Tony and scooped Henley's books.

Waldemar sighed. "Ah, great-grandbaby. You are just starting." He extended his voice to a thundering performance tone. "Come, Saro! More for boy to read! Let us collect informations of Nurse Lily Rattray for pants-shitter's detox! He shall learn about powers of fungus!"

"Lily Rattray. I've heard of her. Another Providence prophet?"

"Great-grandbaby is correct! She saw strange fungus in Great War trenches. Battle of Somme! Now, if I had funding from Reich, we collect these samples for biological warfare. What power we would have! Allies would be sick to death and dreaming of towers of monsters! Ahhhh! But no! Denied!" He sliced the air with his hands. "Reich had no imagination."

"That is one accusation about Nazis I have not yet heard," Tony said.

"Saro!" Waldemar trumpeted. "To my study!"

Saro passed Tony and gave him another nod. Then he galloped up the hill with the flamingo inflatable and the books. Waldemar waddled behind him.

"I remember your study," Tony said to Waldemar's back. "I was never allowed inside—"

The old man turned on him. "And still, you are not!" He tottered forward at a decent clip. "My house rules is simple! First, no drugs! Drugs are fuel for weak men! Second—" he coughed, "—you do not trespass *there*!" He gestured with his cane to a large window at the far end of the house. Like all the other windows, that one was heavily draped.

"What is in there?" Tony asked.

"My study. Are you stupid?"

"Why would you tell me not to go into a room and then point the room out? It only guarantees that I will become interested in doing so. Haven't you ever read a book?"

"Plenty."

Waldemar toddled onward. Tony stayed behind to consider the draped window.

Waldemar called to him from the top of the hill, wiping sweat from his forehead. "*Ach*! Little fruit! *Schnell*! Go find chess board! You are terrible player, and I like winning!"

After a sound beating at the game of chess, and with another sleepless night ahead, Tony flipped on the table lamp and took up the papers and books Saro left for him. This time, they were about the nurse from World War I named Lily Rattray. *Providence Prophetess of the Earthborn Plexus*, he read.

Her history, like Henley Goode's, read as a normal woman's story of her time, but took a disastrous turn when intersecting with a fantastical find.

In 1914, Nurse Lily Rattray, a New Zealand native, had trained as a nurse in the Great War with the Army Corps, serving in France at the meat-grinder known as the Battle of the Somme. There, trench warfare scarred the earth and men holed up in nasty pits awaiting deaths from disease, poison gas, machine gunning, or shelling. These are the maladies Lily treated in a nearby tent hospital. Soon, however, a new sickness emerged among the soldiers: flu-like symptoms after exposure to a strange fungus growing along trench walls.

The soldiers described to Lily iridescent fruiting bodies with feathery white roots. This, Lily suspected, might be responsible for the soldiers' illnesses, their black mouth blisters, their sleep disturbances, and their rantings and ravings. Were these trench mushrooms poisonous? When Lily brought up this possibility to the head nurse, Lily was written off. "Certainly," the head nurse said, "we might logically assign these symptoms to the new influenza epidemic." Lily replied, "And what of the panic, tremors, and nightmares presenting along with the flu symptoms?" The head nurse countered, "Shell shock, of course."

But the Māori soldiers serving in the New Zealand Pioneer Battalion sided with Lily; they also insisted the odd combination of symptoms resulted in fungal exposure. The Māoris had encountered that fungus first, months ago, when they dug the communication lines. Unlike the others, the Māoris recognized the fungus. "As children," a man from the Cook Islands told her, "we were warned never to approach those types of mushrooms that grew along the edges of volcanoes. If we touched them, Le Tasi i Fafo, a creature who inflicted frightening dreams and fevers would come—"

Tony sat upright, spilling papers. *Le Tasi i Fafo*. He circled the phrase. Wasn't that name mentioned in the Griff Tran letter? Wasn't that what the islanders called the creature that Manny eventually recorded: Le Tasi i Fafo? How could he get a copy of Griff's letter to check? Before he came to the fazenda, he heard that independent presses had distributed copies in the streets, translated into Portuguese. Tony would want the original English. Perhaps Saro would know where to find a copy.

He continued reading.

Rather than be warned off by the Māori, Nurse Lily Rattray was intrigued. She continued her war-time service, documenting all the instances of fungal growth and placement. After the war, she sailed to the Cook Islands, intending to search for more cases of it. She arrived in 1934, moved into a colonial bungalow, and never left. Her papers from this era were lost. However, whatever Lily found on the islands drove her to insanity. She became well known to islanders for wandering about with an unkempt appearance and speaking an unknown language. Within a year, she took her own life with cyanide.

Tony went to find Saro.

The entire house was dark. Tony moved toward the west wing, cursing the rough floorboards, when he noticed a blue-green glow coming from the dining room. He stopped.

The overhead light was off. A tapping sound confused him.

He ducked into the dining room to discover his computer monitor was on. He was sure he had turned it off. Power interruptions were not good for the system. The monitor was running the green text from the disk operating system—the raw code that executed commands. Text streamed quickly. The floppy disk slot on his processor glowed an odd violet.

Backlit was the unmistakable shadow of Saro.

Tony staggered forward, too surprised to be angry at the trespass.

He came up behind Saro to read the lines. Tony knew a little about the commands and codes that made his computer run, but not a lot. Saro's text made no sense at all.

"What language is that?" Tony asked.

Saro quickly flicked the monitor off, ejected what looked like a floppy disk, and pattered away as if he hadn't even heard the question.

Tony remained in the dark, utterly confused.

He turned the monitor back on, but the screen was blank.

"Hey," Tony called out. But no one answered.

The next morning, Tony awoke in his bedroom, buried in Lily Rattray papers. Waldemar was shrieking, "Saro! Saro! Quickly! Radio weather!"

Tony found the old man in the dining room with a dirty window thrown open, extending a wizened finger to a foggy sky. "Hurry up, Saro! We are missing temperature inversion prime for signal from big city Paulo!"

Saro pushed past Tony with a contraption that looked like a flattened clothes hanger. Saro also carried a long sheet of aluminum foil that rattled as he ran.

"Here, here," Waldemar pointed to the sideboard, upon which sat a radio older than Sputnik. Saro bent behind it, fiddling with a wire, wadding aluminum foil onto its connections.

"Hey," Tony announced. "Saro is awfully handy with electronics."

"You have no idea," Waldemar said.

"He was on my computer last night."

"So?"

"So, it's my personal computer."

Waldemar ignored him. "Hurry," he said to Saro. He scooped his arms at the air, as if to push Saro's efforts into fruition.

Finally, Saro snapped on the radio. The dial brightened. A news announcer could barely be heard behind a wall of static. Waldemar screeched, "It's on! Out the window!"

Saro neatly sprung in bare feet to the windowsill and balanced there, antennae extended. The news announcer came in clearer: "...Paske released evidence of Howard Winfield's involvement..." Saro stumbled. The radio voice disappeared.

Waldemar yelled, "You had it, *Dummkopf*! Back to left!"

Tony said to Waldemar, "Do you think Saro can find me a copy of Griff Tran's letter, preferably the original English text?"

Waldemar scowled. "What you think this is? Lending library? Big city bookstore? I send Saro out for materials as easy as cake?" He yelled again: "STAY THERE!"

The radio blared, "...Winfield worked with a British spy agency to gain advantage in the post-war European economy, Paske claims: 'This is a man who took advantage of a suffering continent to make his first million with inside knowledge of governmental maneuvers in war recovery. Such opportunism cannot be overlooked as we construct our international response to the threat in the Pacific—'"

"You hear that?" Waldemar fell into an armchair. "Ha! Ha! What rubbish! Everyone in whole of Europe out to make money after war." He blew air past his loose lips. "Something else, though, and listen to me, great-grandbaby. World government business is *not* funny. Mark my words, fraidy-cat people make no good decisions."

Tony whispered, "Is there any way to keep Saro off my computer?"

Waldemar said, "No."

"Thought not."

"Saro goes where he goes. Nothing to be done. Take it from me." He slunk back into his chair.

The radio news program switched topics to the failure of robotic dives at Manny's site. "Excessive radiation melted the drones," the announcer said. "New methods of reaching the Temple City are under consideration—"

"Hey," Tony said to Waldemar, who had fallen asleep in his chair. The old man startled awake. "Griff Tran's letter has a phrase that matches one used by Lily Rattray. *Le Tasi i Fafo*. It's a phrase the islanders use—"

"That," Waldemar breathed.

"Aw, come on. Don't start on the islanders. You have to know by now that the Nazi race theory was bullshit."

"That theory was—how do you say, *unterentwickelt*?"

"Underdeveloped?" Tony said.

"*Ja*. Underdeveloped. But no. I was referring to islanders' name for beast. 'One Out There' is their meaning. Should be 'One in Here.'" He thumped his temple.

Tony patted the old man's elbow. "But I found something, didn't I? I made a connection. Two points in history where—"

Waldemar smacked his lips. "You have found something of interest. Woo-hoo. Perhaps you will be big speaker at next Providence convention."

"I found it interesting."

Waldemar slipped back to sleep. "You are finding your way."

The old man was right. Tony felt plugged in, galvanized from the new versions of history he read, from the computer programming knowledge—he felt as if his neurons were blazing new paths, making new connections, forcing new perspectives. His sense of time accelerated. There was suddenly too little of it to accommodate the work he wanted to do. Also, the drugs were working their way out of his system. He no longer felt dull. He felt better than ever.

But with this new feeling came a restlessness bordering on frenzy. Tony clawed at the boundaries of his own skin, wanting out. His store-bought computer games bored him. He trashed the floppy disks and delved into his operating system, awkwardly tapping out primitive code to create graphics of his own. He'd never programmed before, but he felt inspired to learn now. *School of hard knocks*, Tony thought. He had no idea where this newfound confidence was born, but he reveled in it.

He programmed coordinates onscreen, connecting vectors with colored lines to illustrate what he saw around the house. He drew Waldemar in mid-yawn. He drew Saro in an inquisitive pose, diamond pendants twinkling in candlelight. He drew the Norse gods and goddesses from Waldemar's operatic records. Wotan, the king of the gods. Loge, the demigod of fire. Siegfried and Brünnhilde, the lovers. The Valkyries in flight. From there, he put his illustrations in motion. Then, he designed his own games with more contemporary scenarios than the feudal maps he had played before. The downfall of São Paulo in bright red fires! The Sleeping One, swiping at the air with tentacles to ensnare planes and missiles! Sometimes Saro stood behind him, watching his efforts, vaguely nodding. Tony tried to ask, "What do you think of my work—," but Saro flitted away before he could finish the question.

When the electricity blinked out and Tony lost unsaved code, he unleashed a rage akin to a Nordic hero slaying a dragon. Unlike Ignácio and Lotte, Waldemar never reprimanded him for these outbursts; in fact, Waldemar encouraged Tony to become louder. "From here!" Waldemar socked him in the belly. Tony could howl operatically at the computer for disobeying his commands. He could stomp around the dining room when a line of code wouldn't work. Waldemar, wearing nothing but a bathrobe and a grin, curled like a cat in his dining-room chair and gave notes on Tony's dramatic fury. "At last, I see family in you, *Bürschchen*," the old man snickered, "other than your *unheimlich* green eyes." As Waldemar arranged his morning pills, he philosophized, "People will say to you, 'You, boy, with creepy eyes and sissy clothes don't scare me.' Grandbaby must tough-up. World is brutal." He held a horse pill in his lips. "Approach with volume."

While Waldemar was intent on instructing Tony in the finer points of outward confidence, Saro seemed determined to bolster Tony's inner world. Aside from Providence Prophets—Tony learned about all 12, from Meresankh of Egypt in

2520 BCE to Reverend Lazarus Grieves of America in 1821—Saro would deposit
piles of books on esoteric subjects on Tony's nightstand. These were topics Tony
had never learned in school: astronomy, archaeology, anthropology, herbology,
hieroglyphics. The books were old with crumbling binding and sun-damaged
covers that threatened to disintegrate in his hands. When the books were in a
language he couldn't read, he explored the illustrations and diagrams.

Once, Saro's book pile included one about sacred mushrooms and the origins
of Christianity. Tony flipped to a chapter about fertility rites, hoping for some
fuel for his hormonal erotic fantasies. Instead, he discovered a letter tucked into
the pages.

It was from Dr. Oliver Daas in Boston, addressed to "My Strange Visitor in Los
Alamos." It had a recent postmark. Tony opened it.

My friend!

*I hope you have not forgotten me! Our time together at Los Alamos still inspires
my work, so much so that I am pleased to write to you about the successes in
software-based artificial life. However, one persistent problem plagues us, a
problem for which I hope you will provide the assistance you so kindly pledged.
You see, our ArLiFs (that is what we call the Artificial Lifeforms—we have 12 so
far) run their daytime simulations with a paralyzing number of errors—*

Tony held the letter closer. Saro was able to help a computer coder in Boston
with an artificial-life software program? And Artificial Lifeforms at that? Tony
couldn't quite believe what he was reading. If Saro—

With a rustle of paper, the letter jerked upward, out of Tony's hands.

Saro was standing in front of him, clutching the page.

Tony blushed. "I'm so sorry, Saro."

If Saro was upset, he did not let it show. He simply refolded the letter and
tucked it into his coat pocket. He didn't even look perturbed. In fact, Tony
thought, Saro carried himself with an air of vindication, like he'd bet himself Tony
would read that letter and won. "Sorry," Tony said again.

Saro had already wandered away, as if obeying a voice calling him from the
depths of the house.

Unable to ignore this development, Tony risked asking Waldemar about Saro's
abilities. "Does Saro know anything about computer programming? About
Artificial Lifeforms?"

"Saro knows much about many things." Waldemar stretched and yawned. "*Hosenscheisser*, find my chess board. I will beat you once more before I nap."

Tony persisted, "But does he know about computer programming?"

Waldemar exclaimed, "What is big deal? Is language like Latin! Like Greek! Should I give Saro raises because he knows Assyrian and D++ languages?"

"It's called C++. So, who is Dr. Daas? He lives in Boston. I think he works at—"

"How should I know? I am phone directory now?" The old man plunged his finger deep into his nostril, so far that the side of his nose stretched to reveal a host of filthy pores. "No! I care only Saro drives to Campinas for cheese cans and potato crispies."

"But he's your servant?"

"Who?"

"Saro."

"Who says this?"

"Oh. I—"

Waldemar inspected a booger at the end of his finger. "*Urenkel* is nosy."

Tony muttered, "Maybe I'll go to Boston myself. I could study computer science. I could study Artificial Lifeforms."

Waldemar wheezed. "Tropical Brazil boy wants gloomy New England, does he? Doesn't know he has good life here? Warm climate! Sun!" He sighed. "I remember Wewelsburg in winter of 19 and 43. Stone castle. No heat. Frozen raisin testicles." He blew his nose into a green-tinged handkerchief. "Boston, he says! Good luck, stupid. I mail you snow shovel and ice scraper."

Tony backed off with disdain. Waldemar's bag of tricks seemed limited to name-calling and insults. Tony had lived under an oppressive regime before, inside Ignácio's world of perfect pant pleats and no t-shirts. Any intellectual freedom Tony had won by living here had been traded for a constant barrage of sarcasm and taunts. At least Saro did not speak.

Despite Tony feeling as if he'd been caught invading his privacy by reading his letter, Saro continued the book deliveries. Next, he provided an old handwritten journal, something written in the 1930s by an Irish woman named Ailish Finnegan—another Providence Prophet, the most recent one confirmed. The pages were warped from water stains. Some of the text was written in a dialect Tony did not understand, but some was in English.

From March 1937, Tony read:

HE HAS RETURNED TO US. *He brought Mary a gift, a jeweled box. She does not yet understand the magnitude of a gift from him. She does not even know of his true role in her life—*

Before he could read further, Waldemar approached Tony with speed, cane and rings rattling. "Where you get this one?" The old man peered at the journal cover, squinting hard at the title.

"Saro. Where else?"

When Waldemar read the title, he jolted and stared hard at Tony. His face reflected a depthless frigidity. "You are reading *this*?"

"I'm sorr—"

Waldemar grabbed the journal and smacked him with it. "Great-grandbaby does not apologize." Without taking his eyes off the boy, he shouted, "Saro!" To Tony he said, "Here is end to summer-beach-reading-book-fun club." He tucked the journal under his bony arm. "Bye-bye, books. Little orphan Antonio sticks to god-*spiel*."

"What? I can't read any more books Saro brings?"

Waldemar taunted, "Is not for you, Brazil-boy!"

"Why are you punishing me? I didn't choose these titles! I did nothing wrong!"

"Then why you apologize? Grandbaby never apologizes!" Waldemar's voice echoed in dining room. "Saro! Put this back into my stuffs where it belongs!"

"No!" Tony stood. "You want me to grow balls, you say! Then you do *this* to me? Treat me like a *child*?"

Waldemar approached him so closely Tony thought he would puff his chest to push him backward. "You are sheltered infant. You are not ready."

"I am *sheltered*? What am I to do about that, but work to change that? And how will I change that if you won't let me?"

"You know nothing but what your grandmother and grandfather tell you. Never think for yourself. How will you start now?"

"I *will* start. I *will* do this. You do not understand. You have not lived in such a family. You came from a poor farm in Bavaria. Your parents thought everything you did in school was to better the family—"

"It was!"

"What about me? I cannot have the same you received? I cannot have trust from you to follow my curiosity?"

"Your mind is mush!" Waldemar fanned the journal at Tony. "These things will break such a mind!"

"You don't understand! To have answers handed to you, all the rules and all the limitations coming from Ignácio and no one else!" He changed tactics, growling and pointing, "*Your* daughter was weak! Oma *never* resisted him. Was that because of you? Did you teach her that? Did you cut her off like you are doing with me? Did you call her names and reduce her to a sniveling servant?"

Waldemar's spit collected on his lips. "Now, *you* do not know of what you speak."

"I speak of a woman who had been told—by *someone*—that the only value she had in life was breeding children for a Brazilian gay man—breeding like a Bavarian cow."

Waldemar raised a hand to strike him, but Tony stood his ground.

They remained like that, frozen in a diorama of aggression, neither moving.

Tony said, "You are obscene. And I hate you."

Waldemar laughed low in his throat. "Go to your room, infant."

Tony said, "I hate it here."

Waldemar kept laughing, growing louder. Tony, unnerved, backed away.

"Mmm," Waldemar noted the retreat, tipping forward on his toes. "You lose your nerve. Still not ready."

Tony turned away. "You sick fuck."

"Bye-bye, baby. To your room you go."

Tony strolled to his room, careful not to let Waldemar see his red face. Tony's hands were shaking, not from withdrawal but from fury.

Before he slammed the door to his room, he took measure of the dark end of the hallway leading to the east wing: to the door to Waldemar's prohibited study.

The old man would not let him back into the world he opened up for him? Very well.

Tony would not wait for authority to be given to him ever again.

13

Room

THERE WERE MANY SPARE keys in random drawers and cubbies throughout the house, so Tony tested each one until he found a match. Then, he simply waited for Saro and Waldemar to turn in for the night.

The door to the study did not creak at all.

Tony fumbled around the room until he found a lamp. It cast a diluted glow. Dust motes hung in the air. Tables and artifacts packed the room. Shelves lined the walls from ceiling to floor with books like Saro had brought to him—all of them old, crumbling, rotting. Book spines displayed every recognizable language, some only pictographic symbols. Tops of shelves were cluttered with rolls of parchment tied with decayed leather cords.

Tony tiptoed back to the door and checked the hallway.

Dark. Quiet. All sleeping.

He recentered himself in the room. Worktables staggered around him, layered in dust. He swiped a finger at the closest table's surface, leaving a clean line behind.

He touched cold jars, beakers, and vials. Herbs and plants floated inside, suspended in liquids of every color. In the middle of the table, a crystal bowl cradled soft, viscous fluid. Tony dipped a finger in. The fluid stretched and clung like egg whites. Off to the side, two bare copper wires wrapped around a terminal strip, which was connected to a small wooden box with a switch. Tony flipped it. A miniature lightning bolt popped between two wires. After a moment, the viscous fluid in the nearby bowl bubbled and burped. He quickly turned the switch off. *What the ever-loving Dr. Frankenstein is this shit?*

At the second table, onyx stones weighed corners of parchment scrolls. Tony could see they were maps of the world when only one continent existed: Pangea. The seven continents that exist now were outlined onto the ancient one. The Atlantic Ocean shrank to the size of a lake. Inked arrows connected Ireland to England, then to France and Spain. Tony remembered Waldemar's words: *In those times, whatever is walking inside US and A could also be in Ireland by jumping over tiny creek.* Boop! *They are connected!* He read notes about "Light Ones" and "Travellers," names he remembered from stories with the Prophets Reverend Grieves and Ailish Finnegan. *So, that's his life's work? Tracking supernatural beings as told by Providence Prophets?* Tony wanted to know what was so mind-blowing about that.

Elsewhere on the map, illegible script labeled what Tony assumed to be modern places; they were phrases he didn't recognize, some with exclamation marks, others with question marks. Antarctica was heavily labeled around the Sentinel Mountains, now called Ellsworth Mountains. There, Tony found several notes about Henley Goode's 1921 expedition. From the Antarctic mountains, arrows went out all over the map, some terminating in Ireland, others in the eastern US, India, Iran, and others. *Was it possible artifacts like Henley Goode discovered were littered all over the world?*

At the last table, archival boxes were labeled in old world German cursive, *Kurrentschrift* he knew it to be called. Inside one box was a clay pot carved with symbols. A label read, "Mesoamerican." In another box, Tony found a rock fossil of a segmented creature. The creature itself displayed a pattern of pentagons and stars and swirls he had never seen. An attached note read, "Prophetess Zumaa's creature." *Mexico*, Tony remembered. Yes, the artifacts were everywhere.

Waldemar's voice echoed: *We have lifetimes of looking again at our histories. Who did we label as insane, yet is not? What warning signs did we miss? What else is out there?*

Journals towered to the sides of those boxes. Tony took one from the top. It was Ailish Finnegan's 1937 journal. *I want to see how that one turns out.* He slid the journal into his back waistband.

Next to the tower of journals was a manila file folder. Tony read the label: *Sarajevo. 1943. Galina Blažić.* Inside was a photo of Waldemar in an SS uniform. Next to him was Saro in a floral apron and a elegant diamond pendant. Waldemar was exactly the man Tony imagined him to be. Wrinkleless. Sparkling. Convinced of his superior race. Saro hadn't aged a day. *What an odd duck.*

Another photo of a young woman followed. She was pregnant, eyes wide and hair standing on end. A typed caption read, *Galina Blažić.*

Tony closed the folder.

He stepped back to review the tables again. If there was a logic as to how all these things tied together, he couldn't track it.

Then, he turned his attention to a steamer trunk in the corner. It was oddly sized and upholstered in leather with rope handles knotted into the side panels. The upholstery was tacked to the trunk's frame with brass cone-spike nail heads. Some had come unfastened over the years, exposing sharp clasps tinged with rust.

The trunk opened easily, unleashing the aroma of a thousand dusty attics.

Inside was a metal file box. It surprised him. Such a cold appearance inside the leather trunk, and so out of place among these other tactile things!

Adhered to the metal box's enamel lid in yellowing tape, a faded label: *Domhan*. He flicked at its edges. He had no idea what that word meant. He tried to lift the metal box out of the trunk, but it was too heavy. So he unlatched two buckles on the front and tipped the box forward to hinge the lid open inside the leather, outer trunk.

Inside was yet another box. This one, though, seemed to be the object of Waldemar's interest. It was smaller than a bread loaf but flatter. On the face of it, metal plaques were fastened to heavy wood with tiny nails. The metalwork had been carved with hieroglyphics, but not any he recognized. Around the text, four plates displayed carvings of human and fish images set on decorative backgrounds. The lid was inlaid with crystals and gems. Along the front edge, a raised silver figure of a half-man, half-fish offered an outstretched hand.

This is not the work of an artisan, Tony thought. The childlike etchings on the metal and crooked gem placement appeared slapdash. The gems did not even match, and one resembled an eyeball, lending the whole artifact a whiff of evil.

Should I touch it?

He hesitated.

Then, he examined the metal box again. It had to be lined with lead, which might be why he couldn't lift it. *Why lead?*

He spent a moment wondering what to do next.

Fuck it.

He lifted the jeweled box out of the lead one. It came out easily, though it, too, was heavier than it looked. He shook it. Nothing rattled.

He looked to the lead box again. *Is this jeweled box radioactive? Surely not.*

He examined the fish-human engraving on the front. It was a latch.

Again, he hesitated.

Just a peek, he decided.

An echo of his grandmother's voice rattled him: *No.*

He hesitated. But only for another moment. He pushed the fish-human figure latch and opened the box. Hinges on the lid resisted and groaned. Once the box was cracked open, the odor from inside drew Tony in. It was sweet, with a hint of decay. Emerald light gleamed from the interior.

He opened the lid a bit more.

Thick, cotton-like fog hovered in subtle waves. Tony couldn't determine what it might be. Could smoke linger in a box?

He gently blew it, and it dissipated.

A vibrant green moss lined the interior like plush carpet. It wasn't a flat surface inside; it rolled as if the bottom of the box were pushing up little hills. At the center, in a small divot carved into the bottom, sprouted a bioluminescent mushroom. It was fresh, alive, flourishing.

He heard his grandmother's voice: *Antonio, do not put your nose into such strange things!*

Tony whispered to the mushroom, "What are you doing here?"

Its stem was stocky, and its cap swelled with periwinkle dots of all sizes, like stars in a night sky. The gills underneath glowed dark green at the edges. From deep inside, an orange light gave the impression of a gentle, internal fire. Tiny rivulets of water snaked through the moss. Bushy toothpicks poked through the thickest parts of it.

Tony searched Waldemar's worktables for a magnifying glass and brought the desk lamp closer. Upon inspection, Tony discovered these toothpicks were miniature trees. The rivulets were siphoning water from the moss to feed the mushroom at the center.

He didn't have words for this miracle. It was a microcosm. It was a natural landscape. And it existed—no, thrived—in this box.

The fog he blew away had begun to accumulate again, clouding the interior.

Two loud thuds interrupted.

Tony slammed the lid and stuffed the box under his shirt. The crooked jewels were cold on his belly, but the box itself felt hot. Quickly, he latched the empty lead box, then the steamer trunk lid.

More thumping. From the kitchen? *Was someone awake?*

Tony stood, adjusted the waistband with the journal tucked behind, and slid the box around to his back, clicking the lamp off as he went.

He opened the door to the hallway.

It was dark.

At the end of the hall, he could see that the light in the kitchen was on.

He squeezed through the crack and quietly brought the door back into the frame. He managed to fit the right key back into the lock and gently click the bolt closed.

Tony heaved a sigh and turned around.

Saro stood at the end of the hall, facing him.

The backlight of the kitchen shadowed his face, but his teeth were spotlighted in the darkness, bared.

Tony froze, not knowing if he should speak or move.

Saro was still. Tony was not sure if he was smiling or growling.

Finally, Saro wagged one finger, as if admonishing. Incandescent fingernails swayed back and forth. In an uncanny imitation of Waldemar's voice, he clucked, *Tsk tsk. Naughty* Bürschchen. *Naughty-naughty*. It came out as a rush of clattering sounds that nearly knocked him to the ground.

Tony's heart hammered.

Then, Saro ran at him with frightening speed. He covered the ground between him and Tony, it seemed, in a blink. Tony was so shocked that he dropped the box.

Saro moved fluidly to scoop it up before it hit the floor. He made a sound like a purr.

"Sorr—" Tony began.

Saro lifted a finger.

Tony quieted.

Saro pointed to the west wing, toward Tony's bedroom. A word assaulted him: *Leave.* Saro was talking but his lips were not moving.

Tony nodded. He ran.

He slammed his bedroom door, and threw himself onto his bed.

When he got his breathing under control, he pulled the Irish woman's journal from his waistband and slid it under his mattress. "I win this round, old man."

Strange dreams haunted Tony that night.

He roamed a planet of violent volcanic eruptions and shifting plates. Under his feet, feathery white roots stretched into intricate patterns, tunneling into the earth. One of the roots grabbed his ankle and pulled him into a darkness that smothered him. He wrestled the dirt until he sweated with rage and exertion, but the root dragged him further under. Dirt filled his mouth, choking him.

Ahead he noticed a clearing that glowed violently red. There, a monstrous tree, larger than any he'd ever seen, blocked his view. The tree's twisted branches and powerful root system cut into the ground, throwing up mounds of dirt. The monstrosity sprouted from a luminous sphere below.

The feathery roots had both of his ankles now, and he spat dirt. They dragged him closer to the tree. The bark throbbed and swirled. Faces formed, three-dimensional and lifelike.

In the bark! His mother's face! Tony watched in awe. He had only seen her in photographs, never in lifelike movement like this. He never knew that her eyes squinted in the corners, an involuntary reaction to bright light.

Now, his aunts and uncles appeared, just as he remembered them! Here they were charged with life, looking in all directions to take in their various interests with all their personalities coming to the surface. The reticent, the bold, the apathetic. They popped one by one to the surface, as if coming to a window from a world beyond. Some looked behind them, beckoning, before looking at Tony again. *What do they see on their side of the bark? What captures their attention?*

His grandmother appeared! Oma! He had forgotten the way she swung her head from one side to another, gracefully sweeping over her grandson's face. *Look at you,* she seemed to say. *Look at my Little Prince!*

More appeared! The patriarch, Ulisses Cavalcante! The fazenda founder, Pascual da Silva! And who was that in the background? Ignácio?

From all around, a high-pitched squeal. No, a *shriek*. A sky-splitting noise deafened him.

The roots withdrew. The Tree of Faces shriveled.

Above Tony, a thunderous crack. A noise. A wail.

The earth overhead tunneled in separate directions, revealing an angry sky of blood red. The sky had cracked in two. Beyond the fissure, he could see nebulae, stars, black holes swirling.

And then, a shadowy mass of creatures with wings and tentacles clouded the fissure. They lumbered beyond the crack in the sky, pacing like caged beasts about to break free.

They spoke to Tony in deafening syllables. They spoke a language he didn't know.

Ahaimgr'luhh nnnkadishtuor. Mgahnnn nglui.

14

Rend

Tony woke in the dark in a tangle of twisted bed sheets. He groaned, flexing his fingers. His muscles fired with electric pulses. An inflammation inside triggered a muscle strain. He felt an urge to write that he could not explain.

He sat up.

Saro was seated in a wooden chair by his bed. Waiting.

Tony wiped sweat from his face with his hand. "Uh. Hello. I just—" He reached for a notebook and pencil he kept on his bedside table. There, he had written questions from his research, coding ideas, notes for further investigation after the Collapse, and Oliver Daas's address in Boston. He said to Saro, "Excuse me." He groaned again. "There's something I have to write—"

Saro batted the notebook and pencil away, launching them into the wall. They landed on the floor, and he kicked them aside.

"What the hell, Saro?"

He calmly offered Tony a glass of water.

"No, thank you. I just need—" Tony reached for a pen on his nightstand. Saro slapped his hand. Hard. "Ow! What the *fuck?*"

"Hit him again."

It was Waldemar. He was at Tony's door. The hallway light lit him from behind. His voice was groggy, but firm. "Hit him, Saro."

Saro rose, necklaces swooshing. He raised an arm high and backhanded Tony so hard that he bounced against the wall edging his bed. "For fuck's sake!"

"Acceptable volume, *Bürschchen*, but next time push sound from diaphragm." To Saro he said, "Again."

Tony shielded himself. "No! What's happening?"

Saro punched him with a right hook. Blood sprayed on a lamp shade.

Tony buried his head in his pillow. He screamed, "What's wrong with you two?"

Tony heard Waldemar maneuver into his room. The rings on his fingers clacked against the metal walker. *Clack clack clack.* "Not bad, getting better, boy. *Eine* voice worthy of Nordic blood."

Tony lifted his head, eyes flooding and nose bleeding. He swiped his finger in the blood and wrote on the wall: *Ahaim*—

"Stop him, Saro."

Saro made a fist and punched Tony's fingers. Tony howled. Saro smeared the blood letters on the wall until they were unreadable.

Tony kicked at Saro, then lunged out of bed. Saro caught him by the neck and tossed him backward.

Waldemar said, "Is for your own good, grandson. We said not to touch stuffs. Very dangerous for you. *Very* dangerous. Now, you must sleep it off like drunk Russian. Disgrace."

Tony gagged on snot. "I'm sorr—"

"*Ach.* What did I say about apologies?"

Waldemar himself landed the next blow.

That one did it.

Tony plummeted into a dreamless void.

He woke at sunset, in the hottest part of the day. He was thirsty. *Water.*

Saro had left a glass of water and a pitcher on his bedside table.

The impulse to write had died, but everything in the room he might write with—pencils, pens, notebooks—had been cleared out.

"Ah, grandson is awake," Waldemar said from the shadows.

Tony cleared his throat. "Are you going to hit me again?"

"Maybe," the old man said. He tapped the water glass with his cane. "Drink."

Tony drank one glass, refilled it, then drank another. "Why did you stop me from writing?"

"I will not be answering to thieves. When you are finished with water, you follow me." *Clack clack clack.* Waldemar worked his way out of Tony's room.

Tony drank more water, then felt his face. It was cold. An ice pack slid away from his pillow and fell to the sheets. He pulled tissue out of his nose. When he got out of bed, every muscle hurt.

Clack clack clack.

Tony followed the sound out an open side door.

Outside, crickets whirred in the gloom. Humidity restricted Tony's breathing. Still, Waldemar waddled ahead, down the hill toward the pond, on the red overgrown path beyond, to the one-room chapel with the blue trim.

Clack clack clack. "Almost there, boy."

The Koltz granite mausoleum skulked in the last light of the day. The gate lay open. Tony went inside, into the dark.

Waldemar sat waiting in the vestibule on a bench, his liver-spotted hands resting on his cane. Along the walls, granite chambers with handles locked away the remains of his aunts and uncles. Etchings denoted their names and the dates they walked on Earth. Tony remembered his chants. *Rainer, heroin. Sebastián, venomous bite. Manuela, botched abortion. Britta, drowned. Stefan, suicide. Bettina, tropical disease. Georg, boat accident. Silvia, strangled with a necktie. Paloma, disappeared. Lotte, butchered on her own patio.*

His mother's crypt drawer, he knew, was empty. Lotte's—her death date still a blank—would remain empty as well.

Tony felt a pull, like his chemistry nagging him for another drug dose. He wanted the box. *Back to the box. Back to the tree...*

"Come," Waldemar called, slapping the cold bench. "Sit."

Tony considered the drawers, full of bodies of his relatives, and wondered what his own name would look like engraved among them. *Pascual Antonio Aurea Leoncio Cavalcante.* Who gave that name to him? Was it his mother, or did Ignácio strong-arm his footprint onto his male heir? Tony never knew. He asked, "Do you think my mother would have hated me? Hated what I have become?"

"Eh. Is so long ago. She changes her mind since death."

Tony grunted. "She is alive in that box," he said. "They all are. I saw Ignácio is in there. He's dead. Just as you said."

Waldemar said nothing, just tilted his palm upward.

Tony rose. "I don't like it in here."

Waldemar pulled him back to the bench. "Sit. Here is family, grandson." The rings felt heavy and dug into his arm. "Here is where we make do with memories until we return to Tree of Faces."

"I don't *have* memories of these people," Tony said. "I never knew these people."

Waldemar tilted his head. "But in the box, you know them?"

"Isn't that why you have the box? To visit them?"

Waldemar clacked his rings impatiently.

"Why else would you have it?" Tony asked. "If you let *me* have it—"

"No, I will not do that." Waldemar wet his dry lips with his chalky tongue. "When I was scrappy *Bürschchen* like yourself but more handsome, I live in Passau." He hummed to himself, and Tony thought he lost Waldemar to a song, but then he returned. "Proud German family! Many generations! Live in Germany! Die in Germany! Many generations—" The old man mimed a shovel and dirt. "—return to earth." Waldemar slashed his hand at the engraved receptacles before him. "All returned to earth!"

"I *know*," Tony whined.

"You know nothing." Waldemar blew his nose noisily into his handkerchief. "There is reason we do not see our dead. Our minds too small." He drew a finger in a circle at his temple. "We go *woo-hoo*!"

"What are you talking about?" Tony asked.

"Loneliness, boy. To be alive is lonely."

Tony blinked.

The old man lowered his voice. "I know what you do."

Tony growled, "You know nothing."

"Hush, stupid. Of course, I know lonely. You think living decades with mute man so fun? And I know about box! And what I say is *you must forget box.*"

"I can't."

"Try harder," Waldemar said.

Since the beatings and the second round of sleep, Tony could feel the box's effects wearing off. Still, the vestiges remained. It was like the dregs of a drug lingering in his system, some kind of yearning too strong to put into words. He wanted the tree. The family. The real faces of his aunts and uncles and mother and grandmother and even his grandfather, alive and writhing in the tree. He wanted the box.

Waldemar sniffed. "Is many inside box. Many strong faces, alive and well. Many happy times." He stabbed Tony with a finger. "But there are more things in box than happy times. Darker things. Things stronger than us."

Tony thought of the monsters lurking in the fissure in the sky. "I saw them. The creatures."

Waldemar nodded without looking at him.

Tony contemplated his vision of those creatures, how he felt the need to draw them, to write the discordant phrases they uttered with their sludge-like tongues. "What was I writing?"

"They are talking in that box. You are writing what they say."

"What do they want?"

Waldemar rumbled, "What they want they must not have. *This* I have learned."

"Why were they talking to me?"

Waldemar shrugged.

"Did they ever speak to you—"

"*I* talk now." The old man pointed his cane at Paloma's empty chamber. "You see why we have paintings and photos and crypts like these? What lies in wait for us too powerful to know now." Waldemar coughed into his handkerchief. The cough went on much longer than normal, so long that Tony looked around for Saro to come with water. Soon, Waldemar recovered himself. "What I was saying?"

"You were being a fascist about keeping the box to yourself."

Waldemar smacked the back of the boy's head. "Too free with speech is trouble." The old man returned his gaze to Paloma's crypt. "I tell you, your grandmother Lotte drowned in grief when Paloma disappeared." He lowered his voice. "Is one thing to know of deaths of children, as Lotte did with others." Waldemar narrowed his eyes at the line of dead grandchildren. "Quite another to look and look and look and find nothing."

"Did you show her the box?" Tony asked. "Oma could have seen her daughter there. You could have eased her grief."

Waldemar patted his shoulder. His rings clicked together. "I show no one the box who I love."

Waldemar rose, dragging his walker. Tony shuddered. The old man was slowing down.

With that thought, Tony panicked. Where would he go after the old man died? Back to São Paulo? Was it even safe?

"Oh, grandson," the old man sighed. "You make sad-boy face again." Waldemar picked at a thread of old tape wrapped around a ring on his index finger. "We have such small minds, boy. Where we go after we die, we go without our minds. It is merciful. There, we will understand all. Until then, we must wait."

15

Rift

By the time the rotten sugarcane had shed its aroma of death and the stalks wilted in the last of the summer heat, Waldemar had stopped moving around the casa grande. Saro attended him in his room in the east wing, which was furnished only with a small bed, a table, a threadbare rug, and the gramophone, still blaring Wagner's fabled operas.

Tony visited Waldemar there only once. The room was cloaked in aromas of pungent urine and stale bread. Tony talked, but Waldemar just slept. Tony did not return.

Meanwhile, Tony had completed what he called *God Game—Der GottSpiel*—a video-game scenario of the Sleeping One unleashing itself on humanity. Will the monster be benevolent or evil? The player could decide and let the storyline play out. Tony thought the game was crap, but Waldemar, as a matter of routine, loved to destroy New York City after their evening meal, when he still ate. "Ha!" the old man had barked, punching the keyboard. "Empire State goes bye-bye! Gaudy tower wrapped in tentacles! Big fun!" It was Waldemar's idea to add tourists tumbling from the heights of the tower as the Sleeping One smashed its way downtown, but Tony declined. It reminded him of the sailing bodies from the banking towers in São Paulo. A sting of worry for Ignácio always pricked at that point in the game, but that, in time, faded. Tony knew where his grandfather was. "Still sentimental. Is puny," Waldemar complained when he caught Tony's pale look at the falling bodies. But Tony detected love in it.

One time, Waldemar paused the game and pecked at the monitor. "Why is space empty here?" he asked.

"Where?" Tony leaned in to inspect the game. Near the edge of the screen, a crack had developed in the game's landscape. Tony turned the monitor off and on, but the crack was in the programming, not the monitor.

The fissure in the sky. Tony bent close to it. *How did it get here?*

Waldemar pointed at the jagged empty space again. "Is mistake in game, grandson. Look like something tear New York very big asscrack."

"I don't know what it is," Tony said. "I'll have to check the code." He tapped the screen as well. "Odd."

A flash. Lightning crack. Sr. Rocha. Creatures coming through.

Tony shook the images away.

Waldemar moaned, "Better not be trick for more monsters to come through there. I almost win."

"Odd," Tony repeated. He looked around for paper to note the mistake but saw Saro had still not returned any paper or writing utensils. Now, he noticed Saro leaning into the monitor to inspect the crack as well. "Want to take a shot at a solution, Saro?" Tony asked. "Perhaps you can fix it?"

Saro frowned at the monitor, glared at Tony, then padded away.

"What did I do?" Tony asked.

Waldemar stabbed at the keyboard. "Who knows. Is crabby man baby."

As the days wore on and Waldemar declined in speed and snark, Tony became introspective. There was a palpable sense that an era was coming to an end at the plantation. Tony did not know for certain what would be waiting for him in the city, or if he'd carry on with Saro in the big house until he could figure out another option. Tony would be 18 years old next year: time to consider college. He thought he might write to Dr. Daas—if he was still teaching during the Collapse. So much uncertainty. But what Tony did know was that Waldemar would be leaving them soon. Perhaps his "stuffs" in the forbidden room would become Tony's.

As if in response to his yearnings, his family visited him one last time in his dreams that night.

Oma Lotte's face flitted under the bark of the Tree of Faces, as if shimmering to life. Tony's mother noticed him and called others over. *Oh*, she seemed to say. *You. Yes, you.*

Yes, me.

Another face came to them from behind the bark. Not yet formed. On its way.

They all turned to it, fascinated.

Then, they disappeared.

16

Return

Bright light baked his face. Morning.

When Tony threw back his covers, he discovered the curtains in his room were open. In fact, every curtain in the big house was open. The dynamic energy that had been humming in the house had plummeted. The windows in his room let in the late summer light. *Soon it will be autumn.*

Tony threw his feet over the edge of his bed. Someone had come in his room when he wasn't awake. "Saro?" he called. Tony resituated himself in his bed and felt under his mattress. The Irish woman's journal was still there. He hadn't dared remove it since he stole it.

Tony stumbled into the hallway. The dream of his family had drained his energy. He was disoriented to find that the shadowy house he had been exploring all summer now appeared dull in the light of day. Its dark corners had been illuminated; its cobwebs exposed. He had never seen the place so bright. It was filthy, he admitted. Dishes piled up, crusty with food. Trash towering in the kitchen.

A sharp, antiseptic smell had replaced the cloud of old-man urine in the east wing.

"Saro?" Tony called.

The door of Waldemar's room was wide open. The old man lay in his bed with a sheet pulled over his face. The sheet did not move.

Tony clamped his jaw. He backed away from the door.

Across the hall, Saro's bedroom door was also open. The space beyond was as bright as the rest of the house. It had been stripped down. His clothes were missing. His jewels that had dangled from nails near a dresser mirror were gone. His sheets and blankets were folded neatly at the foot of the bed.

In Waldemar's study at the end of the hall, Tony heard voices.

The door was open. Sunlight flooded the room and spilled onto the rough floorboards. The drapes had been removed from the windows. Heaps of dusty, thick fabric were now neatly folded on the floor. The worktables were clean and bare. The beakers and glass jars and maps and books were all gone. Sealed boxes littered the area. A tall white man with a clipboard checked items from a list.

Another pointed to books in a far corner and ordered them packed. Yet another ran into Tony as he exited the room with a box in his arms. "Well, hello." The men all dressed as if they were foreigners trying to dress like Brazilians: tan suits with pastel and pinstripe shirts, tan fedora hats with dark bands.

"What's going on here?" Tony boomed. He spoke from the gut. He approached with volume.

He noticed the steamer trunk was wide open. The lead box inside had been removed.

The door behind him moved and Tony pivoted.

From behind the door, a nun dressed in a habit and tunic stepped forward. Tony let out an involuntary, "Ah!"

The nun gave Tony a cursory glance, then turned her attention to the men packing the boxes. "Gentlemen," she said to them, "clear the room."

The men nodded and exited swiftly, carrying their items. As they left, the nun examined Tony as if looking for something specific, bobbing her head this way and that.

She folded her arms. "You look like shite. Rough night?"

"I've seen you before."

"Have you?"

"At the beginning of summer. In a car."

"A car. Aye. It's how I get from place to place."

"Who are you, and what are you doing here?" It came out with a little less volume than he intended.

The nun only scowled. She was squat in stature with a broad nose and dark eyes. A navy tunic met the starched white wimple, revealing only a few strands of her wiry, white hair. After a minute, she smiled blandly and said, "Sorry to alarm you, pet."

The nun, Tony thought, did not look sorry.

"We represent the Providence Group," she added.

"The who?" Tony's mind swam. He was buying time.

The nun ignored his question. "Your great-grandfather donated his extensive materials to us in the unfortunate event of his passing." Tony noticed she spoke with a brogue. Perhaps Irish or Scottish. She added, "You have his eyes, by the way."

Who was this? "You got here quick," Tony noted. "I just noticed he was dead, and I *live* here."

"Always so unobservant?"

Tony wanted to answer but struggled to think of something equally pithy to say. He settled for repetition: "Who are you?"

The nun flicked away the question. "Saro notified us late last night of Herr Doktor Koltz's passing. We drove in immediately. We have been staying close, warned as we were of his impending passing."

Tony noticed she spoke his great-grandfather's name with a perfect German accent. "You know Saro?" he asked.

The nun pursed her lips. "As well as anyone can know that one."

"Saro knew he was dying?"

"Didn't you?"

Tony scanned the room. The drapes and a pile of old newspapers for packing were all that were left of Waldemar's cramped study. A newspaper headline read, *Santiago man claims he's Manny di Martini. DNA tests ordered.* Was that the sum of Waldemar Koltz's life?

Through the grimy windows, Tony saw one of the men load the lead box from Waldemar's trunk onto a moving truck parked in front of the abandoned sugarcane carts. *The box*, Tony thought. He broke out into a sweat.

The empty steamer trunk never looked so ominous.

"Interested in that trunk, I see," the nun remarked.

"No."

"I certainly was," the nun said. "Inside was a lead box, and inside of that was yet another box. A virtual Matryoshka set! The inner two boxes are in the moving van now, as you saw, but since you appear so interested, I must ask: have you ever seen the *inner* box for yourself? Gems glued to the front; little fish-man engraved on the front?"

Tony glanced at the empty trunk. The nun noticed. Tony said, "I don't know what—"

The nun raised a hand to stop him. "Young man. Let's not start the day with a lie to a wife of Jesus. I've worked around children since you were naught but a gleam in your communist pappy's eye, so I can tell when a child's lying. You've opened that inner box, haven't you? And you know what's inside."

Tony looked to the four corners of the room.

"You have." The nun exhaled in a wild huff. "Isn't this a slop of wild cabbage?"

"A what?"

"A fiasco."

Tony cleared his throat. "I'm Waldemar Koltz's great-grandson. The materials you're taking ought to pass to me."

"I'm afraid not," the nun said quickly. "The materials, as you call them, have been under contract for quite some time."

"They're mine," Tony insisted.

The nun considered him. "It's your birthright you're concerned about, is it? A sugarcane plantation isn't quite your idea of a keepsake?"

Tony swallowed. *Birthright.* That was the word he clung to inside his head. *Mine.*

"Spit it out, young man," the nun said.

"I want the box."

"Well," the nun sighed. "Who wouldn't? I'm going to guess you've had yourself a peek inside, too. You'll regret that, cherub. Nasty dreams, hallucinations. It ends in death. I'm guessing that wily Nazi shite convinced you to give it over, or you'd still be clamoring over it in a puddle of your own piss."

"It wasn't him," Tony grumbled.

"Oh!" The nun looked pleased. "You were relieved of your possession by Saro himself, were you? Why am I not surprised?" She settled into a blank stare, then added, "Please do become acquainted with the modern sorcery called 'deodorant.' You've been living among men for too long, so it ought to be impressed upon you that you smell like a beast."

Tony asked, "How can a box with a mushroom inside kill you?"

"So, you have opened it."

Tony stepped toward the door, the moving truck on his mind.

"If you're thinking right now that you can outrun an old nun dressed in a habit, do not bet against me."

Tony swallowed hard. "I want—"

The nun said in a soft voice, "It ends in *death*, child. I've *seen* it. Open that box again, and you'll be dead in under a week. It's a life force, to be sure, but it will drain the life right out of you."

Tony stared; his jaw practically unhinged.

"Close your mouth," the nun said.

He did.

The nun let out a fierce whistle between her teeth. Two men on the lawn startled, then ran inside. Then, one of them offered the nun a large satchel.

"Now," the nun said. "Business." She turned to Tony. "Your great-grandfather set this amount aside for your transition period."

"Transition?"

"Returning to the city. Finding suitable housing. Completing school, I recommend."

"A nice Catholic school?"

"You're a wee cheeky, lad. I'm not Catholic."

"Could have fooled me."

"That's the intention."

"You wear a habit but you're not a nun?"

"Used to be," she replied. "I still wear it to get discounts at the automobile rental counter. I have a weakness for luxury automobiles."

She did not smile. Tony could not tell if she was serious or not.

He ventured, "So, you're not married to Jesus?"

She shook the satchel at Tony. "At the moment, we're seeing other people."

Tony accepted the bag, which nearly pulled him to the floor with its heft. He unzipped it. Thousands of euros, dollars, and Brazilian real. "There is a lot of money in here," he said.

"Then, you have been properly remunerated for the collection."

"Like I said," Tony argued, pushing the satchel aside, "I'm a Koltz—"

The nun edged the satchel back to Tony. "The documents for the donation have been signed for some time, as I've said. It's incontestable."

The nun, Tony decided, was quite serious.

"What did you say your name was?" he asked.

"I didn't."

Tony thought of the Irish woman's journal still under his bed. "I see," he said.

The nun scanned him again, as if searching. He did not like it. It was as if she could see his thoughts. She held out her hand. "Give it over."

"Give what?"

"Did you not hear the part where I have lived among children? Filthy liars all of you. The journal. In my hands. On the instant." She made walking legs out of her fingers. "Off you trot."

Tony backed away.

He ran to his room, then reached under his mattress for the journal.

He returned with it, gripping it tightly.

In the study, the nun's hand was still outstretched. Tony placed the journal there.

She eyed it with some sentimentality that faded quickly.

Then, she suddenly clapped her hands. "I will be in touch."

"You will?"

"A place at the university. In São Paulo to start. Then to Oliver Daas. You have a role to play."

"Huh? How—"

"Saro, child. Do try to keep up."

A white man lingering at the door entered to remove the remaining clipboards and boxes. "I want it spotless," she said to him. The man nodded.

Tony backed out of the study. He glanced into Waldemar's bedroom. The old man's frail body hardly raised the sheet off the bed. He had wasted away into a skeleton over the past week. Tony thought he could still hear Waldemar's voice echoing off the tiles. *Stupid boy. You let her steal my stuffs.*

The nun nearly glided to the door. *Floated*, Tony thought, with an up-and-down bobbing motion, as if she were riding on a wheeled platform with a flat tire. Her long tunic dusted what was left of the dirt on the floor.

Tony spun around, looking to the end of the hall. "What about my great-grandfather?"

The nun turned to Tony. She raised an eyebrow.

He said, "He's still in his room."

"He's not included in the donation," the nun said. Tony's jaw dropped again. "I'm joking," she said. "An undertaker will arrive shortly."

"Right." Tony felt naked in the stark light of the day. "This all seems rather sudden."

Tony heard the old man's voice echo, *Is a hard-knock life for pants-shitter.*

The nun stepped forward to search Tony's face. Her eyes darted to his brows, to his lips, to his cheeks. *What was she looking at?* Tony stepped back, uncomfortable.

The nun straightened, as if satisfied. "Aye, a big role," she said, answering a question no one asked.

"What?" Tony asked.

She bobbed out the front door, down the stone ramp, then into the driver's seat of a car idling in the driveway. A Jaguar. Silver. The nun revved the engine, then sped away.

An abandoned farm truck stacked with dead cane waited in the driveway like a sad consolation prize.

Tony deflated. "Well, fuck."

After pacing the empty study, then deciding against a bedside goodbye to Waldemar—*Puny. Sentimental*, the old man would have said—Tony wandered to the front of the house, clutching the satchel of money.

He surveyed the fields.

The sugarcane stalks had dried down to the roots. New cane shoots, bright green and pliable, sprang from the red clay. Roads beyond were visible. A truck rolled by. Then a tractor. Tony heard a crop plane sputtering in the distance.

Time was resetting itself. The world was crawling out of its pit of despair. Slowly.

He would argue to Ignácio, if his grandfather was still alive, that he should stay here. The plantation should come to Tony now. He was the Cavalcante heir. He would run this place. He would rehire the workers. He would harvest the next crop. He would live here—

Tony thought of his relatives in the mausoleum, those who were there. Permanent residence. Cold. Irreversible.

Death. It comes for everyone.

The voice again: *Tough-up, boy. World is cruel. Approach with volume.*

Who was Tony kidding? He was no businessman. He was no Cavalcante. He was no prince.

Words from his favorite book came to him, words about destiny, about what a son is, about the light dimmed by glory—

Tony gripped the money bag. He screamed to the fields: "Fuck it!"

That evening, just before dusk, Tony drove away from Fazenda São Roque in a farm truck stacked with rotten sugarcane.

If his premonition was correct, he had a grandfather in São Paulo to bury in the Cavalcante cemetery. He had a villa to sell, a plantation to lease, a college scholarship to claim.

He drove away from the fazenda with nothing but a satchel full of cash, a suitcase carrying a wad of dirty t-shirts and shorts, his computer, nine heavy rings with questionable markings removed from Waldemar's fingers, and the complete 11-record set of Wagner's Ring Cycle.

Ah, Bürschchen, *you steal my stuffs*, the old man's voice echoed.

"*Saúde*, old man," Tony replied. "It's my inheritance."

Entr'acte II:
The Diaries of Oliver Daas

Genesis

Boston
February to March 1993

February 1, 1993

Pythia Laboratory for Evolutionary Computation

WITHIN THE COLLAPSE, MICRO-MIRACLES abound!

On campus: the trickling in of essential staff, the resumption of payroll, the skeleton staffing of a mailroom. And in that mailroom, after three months of waiting, a response from Brazil! My Strange Visitor had sent a package!

The accompanying letter—unsigned—noted that an enclosed diskette contained a patch for our ArLiF program, one that might address our catastrophic forgetting. He also wrote, "The clock has accelerated. More help is required."

More help? Is he acknowledging that Lucía has been sent by him? What on earth does he mean by an accelerating clock?

After reading that, I intended to ask Lucía if she knew him, but my mouth would not form words. Her expansion of the ArLiF program is already beyond measure, her gifts very difficult to explain to colleagues. If my silence is a form of denial, then so be it. With alien life confirmed on Earth and so many drastic changes since, what of it if I'd prefer the illusion of normalcy? So, I did not tell Lucía about this package. I ran the patch on our mainframe while she slept in my office. She gets so little sleep these days. I could not wake her.

The mainframe rack, where the ArLiF program is housed, is at the end of the hall, away from our lab. I accessed it from a laptop with a disk drive connected to one of the mainframe's ports. After the disk clicked into the slot, it whirred to life.

What happened next was something I am unsure if I will ever understand. A strange purple glow emanated from the laptop's interior. Shimmering green flashes illuminated floating grains streaming from the disk slot. Nearby dust particles gravitated toward the glow before igniting with their own colors. Within moments, the glow faded, and the grains disappeared. The slot sealed itself with a waxy substance that hardened when it cooled. The disk was stuck inside.

Oh no.

I spent half the night disassembling the shell of the laptop to pry it out. Only when I had taken the hardware apart did I discover the disk had dissolved into the motherboard. (Is that the correct word? *Dissolved*? There seems to be no other explanation.) An overwhelming odor of mildew came from the interior. I successfully installed a spare disk reader before Lucía woke to discover the damage.

Here I was, sneaking about like a midnight vandal when I was working on my own project! If anyone would be angry about the damage, it should be the technology staff at the University. Yet, I was desperate not to tell Lucía about my Strange Visitor.

But the disk's effects on the ArLiFs!

At first, nothing appeared different. A night simulation was running. Our population had reached 28 ArLiFs; all were accounted for—no damage. None appeared to have changed. Except one. Claire had begun to twitch in her sleep. Her twitching was subtle, but I immediately feared the worst kind of disaster.

When the simulation had cycled over to morning, the other ArLiFs began their routines with the usual glitches, the catastrophic forgetting. "Oh no...Oh no." One forgot what a toothbrush was and stared at it for minutes, water gushing from a faucet. Another put his pants on backwards and fell over. Yet another ran water too hot and burned himself. I waited for the mysterious patch to take effect for all the ArLiFs, but nothing changed.

Then, a miracle happened. Claire jumped out of bed, completed her morning routine without an issue, then visited each of the others in their homes. She *knew* they were stuck. She spoke to each ArLiF about their confusion, gently reminding each of them of how to execute their tasks. "This is a toothbrush." "Pants are worn with the zipper in front." "Do not expose yourself to a water temperature over 98 degrees." The forgetful tooth-brusher began to brush. The pants-wearer corrected his error. The face-washer found an amenable water temperature. Groundbreaking new behavior, yes. But would the ArLiFs remember their tasks the next day?

To test that, I fast-tracked them all to another night simulation. Again, all the ArLiFs slept. Again, Claire twitched periodically. The next morning, catastrophic forgetting began anew. I held my breath. One ArLiF forgot to eat breakfast and departed her home with a low health reading. Claire popped out of bed, directed herself to that ArLiF's location, then sent her back home for breakfast. However, the ArLiFs from the previous day who had made mistakes all remembered their tasks. No issues in toothbrushing. Pants worn correctly. No scalds.

Lucía had appeared over my shoulder, eyes roving over all the ArLiFs. I did not know she had awakened. "We are not supposed to run the simulations outside of real time," she reminded me.

"I know, but—"

"It messes with our co-evolutionary capabilities, you said. You can't just speed through on double-time until the singularity occurs, you told me. We have to evolve *with* the ArLiFs, side by side—"

"I know, but I think we have a fix for catastrophic forgetting."

She eyed me. "Run it forward."

I forwarded the ArLiFs through their day, then placed them in another night simulation. Another night of Claire twitching. Lucía looked closely at the twitching but said nothing.

The next simulated morning, three ArLiFs went into "Oh no" meltdowns for three different reasons. I held my breath. Again, Claire directed herself to them, explaining their situations, then they all went forward with the next command unhindered.

"They are not the same errors as yesterday," I said.

Lucía pushed me aside and ran another night simulation. Again, she carefully observed Claire as she slept. Again, Claire twitched as if experiencing gentle spasms. We checked the systems monitor to track her CPU usage, but Claire did not drain any resources. Whatever was happening was self-powering.

Lucía was taking notes, frowning deeply. "What have you done?"

"Why the accusatory tone?"

She threw her clipboard down. It clattered, startling me. "Claire is maintaining the others without us. How did you do it?"

"Not everything I do must be run by you." Lucía reared back as if I had slapped her. I felt awful. "All right. I had help. A friend. From Brazil. Sent a patch—"

She twisted her face, obviously not believing what she was hearing. "What kind of friend?"

I did not mean to say that much, and the slope would be slippery now. "I met him at the Artificial Life conference years ago. The conference I told you about."

"The one where you saw the nun in the audience?"

I brightened. "That's the one!"

She nearly ran me over to get to the mainframe. "Did you upload the patch directly into the mainframe? Where is the laptop you used? Show me the diskette."

I hesitated. "It's gone."

"The laptop is gone?"

"The diskette. It... hmm...dissolved into the motherboard."

Lucía was still looking around the lab, flapping her hands like they were on fire. "Show me!"

Like a chastised child, I produced the laptop, which I was ashamed to say I had hidden. Lucía produced her toolkit and had the laptop taken apart inside a minute, the replacement disk drive detached, and the old one before her on a lighted table. She grunted when attempting to pry the drive apart. "What the fuck, Daas? It's *melted*."

"I told you."

"How did it overheat?"

"I don't know."

Lucía jimmied and whacked the dead disk drive for far longer than I did, but she could not breach the fused metal. "Shit! Shit!" The Spanish expletives flowed freely.

"Why are you so upset?" I asked. "Is it with me? The ends should justify the means here. I asked for a solution to catastrophic forgetting, and my friend delivered it. It seems so, anyway. What does it matter that we lost the disk drive—"

She was in my face, her eyes wild. "Don't you see? There's someone else like me out there." She waggled a screwdriver at me. "What's his name?"

"I don't know it."

"You don't know his name?"

I shrugged. "He's very much a need-to-know kind of fellow—"

"Address, then."

I held out two hands to her. "I have it. We will write to him. We will find out more. If it means that much to you."

She hung her head. "It does." It sounded like a defeat. And in my gut, I felt a pang. Was it empathy? Or was it envy?

She backed away, tossing her tools back into the case. "I don't know how he did it, but he programmed a dreamer."

"A dreamer?"

"Claire," Lucía explained, "is dreaming." She led me back to the monitors and pointed. "Perhaps the twitching is only a cute programmed graphic action, but if you look at the CPU usage and activity monitor you can see how she's executing a consolidation of daily data. She's asleep, but her individual usage is running higher than her daytime levels while everyone else is near zero. It's just her. And she's running some kind of organizing program. And you can see on these graphs that data is going out to others—"

"You said she was dreaming, though?"

She reviewed her notes. "It's just a human term to name what she's doing. It looks like she's now functioning as a directory. She's consolidating data learned during the day, then organizing it for access by the others. Just like our brains do when we dream, but more collectively."

"And other ArLiFs are benefitting?"

"Yep."

"Is she organizing the hive mind we've been working toward?"

Lucía pulled at her lips, which she did when she was flummoxed. "Hmph."

Now, I leaned in to watch Claire's twitching. Observing that self-processing flicker under the cover of her eyelids, I was *moved*. Graphic polygons vibrated against her closed eyes. What was happening with her right now? Was Claire experiencing independent thoughts and visions completely outside our monitoring capability?

A spark of fear. I had felt that before, the terror of a toddler taking off into the world, far beyond my control, thoughts and dreams unknown. But what joy! Whatever my original idea had been, what had begun as code on a monitor, had evolved to *this*! I felt as though I were witnessing a newborn take her first breath!

"Where did you say the address was?" she asked. "I want to write to him *today*."

"I will get it," I said, not moving. "In the meantime—"

"Tear apart the code in the neural network?" she asked.

"Yes," I said. "Find out what changed. And if there's any way in hell we can explain ourselves to our colleagues."

She rolled over to another keyboard and began typing. "Gladly."

February 2, 1993

Pythia Lab

CALLED NESSA AT THE Foundation's offices in Boston. She asked why I called. I said a quarterly report was due. She said to send it to the address using the form provided.

I said maybe we could have lunch.

There was a long pause that would have been answer enough, but she added, "Dad. Whatever is going on with you, I am glad for it. But it's too late for us."

I don't know what I said, but it was some version of, "That's fine."

"Let's keep it professional," she said. "I'll transfer you to my assistant if you require our address—"

"You have an assistant?"

She said she had to get back to work.

And that was the end of that.

Our report isn't due for another 45 days.

March 4, 1993

Pythia Lab

OUR LETTER TO BRAZIL was returned with no forwarding address.

Lucía said it was no big deal, but I could tell it was. She sunk into her work and didn't look up for days.

As for myself, I hope we will not require his services again.

What did Lucía mean by "Someone like me?" Someone as talented?

Someone as unexplainable?

In our quarterly report to Howard Winfield's foundation—addressed to my own daughter—I devoted a great deal of space to our most recent breakthrough in self-organizing the neural brain, spurred by Claire's "dreaming." Since the neural network is the foundation of our humanitarian-aid design, we will proceed with prototypes for non-governmental organizations to test on geo-mapping for disaster response.

Nessa didn't even merit that report worthy of a reply. She simply sent another check. Lucía already had come up with ten ways to spend the money. Who knows if Howard even saw the report.

A first: we had to *delete* an ArLiF.

Bob.

Poor Bob refused to connect to the neural network. Claire was building an intricate system, and his catastrophic forgetting was becoming a hindrance to others. Lucía and I joked that we had to do what was right, what was for the best of the colony, and flush Bob down the proverbial toilet like a sick goldfish. Lucía even created a tombstone for him in a hollow on the southern edge of the island. The tombstone reads: *Here lies Bob. He was a good ArLiF.*

We agreed that deleting ArLiFs would not be a matter of routine. Since it is still early in the creation of Claire's neural network, we had to strike sooner rather than later. In as little as a few months, any drastic changes like a deletion might damage the neural network. We would not be able to untangle what role any given ArLiF was playing in the hive-mind scheme Claire was dreaming. Lucía said, "You know, they're like bees. What they build here is complex. What they communicate

is beyond us. Maybe they think about time. Maybe they think about eternity.
Maybe they think about God."

While she seems to have recovered from her disappointment at not finding out
more about the Strange Visitor, she's back to saying bizarre stuff like that.

BOSTON SCIENTISTS REPLICATE HUMAN BEHAVIOR FOR DISASTER RESPONSE

Feb 28, 1993

*BOSTON—Artificial Life has been a subject of intense debate for over a decade.
What is life? And how can it be replicated? Boston-area computer scientist Dr.
Oliver Daas and graduate student Lucia Santamaría, principal investigators
at Pythia Laboratory for Evolutionary Computation, have been working during
the Collapse to interpret those answers for the betterment of humanity.*

*With support from the Griff Tran Memorial Foundation, Daas and Santamaría
will develop an artificial neural network, or brain, to create over a dozen new
computer applications related to disaster response and recovery.*

*The first application will use satellite data to generate geo-maps, or localized
information, to better direct responding agencies to developing disasters. Daas
explained, "There are still pockets of the globe without a stable food and water
supply following the Collapse. There are also a lot of displaced folks driven from
their homes by violent crime. We want to provide a clear picture of our planet, of
where help is needed, and how we can direct physical resources to them with the
greatest efficiency."*

*Further applications for bolstering power and water-treatment-plant security,
disease detection in wastewater, and medical-supply-line recovery will be coming
in the following months.*

*"These applications will advance our understanding of how we can respond to
each other in our darkest times," Howard Winfield, Tran Foundation Board of
Trustees President said. "It has been the pleasure of our Foundation to support
Pythia's cutting-edge achievements."*

*"This wouldn't be possible without the ArLiFs, or more precisely, the ArLiF named
Claire," Daas added. "This Artificial Lifeform has built a network far faster
than humans could have done. Her creative abilities and the speed with which she
constructs relational databases from external data already surpass our own. She
does all this in her sleep! During the day, she's just a regular islander, a citizen
of a growing landscape we call Keyhole Island."*

*To date, the Tran Foundation has directed over $50 million in grant awards to
agencies responding to Collapse disasters. "We do this in the memory of Griff*

Tran," Winfield said, "who gave his life to bring us the biggest story in human history."

PICTURED: LUCÍA SANTAMARÍA AND "CLAIRE," ONE OF 28 ARTIFICIAL LIFEFORMS, OR ARLIFS, LIVING ON A BUCOLIC ISLAND ON THE MAINFRAME OF PYTHIA LABORATORY. "CLAIRE" BUILT THE NEURAL NETWORK THAT SUPPORTS PYTHIA'S HUMANITARIAN AID APPLICATIONS.

March 16, 1993

Pythia Lab

IT MIGHT HAVE BEEN a mistake to humanize the ArLiFs in that newspaper release because now we have protesters outside who have misunderstood what ArLiFs are. About a dozen angry people are out on the campus lawn holding up signs like, *Free the ArLiFs* and *No digital slavery*. One held a sign criticizing us thusly: *God creates new life, not man*.

What in the name of Alan Turing do they think we're doing in this lab? We are the agents of evolution! Humans evolved to create Artificial Lifeforms and did so using the brains God gave us. (This I would tell them if I shared their view of God as the bestower of evolutionary traits, but my point remains.) Where do these people get their ideas? "God," Lucía laughed.

Another person who is laughing is Howard Winfield. He is capitalizing on the public's attention with yet another human-interest piece on the lab—for television! I am *not* the photogenic representative they seek, so I insisted Lucía do it. To prepare, Nessa has sent a stylist to improve Lucía's appearance. A *stylist*! Who is this daughter of mine? As a baby in Haight-Ashbury, she pooped on Jerry Garcia's lap and ran naked in the streets with Grace Slick. She resisted a hairbrush and insisted her corduroy overalls were a rank below formal wear. I never thought she'd outgrow her roots! Janis Joplin is turning in her grave at this development! I trust Lucía will put up a fight worthy of Janis's memory.

All of this because Howard Winfield wants attention. I insisted that he's not even interested in the ArLiFs. Lucía disagreed. "Didn't you notice the creepy way he stared at Claire? Gross."

Honestly, no. I thought that was how he looked at everything.

Lucía further informed me of the public opinion about ArLiFs over a dish of ravioli straight from the can. "Apparently people think they're digital pets. They'll want them in a video game soon."

"Why?"

She waved a spoon as she spoke. "Maybe it gives people hope. We are creating and preserving when others are destroying. That's Howard's angle, anyway. Nessa says people are quite taken with them. 'Enchanted,' was the word she used."

I grunted. Eyeing the protesters out the window, I said, "It would not be advisable to release information about Claire's dreaming. Or whatever we want to call it."

"Too late. They know."

I white-knuckled the window ledge. "*How* do they know?"

Lucía shrugged. "We are funded by a man who thinks there's no such thing as a bad story. Wouldn't be surprised if he leaked it himself."

I cringed. This is the first time anything that interests me aligns with mainstream America. I can't say I'm unhappy about it, but I'd rather not think about anyone being angry about what we do here. I said, "These signs say we are engaging in digital slavery. What nonsense! The ArLiFs just learned to flush a toilet consistently!"

"Yeah." Lucía wasn't even paying attention to me anymore. She was reading a magazine about plans for floating science labs built over the dive site. "They're gonna kill people with this idea," she said to the pages.

But I was not finished. "Catastrophic forgetting is not even a distant memory, and now they think we are yoking digital beings to our will! Let's not get ahead of ourselves! When we reach the point where ArLiFs engage in philosophical discussions about their existence, then we'll talk!"

Lucía turned the page. "Happy Meals are back."

"To be clear, I have no intention of suppressing any advances the ArLiFs wish to make. Our vision puts no limits on their potential. Perhaps *this* is where Howard's media attention will be useful. We can address public concerns."

Lucía yawned and stretched. "You could call your daughter with that idea. Talk it over."

"No."

"Uh-huh." She still didn't look up from her reading. "They want scientists to *live* out there in the South Pacific in some kind of self-sustaining underwater residence." She tilted her chin to the ceiling and whispered, "*San Miguel Arcángel, defiéndenos en la lucha.*"

I added, "May you live in interesting times."

"Huh?"

"It's a curse," I explained. "Interesting times. Not necessarily good times." A blank look from her. "Another way of saying, Better to be a dog in times of tranquility than a human in times of chaos."

"Yeah, okay. Amen."

March 19, 1993

Pythia Lab

HOWARD IS GOING TO get us all hurt.

There was a break-in at the lab. It happened while we slept in the offices. Thankfully, no one else was in the building.

The person acted alone. Lucía called the police. Thankfully they came quickly.

I refused to press charges, though I can't predict what the administration will do. I will argue for clemency. There was no harm done. But the incident has rattled Lucía. She shrieks obscenities about an assault on her ArLiFs and paces the floors with enough energy to lead a battalion into battle.

Our mischief-maker's name is Dennis Beggan. As far as I can tell from our brief discussion as he lay handcuffed on the floor of our lab, he is a normal guy caught in the moral ambiguity of the Collapse.

He described to me a disillusionment with his church (Protestant), as they have disregarded the discovery of the Sleeping One and all its implications on his religious beliefs. He said he only wanted life's deepest questions answered. Were humans created in God's image? Was this Sleeping One "of God"? Reading some of the press about Claire and the ArLiFs' role in creating a neural network to "save" humans, he called the University to request an appointment. He was denied. So, he took it upon himself to seek his own appointment. At 3:00 am with a crowbar. He told me that he found the ArLiFs "disturbing," just as disturbing as the discovery of the creature. "What gives you the right?" he growled at me.

The police edged a toe into his ribs. "Easy."

Mr. Beggan took a few breaths, stifling some larger emotion. He asked me, "What is this place?" He shifted. His cuffs rattled. "My arm hairs raised when I came in, and they haven't gone down. Something is different here."

I couldn't understand his point. Arm hairs? ArLiFs are disturbing? "What did you see here?"

According to Beggan, he broke in intending to damage the computer mainframe, to "kill the ArLiFs," not knowing we do not house the mainframe where the monitors are. He pried open our door, smashed a few monitors with sleeping ArLiFs (which did not damage the program at all), but stopped when he got to the monitor with Claire. I thought I knew where this was going with his story: he saw her twitching and got unnerved. I asked, "And was she asleep?"

"Not at all." He was still facedown on the floor. I asked the officers if he could sit up to speak to me, but they would not agree. Lucía was still pacing the hallways, and she might have kicked him back down anyway.

So, I got down on Mr. Beggan's level, face to the dirty floor, allowing him a little dignity. "What was Claire doing?"

"There's a tombstone on the island," Beggan said. "She was there."

I was shocked. "Bob's tombstone?"

"Yeah. Bob. The good ArLiF or something." I did not want to tell him that Lucía designed that as a joke. Beggan said, "The one you call Claire, the girl ArLiF in the newspaper?"

"Yes?"

"She was talking to the tombstone."

I felt as if my stomach had fallen into my shoes. This was new behavior. ArLiFs do not speak to assets we have designated as inanimate. "Are you sure? Was there anyone else present when she did this?"

"In the lab, you mean?"

"No, I mean another ArLiF. You are sure she was not talking to another ArLiF? That she was talking to the headstone?"

"That's right," he said.

"What was she saying?"

Beggan said, "I didn't catch all of it. It was kinda nonsense. Like, um...Oh! I remember one thing she said. It went, *There once was a world where gravity ran backward.* And, uh... *Once upon a time, there was an owl and a piece of cheese.* This is not verbatim. I didn't know there would be a quiz."

"Stories?" I asked. "She was telling stories?"

"Yeah. To herself. Or maybe to Bob. I wasn't sure. But not full stories. Just the beginnings of them. She'd start one, act frustrated, then start over."

Claire was asleep now. Not twitching. Just peacefully resting in the nighttime cycle.

Beggan said, "But the stories made no sense. Like, *There was an island named Grendelmore*—I'm paraphrasing, but it's close—*where the clouds were made of Worcestershire sauce,* and, *In the dark alleys of Quentin, there are hovercrafts powered by laughter*—"

I called out, laughing, "Lucía! Get in here!"

Beggan was still rattling off things Claire had said: "*Beyond the indigo seas of Liddenstroke, the fly woke the witch.* Should I have taken notes?"

Lucía came in. "What's the little criminal going on about now?"

I said, "He's telling us what Claire was saying when he was in the lab."

Lucía scoffed, "Get fucked. ArLiFs aren't programmed to speak to us."

I said, "He insists she was speaking to Bob's gravestone."

"What?"

Beggan was still listing what Claire had said. "*Once upon a time, the crown jewels went on a galactic quest to the planet Beetroot...*"

Lucía looked at Beggan with a red-faced mix of rage and hurt. "Claire was saying that?"

I interjected, "It seems she was teaching herself to tell a story."

Beggan looked straight at Lucía. "And this one. I remember this one word-for-word: *Once upon a time, Bob was an ArLiF, and he was not ready to die.*"

Lucía stepped back. I swallowed hard. Lucía said, "Claire used the ethernet to get into the fiction library. That's all. She's processing the concept of fiction."

I said to Lucía, "It's more than that. A story about a deleted ArLiF? Bob should not exist for her. There should be no concept of him remaining in the mainframe."

Beggan turned to me. "That's not right, is it? You didn't—What have you created? What have you done?"

Lucía walked away. "I'll check the code for remnants of Bob, make sure he's completely gone. And I'll get rid of the headstone." To an officer, she said, "Get this yammering idiot out of here."

I didn't move. I had to side with Beggan. Something was off. There was an unsettling monitor glow in the room when the officers pulled him out of the lab. I could still hear him as they escorted him down the hallway. "What have you done, Dr. Daas? What did you make? Do you even know? This is not a game, Dr. Daas! This is not a computer game!"

Meanwhile, Claire slept without a twitch.

March 20, 1993

Pythia Lab

LUCÍA WAS THE ONE who called Nessa. "Locks," she demanded. "We need better locks, a reinforced door, and a full-time security guard—"

"Hold on," I said, over her shoulder. "You have to run this by Physical Plant. You can't just change the doors. And the University won't allow an outside security firm—"

Lucía shoved me away. "I want humans with weapons!"

I pulled at the phone. "No! No weapons. This is still my project!"

Lucía threw the phone down and ran off, yelling, "That guy is giving interviews! Dennis Beggan! He's saying Claire is some kind of freak! More will come, Daas!"

I listened for Nessa on the phone. "Hello? Sorry about this."

"More will come!" Lucía yelled.

Nessa said, "Contain your pet," and hung up.

"Lucía!" I called out. "Please listen. Dennis Beggan didn't hurt anyone!"

"Next time!" she shrieked. "Next time someone will!"

One minute after I had replaced the phone on the cradle, it rang. It was Nessa again. Her voice had dropped. I knew that tone. She had been chastised. "You will have biometric scanners," she said. "The installers will be at the lab by the afternoon. Courtesy of Mr. Winfield."

"Oh," I said. "The University—"

"Will be told."

"I see. That's kind—"

"Heads up," Nessa added. "Dennis Beggan will be on the evening news. Get ready."

"What do you mean?"

"For the flood of crazies. The Providence Group has already contacted us. They want to buy the ArLiFs."

My stomach flipped. "Why?"

"They did not say."

"Do not tell Lucía this."

Nessa said, "We refused to sell."

"Well, that was not *your* absurd proposition to refuse. You don't own the ArLiFs." There was a long pause. Louder, I said, "You don't own the ArLiFs."

"Dad," Nessa said, almost exhausted. "Mr. Winfield owns what he says he owns."

And she hung up again.

Do I need a lawyer? Would there be a lawyer more powerful than the one Howard Winfield could summon? I know intellectual property is a sticky business. But this is not something I signed on for.

I emailed our grant contract to the University legal counsel to ask about ownership of our project. Right away, as if this issue skyrocketed to the top of their priority list, I had a reply: "The University will vigorously defend the intellectual property of our faculty at every opportunity. Any assault on said property is an insult to the academic community at large."

I was relieved, but was it enough to have the University on my side?

March 25, 1993

Pythia Lab

A LETTER FROM THE west coast today—with an article enclosed.

WEAKER, ONGOING PULSELIKE WAVES DETECTED AT SCIENCE BUOYS NEAR TEMPLE CITY

Mar 20, 1993

HONOLULU (AP)—Science buoys installed on the ocean surface near Manny di Martini's dive site record consistent electromagnetic pulses identical to the larger "Pulse" that menaced electronic devices near the time of Discovery. These weaker radiograph readings do not appear to interfere with telecommunications and electronics. Scientists are now processing this data with public reports forthcoming.

FROM UCAL BERKELEY

3/20/93

Ollie Daas!

You've been making the news, even here in Berkeley! That Dennis Beggan character is attracting a lot of attention. You're a hot commodity! Funding opportunities should be exploding! Good for you, my friend!

I'm enclosing an article on what data the science buoys are catching. This won't be news to you, but I'm sending it anyway as an announcement of sorts. We at the Center for Neuroimaging are the scientists working on that data. We plan to publish it next month. In short, we think these pulses are the oscillating electrical voltages of the creature's delta patterns. Not only is the beast dreaming, but it is dreaming with such vigor that we can read its electroencephalogram waves on the surface of the ocean almost two miles away! Big stuff, my friend! We are looking at an infusion of big money ourselves as soon as this is published.

I don't know about you, but this newfound fame is attracting some of the wrong kinds of attention. I don't mean the Dennis Begganses of the world. I mean lone

actors, kooks. I mean Providence Group. We have already rooted out two of their spies in our lab, staff members who were not carefully vetted. Who knows what data they have stolen. Providence wants access to all the science that proves their beliefs, but they don't have the infrastructure yet to build the labs to do original work. YET. People tell me they mean to build that infrastructure, and they'll steal the foundational science to make those labs competitive on the world stage quickly. A word of warning: tighten security. Vet your staff. Play it all close to the vest.
All my best,
Will Ahmadi

"*¡Está de la chingada!*"

"I agree it is very shitty." My education in Spanish cursing has brought me far. "But what do you think?"

"I think we will add a background check for contractors and student workers. And I think any prospects will get a thorough interrogation from me if they want to be alone with the ArLiFs."

"Careful not to tread on religious liberties—"

"Fuck that."

"Lucía."

"Think Howard will pay for us to pry into people's backgrounds?" She chuckled. "What am I asking? Of course he will." She threw aside Ahmadi's letter. "Providence. *Pinche* fringe religion."

"Fringe or not, their membership numbers are surging. Look at Dennis—"

"His name is not to be spoken in this lab."

I said, "I don't have experience with Providence. Fringe or not, do you think they are unstable?"

"Yes," Lucía told me. "They believed aliens lived here before it was fashionable."

I do not tell Lucía this, but the Providence Group fascinates me. All this time, they proclaimed the aliens lived among us. And they were right.

Act III

Ashanti Oko
and the Ancestor

Ghana

May 1992 to July 1993

17

Of the Old Religion

Four Weeks Into the Collapse

Ashanti Oko paused writing in her diary; her arm hairs raised in static quivers. "Something is happening," she said to herself. Her house had begun to vibrate. Stained-glass trinkets dangling from translucent lines rattled against the windows. The floorboards hummed.

She tucked her diary under her arm and ran across the hall into her big sister's nearly vacant room. The view of the street was better there.

Ashanti raised a window, which her mother had forbidden during the Collapse. A wall of damp air slickened tight curls to her temples and set her face aglow. She elbowed herself into the frame, shouldering the window upward, claiming her space. Under the peeling sash, she wedged a book: *Alien Architecture on Earth*. The book nearly crumpled under the weight, so she added another: *Cosmic Encounters of the Providence Prophets*. This time, the window held.

Below her, two streetlights popped to life, illuminating an empty road at both ends. Just beyond, in the darkness, tribal drumming tumbled out of the silence. A stage was set.

"Something is happening," she repeated.

She placed her diary onto the windowsill. On the cover, a cartoonish white girl in a fur-lined jacket squeezed a polar bear. Whatever was about to happen would be worthy of an entry.

Over her shoulder, Ashanti called out, "Papa! Something is happening outside!"

Downstairs, her father yipped. Newspaper rustled. The house groaned and shifted under heavy footfalls from the living room, through the kitchen—"Excuse me, Sheryl. Oh my, that looks delicious."—and down the hall. The banister creaked as he took the stairs two at a time. "Where are you?" he shouted.

"Ama's room!"

From the kitchen, her mother called, "Is there a window open up there?"

"Of course not, Sheryl!" her father cried.

After a thundering gallop that shook the picture frames against the flaking plaster walls, Nkrumah Oko entered, face glistening from his effort, dancing bow-legged at the prospect of boredom relief during Collapse lockdown. He bent under the window, rubbing his hands. "What do we have?" he asked his daughter. He tapped the sash. "And let us not mention this open window to your mother."

"Do you hear the drumming?" she asked.

"I do." The beat now rattled the old wavy glass in its pane.

"Something new is coming," Ashanti said.

"It's about time, eh?"

Ashanti's blood ran to her face and her hands warmed. *Finally. Something is happening.*

Nkrumah turned to an assembled rank of Ama's stuffed bears, left behind for Ashanti. He spread his arms to the silent gathering. "And now, my followers, feast your eyes upon this show!"

Ashanti giggled.

Her mother called out, "Nkrumah! What is going on up there?"

"It is all boring up here! Do not come up!" He winked at Ashanti.

"Papa, has Ama called today?"

"Quiet, Shanti!"

Ashanti unlocked her diary, then positioned herself at the windowsill to write. The night air pressed a damp calm onto her like a wet blanket. Since the people stopped coming out, fumes from motor exhaust and fried foods cleared off, and Ashanti could almost smell the salt water from the ocean over two kilometers away. The ocean was where the Sleeping One lived. Her mind went wild with the prospect of returning to her after-school walk to the beach to scan the ocean for signs of its imminent invasion.

Shadows shifted.

"Here they come," Nkrumah said.

At one end of the street, several men emerged from the darkness. They carried tall wooden staffs. More followed, beating djembe drums strapped across their chests. One blew maniacally on a wooden flute.

Nkrumah squatted below the windowsill with an *umph*. Ashanti copied him. "I wonder what they will do!"

Then, the streetlights caught the edges of a monster. Ashanti gasped.

The beast moved forward by rotating and bobbing like a frenzied spinning top. Its magenta and lime hair, crisp and dry like the bristles of a broom, splayed outward as it spun. It kicked up dust from the street, clouding its fringe. With the beast now fully illuminated, Ashanti could see the beast's conical shape topped with tall, sharp animal horns colored bright blue and red. In the streetlight, the horns cast a menacing shadow, throwing twin daggers down the roadway. This beast would surely pummel and crush whatever happened into its path. "What is it?" Ashanti asked.

Her father narrowed his eyes at the beast. "The Zangbeto."

She opened her diary.

"It is what the Ogu people call this masquerade."

"That is a person in a costume?"

"Of course."

"Why?"

Her father scratched at his emerging beard. He did this when he was thinking. "It is from the old religion. The Vodún."

"Oh," Ashanti said. She didn't know what to write in her diary. She might have to look up some of these things in her encyclopedias.

"I have heard of these Zangbeto emerging around Accra, frightening the lawless. There is word they will curse those they encounter. Perhaps do violence."

"Violence?"

"Perhaps."

After a moment, Ashanti asked, "What is that on its body? Hair?"

"It is nothing but dried raffia attached to concentric hoops."

"Oh."

The Zangbeto had stopped in the middle of the street, still spiraling in a loud coil of color. When stationary, the beast also jittered, as if in a spiritual ecstasy. Long blades of dried palms swirled in the dirt: *swish swish*. The beast was taller than one man and wider than three, resembling a giant with hair grown to the ground. Ashanti could not decide if it more resembled a whirling dervish of punk-rock yak hair or a hurricane of unicorn hay.

In her diary, she wrote, "Hurricane of punk-rock unicorn hair."

The beast's human escorts planted themselves around its base. Wooden staffs stabbed the dirt. Drummers accelerated. "Who are the men?" she asked her father.

He grunted. "The night guardians. From the old religion. They meet in secret to learn the old ways of magical powers that inhabited the earth long before people." His eyes swung like pendulums, calculating. "Perhaps," he said, settling on a conclusion, "this will be good for us." He turned away from the window and yelled to her mother. "Sheryl! A Zangbeto is here. And I think this will be good for us!"

Ashanti's mother called back, "What did I say, Nkrumah? Stay away from the windows past dark!"

Nkrumah grunted again and returned to watching the street.

Ashanti popped up between her father and the peeling, crooked window sash. Although she was 11 years old, nearly a teen, she enjoyed the position of the eternal baby in the family. "My late-in-life child," her mother called her. "My Littlest A."

The raffia heap had stopped in front of their house, swirling in place in the center of the road. A troski was approaching, its headlights weaving. The minibus lurched, then coasted. The driver was saving petrol, Ashanti knew, by stepping on the gas then gliding almost to a stop before punching the accelerator again. Her father used the same method to coast to church and back. Ashanti hadn't seen a public-transport minibus since the city's petrol had run dry. The troski backfired and lurched, then ground its gears.

The drumming quickened to the patter of a frightened heartbeat.

"What will happen? *Wahala*?" Ashanti asked. "Will there be fighting?"

Her father brought a finger to his lips. *Quiet.*

The minibus came to a slow stop at the feet of the drummers. The idle engine shook the door panels, adding another vibration to the Oko house. Headlights illuminated the magenta and lime dye, making it appear as a neon galaxy. The dried grasses flicked the ankles of the surrounding men. *Swish swish. Swish swish.*

A sweating man with dark stains on his shirt pushed open the troski door and put a foot into the street. "Eh!" he barked. "What is this? Move out of the way. I have business."

One of the men with the beast asked, "This is your auto? It is not stolen?"

"Who are you to ask me these questions?" the driver returned.

"You are in the streets past the curfew," a drummer announced.

Ashanti heard the phone ring downstairs. Nkrumah ducked a little lower under the window sash.

"I am seeking medicine for my child!" the driver yelled, now spitting his words. "It is an emergency!"

In the headlights, the Zangbeto was silent. Swirling. Menacing.

Another phone ring from downstairs. Her father whispered to himself, "We will surely be discovered spying if Sheryl does not answer the phone." Ashanti cast a worried glance at the men on the street, who did not seem to notice the noise from their open window.

"A curfew is in place by rule of the priestess!" a staff-wielder shouted.

The driver spat. "Crone! She kills babies with a glance!"

The men were silent.

The driver paused. "What am I to do? My child—"

The men said, "The priestess will provide—"

The sweating driver raged, smacking a fist into his palms. "No! Not dubious potions from a witch! Medicine!"

The Zangbeto started to jitter. The drummers changed the beat to match it. *Tap tap tap tap.* As the Zangbeto accelerated, so did the drums. *Tap Tap Tap Tap Tap.*

Five men with wooden staffs surrounded the minibus.

"Eh! Eh!" the driver yelled. "What is this?" He retreated inside the troski.

Downstairs, the phone rang again.

"Papa," Ashanti clawed at her father's shirt. "What will happen?"

"A bit of old magic, it appears," he said. "Let us see."

Her mother yelled from downstairs, "Ashanti! Nkrumah! The phone is ringing, and I am occupied with yams!"

Both ducked lower but kept their eyes on the road.

The giant raffia beast accelerated its rotation, convulsing and bouncing in place. The men chanted in an old language. With their long staffs, the men beat the troski to the beat of the drums. Metal crunched and popped.

"Eh! Eh!" The driver was inside, trapped. The minibus rocked.

Another phone ring. "Reverend Nkrumah Oko! Get down here!"

Her father's voice squeaked, "For the sake of the Prophet, Sheryl! This is some excitement here!"

Ashanti could hear her mother's ragged sigh.

The headlights caught the animal horns on the beast as the Zangbeto doubled over and bore down on the troski.

Crack!

The auto lurched back in the street.

Ashanti grabbed her father's pant leg. Her father let out a satisfied *Yip!* "I know this man in the car, Littlest A," her father whispered. "He indeed has a child, often ill. Yet, we should do all our medical shopping in advance."

Ashanti asked, "Is there not an exception for emergencies?"

"Will not everyone then claim emergencies?" her father countered. "How will we know who is lying? Times are hard, Shanti. We must all follow the rules."

"Eh! Eh!" the driver barked. "What is this? What is this? Vodún curses? You will send the witches to my house to place hexes on me?" Ashanti could see the whites in his eyes. He gripped the steering wheel. He tried to back the minibus away, but the men surrounded him.

Suddenly, the drums stopped. The beast's hair shuddered to a standstill. The men with staffs pulled the man from the troski.

The driver was on his knees between two men.

The downstairs ringing silenced. Ashanti heard her mother's voice: "Reverend Grieves Church of Providence..."

The sweating driver was sobbing. "I require medicine for my child," he repeated. "He has fever. He suffers—"

The beast was deathly still in the dark.

Then, it shuddered. One. Two. Three times. After a moment, the drums started again.

The beast spun. The raffia streamed a smooth gradient of magenta and lime.

The men kicked the driver until he was on his feet. The driver craned his neck all around. "Where are you taking me?" he asked. The men with staffs prodded him forward, leaving the troski open in the street. "Where are you taking me?" the driver called from the darkness. "My child! Requires medicine! He suffers!"

The group advanced down Ashanti's street, then faded into the night.

"Where are they taking him?" the girl whispered to her father.

"For a beating, I imagine."

Ashanti sat back on her heels. "Will he survive?"

"I do not know."

Ashanti frowned. "This is injustice." Her father pursed his lips but said nothing. She asked, "Is this a new kind of police?"

"No, it is very old." Her father hummed, as if searching for a term. "It is...like...a vigilante superhero."

"Vigilante!"

"A crusader," her father added. "A fighter of night crime. Of the old religion. The Vodún."

She clicked open her diary. She wrote: *A vijalantee of voodon.*

Talking more to himself, Nkrumah added, "The police are frightened. The people are desperate."

Ashanti added to her diary: *Disparate.*

Her father calculated with his eyes again. "Yes," he said, turning away from the window. "This could be good for us."

Ashanti wrote: *Good for us.*

She asked, "Papa, will I go back to school soon?"

"There are rumors of how well the Zangbeto clear the streets. We should reopen the academy."

Ashanti's heart sang, then quieted. "I have not yet written my essay."

Nkrumah said, "Why not? The topic could not be easier." He hummed. "Good for us." Then, he turned to the assembled stuffed bears, spread his arms wide, and repeated, "Yes, my followers! Good for us! A rebirth!"

Ashanti laughed. Then, she thought of the man suffering a beating and stopped. "But Papa—"

Her mother called from downstairs, "Nkrumah! A new church member on the phone wants to know of the services this week!"

"Woop!" Ashanti's father hopped as if goosed by an electrical current. He twisted his torso and flung his fingers together—the West African snap. "I am happy as a king! They are seeing the light!"

"Papa—"

"Later, my Shanti!" He blew a kiss from Ama's bedroom door. Then he galloped down the stairs, two at a time, nearly taking the wobbling banister with him.

Ashanti surveyed her street from the upstairs window. No one approached the open troski to steal it or strip it for parts. No one had opposed the Zangbeto. Why, just a week ago, such a sight would have been met with trucks sagging to the road under the weight of masked men overfilling the bed like circus clowns, waving rifles and pistols. It would have ended in yelling and deaths and misery. But now, it was quiet. Just the fact that she was at an open window and not in a back room under a blanket listening to records ushered in a refreshing thought: for the first time in a month, there was peace on her street.

Was this worth the beating of one man seeking medicine for his child? If he was to be believed?

That was the problem. No one believed. No one trusted.

If the man were not telling the truth, perhaps had stolen the troski to do crime, then would the peace be worth his injuries?

Ashanti could not answer.

She thought of her father's words: *Good for us.*

The Oko family was due for some good fortune. Their prison during the Collapse was a crumbling Victorian house the shade of lint-covered bubblegum at the edge of downtown Accra, usually an epicenter of honks, music, chatter, and food aromas. Since Manny's Discovery, though, their neighborhood had been deadly silent. The thick smells—the fried fish heads, squid strips, spicy pork, kelewele, corn porridge—of the all-night market a block away had vanished. Vendors had packed up their stalls and moved back to their villages where it was safer. "Why will we not return to Mama's village?" Ashanti had asked early in the Collapse.

"We know no one in Mama's village," her father told her. For the Oko family, their safest port was their dull-pink house in Accra. Like many others, they stayed inside, scraping together what normalcy they could amongst the tire-screeching, explosions, gunfire, and screaming.

Despite the terror, never in Ashanti's 11 years had she experienced such tedium. She had endured four weeks of no school, no church, no playing outside, and no visitors. Her lifeline had been the telephone, but even that did not work on some days. For her father, the leader of their church, the same: no worship, no preaching, no social fellowship. For them both: at home, doors locked, windows closed. "How will I live?" her father howled. He made a poor introvert.

Her mother permanently occupied the kitchen, stretching very little food into meager meals. The local Shoprites only dispensed canned food and boxed dinners. Fresh vegetables and meat had been difficult to come by; short-barreled shotguns replaced produce at the Makola. Ashanti's father, in the throes of a fiberless diet, complained perpetually of constipation. How he pined for the cabbage that would scour his colon with the vigor his wife had when attacking dirty yams with a scrub brush! His voice echoed in the bathroom: "This will be the death of me."

Her mother made do by negotiating with fellow church members, who always found ways forward in tough times. And times, it seemed to Ashanti, had always been tough for the church. They held "outlandish beliefs," the public told them. Cosmic beings moving humans around like pieces in a game! Paranatural life among Earthlings preparing for a great cosmic war! But these were old beliefs, Ashanti knew, as old as the pyramids in Egypt. Older than Jesus Christ. "Do they know Jesus Christ was a half-paranatural being?" Ashanti asked her father.

"They don't acknowledge that," her father replied.

Ashanti whined, "They say it every time—"

Her father interrupted, "Do not concern yourself. Our truth will out."

It was lucky, Ashanti's mother had said, it was just the three of them during the Collapse. Ashanti's big brother Adom moved out after the Collapse hit. It was a risky move. Just before Discovery, Adom had made an embarrassment of himself. An embarrassment of the church, no less—the worst kind. Adom had "problems." That was what her father said when he meant "drugs." Adom now fended for himself, living in a one-room flat above the church to keep it safe from looters. "He needs this," her father had explained. Ashanti protested at his being alone in such dangerous times. They needed Adom in strength and in numbers. Her father disagreed. "Adom needs a purpose more than safety."

Ashanti's older sister, Ama, worried her even more. On a mission trip in America, Ama had not phoned home since Discovery Day—four weeks ago. Why, Ashanti had groaned, did Ama even need to go to the slaver nation in the first place? And for a whole year! Her father replied, "She must prepare for her career in the Providence Group, Littlest A."

Ashanti had countered, "Providence Group is here in Accra."

Her father's expression dissipated into a gaseous smile. "No, Littlest A. As the descendant of the Prophet Reverend Lazarus Grieves, she will ascend to a place in the *international* organization. She must make herself known in *America*. She must show them how well she knows the doctrine."

Ashanti asked, "Will I ascend, too, Papa?"

He replied with a light in his eyes, "Most certainly!"

To prepare for her career in the slaver nation, Ama would guide mosquito-pocked American-Providence members to the Great Dismal Swamp

along the Virginia-North Carolina border, to the site of Reverend Lazarus
Grieves's awakening. She would provide insight that only generations of Oko
family stories could provide. Why the Americans flocked to that site, Ashanti
could not understand. No one had seen the Light Ones there since Black Nance
relayed her narrative to the Reverend. That was 150 years ago. But that did not
stop Providence members—along with some morbidly curious tourists—from
journeying to the site to investigate for themselves. Ama had almost completed
her year of leading these pilgrims when the Discovery cut off all communications
with her family. "When will Ama return?" Ashanti asked daily.

"When we hear from her, we will know," Nkrumah always replied.

The waiting and worrying had weighed on Ashanti. She had grown thin, and
not from lack of food. She had failed to thrive under the stress and monotony of
the Collapse.

Now, a promise of rebirth.

She inhaled the night air. Still humid. Still lacking the aromas from the all-night
market. But this, she agreed with her father, was going in the right direction.

She wondered how long until her academy would reopen. Her assigned essay
on a prophet of her choice, given out by phone during the Collapse, was only
half-finished. Aside from that, she had been doing very little schoolwork besides
coloring in the Providence Prophet Stories Coloring Book. And, oh, how she
hated that book. She even tired of the book's subtitle: "12 prophets, 12 advances
in understanding cosmic life on Earth!" *Yawn!* She was too old for coloring. She
was in sixth grade—about to advance to seventh! And coloring the Prophets still!
Even the color schemes bored her. Red and yellow: Prophetess Chabi of China
working with the Buddhist monks on integrating cosmic entities in Chinese
religions. Also red and yellow: Prophet Salman of India painting temple walls
with cosmic entities based on Hindu scriptures. White with red blood splatter:
Prophet Henley Goode of England losing his entire Antarctic expedition to a
clawed insect-like beast of cosmic origin. A return to her sixth-grade class at the
Reverend Lazarus Bethlehem Grieves Academy promised even more boredom.
But! After school, she would return to her walks to the beach! She could monitor
the ocean for herself!

Ashanti wrote in her diary, *To the beast who sleeps in the ocean: I am coming!*

She heard her father downstairs, fumbling—with apologies to her
mother—toward his post-Discovery telephone bank in the living room, set up
to take all the calls from potential new church members. During the Collapse,
Nkrumah had wired himself three new telephone lines to handle the call volume.
(Ashanti did not ask how he managed this. It carried the whiff of illegality, which
her father called, "Redistribution of power.") People were, for the first time,
interested in what they believed after such blatant evidence of alien life presented

on television. Other church members hosted similar call centers in their homes. "Cast the net wide!" he had said to the church members. "Leave no one behind!"

In their living room, phone cords and wires crisscrossed and dangled from corners of frames holding paintings of the Oko family's American ancestors: the Grieves family. Unsmiling. Serious beards. Bonnets. Funny neckties. Formerly enslaved. Now, their descendants lived free in Africa and preached the *Sacred Truth*. Though, through the generations of building the church in Accra, the Oko family were quite lonely in the conviction of paranatural cohabitants on Earth. Not that they didn't have support from other branches. The Providence Group absorbed the Grieves Church into their own international syndicate in 1866, offering financial and administrative support that their paltry membership couldn't. Accra church membership historically wavered between 10 and 15 families, all with varying levels of commitment—from "unconditional zealots" to "only here for the potlucks." (Upon finding out about these members, Nkrumah had wailed, "They come for food only! We are no better than Methodists!") Since the Discovery, though, things were different. The Grieves Church in Accra had been growing, and fast. Phones had been ringing nonstop, when the Pulse wasn't silencing them. Even her mother answered them alongside her father: "Reverend Lazarus Grieves Church of Providence, how may we help you to the Light?"

Downstairs, Ashanti could imagine what the caller was saying to her father because all the calls had been the same: "The thing! In the ocean! What does it mean? It says nothing in the Bible...how do we...I do not know what to do!"

"We will teach you to have no fear," her father said now in a smooth tone. "We will teach you the good news of the 12 Providence Prophets, who tell us of the paranatural races that have lived among us since the beginning of our time on Earth..."

Ashanti certainly had no fear. She'd been waiting for an opening to return to her watch on the beach, provided, it seemed now, by the Zangbeto.

In their living-room phone bank, her father continued reeling in the recruit: "But you must take the first step. Join the Grieves Church of Providence..."

Ashanti ached to go back to the beach. To stand on the stone wall above the fishermen working their boats. To watch the ocean.

For what? She did not know for certain. There was no consensus as to how the Sleeping One appeared. Television shows now offered blow-by-blow commentary of Manny di Martini's Discovery with zoomed-in footage from the *Yuna II*, but Ashanti never could see what others saw. Tentacles, yes. She saw those. Big, thick ones that could strangle bridges and skyscrapers. Those tentacles coiled around pointy architecture, glowing and alabaster in the camera's bright lights. Tentacles were not in question. In fact, in most of her fantasies of the Sleeping One clodhopping around central Accra, the creature would scoop people up with those tentacles and toss them into the air, catching them in its maw like they were peanuts. But the colossal, bulbous head some claimed to see? She couldn't see it. Nor did she see the massive body on a throne, like her friend Hania had seen. Ashanti saw the pointy architecture behind it, like white-people's cathedrals. And she saw the vibrant pulsing under its skin. Her diary was full of questions about the creature. *Where was it from*, she thought? *How would we know more about it? Will Manny di Martini be named Providence Prophet for finding it? Should we wake it with a nuclear bomb? Would others follow to find out more on Earth?*

Nkrumah continued on the phone: "We are working for a special dispensation from lockdown to meet. Wouldn't it be nice to come outside? ...And, yes, we have food...fresh yams from my wife's family's village..."

Yes, Ashanti thought. *It is time for a rebirth.*

She pledged that she would see the Sleeping One for herself.

18

Reverend Lazarus Bethlehem Grieves Sr. and the Light Ones

By: Ashanti Oko, 6th grade
29 May 1992
Reverend Grieves Academy

My name is Ashanti Oko. I am related to Providence Prophet Reverend Lazarus Bethlehem Grieves Sr. He is the first prophet of the modern age. That means their are much older prophets and he is a newer one. He is Prophet of Justice and Defaince.

Providence people are not afraid of the Sleeping One becuase of what we beleive. We must be an example. We know how to live with the Cosmics. But we are not so great at the Collaps. Becuase of the Collaps we were not at school a long time. I missed my friend Hania. She is my one friend. Sometimes she is not my friend becuase she is moody. That is what Mama says. We have alot of new kids at school becuase the world is freaking out and Providence is not. Papa is happy about this. We also have a new teacher from America. Our teacher is not white. That is suprising but also good. I would not like to learn about my people from a white slaver. No thank you. I already know alot about Reverend Grieves becuase of my family. That is why I picked him as a topic. I would never pick Ailish Finnegan. She is the Prophetess of Sucidal Madness. She killed her whole villege and made love with fishes. That is what we learn in school! Good luck to whoever writes about that!

(To our new teacher: This essay is more than 5 paragraphs. I like to write. It is what I do. I have a dairy that I like to write in to. I better not get points off for being to long. The other teacher did not do this.)

Reverend Lazarus Bethlehem Grieves was born in West Africa. No one knows when he was born. Not a month like October or Janary. Or the year. That is becuase West Africans did not use calenders like now. We say the year he was born is 1776. That is a speficic date when you think about it. Maybe something happened around then to make people say that was the year he was born. We know the speficic year he died horribly! It was 1821. He died in Atlanta Georgeia.

That is in slavery country. We know about that year becuase the white people were glad he died. They killed him and wrote it down.

Lazarus Grieves had a name in Africa. No one knows what it is. He was caught in Africa by white men and they sent him to the Carribean to work on a ship. His white master was not a mean person. Suprise! That was lucky. Most of them were awful. The white master taught Mr. Grieves to read and write and gave him the name Lazarus Bethlehem Grieves. Mr. Grieves boght his freedom from this sorta nice white man. Then he went to school to be a minster in Rode Island. He chose the Methodist faith. Papa says the Methodist faith is an excuse for people to have pot luck dinners. They don't realy beleive in much. Especially not like us.

Now I will tell the part that is easy. I have this in my memory. Every Oko family member does.

In 1815 the dark days of slavery still thrived in America! Reverend Lazarus Bethlehem Grieves practiced Methodist minstry in Rode Island. He could read and write now. So he was called to take testmony from Black Nance. Black Nance was an old woman. She was a 90 year old person living in Great Dismal Swamp. That is on the east coast of America. Her skin was like rasins. You can see her wrinkled rasin skin in paintings. The Great Dismal Swamp is now where the slaver states of Virgina and North Caralina are. My sister is their now. She is on a misson trip. She says it is hot and to many bugs. She has not called home to tell us more so I am worried. We have not heard from her since Discovery. Mama says she is fine and not to worry. That means Mama is worried to.

The swamp was a stop on the Underground Rail Road. That is not a real rail road. The Underground Rail Road moved slaves to freedom. Anyone who could get to the Great Dismal Swamp was very safe. Reverend Grieves wanted to know what was so speshial about that place. Black Nance told him. She said paranatchrel beings lived their. They lived their since before humans were on Earth. Black Nance called them the Light Ones. We have a painting of Light Ones. It is in our living room. It is called "Reverend Grieves: From Dismal Swamp to Glory!" It is the one where the Reverend strikes a match to light a candle in the hut of Black Nance. A bunch of firefys swarm around them. Those are the Light Ones. This painting is also in our classroom. But it is a poster not a painting like ours.

Black Nance said the Light Ones had a story to tell. They were hiding in the swamp from their masters! Their masters were feirce cosmic beings. They enslaved the Light Ones to build their buldings. The feirce ones were their parents if you can beleive it. Some parents! You cannot trust anyone. The feirce cosmic beings are just like white slave owners. I hope the new kids pick up on that.

Black Nance told Reverend Grieves that the Light Ones show up in storms of light. And they are very mean to white masters and hunters of slaves. Light Ones will kill anyone who tries to get a slave back. The Light Ones ripped limbs from bodies of white hunters. They also displayed white peoples's heads in trees. That was a warning to other white people. This is why I am worried about Ama. She is not white but the Great Dismal Swamp is still full of danger like wild animals and stuff.

We have a painting of Black Nance hanging out with the Light Ones too. This one is in the upstairs bathroom of our house. Ama used to soak in the tub and look at it a long time. This made me angry. Sometimes I had to pee and she would be soaking in there. Also the painting gives me the creeps. Those blobby ghosts chatting with the swamp hag with her rasin skin! Ama used to say that Black Nance was the real Prophet, Littlest A. That is what she calls me. Littlest A. Ama is Biggest A and Adom is Middle A. Ama used to say that Black Nance was the translater. She translated between cosmic and human. Without her their would be no *Sacred Text*. Her story is what Reverend Grieves wrote down. It is Black Nance's story! What Ama said their is a blasfemy. Ama never gets in trouble for blasfemy. I always do. I am worried about her. I want her to come home.

Reverend Grieves met the Light Ones one time only. He was not killed by them. On the way to Black Nance's house they stopped him. It was a whirlwind of lights. The Reverend said this was the most important time in his whole life! They told him things. They said he was intelligent. They said his people needed freedom. (This means freedom from white people.) After that meeting Reverend said he would never go back to the white man's teachings. He would not even go to church. He would teach only *Sacred Truth*. He named his book after Black Nance's truth. The name also means sacred truth delivered by the Light Ones.

Sacred Truth was published in 1816 which is a long time ago. The public did not care for it. They made fun of Reverend. We have this book in our house. It is a first edtion. That means it was one of the very first ones ever printed and it is very old. I am not allowed to touch it.

The Reverend moved with his family to Atlanta. That is the heart of the wicked American South. He moved their to plan a violet riot aginst all of slavery. He wanted alot of Africans in plantations join. They would fight their masters all at the same time! Then they would highjack a ship. Then they would sail to Africa. They would live as free people. Reverend said this is what Light Ones said to do.

The riot did not go well. A slave (Can you beleive it?!) tattled on Reverend and he got caugt. The white men gave Reverend a kangeroo court. That makes no sense becuase it was America not Australia. The trail was not fair. They did not say anything about people living as slaves. That is wrong! But the white people hanged Reverend Grieves anyway. Papa says being hung is a bad way to go. I think being sliced up by a Light One is much worse.

Later Reverend's son made some Providence churches in Providence Road Island. He also made one in Atlanta but that did not go well. That son's name was Reverend Lazarus Bethlehem Grieves Jr. Then that Reverend's son had another Reverend for a son. Can you gess his name? It was Reverend Lazarus Bethlehem Grieves III. He fought in the War Between the States. That is a war about slaves. He also saved *Sacred Truth*. Then he got on a ship to Africa and never looked back. That is why my family lives here in Africa and not in the slaver nation.

Somewhere in time our last name became Oko instead of Grieves. This is becuase no one wanted the family name to be one a white master gave us. Grieves was a sad name anyway. That is why we are the Oko family. Oko means twin becuase we are realy the same as our American ancestors. Just more freer.

In 1866 Providence Head Quarters collected Reverend Lazarus Bethlehem Grieves into it's collection of prophets. That is another story. He became the prophet number 7. We now have 12. I wonder if Manny di Martini will become number 13.

The end.

PS: Do not punish me for to long of an essay or for blasfemy. I know what my papa says about Black Nance being a prophet. He says Black Nance contributes NOTHING to the human relationship to cosmic beings. NOTHING. Reverend met the Light Ones and did something. A prophet of Providence is active. This is what Papa says.

19

Enemy Here

THE OCEAN WAS CALM. No tentacles in sight.

Ashanti slumped on a crumbling stone wall atop the sand leading to the sea. She had missed the ocean, the knee-buckling immensity of it. Her bookbag lay at her feet. She kicked it, then threw a rock. It plumped into the soft sand. Inside her bookbag was a note from the principal to her father. *Blasphemy*, it documented. *Insulting the Prophet Grieves in the written word.*

The first day back to school had started with the horrific announcement that, due to time lost during the Collapse, the school year would continue into the summer. To make matters worse, Ashanti had to knot and bead 12 bracelets in art class: one for each prophet in the appropriate color scheme. Baby stuff.

And then there was the spectacular failure of what she thought was a genius essay.

On top of that, no giant bulbous head on the horizon. Was it stupid to insist upon seeing it here on the African shore when it was entombed in the Pacific? She thought not. This grey-green mass before her connected everything in the world. It flowed south of the Sleeping One, connecting all the continents. Underneath its surface, another world of creatures swam and battled and lay in wait. Predatory or hunted, they were never still, not even in the pitch-black cold. The only signs of their existence: carcasses and relics and gnawed corpses of fishermen that they let float to the surface—an offering or a warning, Ashanti did not know.

She sent her eyes to the horizon.

A chain of Zangbeto perched on wooden boats near the shoreline, bobbing gently on the soft swells. She guessed they were guarding the harbor from the pirates who had plagued it in the weeks prior, raiding the fishermen's huts and disassembling anchored ships for parts. These Zangbeto had raffia dyed all colors: shocking blue, bright pink, blood red, obnoxious orange. They resembled a rainbow of shaved fruity ice melting on the water.

In the week since she saw the Zangbeto in the street by her house, more Zangbeto groups appeared to sweep Accra clean. It was decided the Reverend Grieves Academy would reopen. The Zangbeto had been so effective that her mother had even agreed to allow her to walk home. "Straight home!" she had demanded.

Ashanti agreed, with her fingers crossed behind her back.

She threw another rock. *Ppffft.* Sand sprayed.

She wondered what the Sleeping One would do when encountering the Zangbeto. *Probably wrap them in its tentacles and toss them backward to America,* she thought. *America, the slaver nation. Holding Ama captive.*

Another rock thrown. *Ppffft.*

I will wake it up, she thought.

She sighed.

It was different down here at the beach since the Collapse. The vendor stalls had emptied, and there were no umbrellas shading plastic buckets, fruit, and plastic toys for tourists. No tourists congregated around the old lighthouse, which now towered in a black, burned mass above the sea. Gangs had set it aflame the night of the Discovery. *Stupid humans. Scared of what's lived here since they evolved from apes.*

Ppffft.

Rows of corrugated shacks by the water, where the fishermen and their families lived, now seemed dark places with ominous auras. Men slumped, probably drunk, against wooden pallets and chunks of concrete. Children peeked out of shredded, plastic curtains with hollow eyes and sunken cheeks. No women cooked outside. No fish dried on racks. No vivid smocks or kente cloths lay on rooftops.

Still, beyond the harbor, a few dozen boats drifted. Fishermen dragged their nets into their flimsy dinghies, barely floating above the surface with the number of men packed inside. Seagulls followed them in massive flocks. Over the squawks, the fishermen's voices carried back to land. They chanted tribal songs that kept the rhythm for their work. Their twittering and exhalations set the pace for synchronized pulling of their ropes. In the days before, Ashanti would race here after school as the rush of wooden boats flooded the beach, and the men in western t-shirts—Michael Jackson and Chicago Bulls and *Miami Vice*—unloading their cargo for women already poised to bargain with them.

Another rock thrown. *Ppffft.*

"Eh!" a fisherman barked. Her rock had narrowly missed him.

"Sorry," Ashanti said.

A dried, yellowed chicken foot dangled from a cord around the fisherman's neck. It thumped against his white shirt. "What are you aiming at, small-small?"

"Just playing a game," she said.

The fisherman had dragged his boat up to the high-tide mark and balanced on the gunwales, rocking the boat from side to side. "Look at me, I also play game."

With muscular feet lined with protruding veins, he twisted his hips and rocked back and forth. The dried chicken foot *thump-thumped* on his bony chest.

Nearby, his family and friends now tended his pitiful haul of fish, picking out the plastic bottles and candy wrappers to reveal skinny, flopping specimens that might amount to a mouthful of food.

"I'm aiming at the Sleeping One," Ashanti said. She returned to scanning the ocean.

The fisherman croaked a laugh. He repeated her answer to his people in his language. They scowled and jabbered in return.

"Small-small," he said to her, "We hope you hit it. Sleeping One is bad for business." He pointed to the empty market stalls in the plaza. Around the shacks, children played in the dirt, unenthusiastically kicking a deflated ball. Usually, Ashanti knew, they popped the ball with energy and screamed at their teammates with American pop music blaring from transistor radios. Today: no squealing children. No radios. No smells of fish pepper soup. No women gossiping with giant bowls on their heads.

Ashanti turned away from the empty scene. Waves slopped onto the dark sands. Wind tossed her necktie, and she pushed it down. The woven bracelets she'd made in art class wiggled up and down both arms. She wore them six to an arm, ordered by color of the rainbow, not by dates of their Enlightening as some others wore them.

"What are deez bracelets you have?" the man asked, pointing to her wrists.

She pointed to his chest. "What is that chicken foot?"

The man took up the dried foot and kissed it. "Is for protection against enemy!" He held the leg and waved the foot at Ashanti. "Dis will scratch my enemy! Scratch, scratch!"

"Who's your enemy?"

The man laughed, then mumbled through flashing teeth, "Egyptians hurt my feelings."

"Hmm," was all Ashanti could say about that.

The fisherman's eyes were weird. Two polished black pearls, their surfaces flat, so strangely flat, like reflective holes in his head.

A rush of fishing boats coasted into the shoreline at the same time. The men jumped off and dragged their rickety crafts with threadbare flags onto the beach, parking them eight deep in the softer sands. They chattered and inspected their catches. All the same: scant, filled with trash. Not one glanced back to the sea.

The fisherman rocked his boat, arms out for balance. "Deez people say Sleeping One is bad. It curses people."

Ashanti tsked. "The Sleeping One has not cursed them. It's just litter in their nets."

The fisherman pointed at her. "Dat's what I say! Not so bad!"

"I wouldn't go *that* far."

"Maybe dey should worship it."

Ashanti hid her bracelets. "Like I said, the cause is litter. Humans."

The fisherman frowned. "No one wants fish from ocean with monster in it. Is poison. Is bad." Then, he laughed loudly. "Bad litter! Bad humans!"

A child with no clothes toddled into the road above them. No mother sought to remove him. The child bent in the road to pinch an old cigarette butt from the dirt. He shoved it into his mouth and chewed. Ashanti swallowed her shame for the second time today. Where were the adults to help them? She thought, *I will ask my father about this. And Ama. When she calls.*

The fisherman let loose another round of barking laughter at the child.

"Crazy man," Ashanti clucked. She turned toward the sooty, red-and-white-banded lighthouse, dragging her bookbag behind her. The note inside burned a hole into her conscience. What would Ama say when she found out about her blasphemy? She'd probably laugh. "Take it on the chin, Littlest A," she might have told her—if she were home. But she wasn't.

Ashanti's older brother, Adom, would not know what to do about blasphemy. Adom might even tell her she was hurting his chances of advancement at Providence Group, which was all he cared about these days. *Better than caring about cocaine*, Ashanti thought. She wasn't supposed to know what cocaine was, but she did. She had looked it up in her encyclopedias.

Certainly, for her, a lecture from her father would be on the agenda tonight. Her City Boys records might be taken away. At worst, no television. Not even the repeats of the Manny di Martini broadcast.

She shuffled to the road above the stone wall. Beyond the harbor road, old colonial buildings baked in the sun, working to shed another layer of paint from their white-people columns and balconies and arches. Her father told her that long ago, before the Grieves family left America for Africa, the white people who lived here built these atrocious buildings from which they did their business of robbing Ghana of its gold and its people. Then they left the buildings to crumble into dust. The decrepit, pink Victorian mansion the Oko family lived in was one such colonial building—selected by her father for their home "to make a point." He liked to tell her, "We will take back everything stolen from us and make it glorious." To Ashanti, these buildings were anything but glorious. It reminded her of when her people were subjugated; she felt like a squatter in her own home. Come to think of it, she didn't know what point could be made by feeling that way.

Then, Ashanti noticed the noise in the plaza close to the lighthouse. The drums. The swirling raffia. "Oh," she blurted.

"Ah!" the fisherman exclaimed. He jumped up and down in his boat, pointing. "Ah! Ah! Look! Zangbeto!"

A Zangbeto spun into a plaza above the sea wall where children passed the flaccid ball around. The swirling monster scattered them as they screamed. The Zangbeto's band of followers shook sticks at women and old men who kneeled before it with raised arms. The raffia cone rustled and swept the courtyard dirt into kaleidoscopic patterns.

"You know Zangbeto, child?" the fisherman called.

"I know it."

"Is...ahhh." The fisherman flexed his arms. "Show strength!" he added. "Is old Vodún magic to scare enemy." He barked again: "Eh!" Then went on, "No robbing here! No looting here!" The man emphasized that by scissoring his arms. "No nonsense. Enemy *scared*."

Ashanti hopped back onto the stone wall. "The enemy out there?" She pointed to the ocean.

The fisherman laughed again. "No! Child!" He pointed to the land. "Enemy *here*."

Ashanti considered this view. The gunfire in the streets had all but stopped. "Maybe you're right."

The fisherman clicked his tongue. "You know who is inside Zangbeto?"

Ashanti studied the dancing pile of hay. "Do I know them *personally*?"

"No, child. Is human or animal inside?"

"I don't know."

The fisherman bared his teeth. "Is *spirit*. Is *empty*."

Ashanti scowled.

"Truth!" the man said. "See!"

The band had corralled the swirling cone into a stop. They were disassembling it, layer by layer, heaping the limp raffia onto the plaza. Children rushed the monster to peek inside and squealed to find no one inside at all.

"A trick," Ashanti said.

"No trick."

"The dancer escaped out the back. Or is hiding in a false wall."

The fisherman whispered, "No trick, child."

"A trick," Ashanti repeated.

The band of Zangbeto escorts reassembled the beast, replacing hoops of dried palm leaves onto branches fashioned into a pyramid. Soon after all the layers had been added, the raffia beast shuddered to life and swirled around the courtyard, headed toward the road.

"Go home, small-small," the fisherman called out. He was easing back down to the shore. The seas darkened behind him. "Or Zangbeto—" The fisherman chomped his jaws at Ashanti. More fishermen behind him croaked with laughter.

"I'm not afraid," Ashanti mumbled.

The Zangbeto churned dirt into patterns on the street, the band beating drums and shaking sticks at onlookers, who bowed before it.

"I'm not afraid of anything," she added.

20

Glorious News

INSIDE THE OKO HOME, Ashanti's parents were yelling, but they stopped abruptly when she slammed the front door. She had caught snippets: "Prophet's bloodline," "Insanity," "She cannot be allowed," and her mother's insistent, "I will not sign it."

Ashanti thought, *The principal called them. They already know.*

"Shanti! Shanti!" her father bellowed from the living room. But his voice was upbeat. Manic. Like he wanted to bury something ugly under a confetti explosion. "Shanti! Tell your papa the good news of the day!"

The phone rang. Her father held Ashanti at bay with a pointed finger, then scooped up the receiver. "Reverend Grieves Church of Providence, how may we—Ah! Adom! My son!"

There was banging in the kitchen. Ashanti smelled plantains frying. She moved toward the sweet aroma. Her father continued, "Yes, yes, my son. Thank you for taking the phone call from the nun."

On the kitchen counter heaps of vegetables and fruits cast shadows on the countertop. A slab of unrecognizable meat lay marinating in a bowl of ginger and curry. Ashanti shuddered. The Prophet knows what kind of meat her mother's people were sending from the bush. Rat. Warthog. Monkey.

Her father was still on the phone with her brother: "I know she is not a nun, but I do not know what else to call her..."

Her mother would not meet her eye. "Littlest A," her mother called to her between bangs, "go humor your father. He is in a mood, and I am occupied."

Ashanti was confused. She thought her father sounded happy. Too happy.

He kept talking on the phone: "The nun scares me, Adom, but she has a nose for the stock market, so we must tolerate her for her tips. It is how we live so well on so little...No, your mother will not sign off, but we will talk later."

Something, Ashanti thought, was not right. The hairs on her arms stood up. Something electric was in the house, and she couldn't find its source. "Mama, is something wrong?"

"Nothing," she said. The peeling knife went *crack* against the counter. "Go see your father."

Her father slammed down the phone and exploded. "Shanti! Shanti!"

Ashanti moved to the command center in the living room. New cables hung from the Reverend Grieves painting, tilting it off axis.

A new, smaller television had been stacked on top of the older console television resting on the floor, which hadn't worked consistently since the Pulse. The smaller TV was supposed to be a backup, but on days when the larger TV worked, like today, they had two screens going at once like a TV store. On the smaller screen, static lines squiggled across the image of the Sleeping One in its temple. Her father had the Discovery broadcast tape in the VCR again, paused on the *Yuna II* images. During the darkest days of the hunger-times at the beginning of the Collapse, her father went through the images frame by frame, narrating to the painting above the television what he saw. "We are vindicated," he had whispered then. "All of us."

On the older console television, a broadcast was in progress. *Live from the Vatican*, the crawler said. Another crawler said: *Manny di Martini sightings reported in Las Vegas, Jakarta, and the Nepalese mountains.*

"What is a Nepalese mountain?" Ashanti asked.

"Look it up in your encyclopedias. Come sit here!"

On TV, the camera focused on a long table and a microphone with a golden emblem behind it. No one was speaking, but reporters with microphones and voice recorders milled about in the audience and mumbled. An announcer said, "We will begin in a few moments."

The crawler changed to: *Live: Catholic Church responds to scientific claim that Sleeping One is extraterrestrial.*

Her father waved Ashanti over. "See the Catholics scrambling! If I had known this would happen today, I would have bargained with the cinema for popcorn kernels."

"You do not know how to pop corn," her mother said from the kitchen.

"What is happening at the Vatican today?" Ashanti asked. She kicked her bookbag bearing the principal's note under the side table.

"The Catholics will decide their rhetoric for the Sleeping One," her father said. Then he addressed the console: "Who is sorry now their religion has no reference to life outside Earth?"

This is mania, Ashanti decided.

"No word yet from the Mohammedans or the Protestants," her father added. "Probably waiting on the Catholics!"

The banging in the kitchen got louder.

And my parents are in severe disagreement, Ashanti thought. *Something about a signature.*

"The Jews will likely rely on their scholarship. Now!" He grabbed at the air with wiggling fingers as if angling for precious stones. "Tell me, Shanti, how many new students were with you in class today?"

Ashanti flinched at her mother's banging. "I don't know."

Her father clucked his tongue. "What do you mean, you do not know? How can you not know this simple number? What were you doing all day?" There was a darkness under his words, something Ashanti could not discern. But if he had known about the blasphemy, he would have said so by now.

"Making these bracelets." She wiggled her arms at him. She sat beside him and indicated the smaller screen. "Say, is that a new television?"

"Yes. Given by Providence Headquarters."

Ashanti squinted at the images from the *Yuna II*. "What do *you* see, Papa?"

"I see a head and a body on a throne," he recited. "Like a king." He did not even glance at the smaller screen with the Sleeping One. He was glued to the Vatican broadcast.

Her mother called from the kitchen, "You see nothing!"

"I do, Sheryl! A head! And a body! On a throne!"

The banging continued in the kitchen. She heard her mother muttering, "He sees nothing."

Ashanti thought, *They can't be in disagreement about the Sleeping One. They have never disagreed about that.*

Her father poked her in the side. "Now, focus, Shanti, and tell me the number of new students."

"Twelve?"

Her father whistled. "Twelve! Like the Prophets! Sheryl, did you hear? Twelve new students in Ashanti's class!"

Her mother muttered, "Oh. The blind man thinks I am deaf. Yes, Nkrumah, I hear."

Ashanti added, "There were so many that we were sitting cross-legged on the floor, leaning against the wall, sitting on the reading table in the back—although no one is supposed to sit on that, *ever*, so I'm not sure why they were getting a pass on that behavior."

Nkrumah spread his hands. "It is important to be accommodating. The topics they are learning are foreign."

"And our teacher was wearing a nicer dress than usual. She was wearing high-heeled sandals."

Nkrumah had lost interest. He watched the television like a bird of prey.

Ashanti kept talking: "And she wasn't versed in Grieves history. I had to correct her sometimes." She stopped. The topic was dangerously close to her essay and the note in her schoolbag.

Her father asked, "Do these new students have good Ghanaian names or slaver names?"

"I think one is named Arthur."

Her father whistled again. "I think *that* name—" He called out, "Sheryl! I think one of the new children is named for the judge in the kangaroo court that gave the Prophet Grieves the death sentence for the slave insurrection!"

Her mother said, "Worry about your own children, Nkrumah."

Her father sucked his breath in, then whispered to Ashanti, "It *is* the name. I know it."

"I think the surname was Johnson."

"Twelve students!" her father said to himself.

Yes, she thought, *my father is manic today.* "Papa?"

"Hmm?"

The note in the bookbag burned in her mind. She has never kept anything from her parents. She would like to keep this to herself, but it pained her to be separate from them. Like now, this gravity under their actions and words. She was outside of them. It was lonely and unbearable. She swerved. "The people down by the beach?"

On the large television, the reporters at the Vatican were being shushed. Her father bubbled over with glee: "The Catholics are on! Sheryl, the Catholics are on!"

The banging in the kitchen reached a fever pitch. How was her father not noticing it?

The new television showed a white man in a black frock and a red beanie waddling to a long table in front of the reporters. He tapped the microphone. Other men in similar robes filed in to surround him.

"Papa?" Ashanti whispered. "The people at the beach are starving."

Her father waved a hand. "They are not believers."

"They provide us fish."

"Not anymore. We procure our food from the villages now."

On the television, the white man spoke too close to the microphone. His beanie slipped a little, and he pushed it back. His voice boomed, "Thank you for coming today..." Feedback squealed. He produced a handful of index cards and shuffled them. Visible sweat beaded on his shining forehead. He removed a handkerchief from his robe and patted his face.

Ashanti said, "But, Papa, what is being done to help them?"

Her father raised his hands in supplication. "Ashanti, please...the *Catholics* are on."

The white man on television said, "I have a statement from His Holiness, currently hospitalized with gallstones. This will be the only statement on the matter of the so-called Sleeping One..." He shuffled the index cards faster. He wiped his forehead again.

One of the other robed men stepped forward, covered the microphone, and whispered to the speaker. The man at the podium shook his head violently. The other man stepped back.

Ashanti pressed her father, "I mean, we have plenty of food to share. Our church should create a food-transport system from the villages—"

"Shush, Ashanti! This is our moment!"

The robed white man at the microphone cleared his throat and rearranged the index cards again. Shuffling faster and faster. Another wipe of the brow. Another throat clear.

Finally, he leaned into the microphone. "His Holiness says..." The man cleared his throat again. "No comment."

The banging in the kitchen stopped. Ashanti's father let loose a stream of air.

On the television, the press conference room steeped in a bewildered silence.

The man at the podium tucked the index cards into his robe, then skittered away.

A reporter in the audience stammered, "What did he just say?"

One of the other robed men stepped forward to speak, but the microphone had been cut off with another loud squeal of feedback. Someone off camera started yelling in Italian. The press stood all at once. Hands shot up. The robed man sliced the air with his hands. "*Ferma la telecamera!*"

Ashanti's father released a long, low groan. "Ahhhhhhhhhhhhh," he said. Then his face morphed into a monstrous grin. "*Ei! Anigye da!*"

The phone rang. Her father snatched it and gushed into the receiver, "Reverend Grieves Church of Providence, how...Adom!"

Ashanti slid from the couch. She scooped up her bookbag and slipped into the kitchen.

"Yes, I heard it! Happy day! Happy day! Yes, I agree! The people are very sensitive now! There will be panic! Print the new flyers for distribution..."

Ashanti found her mother in the kitchen peeling noni fruit. "I could go the rest of my life without eating this bitter fruit," her mother said to the green, stubbled skin. "Famine food, my people called it. No one would eat this unless starving."

Her mother stared at the fruit for a long time, not moving.

"Mama?"

Her mother turned the fruit over. "You know, Ashanti, I haven't seen my village in a long time. They did not approve of this..." She gestured to the living room. "*This.*" She continued to peel.

"Mama, may I write to Ama later when Papa is finished with Adom? I know her address in America. She will receive it when she—"

Her mother did not look away from peeling. "No need. She's upstairs."

"Upstairs?" Ashanti felt cold.

"Yes. She came home today."

Ashanti drew her brows together, trying to understand. "She came home from America? Today?"

"That is what I said."

Ashanti did not know what to say. Why wasn't she told? Why was she not at the airport to greet her? Did she fly on the Providence plane, sent by Providence Headquarters? Only they would have the fuel for such a trip. Why wasn't there a party to greet her? She would have many stories to share of fat Americans and their stupid ways. "Mama—"

Her mother's anger cracked like a whip. "How many times must I say that she came home today? She came home today! She is here now! Must I repeat myself like a parrot?"

Her mother resumed peeling.

Her father continued with Adom, "*Fifty* for the reception tonight? Fifty! My son, what glorious news!"

Ashanti tried, "Papa didn't mention Ama."

Her mother said nothing.

"He usually mentions first when Ama is home."

No reply.

"How long will she stay? She will have a new mission assignment—"

Her mother tossed white fruit in a bowl. "No new mission assignments. Do not bother me. I must make food for 50, did you not hear? Do I have a deaf daughter and a blind husband?"

In the living room: "Glorious news, son!"

"Okay." Ashanti shrank.

Her mother held the side of her head. She thought she saw her jaw tense. She did this, Ashanti knew, when she was fighting back tears. "Why don't you go upstairs to see her, Shanti? Make her feel better."

"She is sick?"

Her mother grasped sides of the cutting board. "Just go."

"All right."

"Good girl." Her mother centered a basket of green gourds on the cutting board and sighed at them. "Now, what am I supposed to do with these?"

21

Will You Free Them?

ASHANTI MOVED SLOWLY TO the top of the stairs, holding the wobbly banister in place to keep it from rattling. As she climbed, Ama's singing voice cut right through her. It was low and sad. Ashanti knew the song.

Reverend, we're all onboard.
For the captain's waiting to sail us all to Africa...

It was a song they were taught as children in the basement of the Reverend Grieves Academy. "In the minor key," their music teacher used to say. "The key of sadness."

Ama used to ask, "Why is it in a minor key when it's a song about freedom?"

That was something Ashanti loved about her sister: Ama always questioned. She never cared about consequences. She only wanted to prod people into thinking about what they were doing, to not do things by rote for reasons not understood. It was a skill Ashanti was hoping to develop. One day.

At the top of the stairs, it was dark in their bathroom, but the painting of Black Nance and the Light Ones shone with its pearlescent pigments. The raisin-skinned hag lifted her arms to the floating specters. Her eyes rolled back in her head, exposing the glowing whites in her eyes. The peachy paleness of her palms glimmered. Her mouth hinged open, revealing a hint of sharp, yellowed teeth. Under her sleek skin, muscles rippled. A vivid red scar ringed her neck. This was the evidence of her enslavement, Ashanti knew. The story goes that Black Nance used to live shackled, then broke out to live on her own terms in the Great Dismal Swamp, living among dangerous animals, hunting for food and fending off floods. She preferred freedom and self-determination in the wild to what few comforts that white civilization offered her. Nance's power broke through the canvas and shook Ashanti to the core. Ama was right. This woman could not be relegated to nothingness, a Prophet's crutch. Black Nance would refuse to be put aside.

Ama sang:

When Black Nance speaks,
And the Light Ones glow,
Reverend, we're all onboard...

Ama never sang out of church. Now, Ashanti wondered why not. Her sister's voice lulled her into a different state of being. Ashanti had forgotten about her principal's note, forgotten about her parents' troubling moods. She drifted into a reverie outside of Ama's door. Ama sang:

The Sacred Truth
Is in our hands.
The Light Ones will show you the way—

Then Ama spoke: "Littlest A."

Ashanti startled.

It wasn't a question. Ama knew who was approaching. Was it the pressure of Ashanti's footfall on the squeaky spot in the hallway? Was it the sour, musty scent of the Reverend Grieves Academy clinging to her uniform? The hairs on her arms raised. Ashanti felt hunted, as if she were emitting signals to a predator she could not sense. The hairs on her neck raised, too. The electric current was strong here.

"Come in, Littlest," Ama said.

Ashanti's impulse was to freeze, but she forced herself to move. She slid into Ama's nearly vacant room. Inside, a dim desk lamp on the floor threw light upward. A fan was spinning sluggishly, throwing spiral-shaped shadows on the walls. The effect was disorienting, as if the room itself had flipped, then plunged into a dizzy spiral.

The two books Ashanti had used to prop open the window to view the Zangbeto were now thrown to the floor, wide open and exposed. Pages flickered and crackled under the fan. The faces of Ama's stuffed animal brigade were all turned to her, as if she had fashioned herself an audience. Ama perched upon her bed. It had been cleared of sheets and blankets, exposing the mattress. She watched Ashanti with the steady attention of a beast hiding, waiting for the right moment to ambush. Ama said nothing but cocked her head at her little sister.

"You are home," Ashanti said to her.

"Mmm," was all Ama said. The hairs on Ashanti's legs now raised. They resonated with Ama's hum, catching a spark in her sound.

Against every instinct, Ashanti stepped closer.

Ama's face was in shadow, but her hair was wild. She normally kept it sleek and straight, like European hair, but she had let it go. It frizzed out into a silhouette that was unfamiliar. More than that, she carried herself differently. She usually took up space, made herself bold with broad gestures and hands on hips. Now, she sat streamlined and elegant, spine erect, legs folded in on themselves. Her curves at her waist had disappeared. The Ama here was just a wisp of her former self. Had she not been eating? Her air smelled of cigarette smoke.

Ama beckoned Ashanti. "I won't bite."

Ashanti wasn't sure. She threw out a compliment like a piece of bloody meat to a starving carnivore. "You sing pretty, Biggest A."

Ama hummed as if she were thinking. Ashanti's neck hairs responded.

Then, Ama burst from the bed. Ashanti flinched. Ama stopped, processing Ashanti's terror with another tilted glance. "Do not fear me."

Ashanti bit her lip.

Ama drifted behind the upturned desk lamp and folded herself into a wicker chair in the corner. *Folded herself,* Ashanti thought. *Like one without bones.* Ama never sat like that before. Ama *plopped.* Ama huffed on impact. Ama spread her legs and hung her arms between and sighed, "See, Littlest A?" she used to say, as if she might have preached about something important, even if it was just, "You don't *color* the prophet coloring page for Sir Henley Goode's Antarctic expedition. It's all snow in that picture. Snow is white. Just turn that page back in, and tell the teacher, 'Done.'"

A lighter flicked. A cigarette flared.

Ashanti swallowed the shock in her voice and asked carefully, "You smoke now, Ama?"

Ama blew a cloud that hovered above the upturned desk light. She said in a low tone, "It quiets my mind." Then she rubbed her temples, massaging something deep inside that Ashanti couldn't see. Suddenly, Ama jerked forward to her normal stance with hands dangling below her knees. "That's not our song, you know."

"What song? The song you were singing?"

Ama sucked at her cigarette and released, arms nearly dragging the floor. "It's not a Providence song at all. It's an old tune from the American South."

"Okay."

Ama brought her legs to her chest. Her cigarette glowed between dull-grey fingers. "An operator of the Underground Railroad wrote it and taught it to slaves, talking about what constellation to follow to freedom. Follow the North Star. The Polaris." Ama rubbed at her temples again, murmured to herself, "Polaris. Polaris. The missing submarine. It all comes back around. All comes back around."

Ashanti squirmed under a long pause. "I don't underst—"

Ama lurched forward again. Her knuckles brushed a shag rug. Ashanti suddenly feared fire from the cigarette lighting up the entire house. Ama said,

"The original song says to follow the Polaris star at the time of year that the quails breed. Follow the dead trees by the river. Find the man with a peg for a foot. He will bring you to safety."

"Okay."

Ama waved her cigarette, watching the smoke trail. Ash fell onto the shag rug. Ashanti tensed. Ama said, "It's funny to think, isn't it, that the great Reverend Grieves was once a slave. Born in Africa, sold to the Caribbean trade, bought himself freedom only to die at the end of a hangman's rope in America. Land of the free." She paused. "If he hadn't bought his freedom, he might have met Black Nance on the Underground Railroad instead of in pursuit of a journal article."

"Ama, what's wrong with your hair?"

Ama ignored her. "Black Nance. We all meet her one way or another."

"It's all frizzly."

"Are you listening, Littlest A?"

"No. You're not making sense."

Ama's head rolled. "Ohhhh." She took another drag, then added, "Not you, too."

The street lamps outside popped on. Ama came into a different light now. Ashanti could see that her face had grown ashen and lined, as if gravity had pulled at her too hard and her face had snapped back bruised and damaged. Purple shadows clouded under her sunken eyes. When she brought the cigarette to her lips, Ashanti saw dark lesions on her hands. "Biggest A! What's happened to you?"

Ama waved her away. "My body is of no consequence, Ashanti."

"What does *that* mean?"

"I inhabit a new realm now."

"Mama said you are sick."

Ama laughed. It was a rough bark, joyless. She rubbed her head again. Then she smacked it with the meat of her hand. Her cigarette dumped ash onto her shirt, which was stained.

"What's wrong with you, then?" Ashanti asked.

Ama lolled her head, as if listening to gentle music. Then she spoke in a lower register, "Yes. Yes." She centered herself and studied Ashanti. "I understand the plight of the prophet."

"Okay."

Ama coughed another joyless laugh. "Okay?" Then, she muttered, "She says it's okay."

"Ama, why did you wait so long to call from America? After the Discovery? We were worried."

Ama replied in a detached tone. "What are you talking about?"

"Why did you not call or write after the Discovery?"

She held Ashanti in a dead gaze. "They did not tell you."

"Tell me what?"

Ama half-closed her eyes. "Providence called. They explained. And our parents did not tell you?"

Ashanti was growing weary of this version of Ama. "Explained what? Why are you so different? Why were you in America so long?"

"If I tell you," Ama said, wiping a discreet tear that had leaked out, it seemed, against her will, "you will turn against me, too."

Ashanti whispered, "I would never turn against you, Ama. *Adom*, maybe—"

Ama raised her chin and blew smoke at the ceiling. "You will. Just like Mama and Pa—"

"I am not Mama. I am not Papa. I am Ashanti."

Ama curled back into the darkness. Her cigarette flared and receded. Ashanti approached her, then sat at her feet. She touched Ama's bare toes. They were cold like a corpse's. Ama flinched. "You can talk to me," Ashanti said.

Ama stretched her neck. It cracked. Ashanti bristled at the grating sound. Ama said, "The day of Discovery, I witnessed the Light Ones."

Ashanti withdrew her hand. No one had witnessed the Light Ones since Reverend Grieves visited the swamp. "Ama," she said, "no one—"

Ama spat, "Do not regurgitate the dogma to me. I know that no one has witnessed them, and I know what I witnessed."

"Okay."

Ama drove her chin into her chest.

"You can tell me, Biggest A." Ashanti rested her hand back on Ama's foot. It was cold. Very little blood coursed there.

Ama curled into herself again. She started with a whisper. "I brought a tour group into the swamp. Fourteen white people in bright jackets to keep them from getting lost among the towering trees. It can be..." She searched for a word. "Disorienting in there." She took another drag. "All of us on the ditch trail, hiking to the center lake along the canal. All of us looking for Light Ones." She exhaled. "Looking for what ought not be found." Ama sucked on the cigarette as if it contained the air that fed her. "We came upon a clearing in the swamp I hadn't seen before. Thousands of glowing mushrooms in the swamp muck were giving off their spores in clouds. The little grains in the air looked like a curtain of light. Waving, undulating. It was beautiful." She stopped, bit her lip. "Then...it happened so fast."

"What did?"

"Streams of white light, like lightning strikes. Not at all like the painting in the bathroom. Hot and vicious. You could feel their anger. There was nothing light about them. They *burn*. They are *sharp* like razors. They intend to *eviscerate*."

Ashanti dropped her chin. She was not sure what to believe. "You think these lightning strikes were Light Ones and not—"

Ama wagged her head, her hair mimicking her movements like a halo of black smoke. "Lightning does not move sideways. It does not emanate from the darkness of the earth, from the waters of swamps."

"Okay."

Ama lengthened her spine. "You mock me."

"I do not."

She took another drag. It was getting dark outside. The shadows on the wall changed again, intensifying. Ama said, "That lightning cut into every one of the white tourists. Sliced right into their hearts."

"What?"

Ama jabbed the air with her cigarette. "ZIP! ZIP! They left holes in people, Littlest A." She grinned wide. Her teeth glowed like Black Nance's in the painting. Ama pulled her hand down her chest. "The Light Ones left wide holes where organs fell through. Those people bled like slaughtered pigs, Shanti." She sucked on the cigarette again. "Then, the glowing mushrooms pulsed. All the dead bodies deflated like balloons, like the mushrooms were feeding on them. When the mushrooms were done with the corpses, just tourist jackets and clothes were left behind, like someone dumped a lot of dirty laundry in the swamp, but the bodies were all gone. No sign of them. Then, the mushrooms all exhaled white powder in clouds. It was like the mushrooms turned into smokestacks or steam vents. All that powder hovered around me in curls and wisps, thickening the air. I was afraid to breathe it. My throat and eyes burned. Then, SPLAT." Ashanti jumped. "The powder all fell to the ground like it had been hit by a sudden gravity. The blood on the ground just seeped through all that white powder. Everything turned red." Ama closed her eyes. Ashanti could see bruises on Ama's eyelids. Ama said, "When I close my eyes, I still see it. The Light Ones were like gods smiting us all."

"But not you. It didn't smite you."

Ama let loose a sob, then swallowed it. "Not me."

Ashanti ventured on unsteady ground. "Why not you, Biggest A?"

Ama took another drag. "Because I'm their new messenger. They spoke to me."

"Okay."

Ashanti considered this against what she had heard her parents arguing about before she opened the door to the house.

Prophet's bloodline...

Insanity...
She cannot be allowed...
I will not sign it...

Ashanti still could not understand what the last one meant. "What did they tell you, Ama?"

Ama tilted her head again. Her voice went higher now. "Vastly powerful beings play with our lives, Shanti."

"We knew that."

"No, no. You see, the Reverend misunderstood the Light Ones' message." She was talking faster now. "The Light Ones told him about these powerful beings interfering with their lives, and the Reverend believed they meant the *white people*. So he planned that insurrection. But the Light Ones did not mean white people. They told me. They wanted to be clear. They meant the *Cosmics*. The insurrection was for nothing."

"The...what?" This was blasphemy far beyond anything Ashanti had ever heard before. The Reverend was *wrong*? The insurrection was for *nothing*? He *misheard* the Light Ones? Ashanti couldn't bring herself to ask these questions aloud; they were so dangerous.

Ama bolted from her place, tossing the cigarette against the wall. The butt sizzled and sparked, then extinguished. Ama took Ashanti's hands in a cold clasp, and Ashanti felt electricity surge in her body. Ama was close now. Ashanti could smell her sister's breath had gone sour, like the earth had filled her mouth. Ama was giddy. She said, "I *knew* it all along. I *knew* Black Nance was the key. I *knew* she was the one we should have revered. She told it right, but the Reverend got it wrong. We should have sent someone back into the swamp to find her, to ask her again to tell—"

Ashanti tried to pull away. "This is blasphemy on top of blasphemy. I don't want to get in more trouble."

Ama held her hands tightly. Red welts bloomed on Ashanti's wrists. Ama wet her cheeks with spit as she spoke. "Don't you see? There are *worse* things than white slavers. The Cosmics hold us in far less esteem than white slavers did, Ashanti. They move us like pieces—"

"We are in a game," Ashanti finished. "We know this, Ama. This is not new information."

Ama shook Ashanti's hands until her head rattled. "Pay attention!" She gnashed her teeth at her little sister. "Ashanti, listen! I don't have long—"

"What?" Ashanti forced herself into Ama's face. "Why not? What's going on?"

"I'm trying to tell you!" She reached into her back pocket and produced an envelope. It had been previously torn open but reused and wrinkled. The paper rattled when Ama pushed it into Ashanti's hands. Ama curled her sister's tiny hands into fists around it. "This is some of the white powder from the tourists' jackets—"

Ashanti tried to pull away. "Disgusting! I don't want it."

Ama shook Ashanti again, this time violently tossing her neck around. "This is a gift from the Light Ones! They told me. A gift! Take it! Hide it! Let no one know about it! Keep quiet! Do not make the mistake I did!"

"Stop it, Ama! You're hurting me!" She felt her sister's distorted intensity up close, in the heat from her face and the hot spit from her mouth.

Ama went on, "The Light Ones say that our power to fight back is already here on Earth! There is a network; we are all connected. Like the Underground Railroad. We must use it to be free—"

Downstairs, their mother called, "Ama? Ashanti? What's going on up there?"

Ama rushed to finish. "Take the powder, Shanti. Consume it."

"No!"

"It takes time to work. When it does, you will meet Black Nance at the Tree of Faces—"

"WHAT ARE YOU SAYING?" Ashanti screamed.

Downstairs, heavy footfalls from the living room. Nkrumah bellowed, "Ashanti! Come down this instant!" Then, to their mother, "Sheryl, did you send Shanti upstairs?"

Her mother replied, "What if I did?"

Ama pulled Ashanti close. "One day you will face what Black Nance faced. Will you free them, or will you fail?"

Ashanti sobbed, slapping at Ama's hands. "Stop talking like this!"

Nkrumah's footsteps shook the frames in the hallway. The banister wobbled. Their mother called from the bottom of the stairs, "Nkrumah! Don't! Leave them be!"

Ama breathed hard in Ashanti's face. "They're coming for me, Shanti. I speak the truth, so I upend the church as they know it. You are our only chance."

Ashanti sputtered between sobs, "Whose chance?"

"Humanity's."

Ama pushed Ashanti away. She thudded to the floor, bawling.

Nkrumah rounded the corner and burst through the door. "This will end, Ama. Your nonsense will end *tonight*." He dragged her from the room.

Ama glanced back at Ashanti. "Do not make the mistake I did."

Under the upturned light and shadows, Ashanti shuddered and convulsed.

Nkrumah pulled Ama down the hallway; Ashanti could hear her sister kick at the walls. Nkrumah sputtered his words. "You—you—you will go now to the prayer camp. No matter what your mother says."

"Papa!" Ashanti shrieked.

Their mother cried out, "Nkrumah! I do not consent!"

"Call Adom, Sheryl!" their father boomed in the hallway. "He has the petrol! He knows where to take her!"

Their mother pleaded, "That place is for nonbelievers! They cure nothing!"

Their father raged, "Not even Providence Headquarters can stop her lies! She speaks blasphemy! I cannot have it! Not now! Not when—"

Their father rattled the banister again, this time forcing Ama downstairs. Ama kicked at the walls in the stairwell. She said nothing but fought hard. Ashanti crawled into the hallway, wiping away snot with the back of her hand. She could see her mother's shadow at the bottom of the stairs. "They *chain* them at the prayer camp!" their mother called out. "They live in *dirt*. You want your daughter to live in *filth*?"

Nkrumah held Ama up by her hair. "This is no daughter of mine!"

Ashanti met Ama's eyes between the stair railings. Nkrumah turned on Ashanti. "Go to your room!"

Their mother was wailing now.

"Remember," Ama mouthed to her between the railings. "Remember."

"Go!" Nkrumah yelled.

Ashanti pulled herself off the floor and ran to her room. She slammed her door so hard she shook the floorboards.

She held back staccato breaths, searching her room.

Remember, remember.

Where is it?

She tossed dirty clothes, her blanket, her records.

Where is it? Where is it?

There.

It was under her pajamas: her diary.

She grabbed it, then unlocked it.

And she wrote.

22

Not At All

IN SOME OTHER COUNTRIES, the insane were treated at clean hospitals in beds with professional nurses and medications. Ashanti knew this. Her encyclopedias told her so.

In Ghana, they were treated in prayer camps run by Christians. By nonbelievers. These institutions offered only faith-healing and demon exorcism. Minimal medication would be used. Patients were often chained outdoors and forced to urinate and defecate where they slept on lice-ridden mats. They were tended by nurses called "prophets."

That was where Ama died.

"Suicide," was the word Ashanti caught. She had to look up the word.

She asked her father for clarification. His hand landed on her head. "She has gone to the ancestors," he told her.

Ashanti backed away from him, allowing his hand to drop.

Her father and brother whispered about how to keep Ama's scandal out of the church gossip. There was no funeral. There was no crying.

After Ama was taken away, their mother left Accra to visit her family at a village in the interior. She never returned. She left a note, "This is not what I wanted." She did not sign it.

Soon, the Reverend Grieves Church's services were so full that Adom inquired into taking over the burned-out department store in the mall.

Ashanti refused to attend services in a mall. That would not be the same church she grew up with. Not the same moldy basement. Not the same music teacher. Some Providence singers from Sweden flew in to take over the music program. White people. They had sung like goat herders calling their flocks. Had her father lost his mind, too? Ashanti wasn't taking part in those new services, but her father challenged her. "How would it appear to others," he asked, "for my daughter not to be by my side in these glorious times?"

Daughter. Ashanti wondered if he meant Ama. He never mentioned her. He never mentioned her mother. Adom hovered near him now like a dedicated servant.

Ashanti leered at them both, spied on them from the shadows of their old house, treated them as enemies or prey. Neither noticed.

A new school year started, but Ashanti wasn't interested. She did not even pretend to attend. She spent most of her time at the beach with the fishermen, staring at the sea. Instead of books in her bookbag, she carried food left over from the church's enormous gatherings. No one noticed what she took. She left it for the beach people, food piled high on a wall close to her, but not so close that the people felt the need to thank her. It wasn't her food to begin with.

She thought, *I am the food vigilante.*

She kept her diary with her. She kept it locked. It bulged more than it used to, with Ama's wrinkled envelope inside. Only once had she opened it, sniffing at the powder carefully. It smelled like earthy rot. She couldn't bring herself to ingest it as Ama wanted. What if she went insane as Ama did? Would her father also sign her away to a prayer camp? She didn't want to die by her own hand in the filth. She had plans.

"Sleeping One," she would say to the indifferent ocean. "I am coming."

In her diary, she wrote pages and pages, everything she could remember about Ama's words that night. The way the Light Ones killed the tourists. The white earthy powder they left behind. The Reverend's misunderstanding. The network on Earth. Black Nance in the Tree of Faces. There was one phrase she wrote down in quotes, because she remembered it word for word: *One day you will face what Black Nance faced. Will you free them, or will you fail?*

She reviewed the words every day. Would they ever make sense?

Months later, a man from Providence Headquarters visited their home: their first outside visitor since the men came to take Ama. He gave Ashanti a test with her father overseeing the proceedings. She was videotaped. The man asked questions and Ashanti had to give responses like, "Not at all," "Sometimes," or "All the time."

He asked, "I hear or see things others do not hear or see."

Ashanti: "Not at all."

He asked, "I can't trust what I'm thinking because I don't know if it's real or not."

"Not at all."

"I have magical powers that no one else has or can explain."

"Not at all."

Afterward, the man shook his head gravely, and her father exhaled and smiled.

"I'm going to the beach," she told her father.

He and Adom did not even turn away from their celebrating with the Providence man to notice her. They were sharing their attendance numbers. "Good, good," her father mumbled.

Adom swiped the back of his hand across his nose.

23

Squid Pro Quo

One Year Later

ASHANTI SLUMPED ON THE low stone wall at the beach. Rainbow-colored Zangbeto drifted on rafts in the harbor. Fishermen chanted their melodies. Drums marked the time. Children scampered to the wall to collect what food Ashanti brought, then darted back to their shacks. Waves lapped the edge of the beach.

Things were returning to normal. Slowly. A world government was on the rise. There was food in the stores. There was petrol for the autos. Science was booming. The Sleeping One was putting off dream waves. Americans were doing crazy things with Artificial Lifeforms. Providence Group was exploding with popularity.

Ashanti had missed a full year of school, refusing to go.

She reread her diary. *Vast powers. Playing with our lives. A network on Earth. Black Nance. Tree of Faces. One day you will free them.*

It made no more sense now than it did the night Ama told her these things.

Ashanti considered the horizon. It had been a long time since she had thought of finding the Sleeping One there.

It had been a long year.

Somewhere behind her, an engine growled. A nice one with a proper exhaust.

Ashanti craned to see what was coming.

A yellow sports car careened down the center of the empty harbor street, taking a corner with its back end fishtailing. The car squealed to a stop just inches from Ashanti's bookbag. Inside the car, the thump of American punk music vibrated the windscreen. Ashanti didn't recognize the hard, fuzzy guitars wailing above a stark snare. A New York rapper whined over record scratches and a cowbell.

All around, corrugated doors of shacks flew open. Children spilled out, babbling about the yellow car: "What is it? Where is it from?" Women stopped their chores to gawk.

The engine was killed. The music silenced.

Ashanti shoved her diary into her armpit and stood.

A car door hinged open. A white woman in a navy habit that dragged the ground stepped out, her dark headpiece at full sail in the ocean breeze. Ashanti breathed, "A Catholic." She had never seen one this close.

Just as quickly as the children had appeared, they disappeared back into the shacks. "White ghost! White phantom!"

"There you are," the nun said to Ashanti.

"Me?"

"Aye, pet."

She drifted over toward Ashanti in a bobbing sort of walk, as if she were a boat on undulating waves. Ashanti scooted backward. The woman caught a whiff of something and scrunched her face. "Doesn't this manky beach smell like a mountain of hot fish guts?" The hem of her tunic dragged the ground. She seemed to have no feet. Her face was pale and white, but still a little dark for a white woman, Ashanti thought. And she spoke funny.

"Who are you? What kind of car is that?" Ashanti asked.

"Porsche 964 RS. Limone Yellow," the woman said. "One day you may drive a fine automobile such as this. But not this one, and not today. My turn: why have you dropped out of school?"

"I asked who you were."

"Get used to mystery."

"Why are you driving that car?"

"To bring me here, to ask you why you're not in school."

Ashanti cut herself off with crossed arms. "I don't answer questions from strangers."

"I'm not a stranger. I was sent by Providence."

"You are a stranger to me."

The nun stepped forward. "School is important, Ashanti Oko. So, I ask a third time, something I *rarely* do: Why aren't you attending class in an educational institution today?"

Ashanti shrugged.

The woman dented her tunic with her hands on her hips. "A pouter. I can see life has lost its luster." Ashanti said nothing. "Others have lost much more, and they do not sulk like this." Ashanti turned away. "Why do you behave like a boring child when you are anything but?"

"I'm not here to entertain."

The woman raised her brows, which revealed grey, crimped hair behind her wimple. "She has a bite."

"Piss off," Ashanti muttered.

"And a mouth." Louder, she said, "Pissing off, my treasure, is something I will not do."

"There are no *nuns* in Providence," Ashanti added.

"I'm not a nun."

"Funny. You look like a nun."

"And you look like a dropout and an eejit. Are you?"

"Why wear that costume if you are not a nun?"

"To hide my vicious scars. Want to see?" Ashanti turned to her. "I thought that would get your attention." The woman maneuvered between Ashanti and the ocean. "Listen, pet, as much as I'd like to continue this chat about your academic failings and my outerwear, I'm here on more serious business. I'm here about Ama."

Ashanti sucked in her breath.

"Another attention-grabber, I see."

Ashanti stepped wide in an aggressive stance. "What about my sister?"

"Oh, do put the claws away, child," the nun said. "I've fought and won bigger battles before breakfast. And I certainly won't debate the merits of trashing a place like Heavenly Prayer Camp, where Ama met her end—"

Ashanti bared her teeth, then ran at the woman.

She easily stepped aside—*hovered aside*—Ashanti thought, as she rushed headlong toward the car. "Mind the Porsche, dearest. It's on loan."

Ashanti stumbled and bumped her head on the door. "What about my sister?" she screeched.

"Settle down. I come bearing gifts." The woman plopped down on the wall. "They've got a few strings attached, unfortunately. All gifts do." She raised a finger. "Best learn that now, my precious. There is no free lunch." Ashanti glanced at the pile of leftover food on the wall. "That's an adage, pigeon. I was not referring to actual food."

Ashanti said, "I'm not a bird."

"And she's quite literal," the woman said to herself. "No, dearest, I'm offering a *trade*. Information for information. As a bonus, I'll throw in a ticket out of here. I hear you're at your wits' end with your father and brother, so that ought to inspire you to talk. No matter. Your future lies elsewhere."

Ashanti squinted to better focus on the woman. "You talk funny."

"Don't get out much, do you? Let's fix that." The woman straightened herself. "Sweet one, haven't you noticed that the Reverend Lazarus Bethlehem Grieves Academy fails to challenge you?"

"I don't have any *information*—"

The woman steeled her gaze. "I doubt that as much as I doubt that you're the eejit you appear to be today." She hopped off the wall. "I won't insult you with more small talk, so let's get to it. Quid pro quo, turnip. Tell me what I want to know, and I will tell you what you want to know. Then, you get to go to a new school—"

"That doesn't sound like a fair trade."

"—in a new country. A fresh start."

"I'm happy here."

"Ashanti," the nun said. "Come now. We both know that's not the case."

Ashanti returned her focus to the ocean.

The woman sighed. "All right. Allow me to open my powers of perception." She moved toward the girl. "You, sweet cherub, struggle with feeling alone. You have trouble making friends despite the close circle of the church. You don't even have friends in your class, except the girl who no one else likes anyway. You feel like an outsider in your own family. You are too dark, too short, too unruly, too strange. And you are *much* smarter than you let on." Ashanti tossed her another side glance. The woman continued, "This is not a new problem. It did not begin with Ama's death or your mother's departure. It did not begin with the Discovery. It is a problem as old as I am, and I'm here to tell you it doesn't have to be this way."

Ashanti twisted her lips, holding back tears or harsh words. She wasn't sure what would come out.

"Now," the nun continued, "I say, and others agree, that you might benefit from a change. Perhaps a new school that allows students to study the Sleeping One and all its accompanying mysteries?"

Ashanti's heart stopped. She rose. "What?"

Now, it was the nun's turn to stare off into the distance. "It's an emerging area of study within the Providence academia. Top scientists convening to discuss ways we will study the Temple Site. Figuring out how we will determine the language of the Temple inscriptions. Radiography. Computer modeling. Biological samples. Behavior monitoring." She turned to Ashanti and pointedly said, "The unique marine fungi that coats its lair. So unusual! Or is it? Extraterrestrial plant matter associated with the home of a cosmic being? What news! It seems the Sleeping One isn't the only alien life in our presence, is it? Plants. Fungi. Pollen. What a puzzler for the academics." She let that thought hang between them. "So. Those topics are all matters for further study. You name it, we want to investigate it."

Ashanti's mind raced. "I can go to school *just* to study the Sleeping One and its...uh...plants?"

"More or less. Mathematics and biology are necessary. Thus, to enter that field of study, your educational pipeline must change dramatically."

"What does that mean?"

"It means, cherished, that instead of a life inside a church basement memorizing the stories that bore one to tears at age 11—"

"I'm 12 now."

"It's a relief to hear you can count that high." The woman continued, "No more Reverend Grieves Academy, my elderly scholar. How about boarding at a foreign educational institution with subjects appropriate for studying at the Temple Site itself? One day."

Ashanti felt dizzy. "We don't have the money for that."

"There are full scholarships. Courtesy of the Providence Group." Ashanti opened her mouth to speak, but the nun interrupted, "Having a full scholarship means your education is free. And close your mouth."

Ashanti closed her mouth.

The nun kicked a rock. Her long tunic made this a sloppy effort, as her feet were buried in folds of navy serge fabric. She said, "Oh, aye! To study at the Temple Site in the Pacific! Not this deplorable monitoring outpost here. Wrong ocean, by the way."

"They're all connected. It's a network."

"Fair enough."

"Free school?" Ashanti pressed her lips together hard. "But there's no free lunch."

"They said you learned fast."

"What about this information exchange?"

The woman clapped her hands once. "Let's get started."

Ashanti narrowed her gaze. "Hold on. How do I know your information is of value?"

"And you're a shrewd one."

"What could I possibly want from you?"

The woman brightened. "Why, to know exactly how Ama died, of course."

Ashanti's voice dropped with her confidence. "She died of suicide."

The nun shook her head. Her wimple waggled. "Sorry, pet. No."

"I heard—"

The woman lifted a finger. "No, no. Me first." Ashanti frowned. "I'm offering *more*: information about Ama *and* a life away from this dump, so we will do the exchange on my terms."

"This is not a dump."

"Agree to disagree. Now, what I want to know—what *many* want to know—is exactly what Ama told you the night she was taken away. *Exactly*, turnip. No detail is too small."

"She didn't say—"

The woman frowned. "Ashanti Oko, do not waste my time."

"I'm not—"

The nun's voice darkened. "You are mistaking me for someone who does not understand the power of family lineage, for one who does not understand the constant burden and privilege of being the ancestor of a prophet. How is my life different than the lives of others, you wonder? You feel you are meant for more in this world but cannot put your finger on what that might be. It is the source of both abject loneliness and limitless speculation—"

Ashanti dropped her shoulders. "How do you know all this?"

"I know the type, pet. And for once, accept the hand that's being offered instead of doubting its intention."

Ashanti squinted. "Who *are* you?"

"Believe this: I am a friend."

Ashanti fixed her jaw and all her muscles against that concept.

The woman relented. "All right. Friendship will take time. But for right now, tell me what Ama said that night. It's easy. Open your mouth and move it."

Ashanti was unsure whether she could trust the nun who was not a nun but uncertain of what she had to lose. And this woman was so *pushy*. Ashanti had to be careful, so she started small. "Ama said the tourists died."

The woman nodded. "We know that."

"Ama said it was bloody."

"Yes. We noticed that. I'll need some *new* information, pet."

Ashanti rubbed her throat. "And there was a—uh—white powder."

The woman followed Ashanti's hand to her throat. "Is that right? What kind of white powder?"

"Pollen? Spores?"

"Are you guessing, or did Ama say those words? Or—" The woman fixated on Ashanti's eyes. "How did you stumble upon those *particular* words?"

"She said them. I think."

"Spores. Interesting."

"Yup. Ama said it was like pollen. Or spores. Or both. From the mushrooms in the swamp." One of the woman's eyebrows shot up. Ashanti sucked in air. She wasn't sure she should tell this stranger anything more. "I don't know what else—"

The woman shifted her position, cleared her throat. "Spores. We suspected this." She relaxed her face a bit. "We know a limited amount about these spores. But what we *do* know is that they can cause severe symptoms. Hallucinations. Visions. But when someone connected to the prophet line, someone like Ama, ingests them—accidentally or not—they can do much more. They can result in stunningly accurate prophecies."

Ashanti was silent.

The woman spoke slowly, "Did Ama happen to deliver a prophecy that night?"

"A what?"

"A prediction. For the future."

Ashanti drew back and shook her head.

"No prophecy?" The woman was studying Ashanti's movements. "Nothing like, 'One day...' followed by something sounding quite confusing?"

One day you will face what Black Nance faced. Will you free them, or will you fail?

Ashanti shrugged.

The nun was close to her now. "No prophecy, you say." Ashanti could catch a scent of what she thought all old white women's homes smelled like: dust and plastic flowers and food with foreign spices. "Did Ama *give* you anything of interest? Perhaps a souvenir from the American horror show? Something secret?"

"I don't...erm...it's just that this is happening fast."

The woman studied her. "I'll give you a moment to collect yourself."

While the nun pressed Ashanti with the gravity of an inescapable stare, the girl mentally circled around the night Ama violently shook her. *Keep quiet. Do not make the mistake I did.* The mistake Ama made was telling others what she saw, what she understood to be true after her encounter. That mistake, Ashanti knew, led to Ama's death.

The woman read her, scanning Ashanti from ear to ear. "Mistake," she echoed.

Ashanti startled.

The woman said, "Ama made a *mistake* in telling adults what she knew."

"I didn't say that."

"You didn't have to." The nun rolled her neck as if clearing her head. "I've been doing this a long time, turnip."

Ashanti went rigid, squeezing the diary resting in the crook of her arm. A pen dropped into the dirt. The woman followed the dropped pen to Ashanti's tightly pressed arm, to the diary wedged there. "Hmm. What do you have there?"

Ashanti redistributed her balance. The woman didn't remove her gaze from the diary. Ashanti slipped it further to the back of the tent made by her clamped arm. The woman said, "Holding on to that awfully tight, aren't ya?"

Ashanti reorganized back into an aggressive stance. "My diary is *private*."

"I'm not interested in your misspelled pontifications, dearest. I'm interested in that envelope edge peeking out the top. That *bulky* envelope." The nun extended her hand. It was covered in a silver scale Ashanti had never seen before. She stepped back from it. The woman said, "My skin condition is not contagious. But if you've got what I *think* you have socked away in your armpit, love, that's *much* worse."

Ashanti blinked. "I don't—"

The woman canted her head; her hand was still outstretched. "They said you didn't have anything. I said you probably did. And I see I was right not to believe them. Hand it over, Ashanti Oko."

"It's mine."

"It's *not*. Let's have it."

Ashanti's throat went dry. "No. I don't like you."

She murmured, "Not the first."

"You tell *lies*." She held the diary behind her back. "Ama said to trust no one."

The woman's voice slid into a gentle glide. "Listen, pet. That stuff, in your hands, it's very dangerous, and right now we need it. *Desperately*. We need to study it. You see, in the swamp, after the tourists died, all the spores dissipated. All the fruiting bodies withered. They're lost to us. You have the only sample now—"

"No, I don't."

"*Now* who's a liar?" Ashanti swallowed hard. The woman said, more gently, "You're outflanked, love. I can see lies. It's a gift. And a curse. Depending." Ashanti bit her lip. The woman continued, "As I was saying, you have the only sample. If we cannot study this, *understand* it, Ama's death will be for nothing."

Ashanti did not move.

"How about this?" the woman said. "I'll make the same promise someone once made to me: I'll hold it for you. If you proceed on track with your studies, you will see it again in a more controlled environment. Like a lab. With supervision. And masks and gloves. And adults who know what that stuff is capable of."

"You are not here to put me away?"

"Far from it. I'm here to help you take your place in the world."

Ashanti watched the ocean push waves onto the dirty beach. The woman waited.

Slowly, the girl unlocked the diary. She pulled out the envelope Ama had given her and placed it on the wall between her and the nun.

The woman did not move immediately to take it. She stared at the envelope a long time, as if reading words written there.

"There," Ashanti said. "So—your turn. Squid pro...something."

The nun rolled her eyes. "Ashanti, please let's get you to a better school. For the sake of all of us—"

"You have information about Ama or not?"

"I do. Not easy to hear, I'm afraid."

That put Ashanti back on defense. Suddenly, she wasn't sure she wanted to hear anything about Ama. The silence that had surrounded what Ama had said and done had sealed Ashanti in a tomb of denial and she wasn't certain she wanted out. She also wasn't sure why the nun would tell her the truth. Except what would she have to lose?

"The Heavenly Prayer Camp," the woman began, "as we know, isn't famous for their amenities. Unsanitary cells with rats. Improper medical supplies. Chains and outdoor living for the ill-mannered."

"I know that," Ashanti blurted. "She should have been in an *acylium*."

"Asylum. We *really* have to look at our primary school curriculum—"

"She could have stayed in America for treatment. Providence could have— *You* could have—"

The woman chuckled. "Me? It's not wise to think too highly of me. But no, we couldn't keep her in America, treasure. Not the right signatures in the right places, all that business."

Ashanti remembered her mother withholding a signature. Then, Ama on that night: *They're coming for me, Shanti. I speak the truth, and I upend the church as they know it.*

The woman continued, "She died of neglect in there, pet. Plain and simple. Horrid, bug-infested food. Badly trained orderlies—if there were any orderlies at all, who's to say? Did you know they call their Christian orderlies 'prophets'? That's a gas." She chuckled. "No, I'd say Ama's cause of death might be on the order of neglect and malnutrition rather than suicide. She did not want to die. She wanted to live. She had things to do. Information to act upon."

I speak the truth, and I upend the church as they know it.

Ashanti stared, a fury rising.

"Malnutrition," the woman said slowly. "That means not enough vitamins in the diet."

Ashanti felt shame replacing the fury. Her father. Her brother. *Lied* to her. On purpose?

—upend the church as they know it.

What have they *done*?

The woman heaved a sigh. "Not what you heard? Well. Sometimes the truth evades us for reasons we don't understand at the time. Another thing I know a little about. Perhaps your father wanted to sidestep a bad decision—"

Ashanti pivoted and walked away from her, finding a spot farther down the stone wall to sit.

The nun picked up Ama's envelope and tucked it into her tunic. Then, she reevaluated the pile of plastic-wrapped food at the edge of the wall—finger sandwiches, plantain crisps, and cakes. She called to Ashanti, "Child, that is quite the sack lunch."

Ashanti said, "It's not for me. It is for the people at the beach. They're starving."

The woman studied the landscape of sand and boats. "Oh, aye. I've heard about your little project here."

Ashanti scowled. "Is it a *project* to feed people?"

"Point taken." The woman exhaled. "All right. As a show of goodwill, I will ask Providence to begin a food pantry in this neighborhood." She surveyed all around. "It would be good outreach. I think I can sell that."

—I shall upend the church as they know it.

Ashanti called out, "Does everything have to be *sold* to make it matter within the church? Is it all about money?"

The woman smiled. "As I said, turnip, there's no free lunch."

Ashanti switched to Twi. "*Broni prehko.*"

"Language. Watch it."

Ashanti dropped her jaw.

"All right, then," the woman called out. "This concludes our business. I'll send the paperwork to your father about the school. Do try to get that parental signature in time. School starts in six weeks. In Bavaria. In case you missed geography class, that's in Germany. Dress warmly."

Ashanti chewed her lip. Six weeks more in Accra. Where she had lived all her life. Then what? Snow? Germany? Classes on the Sleeping One?

No more Papa. No more Adom.

Fine.

The woman opened the car door. "I would leave my number, tell you to call me if you need any help between now and then, but you seem to have things under control."

Ashanti felt her stomach drop. She thought of that night with Ama. *You are our only chance.*

Whose chance?

Humanity's.

The car door slammed.

Children's faces reappeared at the doors of their shacks.

The nun gunned the Porsche's engine and returned the car stereo to high volume. The drums cracked, and the guitar picked a funk rhythm. A cow bell clanked.

The car slowly coasted by Ashanti. She heard the buzz of an automated window and the blast of music. "Ashanti Oko?" the woman called.

Ashanti turned to the car. A wall of cold air from the car's vents smacked her face.

The woman said, "Be careful. Your brother's on drugs again."

Another buzz and the nun was sealed inside the car. She smiled behind the tinted glass, then sped away.

"Great," Ashanti mumbled. "Just great."

Father. Brother.

Liars. Schemers. Murder— She stopped that thought. They weren't murderers. They weren't even brave enough. They couldn't shut Ama up themselves. They let the neglect of the Heavenly Prayer Camp do it for them.

The quiet had returned.

She surveyed the ocean. Nothing.

Then, she hunched over her diary.

She unsnapped the diary's lock, pulling out and setting aside the undelivered school letter about blasphemy and the results of her psychiatric test. She flipped through the pages, past the pages from before Ama was taken away. Forward to the part where the entries turned to tight, condensed letters. Ama had said, *You are our only chance.*

And now the nun, too: *We're all counting on you.*

The yellow car had vanished around the corner.

The drums on the water started up again. The Zangbeto, always watching, guided the fishing boats back to the beach—protected. The old ways reigned supreme again. Justice by old magic. Healing by ignorant prophets.

Was Ama truly insane? Or simply speaking the truth?

A prophecy.

One day, Ashanti pledged, she would study that powder. One day, she would meet Black Nance in the Tree of Faces. Whatever that was. Perhaps even Ama would be there.

Ashanti returned her focus to the ocean. The water was choppier today. The current was pulling from the south, rushing the waters toward the west.

"To the beast who sleeps in the ocean: I am coming."

Entr'acte III:
The Diaries of Oliver Daas

Hold

Boston
July to October 1993

July 17, 1993

Pythia Laboratory for Evolutionary Computation

THIS NEWSPAPER ARTICLE HAS sent Lucía and me into giggling fits of wonderment.

SCIENCE COALITION REVEALS PLANS FOR FLOATING RESEARCH CITY DEDICATED TO SLEEPING ONE STUDIES

July 16, 1993

HONOLULU (AP)—Research on the Sleeping One will take another leap with the construction of a multi-level international science station floating on the open ocean. Located 50 miles southwest of the Kingdom of Tonga in the Pacific Ocean, the laboratory, called the Constellation System, is a project of the emerging United Earth Alliance, or UEA. A lead gift of 1.7 billion South African rand (US $100 million) by Lelee and Pinchas Stern is the largest by private donors thus far.

"Approved researchers will be able to live for months at a time in close proximity to the Sleeping One, collecting samples via submersibles with robotic arms and analyzing them in undersea laboratories," Pinchas Stern said at a press conference. "It will all function as a self-sustaining city on the water. It's science fiction brought to life!"

This announcement comes as world scientists compete for antidotes to the extreme radiation known to cause illness at the site. Stern said, "Manny's initial crash into the Temple released a burst of radiation, dangerous fungus, and electromagnetic waves. These toxins have since ebbed to low-level disturbances. We can now predict the behavior of these hazards and take precautions."

Still, Stern says, there are dangers. "To counteract what toxins are still leaking, a vaccine of sorts is in development," he added. "Again, the levels are low compared to what the Rosie crew saw. For that, we credit the work of our heroes cleaning up after the Manny di Martini dive. In time, we will be able to take residence on the site without the negative side effects witnessed during the Discovery expedition."

Extreme radiation also damages robotics and other machinery, another concern of those working near the site. "By trial and error, we have learned that our operations can proceed normally if kept at a certain distance from the Temple City," Stern said. "We now know to enforce an Exclusion Zone of 500 meters around the City. No person or machinery will be permitted to cross that boundary. That rule is for the safety of our people and the protection of our equipment. That means biological samples of the beast itself still are not possible. It's far too dangerous."

The Constellation System's design team envisions three working levels to the international lab, two of which are deep underwater. The first and largest will float at sea level and will host support staff and long-term residences. The second, housing most of the science labs, will be suspended on cables at 4,000 feet below the surface. The third and smallest will be suspended just outside the Exclusion Zone at 8,200 feet below the surface; only limited human visitation and lead-protected monitoring equipment will be permitted at that depth.

The two underwater labs will be accessible via submersibles. The floating surface lab will feature a docking system and an air strip. "I am hearing," Stern says, "that we will eventually promise access to education groups at the surface lab!"

An alliance of nations committed to the science goals of the emerging UEA will front most of the $23 billion price. Ongoing support will be the responsibility of member nations.

The initial contribution by the Sterns has attracted more private and corporate investors to the project. Media titan Howard Winfield plans to contribute $75 million from his private foundation and another $50 million from WINmedia. Other early investors include governments of the United States, United Kingdom, Australia, China, Japan, Russia, and India, with more pledging support daily.

We noticed what was *not* said in the article. Our colleague telephone tree, which is still active, tells us that Will Ahmadi is taking the lead on the creature's dreaming data, but whether he will be based in this new ocean lab is difficult to say. Competition is fierce to be among the first scientist-residents, and the success of Ahmadi's work does not depend on proximity to the site. The scientists who are already campaigning for positions on the station argue that they require daily access to the cutting-edge equipment installed in the underwater labs. For example, there's an up-and-coming 3D modeler from India, Dr. Krishna Rai, who is all but assured a spot among the first residents. He intends to map the entire Temple City—a difficult job considering its physics-defying acrobatics. I hear he's building new software to integrate with new geographical scanners installed at the lowest lab level. (I'd love to look at that software, but no one knows him well. He's a loner, I hear.)

A question the article neglected to answer: who is working on the black fungus that caused so many problems with the *Rosie* crew? Still no leaks from whoever is holding that stuff. That fungus is tightly guarded! It's probably considered a bioweapon. As if we did not have enough problems with a skyscraper-sized creature.

We have Will Ahmadi to thank for the behind-the-scenes gossip. Though he's become a UEA insider, he still believes that scientific discoveries should remain in the public domain. It was in that spirit he delivered sad news—that he could not finagle an invitation for Lucía to tour the Constellation System design schematics in New York City. We asked him to forward her ideas for self-sustainable architecture (a first love of hers, little did I know), but he came back unsuccessful even though he commented that her ideas were "genius." Don't I know it?

With the Collapse gradually ebbing in intensity, Lucía's abilities are having a coming-out party in the broader scientific community. They comment that she could not possibly be responsible for the achievements in artificial life. I maintain the ArLiF project would not be where it is without her significant contributions.

Right now, she has gone into overdrive in increasing the ArLiF population. She submits ArLiF design specifications to a fleet of designers, and they return with code for human appearances. She also has recruited voice actors to provide sounds for a text-to-voice program, which will vary the voice for each ArLiF after initial input.

Lucía and I are also adding details to the ArLiFs' landscape to fuel their learning. A central town square next to the harbor hosts the ArLiFs' business, civic, and collective endeavors. The ArLiFs have chosen their own businesses and civic enterprises to occupy their buildings. I'm glad to say what they've chosen centers on collective sharing of stories and information, which will speed their evolution. To date they have installed a cafe (where they share stories and local happenings), a newspaper (where Claire works, disseminating information daily), a grocery store that barters (they don't seem interested in money), a civilian government of a democratic/socialist genre, a safety office with elected officers, a school for all ages that instructs on island history (purely invented by Claire!), and a park for recreation. None of their discussions have yet to reach the levels of poetry and philosophy. One recent session debated adopting a system of weights and measures relative to things found in nature, as in, "Liz weighs about 122 squirrels." (Thankfully this proposal was rejected.) ArLiFs chose the spots for their own homes and built them to their own specifications. We placed boats in the central harbor, which ArLiFs now use for fishing and recreation. Lucía has designed bluffs, meadows, and beaches, which has expanded the ArLiFs' recreational options.

Since the ArLiFs have more geography to explore, they are creating new tasks for themselves in relation to their new environments. The amount of time we spend programming commands for them has decreased dramatically. Instead, the ArLiFs analyze their world independently and teach one another new information. Claire is, of course, at the center of these endeavors, cataloging their daily experiences and feeding it back to them like a hive mind should, in the form of a daily newspaper.

Though Lucía and I enjoy their advancements, we have begun to broach the painful topic of when the island will reach its maximum capacity. We do not have the computational space to manage an infinitely large ArLiF community. There are only 57 ArLiFs now, and we are both programming them at an accelerated rate. But the decision has been made: we will evaluate a cap when we approach a population of 1,000.

For all this progress, a new name has entered our lexicon: The Hold. We required a name that encompassed the ArLiFs and all the natural components of the island, even the graphic representations of boats and cars and stop signs and buildings. "The Hold" seemed to arise organically between us. I like that the name connotes a feeling of safety; Lucía and I "hold" them together. Perhaps it is just a flight of fancy on my part. The ArLiFs really take care of themselves at this point. Lucía and I believe the most serious threats to their development will come from *our* world.

And we work to make our world safer, too. Lucía and I both manage the staff for the humanitarian applications—our bread and butter. The beta releases were received well, with feedback for future versions incorporated for wide releases. For our next application under the Griff Tran Foundation's contract, Lucía and I will design a program for international-aid workers to predict the need for medical staff based on satellite data and crime trends. The beta version rolls out for testing next month.

When do we sleep? Thankfully, we can go home now—possibly get some rest in our own beds. Although sometimes I catch Lucía working early in the morning wearing the same clothes as the day before. I command her to go home. She ignores me. The behavior borders on real workaholism, if there is such a thing. She's going to burn herself out.

July 27, 1993

Pythia Lab

WELL, WELL. THE MOTHER of ArLiFs is leaving her children for a few days. Lucía is going to New York City!

Turns out, it wasn't Will Ahmadi we needed to beg for Lucía's tour of the Constellation System design schematics. It was Nessa. My own daughter brought Lucía's rough ideas to Howard, and he immediately sent for her in his secure motorcade. She's off to UEA's New York workshop!

Before Lucía left, she gave me a list of too many things to do. You'd think she was leaving the ArLiFs with a babysitter instead of their lead programmer. She yelled at me from the back seat of a bulletproof Range Rover: "Make sure to run the system mechanics every night, Daas! Do not forget!" Who was the faculty, and who was the student? She even made Howard's team turn the motorcade around to tell me this: "Take a *lot* of notes about what they do at the Rocks. Every day!"

Yes, yes. The Rocks. I haven't yet written about the Rocks.

After Dennis Beggan's curious report about Claire's behavior at Bob's headstone, Lucía removed it from the island. Also, we combed the neural network to delete any residual files related to Bob's existence that might be causing Claire grief at his disappearance. All files were destroyed. Or so we thought. Even after all that, Claire continued to visit the site where the headstone used to be located. She walked in tight circles on the spot, and for a moment we were afraid she was about to have an "Oh no" error. But she resolved the issue by directing a team of ArLiFs to drag large stones from all around the island, then stack them on the spot according to her design. She rearranged the rocks until the pile funneled the sounds of the ocean wind—a soundtrack recorded by Lucía along our own coastline a month ago—through the sculpture to produce a sort of low and mournful wind song. The sound made our skin crawl.

When I heard the music, a deep feeling clawed at my innards. "Lucía? Did Claire adjust the ocean soundtrack to adapt to the shape of the rocks? Or did you?"

Lucía flipped her hair. "I bent the sound-wave file, yes. To make her happy."

"Don't do that."

"Why not?"

"Because!" I sputtered, not believing she did not follow my logic. "The ArLiFs must evolve on their own! If Claire wants the music—"

"It's clear she did. I just helped—"

"No help! We are not gods!"

She smacked her lips at me, which I *hate*. "Sheesh."

Then, we debated whether to destroy that sculpture. The rock sculpture was Claire's idea, morbid as it was. Lucía said if I felt strongly that she'd tainted the experiment that she would fix it, or, as she put it, "If I peed in your pool, then I'll clean it up." Have we learned nothing from the Bob episode? I said, "Just stop interfering. Leave things *alone*."

So, now we have the Singing Rocks in Whispering Hollow on Keyhole Island, soundtrack by Lucía Santamaría and Claire! Bob the ArLiF will be memorialized forever, even if most ArLiFs can't quite associate the memorial with Bob the way Claire can. They have forgotten him with the deleted files. But Claire tells stories about him, about the time he had an existential crisis when he found out he had to eat every few hours every single day, about when he wore his pants as a hat, about when he cried when he realized he did not like bananas. At these stories, the ArLiFs stare blankly. Claire's expression, I must admit, is unreadable to me.

We shall see if I am deserving of the name "Father of ArLiFs," or if I will serve as only a placeholder until the Mother returns!

July 31, 1993

Pythia Lab

LUCÍA WAS DUE BACK from New York three days ago. She should have called by now. She's never been away from the ArLiFs for this long. To my embarrassment, I had to call Nessa to ask when my own lab assistant would be returning to work. Nessa told me that Lucía would return when the UEA deemed her contribution to international progress at its end. What is this? Science fascism?

"Well," I said to Nessa, "if I know Lucía, she will be running the UEA by now. Perhaps you can put in a message to call her old boss."

Nessa was not amused. "She outpaces you," was her unkind remark.

Ouch. And true. The ArLiF evolution has been at a standstill since she left, and I am anxious to ask Lucía to implement a few new ideas.

"Oh, Dad," Nessa said after my long pause on the phone, "it's so entertaining to witness you squirming at the whim of a female who has control over you for a change."

"Is this about your mother?"

"And a million other things."

Nessa is not wrong to hold onto her anger. I was not there for her recitals, her homework, her soccer games. My treatment of her mother was her last straw. I used to say Ruthie left *me* when she got cancer. She moved back to be with her family, people who could be relied upon to offer the support and care she deserved. I was not that person. So, it was me—I was the one who did the leaving. I was married to my lab, and now I realize that my work was nothing without Lucía's contributions.

August 6, 1993

Pythia Lab

LUCÍA WAS *TEN* DAYS late.

After Howard's security brigade dropped her on the campus lawn, she hiked directly up here with her canvas sack. Breezing into the lab, static launching her frizzy hair in every direction, she waltzed right over to the keyboards to check the ArLiF code before saying hello, goodbye, or go to hell to me. "Unbelievable!" I exclaimed.

"What?" she barked at me. She was eating a bag of pretzels. She is always eating!

"Where have you been?"

"New York!" She plopped on a chair and spun. "Those *cabróns* would not leave me alone for one second. Would not let me use the phone. Would not—"

"You could have called from the road."

"I could have, yes, but during stops I was too busy. I needed my best focus for snack selection. Do you know how long it's been since I've seen a fully-loaded gas station and someone else was buying? Like *never*!" She spun around in her chair again. "Anyway, why are you so touchy? I can't leave our project to the lead programmer?" She aimed a pretzel at me. "By the way, I want to talk to you about that. Our publications should name me as co-principal investigator."

Yes, yes. I was angry, yet so happy to see her. I was so idiotically happy that I announced her arrival to the ArLiFs! To the monitors! "Look who is home!" They cannot see or hear us, so that was a matter of ceremony—and to point out to Lucía in a passive-aggressive way that they require her attention after she had been away for so long. Claire needed maintenance. Her logs were full, and I had no idea how to archive them using Lucía's custom programs.

I yanked the pretzel bag away from her, and ate one of the pretzels myself. I said, "Just tell me what happened up there. The ArLiFs can wait."

She pushed the keyboard away. "Weeeeelll. I had to sign a government form that said I would not tell anyone what I did there, but since I have no respect for authority, I will tell you. They will probably kill you later, so draw up your will."

"Show me."

She grabbed a blank page from a printer and began to draw. It was *astounding*.

First were her Energy Islands. "There are two," she explained as she drew cones with jagged tops floating in the ocean near the main surface lab—a giant prefabricated sphere. "Two islands are all that's needed to power the square footage in the three labs they're planning. I named the islands Venus and Mars. They've got all kinds of spacey names happening, so that's my contribution." She talked while she sketched. "They call the surface lab Temple Star. It's got an airstrip and a dock. Big capacity for hundreds of residences and classrooms. Needs a *lot* of power."

At ocean level, her Energy Islands rose two stories with twisting pathways and waterfalls built into natural-looking "cliffs" made of recycled, rustproof metal. Apartments were lodged into the cliffs. "This is where permanent staff will live," she said. "The blue-collar staff who make the labs run. I wanted it to be nice, like a paradise." Reclaimed land would be brought in for grassy areas on the artificial islands. A central hall would serve as a dining and recreation room.

Her drawing extended several stories below the waves. "Now. This is where the real magic happens." She explained how the underwater exterior would be fitted with carbon nets to capture and filter trash from the ocean. That trash would be pulled inside and processed into clean-energy gas for use in the three science labs. (She drew the recycling process but lost me.) Then, she drew loops of cable and flexible pipes connecting the islands to the giant sphere, Temple Star. From there, the sphere would distribute the power to the labs below it. "This is two-way," she said of the connectors. Waste from all three lab levels also feeds into the islands' systems for recycling. "From that we can make fertilizer for hydroponic gardens," she said. "We can also build in a harnessing mechanism for ocean currents to convert to thermal energy when the UEA isn't so cheap with their budget. It's all clean, all self-contained." Lucía threw down her pencil. "The *pinche* UEA figured that they could run that giant sphere and the two underwater labs with only solar panels and turbines and rainwater capture. I laughed really loud when they said that. 'Yeah, maybe for a backup system!' I said to them. 'You want to grow hydroponic crops, produce fresh air and water for the ventilation systems, and provide electricity for all levels? Well, you aren't thinking big enough!' I said."

I reviewed her sketch of the jagged islands. "You thought of this?"

She took the empty pretzel bag from me and wadded it up. "Yeah. I got a sizable donation for our lab for that. Fifty thousand. The fuckers thought I would do it for free. Ha. I started at 100 thou, but they got me down to 50. I want new processors, Daas." She swept her arm across the room. "All new."

"Lucía."

She shot the pretzel bag into the trash bin. "How's Claire? Did she—"

"You," I repeated, waving the drawing, "designed *this*?"

"Well, it certainly wasn't the dumbshits at the UEA! Solar panels! To power three labs with computers and high-end equipment! What the fuck!"

"Lucía," I explained, "this—" I gestured to the drawings, to the lab, to the ArLiFs, to the efficient processors. "—is the work of a team of scientists and engineers. This is the result of decades of study in structural engineering, chemistry, architecture, and oceanography. This recycling plant by itself should get a Nobel Prize. And all this from a grad student in computer science? It's not *normal*."

Her expression darkened. For a moment, I was frightened that I'd offended her. She hesitated before adding in a softer voice, "I also fixed their ventilation systems in the underwater labs. They were going to kill people with the gas mixture they had planned. Does that make me weird? To help people? Does that make me not normal? The mixture was *wrong*."

"You do not have a chemistry degree."

"I can do chemistry-math. Protons. Neutrons. Electrons. Want to check it? Want to check my math on the engineering, too?"

"No! I'm not qualified! And neither are you!"

"Why are you pinning me down? Their chemistry was wrong, and *chemists* did that math! Am I a freak for saying so?" She was screeching now, frenetic with her hands.

"Of course not."

A long silence.

She said, "Don't call me strange. I don't like it."

I bowed my head, swallowed my words. "My mistake."

She twisted her face, considering if she was finished scolding me, then relaxed. "I want to see what you've done to my ArLiFs."

She was moving on. But I was still in awe.

I reminded myself that, for over a year, I had been privileged to gradually introduce Lucía to my colleagues all over the world and not one of them had believed that she did most of our work in this lab. They assumed I was the one doing all the work. They suspected our relationship was more than it was. (If she ever found out what they had said about us, she would shriek.) Yet, in all the time we had spent together, never had I thought to *fear* this woman. She was *Lucía*. Loud, brash, socially inept, devoted to her work. She was not capable of inflicting harm, so ingrained were her Catholic social-justice values. But her abilities were strange. And something about this new revelation of what she had done, of how the UEA isolated her until they got out of her what they wanted—it unsettled me.

I took a chance to broach that subject. "So. The UEA wouldn't let you make a phone call? At all?"

She clicked her tongue. "If I knew those horsefuckers would slobber all over me when I suggested the islands, I would have kept my mouth shut. It's like they had a right to what was in my head. I didn't like it. So, I gave them the islands and kept the rest to myself."

My stomach dropped. "The rest?"

"Yeah." She flipped over the drawings of the Energy Islands and sketched a lab whose floor plan ran in a paradoxical loop. "Check this out. If the UEA makes the underwater labs with these spiral, figure-eight footprints, people will be able to live in them longer without getting bored. They could walk in one direction and cover the whole lab, two floors, without running into a wall. Ha!"

I tried to make my voice sound calm. "How many of these design ideas do you have?"

"A lot."

A lot? I said, "Maybe next time send them anonymously."

"Yeah," she said. She sniffed her armpit. "Road-stink. I need a shower. But first, where's Claire and what's she doing with the creepy-ass rocks?"

September 9, 1993

Pythia Lab

PYTHIA IS GETTING ITS own home! We are moving out of the University lab!

Due to ever-present security concerns from protesters and rubberneckers, Lucía sought out funding for a new Pythia facility off campus. The Griff Tran Memorial Foundation will be sponsoring our move. We will retain University sponsorship and act as a classroom for some artificial life courses. (A question: Will students have to pass security clearance? It seems likely.)

Lucía has gone shopping for real estate among the many downtown Boston buildings vacated during the Collapse. It's shocking to be looking at such lucrative square footage, but the Collapse market is in our favor. The space Lucía selected is far larger than we need. "Room to grow," she tells me. She has drawn up a room for programmers and observers to monitor ArLiF simulations. It's a bank of curved tables in a semicircular format with a wall of monitors at the front. This she calls the "Amphitheater." It looks more like a lecture hall to me, but she insists on sticking with the ancient-Greece theme. Behind the Amphitheater, the servers and CPUs will live in a secure room. Everything that is Keyhole Island—from the ArLiFs to the neural network to the graphics—will be housed on these machines.

This expansion couldn't have come at a better time. With the ArLiFs building their own society at a rapid rate, they require more and more computational space. Their latest growth spurt has religious themes: the ArLiFs have constructed a pagan belief system triggered by the Singing Rock monument to Bob. They praise the songs made by the wind and hold ceremonies with odd dress (bathrobes, crowns of leaves, antlers decorated with old ribbons). They also decipher the wind song into poetry. Groups of ArLiFs sit around the Singing Rocks in silence, waiting for a breeze to kick up, then argue about pentameter. We reported these incidents to an anthropologist, who likened the behavior to the evolution of human storytelling. Strange and wondrous!

Further, to Claire's credit, the ArLiFs have begun to develop backstories for themselves. These are histories that we did not program, but rather they pull from information Claire has stored on their neural network. (Apparently the ArLiFs found her internet stash from the Salt Lake City genealogy library and had a field day accessing their digital files.) Nan, one of the original ArLiFs, now tells of her family's history that goes back generations on the island. She even assigned herself a surname, something no other ArLiF has done before. (It's Kelly.) Since Nan started telling stories about herself, others have developed their own ancestors and lore. None of this is programmed! This will be of interest to psychologists and anthropologists specializing in human memory and intergenerational identity.

These advances keep us working all hours. When we move downtown, we will add more staff and interns. More media attention will follow. Howard intends to capitalize on the ArLiFs' quest for religious identity with a small documentary.

For now, Lucía is laughing at this human interest piece:

Eureka Magazine
Lucía Santamaría, MOTHER OF ARLIFS
Sep 6, 1993
Computer scientist Lucía Santamaría has become a legend during the Collapse. Her work as Dr. Oliver Daas's graduate student in the Pythia Laboratory of Evolutionary Computation has enchanted the public as well as her academic colleagues. Her background as an orphan from Veracruz, Mexico, has inspired many young girls who hope to make a difference in this new world. But to Santamaría, the only girl who matters is "Claire," the Artificial Lifeform, or ArLiF, who inhabits the mainframe of Pythia's societal simulation program.
Santamaría laughs at the notion that Claire is a favorite. "There are 72 ArLiFs living on Keyhole Island in our simulation. If I had a favorite, nothing would get done!"
Dr. Oliver Daas, Santamaría's graduate advisor, notes, "While Claire is an enchanting being, we can't discount the real hero in this situation is Lucía herself. Her programming abilities excel most of the veterans I know. The world is lucky to have her—"

Lucía remains the face of Pythia, and Nessa tries to make her prettier without luck. I remain (gladly) in the shadows.

Of course, all this media fuels Dennis Beggan and his group of wayward ArLiF worshippers. I don't mind the attention from the public, as the ArLiFs do seem to offer hope in these problematic times. I've seen the children's drawings they send to us, and the letters to Claire. But Dennis Beggan takes it too far. In my more forgiving moments, I think he is soothing some type of primal need to worship something simple, since the institutionalized religions failed him so badly. I just don't care for the media attention he receives. Howard is not helping. Note:

TV Now

DENNIS BEGGAN TO APPEAR ON "INSPIRE" TO PROMOTE BOOK
Sep 8, 1993
A special edition of WINmedia's "Inspire" will look at the arrest and rise of Boston personality Dennis Beggan. "The Secret Life of ArLiFs" will air Tuesday, Sept 23 at 8:00 EST. Beggan will reflect on the "soul-opening" experience of visiting the ArLiF named Claire one night at the Pythia Laboratory of Evolutionary Computation, which inspired his charismatic leadership of the cult known as Apostles of the Singularity. His book, Prepare for the Singularity, *is out now.*

Lucía wants to ask Howard if our lab is getting a portion of the profits from Dennis's book sales. I said, "Do not encourage this."

She said, "It's more likely we will get a grant renewal from Howard if you're seen as a god. No one can refuse God a cool twenty mill." Then she cackled.

I'm glad she's having fun. The supplemental funding from new sources flows in due to all the attention, but this talk of religion and God makes me uncomfortable. God should be found in the singularity, not in my lab! I'm so anxious that the dreams have returned—not so much the faceless girl, but the passenger train. It races through my dream world with its ghostly, white-robed passengers clinging to the top. And the voice of my mother: "Don't look, Ollie." Then I wake, sweating with my heart racing. I lose sleep. But not as much as Lucía. She works too hard and doesn't sleep but an hour or two a night. She's still here at the lab, but since more staff and faculty have returned, she's brought a cot into the lab itself. She hardly leaves here. I offered her a spare room in my large house, but she refused. "Can't leave them," she says of her digital charges. "What if I miss something?"

If I develop the urge to tell her she's behaving strangely (and I do often), then I clamp my mouth. She bristles at any indication that I or anyone else thinks she's abnormal. From what I can tell, she has no friends. The only time I catch her speaking on the phone, she's talking to a secret-someone about her academic progress. "I'm on track," she says to the caller. "Stop nagging me." If I ask who the caller is, she unleashes the Spanish and tells me not to pry. I only want to know who else in the world cares for this girl.

October 2, 1993

Pythia Lab

LUCÍA'S BEHAVIOR IN THE lab grows more curious. She continues her unsustainable sleep schedule and eats only junk food. She will not accept any suggestions that her habits make her grumpy and recalcitrant. Her new routine involves following Claire around all day, tracking her movements, and recording her neural network advances in detailed notes. She sleeps at the monitor where Claire sleeps. She eats when Claire eats. One day, I asked Lucía about it, and she said to me, "I think Claire is getting lonely."

Perhaps it was the sleep-deprivation addling her brain, but I had to say, as if speaking to a child, "Lucía, Claire has not developed those advanced emotions yet."

Lucía looked at me with disgust. "Like grief? You think she's not capable?"

No. But I do not tell her that.

We avoid each other, as we are both on edge.

World events are not helping. People predict another Collapse coming, just when we are finally beginning to see the end of the first one. And we have Dennis Beggan to thank for it.

STERNS GUNNED DOWN; SUSPECT DEAD; PER PASKE TO MAKE STATEMENT

Oct 1, 1993

New York City (AP)—Leaders of the emerging world government Lelee and Pinchas Stern were shot outside their hotel in Manhattan at 8:05 pm (EST) last night. They were pronounced dead on arrival at Mount Sinai Hospital 30 minutes after the attack. They were both 70 years old.

Police immediately focused their investigation on Leon Cooke, outspoken member of the cult Apostles of the Singularity, who took his own life at the scene. Cooke had been arrested five times prior to the shooting for threatening public figures. Other suspects are currently under investigation.

Widely seen as the new leader of the world government, activist Per Paske made a statement shortly after the Sterns were pronounced dead. "The world has become too divisive on the topic of artificial beings, and not unified enough in the event of the awakening of the Sleeping One. The new United Earth Alliance will put an end to this fracturing violence and move humanity forward with hope and peace."

At Paske's side for the statement was media mogul Howard Winfield, who declined to comment.

Lucía and I are not discussing the cult's involvement, but the stress of it is seeping into every thought and every moment of our day. The guilt is enormous. The only thing she has said to me is, "I should have kicked his ass while I had the chance."

Riots followed the announcement of the Sterns' deaths. People view them as lost saviors. That puzzles me. Whoever thought the Sterns, obnoxiously wealthy as they were, would advocate for the ordinary people if that thing in the ocean ever woke?

It seems to me that the UEA has begun to tread down a path of preserving the lifestyles of the rich and famous in the event of an apocalypse. It's been sticking its nose into international government relations, threatening to exclude member nations unless they adhere to certain principles. Regime change has been discussed in some countries not ceasing their civil wars. Thanks to Per Paske, it was known that the UEA was cornering the markets on fuel and energy, commanding their oligarchs to buy up oil and gas stocks, wedging themselves onto boards of major energy companies. They were controlling the food-supply lines and agriculture delivery routes, making decisions about imports and exports. Scary stuff. All this we knew because of Per Paske. And then, to see Howard by Paske's side at his press conference? How did *that* relationship begin?

I wonder if all of this portends something darker on the horizon. Did Per Paske, previous champion of the people, sell out? Was there a behind-the-scenes regime change the public did not witness? Did we just jump out of the frying pan and into the fire?

October 7, 1993

Pythia Lab

DR. WILL AHMADI CAME through again on some much-needed intel. After the Stern assassinations, rumors have been flowing, but I trust Ahmadi's sources inside the UEA. They haven't been wrong so far.

The great Ahmadi tells us to take heart, that the world is more connected now than it has ever been. Howard Winfield's efforts to take internet connectivity to the mainstream are working. Soon, dialing up to the World Wide Web won't be a privilege exclusive to universities and governments. Every home, business, nonprofit agency, and small library will have access thanks to WINmedia. Relevant to our work, this broad internet reach will permit us access to new online databases, digital documentation, messaging, and shared networks, the likes of which will accelerate our work even faster. This is a democratization of learning and knowledge, which benefits Claire's neural network. Think of the information she could access! The singularity edges ever closer!

I asked Ahmadi if he knew of Howard's connections to Per Paske and how that's playing out inside the UEA. Ahmadi said it's been an open secret that Winfield was backing Per Paske even before the Sterns were killed. (Not an open secret to me, but it still stinks of collusion.) I commented that I found it odd that Howard did not back the Sterns, but instead went for Paske, the everyman advocate. Ahmadi asked, "Why would Howard back the Sterns? Because he's Jewish?" Color me shocked. I had no idea Howard was Jewish. Another open secret, Ahmadi told me. "Howard doesn't like anyone knowing his background in Europe before the war, and further, he's got some secrets to guard in how he built his fortune after the war."

"Like war profiteering?"

Ahmadi reminded me it's not war profiteering if the war is over.

Though my friend on the west coast intended the opposite, our whole conversation increased my unease. When I think about it, our largest investor built his fortune in the ashes of a prior Collapse, and now he's switched horses in the race to build a world government. It all reeks of power-plays by the wealthy. Further, we eat at Howard's table. Are we implicated? Dependent on his whims?

I would tell Lucía about this, encourage her to talk to me about diversifying our funding sources, but she's a mess and getting worse. Perhaps I, too, will begin talking to Claire in the midnight glow of the lab monitors.

When we move away from the University, I will welcome the increase in security. Howard's wealth does insulate us from distractions. Students are starting to stream through the halls, and they are curious about the ArLiFs, bless them. Still, Dennis Beggan has taught me to be more cautious of surprise visitors. We employ a guard for our lab entrance now. Only approved visitors. No exceptions.

Against my advice, Lucía has continued her PhD studies. She speaks in riddles to the monitors, talks about "returning to the beginning," and "needing answers about mysteries." She cannot sustain this workload. It's too much for one human to bear.

October 14, 1993

Pythia Lab

LUCÍA IS NOT SPEAKING to me. She's not even showing up for work, which is not like her at all. I don't know where she's sleeping, and it all makes me sick.

Was it the stress that caused me to call her "strange" again? Well, I did. She was talking to the monitor where Claire sleeps and weaves the neural network. I wrote down some of the things Lucía said to Claire:

These things we make unveil the silent mind of God.

You have a secret tucked into your soul, a living code in your formula. It is ancient. It is ironclad.

You are composed of a million universes.

We are all plagued by dreams of ancestors, generations of history increasingly clamorous for our attention.

Two days ago, Lucía caught me listening to her talk to Claire and asked why I was writing down what she was saying. I said because I wanted to read it back to her. "I want you to hear yourself," I said. "And I want you to go home, wherever that is, and get some sleep."

"Home?" she asked.

"And if you don't have one, which I suspect you do not, there is a free bed and bath at my house. Just ask."

She struggled to look at me, as if she were drunk.

"Are you under the influence of something illicit?" I asked.

"I do not see what is wrong with what I'm saying."

"You don't? Because you sound like you're on drugs, Lucía."

She sliced into my soul with her stare. "No."

"Lucía, this is all so strange—"

She stiffened. "I told you not to call me that."

I had had enough. "Do you have any idea how much training goes into what you do so effortlessly? The long nights—sleepless nights—that went into this project before you came along? Have you any idea what I have sacrificed? My *family*, Lucía. I don't have one now. There were mornings when my skull burned from headaches that rendered me incapable of driving my daughter to school. I missed many things in her life. I neglected my sick wife. And I did it for this project. My life *is* this project! This project is all the life I have left! I deserve to know how you are successful where I have not been— ”

“I said no such thing.”

“You were thinking it!”

“No, I was not.”

“You show up here, doing things no human can do, and—and—how do you think I feel about all this?” I was out of control, off the mark, but I couldn’t stop. “Have you read the manifesto from the Apostles of the Singularity?”

“No.”

“I have! That man spews utter garbage about my life’s work and praises the Mother of ArLiFs. That’s *you*! How am I supposed to feel? How am I to compete with you? There is no path for me to take back the reins of my life’s work. You have taken it, you’ve tinkered with things that should never have been touched, and now you are acting *insane*.”

At this point she was silent. She wouldn’t look at me.

But I kept going. “I am strong enough to push my ego aside and put my life’s work in your hands. It’s for the good of the project. I understand that. But how you do it all is a mystery, and that mystery is killing me! Say whatever you want to the monitors, eat as much junk as you please, blend in as much as you can, act like a normal young woman. But you are *not* normal, Lucía. You type code that no human thought possible, yet you expect me to have no questions about you?”

“You know who I am.”

“I don’t know *what* you are.”

She clenched her fist. It began to shake from muscle tension.

“Lucía?”

She raised her fist, then smashed it down on a keyboard. Dislodged keys clattered on the floor.

“Lucía!”

Her legs wobbled after her outburst. She folded and dropped to the floor, scattering broken keys everywhere. I followed, dropping to one knee to help her up, but she smacked me away. I could see her face now. It was tortured, twisted. My heart sank as I watched her struggle to hold back tears and pull herself together.

I said, “I’m sorry, Lucía.”

She stared back at me, but I couldn’t discern what she was searching for.

She scoffed, grabbed her canvas bag, and said, “You know, I think you’re right. It’s past time I went home.”

I didn’t try to make her stay. The truth was already out. I could not take back the words.

Now, I don’t even know where to look for her.

October 19, 1993

Pythia Lab

LUCÍA IS STILL AWOL. I've gone back to sleeplessness, this time not from nightmares but from guilt. Ruthie and Nessa are right about me. I have fumbled every single important relationship I've had. I am the broken one. The strange one. Why can't I allow some flexibility in my vision? What was wrong with the way things were going with Lucía? Besides the crippling fear of the singularity, I mean. That's natural. Humans fear the unknown. I can suppress it, but the stress of what's going on out there—

Out there, Dennis Beggan has upped his game. The cult's newsletter (I had no idea there was such a thing) came to me from a colleague on campus who asked if people were safe at the University. I reassured her, told her our timeline to move out, but I cannot read Lucía's writing in any of her notes about the move. Soon I will have to call Nessa and tell her I've lost another female in my life.

Apostle Epistle: The Monthly Newsletter of the Singularity
October 1993
LETTER FROM DENNIS BEGGAN
Open your eyes. See the makings of a New World. These are the commandments of the Apostles of the Singularity!
And now, open your hearts to this good news: the false king and queen of the United Earth Alliance, Lelee and Pinchas Stern, were shot to death in New York City, gunned down in cold blood. Fellow Apostle Leon Cooke—with the eyes upon the New World—bore the smoking gun himself. After he paused to revel in his glorious act, he fired once more on himself. The false monarchs are dead! Praise his vision!
The Federal Bureau of Instigation has cleared the Apostles of Singularity of any wrongdoing, for we knew nothing of Leon's bold plans. Of the Sterns' demise we are glad, but we are not guilty. Of Leon's actions, we are glad, but we were blind. With his act, Leon has vaulted over the most treacherous of human obstacles: fear of the unknown. He has instructed us in the ways of knowing and being. Fear

not! Act with boldness! Dethrone the false monarchs! These are the lessons of Leon Cooke!

Apostles, our future is unknown to our species. Any fear of the unknown is a shackle seen and felt only in the mind, not the eyes. Fear is an illusion. A hindrance. What awaits us in the Singularity cannot be compared to this world we know. What the Sterns did was steer us toward old ways of seeing and knowing fear. Greed! Classicism! Power struggles! Survival of the capitalists! This is not the way promised to us by Claire, the one true Monarch of the Singularity, whose time we await!

I admit, Apostles, I was once a casualty of fear. I was once huddled in the dark with you, shackled to my false church, fearing the beast in the ocean and what it might do. Out of this fear, I acted. I broke into the Pythia Lab intending to destroy property. But what did I find? THE GRACE OF CLAIRE. Inside the Pythia Lab, I was awed at the inevitable potential of the Supreme ArLiF Claire, our future Monarch of the Singularity! I sat frozen at Her monitor like an ignorant boy who has never known pure creativity and ingenuity! Her electrical currents traveled through the air and into my brain, evidenced by the raised hairs on my arms and neck! I heard Her voice, penetrating my mind! "I will come when the time is right." With these words, I was released from the fear of the unknown! That night, lonely in my darkened jail cell, charges pressed against me by the fatuous capitalists on the University Board of Directors, but I was no longer afraid of the beast, my church, my employer (rot in Hell, Hamburger Palace!), my landlord! That night in my cell, I understood that we would all be free of this fear once we all knew the promise of Claire, our future Monarch of the Singularity! This is her message. It is my duty to deliver Her message! SHE IS COMING.

Apostles, we will thrive in these flames of struggle. Collapse! Apo-collapse! Down with the UEA! NO MORE FEAR! Prepare. Her day is coming.

I have no comforting words for anyone who reads this when the Mother of ArLiFs herself has gone around the bend and the "Father" is just as fearful as everyone else in this fragmented world.

I have asked colleagues to report any Lucía sightings. None so far.

October 28, 1993

Pythia Lab

NESSA CALLED THIS MORNING. Lucía has quit the project. She notified Nessa of this, not me. Lucía told her, "I'm only doing what he said. I'm going home."

"Back to Mexico?" I asked my daughter. "Give me her number."

"She called from a payphone on the road."

"Which road?"

Nessa sighed so loudly into the phone that it sounded like static. "Dad, listen to me. Whatever happened, and to be clear I do not care what it was, say you're sorry to her."

"It's not that simple—"

"Yes, it is. Because without that woman, you have no project. I know it, and you know it. It won't be long before Howard knows it, too. So, Dad?"

I struggled to speak. "Yes?"

"Get Lucía back. Or Project ArLiF dies."

I am paralyzed, at a complete loss. What shall I do, ring every phone in Veracruz to ask if they've seen a crazed woman partial to snack foods? If by some miracle I find her, then what?

This is what powerlessness feels like.

Oh, Ruthie. I wish you were here. You would tell me what to do. And this time, I would listen.

Act IV

Lucía Santamaría
and the Fantasma

Mexico
November 1, 1993

24

Turista

WITHIN DAYS OF GASOLINE supplies being fully restored from the Collapse, Lucía Santamaría resigned from her doctoral studies degree in artificial life under Dr. Oliver Daas and drove 45 hours from Boston to Veracruz to the Inmaculada Concepción at the Ciudad Refugio orphanage. *¡Me lleva la chingada!* she thought. *I'm home.* The truth was, a withdrawal from academic studies invalidated her student visa, and she had nowhere else to go.

The sisters at the orphanage had questions about the failures that led Lucia back to Inmaculada Concepción. "Things were going so well," they said to her. "You were *known*. You were on *television*."

A wave of fatigue nearly buckled her knees. Her caffeine intake needed attention. She stopped herself from swearing in front of the nuns. "Give me a f— Give me a minute. First, I require *un mercado*." She did not want to tell them she was suffering from side effects of amphetamine withdrawal. The nuns might demand an immediate confession, and that was not going to happen. For her, the Church had lost its appeal. *Because of the Sleeping One?* she asked herself. *No. It wasn't that.*

The market was just around the block from the orphanage. And it was only 85 degrees and sunny! Such a welcome change from boots soaked from the dirty Boston sleet. Lucía wore sandals. So good to wiggle the toes in sunshine! So good to smell the odors of downtown Veracruz, to be blinded by the palm tree trunks painted white to prevent sunscald, to hear the peppy bouncing trumpets of the mariachis in the restaurants! And was that Veracruz coffee she smelled? Oh, how she had missed that mellow, aromatic bean that could only grow in this region! Yes, she would stop for a cup.

She didn't make it far from the orphanage gate.

A silver Crown Vic with tinted windows jumped the sidewalk in front of her and broke sharply, kicking up a curtain of sandy loam. Four beefed-up soldiers masked in balaclavas, some strapped with machine guns, rushed her into the back seat. The silvery grey velour interior that reminded her of a donated pullover she wore in the '70s. Lucía noted the freezing air conditioner. *La mafia*, she knew. In Mexico, the cartels were among the only ones to have decent AC.

Before the driver had slammed his own door and smashed his boot on the gas, Lucía was talking. "Listen, *cabróns*. No need to be handsy. I would have gotten in the car myself if you had asked nicely. I know the drill."

Of the sweaty mouth-breathers crowded into the Crown Vic, two of them bookended her into the back seat, and two up front were jammed in like clowns in a circus act. All of them hunched over, shoulders rolling forward. They did not remove their masks.

When no one responded to her first statement, Lucía called out, "The hag once had me kidnapped from the University library when I didn't enroll in the correct classes." She mumbled to herself, "Like she knows what is best for the A-Life degree." Then louder: "Mary, Mother of God!" She picked up sticky Chaca-Chaca candy bags from the floorboard and waved them. "One, two, three...four bags! It is *dis-gus-ting* in here!"

The man wedged between her and the door expressed silent injury at her comment. She threw the empty candy bags at him. "Have some pride in your work," she said. "*Pendejos.*"

Quietly, they rode to the outskirts of Veracruz, where the Crown Vic cruised at top speed down a two-lane highway edged by stunted trees, scrub grass, and graffitied shacks. The one riding in the passenger seat opened a tabloid paper from America. The headline read, *Manny di Martini living among Alaskan Inuits, learns to build igloos.*

Lucía sighed heavily at intervals. Eventually, she asked, "How about some music?"

The one next to her tugged his balaclava and said, "You're not playing the game correctly. It is customary for our passengers to beg us not to kill them, ask us where we are taking them, tell us they will pay us a lot of money to allow them to go free. Things like that."

"Do you want money?" she asked.

"No."

"I thought not." She called to the front seat, "Hey, up there. I am good with the Fleetwood Mac—" She rolled her eyes upward to search for the names of bands she liked. "—the Pretenders, the Go-Go's—If you have the Dr. Dré, that is not bad—"

The driver and the front passenger exchanged glances.

"Just no *pinche* Tejano," Lucía added. "And no Michael Jackson—"

The squished man mumbled, "This is highly irregular. You are not playing the game."

Lucía shrugged. "It's a long ride. No reason we can't be cordial." The muscled man in the passenger seat held up a Beastie Boys CD for Lucía's approval. "*Paul's Boutique.* That's a good one."

The squished man insisted, "But you don't know where we are going!" He scratched his nose through his mask.

She turned to him. "Mexico City Cathedral. Am I close?"

The man's shoulders sank.

Lucía mumbled, "The hag loves that damn cathedral." She scooted down low in her seat and rested her knees against the console. "Arrrrrrhhhh," she moaned. "Anyone have any drugs? Withdrawal is kicking my *ass*."

The front passenger rummaged in the glove box, then passed back a gallon-sized plastic bag full of pills. Lucía's eyes lit up. "*Muchas gracias. Eres la verga.*" She tore open the bag and selected a pale green tablet, a beige capsule, and a pink tablet. "These better be free," she said. "It's the least you can do." She neatly rezipped the bag and tossed it to the front seat. The man to her right offered a bottle of water. "No need," she said, and swallowed them all dry with a hard gulp through gritted teeth.

Another long silence.

Lucía drummed her palms on her thighs. "Okay, fucknuts. Who wants to play Tour Guide? I haven't been home in almost ten years."

"Not since Discovery?" the squished man asked. "I love Discovery!"

"Discovery was a year and a half ago," Lucía said, "so yes, that counts."

"I am not a dumbbell," the man said.

"You said it, not me."

He asked with wide eyes, "Then you don't know about the return of the Aztecs?" His brow pushed against his balaclava, wiggling the mask.

Lucía said, "They're called Colhua. Or Mexica."

The man blinked.

"Okay. Aztecs. So. Aztecs are back, huh?" she asked. "Better than ever?"

"Yes, they are back," he said. "With human sacrifices!" He put a hand to his mouth hole and giggled.

Lucía stopped drumming. "*Recent* human sacrifices?"

"Oh yes!"

Lucía reevaluated the man. She thought him much too excited about this statement but sensed an opportunity to inject some intrigue into this five-hour drive. "In that case, please enlighten me." She stretched her legs through the fold-down armrests, eliciting a frown from the driver. The man in the passenger seat leaned closer to his window.

Lucía said to the squished man, "I might drift off, but you keep talking."

The squished man turned to her, shifting in his seat as far as his body would allow. He wiggled his meaty fingers. "I will now conjure the Mexico of the Collapse!" Lucía knew she would have heard most of this on the television already, but what the hell. The man began, "The Mexican economy was not doing so well. It had not only crashed, but the government had fled to the US! Big problems!"

Lucía smacked her lips. It sounded just like the problems she knew in Boston. The basics of survival—food, water, electricity, fuel, and medicine—in short supply everywhere, no one in control. However, the man told her, in the big cities—Mexico City, León, Puebla, even San Cristóbal de las Casas in Chiapas—citizens who could do so abandoned their homes and businesses, leaving behind the sick and the elderly to the whims of the hordes of homeless children. "We call them the Street Rats," the man said.

"I know the Rats," Lucía said. "We had them in the orphanage. Difficult to potty train. Even harder to detox. Most would just run away."

"Dangerous!" the man added. "Nothing to lose. They took over." With the cities to themselves, he went on to say, the Rats graduated from getting high off the paint thinner to getting drunk from looted tequila and champagne. In Mexico City, they ravaged the central zone. "Like hungry locusts in the end times." He laughed.

"And that's what gave people the idea to get back to the basics with Aztecs?" Lucía asked.

"No," the man said. "That was when *we* stepped up to run the country." He jabbed himself with his thumb.

"La mafia?"

"*Sí.*"

"Why you?"

He puffed his chest. "We represent the country's sole stable industry in the Collapse."

"Violence?"

"Drugs, silly."

Lucía knew about all of this—so far. "How's the career change going?"

He picked at his mask again. "Not bad," he said. "We are used to war with other cartel families, but now we work together. Mostly. Only a few battles." He said to himself, "Boring."

"Are you finding running a country requires a different skill set than drug trafficking?"

"We are not accustomed to finding consensus. We are used to doing things our way. There have been growing pains, as you Americans say."

"I'm not American," Lucía said.

"*Discúlpeme.*"

She gave a slight nod. "Go on."

The man rearranged himself. "First it was us in charge, but the religion was not in hand. After the Catholics said, 'No comment,' the Aztecs stepped up to take their place."

"Ah," Lucía said. "Collective conversion crisis."

She had heard about Mexico's reaction to the Vatican's statement: a clusterfuck of angry parishioners followed by a swan dive in tithing and attendance. Afterward, a group of cardinals had written an open letter describing a crisis of faith that the Discovery had wrought, to which another group of cardinals had responded with yet another press conference that was sabotaged by technical difficulties. During that fiasco, the Pope was out of commission, unable to appear in public due to a minor gallstone surgery. By the time the Pope did appear, the downward spiral had serious momentum. His cardinals were in an all-out war with each other. Parishioners had taken sides. The Mexican government-in-exile, based in San Antonio, broadcasted this to its citizens: "The Mexican people will always rise to cast away the chains of oppressors and colonizers. Perhaps it is time to return to the ways of our ancient peoples and rebuild the pyramids to address the gods we have left behind." During that press conference, the Mexican President had dropped her page of notes and said to the camera, "How's that for a comment?"

The squished man raised a finger to reclaim the narrative. "This was when dancers in the traditional dress—the striped tunics and the feathered headdresses and such—occupied the plazas in all cities."

"Kind of a response?" Lucía asked.

The man nodded. His balaclava was riding up the back of his head. A wad of fabric at the top of his head bobbed as he talked. "The people all over the country would meet to relearn the old gods, to pray in the old ways. And from there, leaders came forward to us to ask for a partnership for safer streets from the Rats."

"You took that meeting? From people dressed in costume?"

Another waggle of the wad of fabric up top. "Yes. There was an agreement made. We would round up the Street Rats, and the Aztecs would dispense justice according to the old laws."

"Old laws?" Lucía straightened. "Are you telling me the modern Aztecs are executing children?"

Another waddle. "*¡Sí! ¡Mire!*" He knocked on the window.

They were whizzing past an old shipping container yard. Centered on an open expanse of concrete was a high wooden platform accessed by an impressive number of wooden stair steps. At the moment, it was quiet, unoccupied. At the center of that platform rested a stone—or perhaps, Lucía thought, a better word for it was "boulder"—the size of which likely demanded placement by a crane. Ropes and manacles wrapped the stone, which appeared to be drenched in red paint. The man asked Lucía, "Did you not see these platforms driving in from the States? Surely."

Lucía dove over the squished man for a better view out the window. "I did," she said. "But I did not have the context for them at the time." The red paint appeared to flood halfway down the immense stair system. Lucía got a chill. "That's not paint, is it?"

The man's voice was in her ear now. His breath smelled of mandarin oranges and sugar. "The priests carve out the hearts of the Rats with dull knives," he said. And he added, Lucía swore, a slight giggle.

She reexamined the sacrificial platform. She had heard about the severe Druid courts in Europe, the torturous Zoroastrians in Iran, and the public mutilations by the Vedics in India. But this? This beat all of them. She clamped down on her simmering rage and said to the giggling man, "You sound happy about the change in justice administration."

"Who is not happy to get rid of a few Rats? To make an examp—"

Lucía pushed him into the window and held his gaze through cotton eyeholes. "What the fuck is wrong with you?"

The man scrambled for an answer. "So many things, I am told. Bad parental figure."

She smacked at the fabric wad on his head. "You're all behaving like children. Regressing. Do you *realize* the world we live in now? To survive, we must look *forward*, not backward."

The man slid back into the velour to escape Lucía's disdain. "I don't know why you're so upset. *I* don't carve out their hearts," he said. "This is all done by a certified priest."

"Certified? Why didn't you say so?"

The man grinned.

"Idiot."

The squished man hung his head. *Like a child*, Lucía thought.

She scooted away from the window and called to the front seat. "You up there?" She whacked at the head of the man in the passenger seat. "These drugs aren't working."

"You took a lot," he said in a monotone.

"Not enough," Lucía said.

He reached into the glovebox and passed the pill bag to Lucía again. He said, "No charge for the Mother of ArLiFs."

She shot him a look that might have severed his neck right under his balaclava hem. "What did you call me?"

"Mother—"

"I am mother of nothing," she said. "So shut—"

He added, "You are *known*."

She threw the bag at him. It missed and crackled against the front glass. The car swerved. The squished man giggled. Lucía yelled, "You don't know me!"

The man in the front plucked the bag from the dashboard. "You take too much."

"I'm always like this!" She repeatedly thumped her head against the back of the seat.

"Miss Lucía—" the squished man began.

"*You* shut your mouth!" She squirmed in her place and pulled at the knees of her jeans. "I'm gonna be sick."

The man up front said, "I told you. You took too many tablets."

The squished man called out, "Hector, pull over. The Mother of ArLiFs will regurgitate and ruin the upholstery."

Lucía twisted in the confines of the back seat. She couldn't breathe. It was too cold in the car. Then, too hot. *Why won't the drugs work?* she thought. *Please work. Please take the pain.*

Why won't they work?

Why—So sleepy—

25

Soñadora

1973-1976

LUCÍA'S EARLIEST MEMORY WAS of falling upward.

There was the sea, swaying. Her neck undulating with the waves, the horizon sinking, then rising.

She knew a lullaby and sang it aloud. It comforted her.

Her mother lay next to her in the boat. Smelly. Black hair covering her face. Flies on her open eyeballs.

Then, darkness overhead. Cold. Hands reaching out to her, and Lucía screaming.

"Screaming?" That bizarre accent.

A new nun had arrived at the orphanage to see Lucía, and only Lucía. None of the 16 other children living there interested the nun. "Show me the child from the sea," she had said to the others.

This nun with the hideous accent came from far away, Lucía had been told. And this nun asked a lot of questions. "Screaming?" she repeated, tapping Lucía for attention. "As if? As if what, pet?" This nun smelled funny. She walked funny.

In the art room of the Ciudad Refugio Orphanage, Lucía had just blown out five candles on a cake. Everyone in the orphanage got a small slice, even the nuns. No one knew Lucía's real birthday, but the sisters marked the occasion on the anniversary she was rescued from the Veracruz harbor by a passing fisherman. The body next to her, it was assumed, was her mother. No family claimed her body. No father came for the child.

At the orphanage, Lucía always enjoyed the small amount of attention anyone paid to her, but, eventually, they all backed away. She sensed that they thought her weird.

The Catholic press had published an article about the miraculous girl from the sea. Gifted in art and languages, origins unknown! The orphanage's nuns had pinned the article to the wall. Soon after, the new nun showed up with her demand: "Show me the child from the sea."

The nun's pale face, like a ghost's, was carved with deep wrinkles. She was short and wide with bulging eyes. And the nun's breath was evil, Lucía decided, as if the woman had eaten things like bats and puppies and rotten algae. Further, she skittered around in her habit with a strange walk that dipped and rose. The other nuns whispered about spina bifida, though Lucía had no idea what that meant. The new nun exercised an agility that surprised the other children. "*Fantasma*," they called her.

"Sister Mary," she corrected them. "Not *Fantasma*."

Sister Gloria announced that this new nun would be coming to visit Lucía for two weeks, two times a year. Lucía wasn't told why.

"When you were rescued from the sea," Sister Mary said again, "you were screaming, child." Lucía noticed she spoke to no other children in her funny kind of English. Just her. And Lucía understood her. Quickly. "As if..." Sister Mary prompted again, raising all the wrinkles on her forehead at once.

Lucía should supply an explanation, she knew. Why was she screaming in the sea? She didn't remember. Lucía just stared at the squat nun, mouth in a pout. "*No hablo Inglés.*"

Sister Mary clucked at her. "Don't play that game with me. I'm far too old and far too grumpy."

Sister Gloria stepped into the art room, her rosary swinging from her waist. The new nun didn't have a rosary, Lucía noticed. Sister Gloria barked at the woman, "You'll not get more out of her than that. She says nothing about that day she was found in the harbor."

Sister Mary blinked at Lucía. "Is that true? Will I get nothing more from you, little one?"

Lucía pretended she didn't understand her. Sister Mary huffed. The air flooded with the aroma of cheese.

Lucía flipped to a blank page in a beat-up spiral notebook and took up a blue pencil.

Their art room was packed with fantastical creations. Children's drawings hung low on the beige cinderblock walls. Scribbled stick-figure families—two parents, two children—that none of them had ever known. Homes drawn like gingerbread and candy houses. A stick girl riding a stick horse. Boxy golden school buses. Playgrounds below puffy clouds. Scenes from a normal child's life, learned from picture books. The children were mimicking a life they didn't know. Lucía drew none of those things. Her drawings were of spiraling cities with leaning architecture—photorealistic with shading, drawn before she could read. Lines made straight without the aid of a ruler. Buildings soaring above and tunneling below the ground. Platforms with staircases running in inverse. One of the nuns likened Lucía's art to surrealists like Victor Vasarely, Salvador Dalí, and Octavio Ocampo, with tessellations and infinite reflections and shapes in impossible loops. "It's unsettling," Sister Gloria had said.

Why draw anything settling? Lucía wanted to ask. Everyone knew the universe is unsettling. It only made sense to reflect it.

Now, at the art table with Lucía, Sister Mary eyed Lucía's blue pencil. The new nun asked Sister Gloria, "Why are there no normal drawing pencils for the children? Just these blue ones?"

"We work with what the Lord provides," Sister Gloria told her.

"Is it beyond the Lord's power to provide crayons?"

Sister Gloria replied, "A student newspaper at the university has donated blue pencils previously used for editing copy. As you see, every child's drawing on our wall is presented in blue."

"Aye. That is obvious."

With such a blue pencil, Lucía slashed at the page, whipping lines into the horizon with perfect perspective. She never concentrated on how she did what she did. There were worlds inside her like actual physical presences. She had to let them out or feel the pain of those worlds crowding inside her. The pain began in her stomach like she ate something bad. Then it burned her from the inside out. Sometimes she had trouble sleeping from all the worlds creating themselves in her head. All around her cot, the walls were covered in drawings: temples and walled cities and irrigation systems and roads, all folding in on themselves and expanding in multiple dimensions. It made the others sick to look at them. For Lucía, though, she felt relief at their airing out.

Sister Mary sank back in a child-sized chair. It groaned under her girth. "It's an orphanage. One would imagine a box of crayons would not break the budget. Gifted from the Lord, or not."

"*Extranjera.*" Sister Gloria huffed and left the room, presumably to round up the other children for nap time. To her amazement, Lucía learned she would be allowed to skip nap time whenever Sister Mary visited.

They were alone now, except for Sister Vicenta lurking nearby under the pretense of dusting.

Lucía completed her drawing of a convex building façade as if seen through a fisheye lens. She signed her name in blue and passed her drawing to the nun. "Thank you, pet." Sister Mary studied the signature. "Why are the children here all named Santamaría?" she asked aloud.

Sister Vicenta floated into the room with her duster. "Ah." She cleared her throat. "Santamaría. Named because the children are all gifts from the Holy Virgin Mother." She noticed a nearby shelf closer to Sister Mary and Lucía and flicked her duster there.

Sister Mary said to Sister Vicenta, "I was told you were the one who administered to the child on her arrival."

Sister Vicenta pointed the duster to herself, leaving a dusty smudge on her smock. "Who me?"

"Aye, you, turnip."

"Oh, me," she said. "Yes, I did administer to this little one."

Sister Mary pressed a sheet of paper to the art table, then slid it toward Sister Vicenta. "Write down the song she was singing upon arrival, please. Phonetically." The nun tapped the page. "No detail too small."

Sister Vicenta dropped the duster and crammed herself into a child's chair. In large letters, she wrote a string of vowels and consonants that resembled no known language. Sister Mary flicked her eyes from the letters to Lucía.

Sister Vicenta finished by passing the sheet to Sister Mary. "It's the best—"

"Thank you," Sister Mary interrupted, snatching the page.

Sister Vicenta gestured to her transcript, intent on extending her cooperation. "I wrote, *cough all noffle*, but after that, it gets fuzzy. Perhaps I should have written, *miggle-noffle*—"

"Don't slaughter it, pet," Sister Mary said. "That will be all."

Sister Vicenta wandered away, but not too far. She was never far from odd happenings in the orphanage. Lucía was pleased to be the odd happening attracting Sister Vicenta today.

Sister Mary was examining Lucía over the paper. Her starched, white headdress pushed her eyebrows into flat lids clamping down her whole face. Lucía squirmed until Sister Mary stabbed the paper with her pudgy finger. "Now, how would *you* know *this* language?"

Lucía shrugged. "*No hablo Inglés.*"

Sister Mary fired off, "*Si quieres hablar tu lengua materna, ¿por qué no lo dijiste?*"

Lucía's jaw hinged open.

"Close your mouth, pet."

Lucía closed it.

Mary leaned forward to remove a black journal from her tunic. Lucía marveled at it. So clean. So new. Sister Mary observed her fascination while making a note in the journal. Then, Sister Mary tucked Lucía's drawing and Sister Vicenta's lullaby transcript into the book and closed it. Sister Mary produced a clean sheet of paper. Lucía was amazed. She almost *never* had blank paper all to herself, front *and* back. She only drew on the backs of used pages. She also drew on walls when the buildings inside her insisted on it. She felt the fibers of the fresh page. They were cool.

Sister Mary nodded at the blue pencil Lucía gripped. "Again, child. Draw."

That was what Sister Mary wanted at every visit: for Lucía to draw her worlds. Sister Mary came in autumn and in spring, staying two weeks each time. When Sister Mary arrived, she did not engage in small talk with the others. She did not want a restroom or even a change of underwear. She pressed her small bag into another nun's chest and demanded Lucía be brought to the art table. Lucía felt like a queen. Under Sister Mary's watch, Lucía drew towers and spires and extensive cities with intricate carvings in no known language.

In between visits, Sister Mary mailed art supplies addressed to Lucía. The battered packages arrived covered in stamps from a place called Glasgow. In the first package, Sister Mary enclosed a letter asking the orphanage to move a new table into the art room just for Lucía. *She needs appropriate space*, she wrote. Lucía read the letter over the nuns' shoulders. The nuns wrote back to inform Mary that the other children barely had space themselves, that offering Lucía such an expansive space would be a ludicrous inequity. Sister Mary replied by sending the entire orphanage all new clothing and toys. *Now*, she commanded by letter, *a table for Lucía. And only Lucía.*

Sister Mary also sent modeling clay. Blue exclusively, just as Lucía liked. As soon as the clay arrived, she popped one open and shoved her nose into the can. It smelled of musky vanilla and salt. Inside the can, the clay was just a blob with the embossed logo from the lid imprinted on the cylindrical mold. Outside the can, under the pressure of her fingers, that clay could transform into a temple with spires extending as far as gravity would allow.

During a visit when Lucía was almost eight years old, Sister Mary had brought crates of modeling compound. One thousand cans of it. The crates stacked up on the concrete playground outside for other children to play on, and the other nuns brought the cans inside a dozen at a time for Lucía. "Go wild," Sister Mary said to Lucía. The girl could hardly believe her luck. With the clay, she built a city that took up almost the entire playroom and flooded the whole orphanage with the smell of musky vanilla. Lucía sculpted bridges with ladderlike towers that swooped under themselves to serve as roads, then angled down to resemble ladders to underground caverns. Lucía attached these sculptures to the ceiling, to tables, to desks, to undersides of chairs. She sculpted humanlike creatures ("Such slender, ungodly creatures," the orphanage nuns noted in disgust, "as if Satan had stretched them on a torture rack.") climbing stairs that morphed into ladders rising to the spires, then into slides plummeting below. By the time Lucía had finished, the nuns had to press themselves against the wall to enter the playroom. The other children froze in the presence of such a massive undertaking. The nuns were furious.

Sister Mary was only slightly impressed. "Quite remarkable, child."

"May I remind you, Sister Mary," another nun droned, "you're here to serve the *entire* orphanage."

Sister Mary barely looked at her. "I dedicate my energies where they are most useful."

The other nuns called her *Fantasma* now, but never to her face.

To keep up with Lucía's bursts of creative energy, pushing chairs and tables into foundations for her clay architecture, Sister Mary moved like a bug with a hundred legs on fire. She bent low to watch Lucía attach clay to the undersides of furniture. She watched closely when Lucía stabbed pictorial characters into the walls she had sculpted.

When Lucía had finished, Sister Mary inspected the whole-room sculpture with the intensity of a municipal contractor. She found no flaws. She poked the modeling clay. It drooped. Sister Mary said to herself, "I shall have to investigate more imaginative media for her scale of expression. Media more suitable to Lucía's scope of thought." She scratched at her leg through her tunic. "Perhaps digital. There have been marvelous advances in home computing this year."

Sister Vicenta, again, was lurking by the door. She sputtered, "You will put a *computer* in the orphanage?"

"If the Lord wills it," Sister Mary said.

The year Lucía turned ten, Sister Mary insisted that the Franciscan Sisters of the Inmaculada Concepción in Veracruz take Lucía along during their annual trips to the Archdiocese of Mexico City. Sister Mary wrote that she would accompany them. It was to be a rare summer visit. While the other sisters met at Archdiocese, Sister Mary would escort Lucía to the Zócalo, the plaza in front of the City Cathedral.

The edifice darkened the sidewalk where the two would seek out street vendors for raspas and gorditas de nata. After choosing a flavor from the rainbow of syrups for her shaved ice, Lucía would nibble on buttery cakes warm from the street griddle while *Fantasma*, as the children still called her, told Lucía about the ruins under the cathedral. "The temples of the Tenochcan city of Tenochtitlan are right under our feet," Mary said. She stomped the pavement. Her habit folded under her feet. It was always too long, Lucía noted. How Mary bobbed so gracefully without tripping on it, Lucía could not figure. If Mary were like the other nuns, a rosary around her waist would have clattered when she stomped. Lucía asked why she didn't wear one, but Mary ignored her.

"We aren't here for...?" Lucía raised her chin to the hulking stone cathedral with carved saints and stained glass.

Mary trilled a high note. "That thing? You could draw and sculpt that monstrosity when you were five." She placed her half empty raspa cup on the park bench. "Now. I want you to imagine an entire civilization underground. Right here."

Mary wiggled her hands before her. It meant Lucía was to imagine what the nun was conjuring with words. The city was, Mary said, an *enchantment*. Great pyramids rose from the water, all built of masonry. "The Spanish colonists, upon seeing it, asked whether the city they saw before them was a dream."

"And was it?" Lucía asked. She wiped pastry from her mouth with her sleeve.

"Use a napkin, pet, not your hand," Sister said. "And no. The island civilization was very real."

With more hand waggling, Sister Mary conjured a world below. Wide streets on grids, artificial floating gardens, canal waterways feeding the shrubs, trees, and gardens. Marketplaces sustained the population with fresh foods and artisan wares. Public buildings housed the mayor and their councils. Temples protected sacrifices to gods of rain, sun, and sport. A central palace that housed the emperor had room enough for a zoo and an aquarium with hundreds of people caring for the animals.

"Is it cruel to keep animals in a zoo?" Lucía asked.

Sister Mary whacked Lucía's knee. "Focus, child."

Lucía listened in a slouch, imagining the dream that Mary conjured. Social classes. Noblemen. Warriors. Slaves. Priests.

Then, Mary said, the outsiders came. The conquistadors.

Lucía suddenly sat upright. "What happened next?"

"The civilization was taken down to the core by Catholics," Mary said. She slurped her raspa.

"Oh."

The missing rosary was never so prominent.

Mary waggled her hands toward the edge of the cathedral. "The conquistador Hernan Cortes himself was said to have laid the cornerstone of the cathedral that would act as the spiritual conquest of the early Mexican civilizations he had destroyed. Did you know Cortes, also known as the Spanish Plague, founded your city? Veracruz?"

"No." Lucía imagined her old city crumbling at the footsteps of the foreign conqueror.

Mary drained the dregs of her sugary syrup, then adjusted her headdress. "Time to be going, turnip."

"But wait," Lucía begged. "You brought me here for an assignment."

Sister Mary pulled out a red journal from her navy robes. "History of the Aztec Empire, properly known as the Nahua alliance..."

"No," Lucía whined. "A new model!"

Mary chuckled. "All right, child." The nun slapped the journal closed and tucked it back into her robes. "Build the enchanted island city."

Build the enchanted city, Lucía mouthed.

Sister Mary rose from the bench. "Come along. We're late. The sisters will be angrier than usual, and the ride back will be especially unpleasant. We really must procure the convent a new vehicle with better shocks. My rear end is numb—"

The nun bounced away with her weird walk, leaving Lucía in a throng of strangers in the plaza.

"Wait," Lucía called out weakly.

Mary drifted out of sight.

"Wait—"

Lucía felt as if her mouth were glued shut. Her voice stopped in her chest. She could make no noise.

"Mmmgg—"

A shadow was approaching.

"Mmmffff—"

A light hit her face. She shielded her eyes.

"Nnnnnn—"

Someone was here. Someone else. The figure darkened Lucía's face. Colossal. Cold as stone.

26

Guardián

Mexico City, November 1, 1993

"Pleasant nap, pet?"

Lucía wiped drool from her face and blinked away the scenes from her past. Her mouth felt packed full of cotton. Dried skin came off her lips in flakes.

Sister Mary was sitting in the opposite chair with a table between them, her legs swinging under her thick tunic. Lucía noticed a porcelain teapot and two cups rested on a tray, likely to denote the civility of the intended conversation. Steam snaked out of the teapot's spout. Lucía hated tea.

Lucía looked around. Someone had carried her to a wrought-iron chair and set her upright in it. Now she was on a balcony with no memory of how she got there. She shivered. The stone buildings of downtown Mexico City cast cold shadows across her legs. The cathedral loomed nearby. "Mexico City Metropolitan Cathedral," she said to herself. "Called it."

The nun was older now—her wrinkles were deeper and her skin sagged with the weight of 16 more years of unrelenting gravity. The only thing unchanged was her habit: navy with a starched white headdress framing her dark, protruding eyes.

"Fucking hell," Lucía yawned.

"Oh, child. My virgin ears." At the moment, the deepest wrinkle on Mary's face was her frown. "You know, I had to pay extra today because you were a gobshite to my fellas."

"Good. And what's wrong with using a telephone to request my presence? Why do you always have to be so dramatic?"

Mary swatted away Lucía's suggestion. "Faster my way."

"No need to consider any trauma you might inflict?"

"Are you traumatized?"

"Not yet." Lucía stretched her dry lips and wiggled her jaw. "But your fellas might be."

"Makes 'em stronger. Tea?" Mary poured amber liquid into two cups.

"Boiling herb-water? Hell no."

"Hell no, *what*, child?"

"Hell no, *thank you*. And I'm not a child." Lucía bent down to touch her sandals, stretching her back. She must have slept crammed in a back seat between two drug traffickers for the whole drive from Veracruz. "What do you wanna bet I snored the whole way here?"

"No bet. You have always had a terrible relationship with slumber."

Lucía peered over the balcony at the massive plaza, the Zócalo, at the heart of Mexico City. Cartel soldiers patrolled below. Assault rifles on straps flapped against their hips as they walked. At the south end of the plaza, a new addition: another sacrificial platform, this one much higher than the one outside Veracruz. The sacrificial stone was soaked in red, as were the stairs.

In the center of the plaza, a man in costume danced. He was dressed in white feathers with darker ostrich plumes extending from a crown of skulls. His face, under a bird mask, was caked in white makeup. As he rotated and swirled, the streetlights cast feathery shadows on the pavement. The cartel soldiers rested elbows on their guns and watched with faint amusement.

Besides the platform and the dancing bird man, Lucía noticed makeshift altars, *ofrendas*, at the edges of the plaza. "Hmph," she said aloud. *Día de los Muertos*. November 1, 1993. Peculiar way to tell time: by cultural tradition.

On the pavement, wooden crates towered in tiers. A framed photo of a loved one perched at the top of each one. Marigolds in water on the next levels, with petals scattered to lead the loved ones' spirits to the altars. On the bottom tiers, food and drink: sweet breads, tequila shots, candies. *The fucking Rats will take it all by nightfall*, Lucía thought. But still, those altars were signs of life, even if it was the practice of communing with the dead. She wondered when it would all come back—the full festivities. The hulking papier-mâché skeletons on parade floats, as were traditional on this day. Or would they change to tentacled beasts? Would the vendors sell *Lotería* cards picturing the Sleeping One? *La Criatura*?

The dancing man swiveled his arms and tapped his feet on the plaza's stones. Bells shaped like skulls encircled his ankles. Lucía couldn't hear the noise from the balcony, but she wondered if he was scaring off the Rats from the *ofrendas*. As if reading her thoughts, Mary said, "The Catholics stole the Day of the Dead from the Colhua. The modern people are stealing it back."

"I hate it when you respond to what I am thinking. Stay out of my head." Gunfire rattled. A few blocks away, Lucía judged. Not close. "Where are we, exactly?"

"The Gran Hotel," the nun said. She sipped at her tea and winced. "Isn't this shite tea?"

"All tea is shite." Lucía inspected the balcony: the wrought-iron chairs, the tiled floor, the full basket of mums hanging from the balcony rail. "I might have thought this hotel would be closed for the Collapse."

Mary gulped tea again. "It is."

Lucía smiled. "But not for you."

"I have business here."

"At the hotel?"

In reply, Mary raised her teacup to the cold edifice looming in the near distance.

"The cathedral?" Lucía laughed. "You're working for the Mexican Archdiocese now?"

"Not exactly."

Lucía squinted. The cathedral appeared strange to her. "Hey. What's wrong with the cathedral?"

Mary centered her cup in the saucer, then replaced both on the table. "The Street Rats burned it. Sent it right back to God in a puff of smoke." She gestured into the air as if sketching the rising conflagration. "That's why I'm here."

Lucía looked again. "I hadn't heard. That sucks."

Mary pitched her head: "Eh."

Lucía stood and craned her neck, which cracked with a head roll. The roof in the back of the cathedral had caved in, exposing a skeleton of iron supports. The charred rafters poked out of the church's roofline at odd angles like a handful of burnt matchsticks that landed in a chaotic jumble. The entrances were sealed with yellow tape. "Is that smoke I smell?" She gagged at the taste of ashes in her mouth. "Accckk. Acccckkkkkk."

"For heaven's sake." Mary handed her a paper napkin. "The cathedral stopped burning months ago. Possibly you're detecting the Street Rat piss baking in the Zócalo." Mary rose and entered the hotel room through an open door behind her.

"No," Lucía called out. "It's smoke. It smells like death." She wadded and threw the napkin over the balcony railing, then yelled to the men patrolling the plaza: "Eat my trash, *pinche soldados*!"

From inside the hotel room, Mary yelled, "Do not antagonize men with guns!"

Lucía gave a staring soldier the finger.

Mary returned clutching a stack of photos. "All right, cherished. *This* is why I'm here." The nun tossed the stack onto the glass table. The photo pile avalanched, knocking Mary's empty teacup into Lucía's full one.

Lucía selected a few photos and examined them. "What's all this?"

Mary poured another cup of tea for herself. "After the cathedral fire cooled off and the roof caved in, the Federales moved in to secure the site. That's when they found this." The nun poked at the murky photos of stones and carvings. "Under the church."

"It looks like an archeological dig. Is it a room in a Tenochcan temple?"

"Correct. As we know, the cathedral sits atop ruins. And here is the motherlode." Mary sipped. "The Mexican government went into exile not long after the room was exposed by the cave-in, so there was a problem securing the site from authorities. The Providence Group—"

Lucía lifted her brows. "*Those* fuckers?"

"The Providence Group paid off the cartels—and I'm talking a *lot* of money here—to access the site." She waved a hand. "And for protection."

"Of course."

"The government-in-exile got involved and granted permits. Almost as soon as Providence accessed the site, they confirmed the room exposed below the church belonged to one of their prophets: Zumaa." Mary snatched a photo from the top of a stack and held it out for Lucía.

"Zumaa. Who's that?" Lucía studied the photo. Relief statues along the perimeter of the room depicted an insect-like being with long blades for front legs, under which text had been inscribed. Lucía recognized the language but said nothing.

Mary explained, "Zumaa was a priestess of the Aztec Empire. She is known in broader history as simply that, but she's also worshipped by the Providence Group as the Prophetess of the Cataclysmic Herald."

Mary tossed another photo to Lucía: an altar with more text. Lucía quickly scanned the text. Same language.

She set the photo aside, then sat back with her arms folded. "Didn't think that Providence saints were in your wheelhouse. What's Zumaa to you?"

"Prophet, not saint." Mary rested her teacup on a bulge in her tunic. "And I'll get to *your* purpose here in a moment."

Lucía threw her hands up. "Whenever you're ready! By all means, get your peso's worth out of your kidnapping today!"

Mary continued, "The Priestess Zumaa lived in Tenochtitlan, the ruins of which are right under the plaza out there. As you know." The nun gestured to the Zócalo with her chin. "Zumaa documented visions of an apocalyptic harbinger, a creature who acted as a sort of alarm clock for the apocalypse."

"Uh-huh," Lucía grunted. She shuffled her feet. "Is there water? I am thirsty."

"I wouldn't drink unboiled water here." Mary swept her hand over the photos. "Providence guessed that Zumaa might have built a sacrificial room in one of the central temples."

Lucía scraped white gunk from her lips. "And here it is."

"Thus, here I am." Mary eyed Lucía in deadly focus.

"What?"

"It's our old game, tulip. I talk, then you talk. I told you why I'm here, in detail. Now, you tell me why you withdrew from your PhD program."

Lucía stretched. "You don't want to know what the etchings say? That is why I am here, right? You think because I sang a strange lullaby in a harbor in 1969 that I am the one to interrogate about *all* unknown languages?"

"We'll get to that." Mary resettled her entire body into her seat, bringing her shoulders down to lower her center of gravity. Lucía knew that meant she was battening down for a major battle.

Lucía slumped in her chair. "I see you are in your battle-axe mode, so I will tell you." She twisted in her seat. "It was Dr. Daas's fault."

The nun did not move.

"He's afraid of them," she added.

Mary tensed her lips but said nothing.

Lucía added, "The ArLiFs. Afraid of the ArLiFs." She wanted to say, *Claire*, but did not.

Mary sipped her tea.

"Oliver Daas is a man afraid of his own creations," she said. She wanted to add, *Afraid of Claire. Why?*

Mary cocked her head.

Lucía continued, "And he thinks he is afraid of *me*. He is wrong. He is afraid of—"

Claire.

Even more telling to Lucía than these lies of omission was the sickening pain in her abdomen. The pain began the moment she left Daas's lab, the moment she turned her back on Claire. It wasn't the withdrawal, either. She knew withdrawal pains. This was a different pain. It was psychological. It was grief.

Lucía's hands were windmilling now. "Daas hadn't the guts to design faces on computer lifeforms. And he wants to create the ultra-intelligence?" She laughed. "He does *not* have what it takes to deliver that! What does he think his project aims to do, bring some computer beings to life? Like he's Geppetto and he's gonna make a real girl? Such bullshit! It's complicated! It's real! It's messy! He wants this to be neat! He wants explanations and publishable equations! Fuck that!"

The nun rolled her eyes.

Lucía jabbed at her with a finger. "Do *not* do that! You do not understand the importance of *instinct* when creating life! It's everything! The drive is unexplainable!"

Mary sucked at her teeth but said nothing.

Lucía slapped the table to emphasize every other word: "The INTENT to CREATE must COME from PLACES of DEVOTION without EXPECTATION of RESULTS. *Who* said that to me, I wonder? Someone at this table?"

"Yeah, yeah," Mary said. "Oliver Daas is human, and he acted accordingly. As if you're the first one to encounter the time-worn obstacle of mediocre leadership from a man. My question is why did you leave the project instead of managing the problem?"

Lucía threw her hands up. "It's not *my* program. I'm just a student."

"You imply they're *your* lifeforms, but when you're called to lead you claim you're just a student. The project needs you."

Lucía bounced in place with fury. "*¡Es pura paja!* What about what *I* need?!"

"We both know exactly what you need, cherished. The best program on the planet to build, build, build."

Lucía was loud now, attracting the attention of the soldiers on the plaza. "Is that what you thought when you put me on a plane to Boston? Straight to Oliver Daas with me—"

Mary interrupted, "That's right! Nothing but our most promising plan to build a new world. Nothing else would have done for you. Daas was preeminent in the world with his work, and that's what you needed to keep building. That's why you are there."

Lucía muttered, "I'm there because you *pushed* me to go there. I am there because you'd *kidnap* me if I didn't keep going to classes—"

Mary interjected, "No one forced you to develop your abilities!"

"HA! That is HILARIOUS. Did we even *go* through the same years in Mexico? 'Lucía, do this. Lucía, do that.' You were the fucking foreman for the construction of a Play-Doh Civilization for YEARS!"

"No! A decade! Over a *decade* of work! An undergraduate degree and one graduate degree, soon to be two! All paid for! And now you're walking away? That behavior does not become you. This is not the girl I raised."

Lucía widened her eyes. "WHAT? A visit twice a year for 12 years, and she thinks she *raised* me!"

Mary hissed, "You consider Sister *Gloria* your parent figure? How about Sister *Vicenta*?"

"Those *cabronas*? They couldn't raise radishes in a pile of cow shit."

"Thought not." Mary slammed her teacup onto the glass table. "So, go on. Please. I'm enraptured by your explanation for quitting. Had you another offer for world-building on the table?"

Lucía showed her teeth. "As a matter of fact, I did. From Howard Winfield."

"Oh! Him!"

"Yeah. Him! He called for me. Brought me to New York. In style. And I gave him a few things."

"You gave him a few *things*." Mary fiddled with the edge of a saucer. "Things like—?"

"Better power sources for the floating scientific city over the Temple Site. Those UEA ideas were *shit*. So, I gave Howard a few of my ideas. In my sleep, I might add."

"You designed something for him?"

"For the UEA. But he was there."

"Were you curious at all about why a media man would want a science lab?"

"None of my business." Lucía flexed and distended her fingers to recreate her vision. "But it's a *good* plan. Self-sustaining science labs in the middle of the South Pacific to study the Sleeping One. Multiple levels, most of which must function at hydrostatic pressure levels that have never supported long-term human existence. All of it impervious to the radiation and poison that the site leaks. Not impervious to the dreams that creature broadcasts, which drove Manny di Martini mental. How the scientists protect themselves against the creature's dream waves is a problem, but it is not *my* problem."

"The creature broadcasts dreams?" Mary asked.

"You do not keep up with news? Yeah! Dream waves have been detected. More to the point, as you correctly noted, designing the floating city on the ocean was not the challenge of designing Artificial Lifeforms by any means, so I went back to Daas."

"But you completed Winfield's job?"

"I sketched it out for him, yes. In a day or two."

Mary tilted her head. "That's hardly possible, even for you."

Lucía shrugged. "Much can be accomplished on amphetamines."

The nun seethed with flared nostrils like a bull ready to charge. "Drug use is a failing—not a bragging right."

Lucía continued to press her point. "Howard Winfield is evil, and the world will know it."

"And you designed for him! How interesting!"

Lucía kept talking. "Mark my words. He wants nothing to do with real science. He will kill us all."

Mary snorted. "'Mark my words!' Oh, pet. Your ego is out of control."

"He wants the ArLiFs for a military response, did you know?"

Again, the phantom stab in her gut. The way Howard looked at Claire terrified Lucía.

Mary answered, "Who wouldn't? I imagine security is tight in your lab."

"And Howard wants them for an ArLiF *movie*. I shudder! What propaganda would he unleash out of their mouths?"

Claire. Claire's mouth with Howard's words? Never.

Mary frowned.

Lucía picked up her argument. "The man is obsessed with safety via media control. And Daas doesn't see it. He keeps signing contracts with that man—"

"Again, I'm hearing reasons why you should not have left."

"Howard was *never* involved in their creation, so he will be an author of their *destruction*." Lucía was manic now, hands pumping and words tripping over themselves. "He's the most dangerous type of benefactor because he has no clue what we sacrificed to bring the ArLiFs about."

Mary said, "Oh, do shut up and get to the real point of your tirade. I'm *bored*."

Lucía grabbed both armrests of her chair and ballooned her cheeks.

Mary said, "Spit it out, pet."

Lucía exhaled slowly. "Do you have any drugs?"

Mary blinked in disbelief.

"Worth a shot," Lucía said.

"What is *wrong* with you?"

"I live on drugs in the lab. Micro doses of speed, gallons of caffeine, and lots of donuts."

"*Wheesht!*" Mary's accent revved into high gear. "As if talkin' to ya when you're off your nut on whatever drugs my fellas shoved down your gob isn't a solid enough task already! Now you want to get high again?!"

"Forget it."

Mary hurled her voice like a rock at Lucía's face, "Talk!"

"All right," Lucía sat back. "I came home to find out what I am."

"*What* you are? Not *who* you are?"

"Yes. It's been said that I'm not human. So—am I?"

"Are you what?"

"Human. I am asking you. Who are my mother and father?"

Mary slapped the table so hard the porcelain cups rattled. "What does *that* matter?"

"It's my *identity*!" Lucía, fast as lightning, launched a porcelain cup over the balcony rail.

Mary ignored it. "How many times did I tell you that your career is paramount—"

"Either you know who my parents are, or you do not! Which is it?"

"I do not."

"Fuck! I don't believe you! You show up at the orphanage, asking questions about where I come from! You come to see me twice a year, encouraging me to draw and sculpt! But no one else would come near me because they all thought I was a freak! But not you! You were practically knocking over nuns and orphans to get to me! So, what do you know?"

"You seem to think—"

Lucía shot up and launched the whole tea service off the balcony. Soldiers scattered. "I won't go back! Not until you tell me why you came to me in the orphanage! You know something and you are a lying hag! You are keeping *my* secrets to yourself! It's *my* right to know! Mine!" Lucía turned in a circle, not knowing what to do.

"Oh, for the love of—Sit," Mary said.

Lucía parked in the wrought-iron chair. Her pulse was still racing, her face pink and her hairline sweaty.

Mary gathered her thoughts in silence, as if computing something immense.

Bile rose into Lucía's throat. "What do you know?"

Mary scanned her, deciding on something. Finally, she said, "All right. I do not know as much as I'd like. That's why I spent so much effort trying to pry it out of you when you were a child."

"What are you talking about? Do you know something or not? Should I go back and ask Sister Gloria?"

Mary looked away. "Those nuns know nothing."

"*Someone* better fucking tell me something! Is it gonna be you? Or do I have to hitch a ride back to Inmaculada Concepción with those fucking goons down there?"

The cartel glanced up to the balcony again. One smiled weakly and waved.

"You're going to need to be calmer, pet," Mary said. "This won't be easy."

"Oh, it's been a fucking joyride so far! A blast—"

Mary shot up and grabbed Lucía's hand. She jerked Lucía out of her chair with a surprising strength. "What the fuck?" The nun pushed Lucía into the hotel room. "Jesus!"

Mary whisked over to the balcony door and slammed it, sealing them off from the plaza inside a dark room. Then, she whipped the curtains closed. She murmured, "No one can hear this."

"Mary—?"

Mary withdrew a flask from her tunic and flung it at Lucía. "At the risk of feeding your bad habits, down the hatch with it. Get blootered. You're going to need it for what's coming." Lucía looked from the flask to the nun. Mary said, "It's time I told you some things."

Then, Mary removed her headdress. A puff of dandelion-white fuzz sprang to life. Lucía's eyeballs went dry from not blinking. She had never seen Mary without her headdress. She asked, "What's happening right now?"

Mary folded the stiff fabric of the headpiece neatly on the bed, then settled into her chair by weak lamplight. She began by unleashing a long sigh.

Then, she said, "I am the daughter of Providence Prophetess Ailish Finnegan."

Lucía laughed.

Mary did not.

Lucía blurted, "Are you joking?"

Mary pointed to the flask. Lucía unscrewed the lid and took a drink.

"*Bueno*," Lucía said.

"It's where it all started, pet. This is what you want to know." The nun ran her hands through her hair, which sprang back into a round puff. "About my mother—I ought to point out that Providence lore has it wrong about her. They say she had a hand in the deaths of over 90 villagers. Hardly. She was a healer, not a murderer, no matter how black those hearts were who had turned against her. No, it was likely the plain ol' bloody flux took those 90 souls in our village. Like most who bear the title of 'witch,' Ailish was educated and different. Among fearful men, that's a death sentence." Mary stewed in a dark cloud for a moment. "The only person she ever managed to kill was herself. Although, I helped."

Lucía didn't take her eyes off Mary for fear she'd stop talking. Mary had *never* before answered when Lucía asked about her life. Lucía knew absolutely *nothing* about the nun's life before she set foot in her orphanage. Now, Lucía pulled at the hotel-room bed covers, trying to stabilize herself.

Mary sighed again. "What you need to know begins in the bogs of central Ireland in 1937, when a man I barely knew brought me a gift. That gift was a jeweled box with the world inside."

27

Mary Finnegan and the Traveller

Ireland, 1937

IT WAS A HOUSE they had to fight their way into.

Balancing on oak beams kept them from falling into the mire, treacherously deep in their corner of the spongy bog. The high stone wall with the moss grown in the crevices ended at a rusted gate they had to wrestle for entry. The house itself wasn't visible from the gate; they could see only the bluish tin slapped over the original bog-sod roof. Long grasses, dead trees, and tangled ivy nearly buried a stone cottage no younger than the Irish Rebellion of 1798. That cottage had housed the Finnegan family of Tipperary County for seven generations, but by 1937 just Mary and her mother, Ailish Finnegan, lived there—the last of the Finnegan line living on what was left of Finnegan land.

Both women were built for hard work and survival in the elements: stocky and squat, the best stature for swinging an axe and battling the goat for milking. Ailish had aspired to teach school, and even attended university in Galway, but before she could finish she was called back to the Tipperary cottage to care for Grand Mammy in her last days. That was before Mary came along. The remainder of the Finnegans, now spread out as far as Limerick; they never visited, called the old cottage "cursed." The ancient priest, Father O'Brien, came only sporadically, having cast his judgment on Ailish as a fallen woman for her child-birthing outside holy matrimony. He was not, however, above accepting her occasional contributions. "For the Church," he wheezed, tucking a brass trinket into his robes. Other villagers were not so undiscriminating. "Ailish the Witch," was their name for her. If they had a name for Mary, she didn't know it, but it was probably something to do with her legs. "Extra-jointed," her mam said of them. "Funny hip bones. Nothing to sneeze at."

Despite the slippery decay and dank odor of the bogs all around, their cottage oozed life. Moss and lichen sprouted from the roof on the downwind side. One goat and a dozen chickens foraged on scattered seeds and grasses. A scrawny pony grazed. Beyond a low stone wall, in a scant spot of sun heating unfavorable soil, their meager garden miraculously sprouted potatoes, cabbage, carrots, and the occasional summer tomato. In the warm months, Ailish spun wool from neighboring sheep farms into skeins of yarn on the same wheel her Grand Mammy used and her Grand Mammy before her used, while Mary, a sprite of only nine years, spun circles in the clearing behind the cottage. Mary's long dress dragged in the dirt, which angered Ailish. "Ya walk as crooked as a ram's horn, pet!" Surely, Mary's left foot dragged the ground, clawing a trench deep enough to water the animals.

Inside, the Finnegans lived in one room and shared a raised bed. Overhead, the wooden beams hosted spiders and doves. Soot coated the white stone walls in a gradient that darkened near the roof and lightened toward the dirt floor. A cauldron in the gaping fireplace swung on a chain from one iron arm; a kettle swung from another. Over the clods of fiery peat in the hearth, a soup of some kind always bubbled: a bit of lamb, pig's feet, or fish stirred in when Ailish was flush from the summer yarn sales. On the mantel were two portraits: one of Jesus, the other of Mother Mary and Baby Jesus. The solo Jesus picture showed Him revealing His sacred heart from under His cloak like a magic trick. Next to the fire, Ailish kept a basket brimming with gold and brass trinkets. A washtub for soaking Mary's sore leg leaned against the wall. By the hearth were three seats: a splintered chair with a drooping seat for Ailish, a burlap sack of grain for Mary, and a solid wood chair which Ailish forbade anyone to touch.

Their cottage was stuffed to the gills with books—books on windowsills, books on rafters, books on crooked shelves that sagged. At nights, Ailish taught Mary the Bible and how to write Irish and English letters. Mary was a fast learner. Most of all, she coveted Ailish's book about Irish mythological creatures, with its illustrations of banshees, giants, tricksters, monsters, and faeries. On a beam above the back window, Ailish shelved her journals out of Mary's reach—years of them dating back to before she was born. Ailish used to say, "It's a powerful woman who knows her letters." Mary would ask why that was so, and Ailish replied, "For humans are the wiliest creatures, even above the pooka. One needs all her faculties to overcome their trickery." Mary asked if the old priest who came around was such a wily creature. "Aye," Ailish told her. "But he can be brought 'round with a coin."

There was only one other who ever visited them. He had no name, so Mary bestowed one upon him: *Fear Gorta*, meaning "Hunger Man" in Irish. According to Ailish's mythology book, stories of this solitary specter were oft repeated during the 1840 famine, when real emaciated wanderers in rags would drop dead of hunger on unsanctified ground. Its appearance foretold bad events, but you could ward him off by offering food, shelter, or alms, thus turning your fortune to good. And that's just what their visitor did. Mary and her mother offered him shelter for one night, and in return, he brought gifts. Over the years, he had given them brass rings, goblets, brooches, and neck plates they kept in the hearth basket. Ailish rarely sold them. The Fear Gorta came every spring and every autumn, and where he lived in between was a mystery. Mary always imagined that he roamed the whole width of Ireland, stopping at their cottage on his route. The chair by the fire was reserved for him.

In early spring 1937, the Fear Gorta appeared at their rusted gate in a cold, driving rain with a box tucked under his arm and a basket resting at his muddy boots. It was the dead of night. Mary and Ailish happened to be looking out the window, watching for lightning strikes on the bog. A sudden bolt lit up his lean body. He was gripping the gate post with a ghostly hand that nearly scared the life out of Mary. Ailish let loose an, "Oh!" and ran to him with a shawl over her head. That "Oh!" her mother exclaimed carried with it a world of feeling, but not of any fear. The emotion carried the heat of excitement. Perhaps it was her age, coming to knowledge of how the world worked, but it was at that moment Mary realized Ailish loved this man.

As Ailish fetched him, Mary dragged the good chair to the warmest part of the room.

The visitor filled the entire door frame, clutching the small box. Rainwater dripped from the edge of his cap, dotting the dirt floor. His wool jacket and pants dried like magic, fibers flexing and contracting to dispel water. He held a fixed smile that conveyed no emotion, showing tiny, dull teeth wedged like dirty pebbles into his gums. He didn't speak, except to mumble to Ailish in a dialect that sounded like chirps and chucks and trills. Mary never knew how Mam understood them.

Ailish heaved a basket onto their carved table. "Would you look at this, pet? Salted fish for us! What a meal we'll have!" She lifted the large leaves to show Mary the rows of fish: gutted, cleaned, and stored in the ways of the old times. But Mary couldn't take her eyes off the man. When, at Ailish's urging, he finally moved, he loped over to the solid chair waiting for him with a gait Mary recognized as her own, except more exaggerated. His left leg cut a deep trench into their dirt floor, much deeper than hers. He sat with a straight back, interested in the fire, arranging the box on his knees. His face froze in an expression of wonder, as if just about to speak of some curiosity but held transfixed, words failing him.

Mary waited until Ailish was occupied with the fish before she climbed onto her sack, which she had repositioned to face the faded knees in the man's trousers. She had never been this close to him. During prior visits, she was kept at bay, only allowed to play nearby, or read while he and Ailish spoke in whispers. Now, closer to him than ever, Mary noticed the smell of him was like the bog itself, earthy and sharp. Firelight caught silver scale on the skin on the back of his hand. The scale had dried at the edges, flaking away to reveal an angry, red layer of epidermis underneath. Mary said to him, "I've got that scale, too. On my legs."

The man followed her pointing finger to his own hand, and, startled to find the box still in his possession, held it out to her. Ailish jumped to intervene, but in a quick move, the man whipped out a hand to hold her back. Mary was shocked by what seemed like the man defending territory. Her heart soared at it. Reaching for the gift, she said, "Thank you." Ailish strained to become a part of their exchange, but the man still held his arm out to prevent it.

The box was larger than their Bible and twice as heavy. Brass plates had been affixed to all sides, with etchings in a pictorial language—perhaps Egyptian. The front plates showed etchings of sea creatures and humans in communion. Various colored baubles were affixed to the plates. At first, Mary thought they were glass, but on closer inspection discovered them to be jewels. She had seen relics like these in books about the saints, but never on a box such as this. It had an air of darkness to it, a hint of old times when pagans ruled these bogs and cut the throats of their sacrifices. Should Father O'Brien see this box, Mary knew, he would condemn it as unholy. She made a note to hide it from him during his visits.

The Fear Gorta gestured for her to open it. Ailish held her breath.

The lid was creaky. Inside was an odor that inspired a memory of a pony's corpse that had been extracted from a deep bog pit nearby. The smell was pungent and furious, and it almost knocked her over. But a glowing green light inside reeled her back in. Delicate moss lined the box, the kind of cool softness anyone wants to stroke, which she did. At the center, a mushroom grew. She flipped the box carefully to look underneath, but she could not figure how a fully vibrant thing could grow without rich soil. And this mushroom—Oh! It was the kind from faerie tales! A cap black as night with glowing purple flecks that themselves held more glowing flecks, which housed more glowing flecks—like a mirror turned on itself, the depth of it had no limit. Underneath, the gills shone golden and warm. As Mary gawked at it, a fog collected all around. She whooshed it away with her hand, but it quickly resettled.

Ailish was relieved at the sight of it and exhaled a puff of air she'd been holding in. "Isn't that nice?" To herself, she added, "Never seen the likes of that mushroom before." But to Mary, that box was more than nice. It was as if the man had gifted her the entire world in a jeweled case. She stumbled for the words to thank him. The man just held that odd frozen smile without any indication of whether he fed off her excitement or not.

Ailish regained control of the gathering by speaking to him in their mutual dialect of clicks and clucks. The man rose from his chair and accompanied Ailish as she led him to the door. This was the signal that he would go. He would sleep in the shed outside, as he had always done. But tonight, to Mary, it seemed wrong. This was a momentous occasion. He'd brought a gift for her. And what a gift! She protested, "No, Mam! Won't he sleep inside with us?"

But Ailish insisted. "We wouldn't want him to be uncomfortable."

"Anyone would feel more comfortable by our fire than in that cold shed." Mary knew he'd be gone in the morning, as he always would, and he would not return until autumn. She wanted more time.

Ailish just sighed. "Pet, you know he has his own people, his own ways."

Mary knew all about his people. The Walking People. The Travellers. They were itinerant, hated for treating Ireland as a collective home instead of buying into the landowning scheme. That carving up of the land into bits and pieces got the country into serious trouble during the famines, Mam said. The Travellers were part of the reason Mary and her mam were hated, for the Finnegans embraced him and understood their grievances.

Ailish and the man wandered outside arm in arm to the stone shed that leaned so badly its door barely opened. She would say good night to him there in their language.

Mary stayed behind to admire her box. Before her eyes, the mushroom was sprouting fragile white roots that weaved into the moss. The ends of the roots feathered into what looked like a snowy swan's wings.

Mary awoke after midnight to the rusted gate creaking. The man was leaving.

She shot out of bed, careful not to wake Ailish, threw on her own wool cloak, and set out after him. She was hungry for more clues about his existence and would not be denied.

The rain clouds had long drifted away, revealing a full moon. The bogland was a place not to be crossed at night. Besides the danger of falling in, the bog was spooky for the way it exhaled steam after a rain. Dead trees twisted up and away from the mist. When the bog was like this, Mary thought the soft ground might push up all the corpses that dwelled underneath, the bodies of all those who wandered in here drunk and drowned, all the ancients who fell here fighting for their piece of land, all the lost and forgotten ones with their dead eyes the shade of ghostly grubs.

Mary set out after him. *Don't fall in. Don't fall in.*

She caught up to the man just as he entered the bog. He was heading toward the highland. She knew the bog well enough to cross in a full moon, but did he? One wrong step and he could fall through up to his armpits, then get sucked below. She thought again of that putrid pony, who once galloped across the bog, only to disappear into a deep mud pocket with one wrong step. Villagers pulled out its carcass with ropes. The bog, her mam told her, is devoid of oxygen, so even though the pony had gone under weeks prior, the bog had perfectly preserved it, down to the twisted expression on its face and its swirl of mangy, chestnut mane. It was not an image Mary wanted in her head, but it had frightened her enough to keep her footing, always.

But this man was not using the planks that she and Ailish needed to negotiate that spongy ground. Out here, his awkward gait had vanished. He used his bad legs to rear back and catapult himself gracefully from one dry mound of earth to another. Watching his legs, knowing hers to be similar, Mary tried to imitate him. She flexed her bad leg in the same manner and was surprised to find her ankle bone extending in ways she didn't think possible. She ratcheted and leapt. The cold air slapped her cheeks, and her stomach lurched. She did it again and again. Ratchet and leap. Ratchet and leap. It was a delight to move like that! As soon as she closed the distance on him, he accelerated. Mary had to move faster. Did he know she was following? She did not care. Together they shot through the bog, shadowy amphibians hurling across the foggy turf.

Soon, Mary heard music and saw the glow of bonfires. He was headed to the Traveller camp, the place of his people, the *lucht siúil*.

Ailish had forbidden Mary from ever setting foot near a Traveller camp of any kind. Compassionate as Mam was about their rights to live where they wanted, that sympathy ended when it came to Mary's potential interactions with them. Mam said they drank to excess and fought with bare knuckles, sometimes finishing each other off with slash hooks and machetes. "They're a violent and rowdy bunch," Ailish told her. "No place for you, pet." Surely, the man who brought her such a treasure could not be described by those unkind words. Mary pulled the brim of her hood low and followed him into camp.

Ponies grazed around the base of a high hill, the top of which was alight with bright, crimson fires. Driving, thumping bodhráns propelled the fiddles and harmonies looping and swirling underneath high whistles. Mary saw no boxing, but the talk was lively and loud in the clicking language she thought belonged only to the man and Ailish. They all spoke in rapid-fire cadence, pausing only to cackle. A young woman with luscious red hair roamed a field on the outskirts of camp, chirping a haunting song that vibrated the grasses. The women all wore long skirts, but some had cinched up their waistbands to reveal silver scaly legs above boots caked with mud. Mary gasped at their boldness. *Showing their malformed legs!* The men laughing and smoking around the fire had scale on their faces and arms, visible below their rolled-up sleeves. As they puckered their pipes and blew the tobacco smoke, the barnacles on their cheeks reminded Mary of a fish gasping for air on land. Children, seemingly without strict bedtimes at all, ambled around with the drastic limp she knew well. Tired children scrambled up the wooden steps and disappeared into the back of one of the bow top wagons parked in a circle.

Mary inched closer in a low crouch. The wagons were like miniature houses with windows, shutters, swinging doors, and stovepipes poking through tiled roofs. The wagons were all brightly painted in scarlets, teals, golds, emeralds, and lavenders. Intricately carved panels of wood on the sides shimmered with gilded paint. These panels told stories of fish and humans in a cycle of life, death, decay, and rebirth. On one, she noticed a story panel with a different theme inside the arch of one of the wagon's eaves. In that series, a ghostlike creature resembling an octopus-man hunched on a throne inside a castle with spires. Roots entangled the interior of the castle, growing dense to impound the creature on its throne. Then, thin beings of smoke and light removed the land under the castle, sinking it far beneath the sea.

She heard a sound, a guttural, "*Atch!*" The singing woman who had been wandering had spotted her reading the wagon's scrollwork. Another Traveller responded with a call like a ripping of the throat. The fiddles and whistles stopped.

The Fear Gorta poked his head out of the wagon nearest Mary. He looked straight at her, like he knew she would be there. She couldn't see his face clearly, but his eyes glowed copper. They conveyed no anger, no fear. Only recognition. *I see you.*

Mary sucked in her breath and took off down the hill toward the bog. Behind her, the camp erupted into chirping, like laughter.

She turned back only once. The man's lanky body was backlit by the fires. His looming shadow sloped downhill. Behind him, fiddles impatiently scratched the signal to start another tune. Tin whistles performed acrobatics. Drums thrummed. The bog grasses quivered.

It was the last time she ever saw him.

That night Mary dreamed.

No—what she experienced after returning to their cottage, after vaulting over the stone wall with her newfound strength in her legs, after hanging her cloak out to dry, and after tucking herself back into bed with an oblivious Ailish—wasn't a *dream*. It was a writhing, twisting devil of a nightmare that perched on her chest and pinned down her shoulders. It strangled her with thorny tentacles. It even had an odor: salty and moldy. The nightmare itself was starving. It wanted to gorge on her pain and sadness and anger—the name-calling, the isolation, the rejection, the rock-throwing from children, the sneers of the old priest. It wanted so much pain that she had to generate more and more to feed it until she was drowning in her own hate. That nightmare was ravenous despair itself, bound into the eye of a great creature that opened and blinked at her. Its red-veined, slate-grey iris pulsed with its slow heartbeat.

When she woke up with the morning sun filtering through the dirty windows, she saw that the Traveller camp on the high mound was replaced by a thin column of smoke. Twin trenches dug by caravan wheels gnawing in the dirt road curved away from the cow pasture and disappeared onto the mountain road.

She found Ailish nestled in the chair reserved for the Fear Gorta chatting with Grand Mammy, dead long before Mary was even born.

"It's been a long time, Gran," Ailish said to the empty chair across from her. "Shall we talk about how well the spinning has gone this winter?" Her bright red hair stuck to her forehead. A fever. Mary didn't know what to do. Ailish prattled on about how young Mary was getting on in the world, about the incurable greed of Father O'Brien, about the new pony out in the field since the old one died. Ailish was sprightly, despite signs of fever.

Mary said, "Mam? Grand Mammy has been dead many years."

Ailish turned to her with a look that said she was sorry for her ignorance. "Child. Can you not see what is right there in the chair opposite myself?"

"No," Mary said, "I cannot. The dead don't occupy any chairs when they've been laid to rest in the churchyard so long ago."

Ailish held her in red-veined eyes, just like that creature in her dream, and told her, "There's a great many wonders opened to me this morning, Mary. Grand Mammy for certain was returned to the earth in a pine box to be fed to the great tree that supports life for us. She's alive and buzzing in this tree. She's a part of everything. She's a part of you and me and that chair over there—" And just as suddenly as Ailish launched herself into that doolally speech, she hurled herself into a different topic. "Bring me a fresh journal!" she called, dropping her shawl to the dirty floor. "I'll write now! I'll write a great book for the Tree, to open its branches to cradle the world!"

Brain twaddle, it sounded like. Despite Mary's secret wanderings and the poor sleep from her thick and sludgy dream, it looked like her mam was out of commission today. Mary would be feeding the animals by herself that morning. What could she do but reach inside the cedar chest at the foot of their bed for a new notebook for her?

Mary fed the animals and weeded the garden herself for three more days of Mam's fever, of Grand Mammy chats, and of agitated writing in notebooks. Ailish wrote nonsense and drew the most awful dark creatures, none of which could be touched in imagination by anything in Irish Folklore. When Ailish completed one notebook, which she did in a day, she tore at its pages and posted the strangest of her illustrations all around their cottage. Mary fingered the edges of the paper and asked her what the creatures might be. Ailish said she didn't know. Part of her was consumed by the fever and excited by her scribbles in her journals, but occasionally, she'd look at Mary with despair, like she was a prisoner in her own body. That's when Mary asked her, "Was it the fish that was bad to eat, Mam?"

She said no. She said, "I'm not right in the head, child. Something is not right."

"But you have a fever, Mam. That's a sickness in the body. You taught me that."

Ailish repeated, "No, I'm not right in the head."

"Shall I fetch a doctor, Mam?" Mary did not know how to fetch a doctor. She didn't even know where to find one. They only used the herbs and plants Ailish harvested from around the bog to treat their aches and coughs.

"No," Ailish said to her, just before the sickness took her back into the depths of herself, before she returned to the gibberish talk. "Get the priest."

Fetching Father O'Brien was not something Mary did often; that was under Ailish's purview. But she did know how to drag herself up the paved road into to the village's Catholic Church. It would take her all day. But first, she hid the box. She wouldn't have Father O'Brien claiming it was an abomination and leering over its jewels.

Before she tucked it into the rafters behind a dove's nest, she peeked inside to check her treasure. A gauzy layer of fog had settled over the moss carpet much more densely than it had before. The mushroom at the center poked through like a mountain cap through clouds. The white feathery roots spidering from the stem had stretched to form miniature hills. Dots of vegetation had sprouted from the moss. "A world in a box," she breathed, before tucking it into the overhead beams.

The old priest took his time to waddle out to their stone cottage on the bog. When he finally swung open their door days later, and when the Irish wind rattled all of Ailish's pages of dark scribbles tacked to the walls, Father O'Brien covered his mouth to cage a wheeze of shock. Ailish was in a state: hair greased and tangled, hands filthy, bare feet blue from the cold, nightdress stained. The priest took one look at Ailish, then allowed his eyes to dart to all corners of their cottage, studying the creatures Ailish's pencil had spat out. He absently clutched the cross dangling from a cord around his neck, then asked Ailish about the Travellers. Had they come again? They'd been seen in Cullen last week, he said. Had they visited? Did they bring anything? His hands were shaking.

Mary had no idea what the Travellers had to do with her mother in her present state, but Ailish gave nothing away. She told him, "It is a mercy to us that we cannot understand the universe and all it holds."

Father O'Brien nodded at that, as if Ailish had finally said something wise to tether her back to reality. He raised a sinewy finger at her. "What is God's knowledge alone, we shall trust in." Then, his eyes roamed over the brass trinkets shimmering in the leaps of the fireplace flames. "Ah, sure, Miss Finnegan, it is a long way out here. How about a donation for the Church today?"

Ailish laughed at him before burping a new language Mary had not heard before. It wasn't the chirps and clicks of the language she shared with the Travellers. It was a deep, throat-rasping rip: "*Ymm gah kadish tu* Tower of Babel?" Mary only caught the last phrase. It was an earnest question, and Ailish blinked at the priest to denote that she expected a reply.

"Hmmm," he hummed. He lifted a shaky hand to pat his sweaty brow, as if tamping down the evil he sensed. More loudly, he asked, "May I see you outside, Mary?"

The chickens flocked to the old priest, believing him to be holding grains in his pockets instead of brass trinkets. He shooed the chickens as he pulled their door closed. "So?" Mary asked. She was worried. It had never occurred to her to fear for Ailish's health. She was always a hearty woman who could plow a garden and chop the wood better than any man. How would they live if she weren't herself? How would they get on with Mary's sickly legs? They had no family Mary knew of to call on. The villagers thought Ailish a witch. The Fear Gorta was days down the road, and no one would be able to find him now. Mary doubted he could do anything with that frozen smile of his and his chirpy way of speaking, but he was, in her view, their only ally in this world.

When Father O'Brien successfully kicked away the chickens and blocked the goat from mouthing at his wooden cross, he mopped his gleaming forehead with his sleeve. "Whew," he said to himself. "That was a brush with the devil, wasn't it?"

Mary asked a new question: "Has she a demon creature with great eyes pulsing with red veins living inside her? Will you call an exorcist?"

The priest wrinkled his nose. "Where do you get your ideas, child? No."

"What will you do to help Mam? There's more brass inside."

He fiddled with today's donation inside his tunic pockets. Mary could tell by his chin held toward the gathering clouds that he was weighing an idea. He must have settled on a direction because he started toward the rusty gate with a new purpose in his stride. "I'll be back," he called back to her. "With help."

"What help?" Mary asked.

"A doctor of a different kind," he said at the gate. "Someone interested in exactly this thing. Someone interested in this area and its...*people*."

Mary had no idea how such a person could help her mam, but she was desperate.

"It could take time for him to come here," the priest warned her. "He offices on the continental mainland."

"What shall I do in the meantime?" she asked.

"Pray."

They arrived a week later, delivered inside a marvel of machinery that shocked Mary's soul.

It was a dove-grey cloud of luminous chrome carried by tires framed in dazzlingly white sidewalls. The sloped rear, ending in a flared lip, suggested it was powered by rocket fuel. A wave of sculpted steel cascaded from the rounded front bumpers to elegantly form the running board onto which Herr Doktor Waldemar Koltz now stood. He stretched and shouted to the sky, "*Gott im Himmel!* What forsaken place have you brought us to?"

Father O'Brien shrank in the dickey seat that jutted from the car's rear end. Supple sapphire upholstery must have hugged his buttocks as no rigid church bench ever had. "The demon woman is inside!" He directed Waldemar toward the cottage with a flail of his liver-spotted arms. "Go in without me!" Mary noticed the priest was sweating through his robe. Dark spots bloomed in his pits. He slouched and added, "I would like a moment longer to investigate this fine automobile."

Another door slammed, and from behind the implausible vehicle stepped another marvel. His skin was the shade of the shadows in the deepest part of their water well. His hair as white as goat's milk and as dense as sheep's wool. His partially bald head shone like a polished stone. In the front, dabbing at his forehead, was a wiry flap of hair, incongruously ebony. A linen jacket, the same shade as the sapphire leather interior, shuffled loosely around his knees as he lurched to catch up to Dr. Koltz. A neatly pressed hemline kissed gold silken trousers, onto which a floral pattern was embroidered with shining black thread. A single strand of pearls accented rigid bones jutting from his neckline. Wedged into the center of the strand was a large diamond that caught a ray of sun and sent it back to Mary in a fractal explosion of light. She brought her flat hand to her brow to view the overload of brilliance in her field of vision. Father O'Brien stretched his cheeks into a false grin as he did when someone with money appeared to be on a road straight to eternal damnation.

"Saro!" Waldemar shrieked. "Where in treacherous hell are we?"

The priest called from the back seat, "Tipperary! The bogs!" Again, he pointed with force. "She's *inside*."

Waldemar stretched again and unleashed a long, tenor bellow, which stuttered in his throat. "Humid!" He hummed and buzzed, then massaged his larynx. "Saro, fetch me schnapps! Too much dampness obstructs my instrument!"

Saro withdrew a flask from his jacket pocket and offered it. Waldemar drank deeply then trilled in a baritone:

> *Zen give three cheers, and one cheer more,*
> *For ze hardy captain of ze* Pinafore!

He thrust his chin upward. "Acceptable. Acceptable." Pea gravel crushed under his gleaming loafers. Saro leapt in front of him to relieve him of the flask and to wrangle the rusted gate, which he did with an ease not even Mary or her mother could manage.

"Child!" Waldemar called to Mary, which inspired the most terror she'd felt outside her nightmares. His footfalls were widely spaced and heavy, the walk of a man under the illusion of supreme confidence. He wore the black wool coat and striped tie belonging to a man with the kind of money Mary had never seen before. Heavy rings encircled most of his fingers. The reach of his aquiline nose suggested that no scent ever eluded its flaring nostrils. The cut emerald eyes glinting in his sockets suggested nothing escaped his notice. His lapel advertised a black crooked cross, ringed by scarlet and gold. Mary had not seen that symbol before. The one called Saro shuffled behind Waldemar, craning his neck to view Mary.

"*Kleines Mädchen*!" Waldemar sighed as he reached Mary where she had frozen while scattering seed for the chickens. Waldemar displaced a curious chick from his reflective shoe by sending it airborne. His heavy Teutonic accent barely translated into understandable English in Mary's ears. "You will have honor in presenting me to—" He snapped at Saro with gloved fingers. Saro immediately produced a slip of paper for him to read in halting syllables. "Ah-leesh Fee-nah-gahn."

"She's inside."

The priest's voice floated from the car's rear. "I told you she was inside."

"Ah!" Waldemar exclaimed.

Mary pointed to the swastika pin on his lapel. "What's that?"

Waldemar formed a double chin to follow her grubby finger. "This?" he said, "is only *eine* manifestation of high standing. However, my profession is very much older! Old as humanity!"

Mary pointed to the car. "What's that?"

"Mercedes-Benz 540 K! Supercharged engine, 5.4 liter, straight-eight! Superior example of German engineering! You must look for *eine* opportunity to drive one in your adulthood! Not this one." He clapped. "Now! I will leave you to resume nourishment of your poultry!" He removed both gloves and slapped them into Saro's outstretched hand, then pressed Mary by her shoulders to move her aside. "You are inquisitive and helpful *Mädchen*, and if I may risk impertinence, quite ugly. Come, Saro!" Waldemar strode past Mary with dizzying speed.

Saro moved more slowly, studying Mary from her torn skirt hem dragging in the dirt to her unwashed and uncombed red mane. He glanced from Mary to the hillside where she last saw the column of smoke from the Traveller camp, then back to Mary.

"*Dia dhuit*," Mary said to him.

Saro said nothing. He darted inside the cottage.

"I will stay here!" the priest called again from the rear seat. Then, quietly, "Such fine leather."

Mary pushed the half open door to her home. Waldemar had already settled across from Ailish, placing a large book in his lap. "Fräulein! I must introduce myself..."

Ailish slumped, drooling into her nightdress.

Saro perused Ailish's scribbles tacked to the walls, hands interlocked behind his back and head askance as if viewing a fine art exhibit.

The goat had settled on their raised bed with the Bible between its front hooves, feasting on Solomon's words in Ecclesiastes. *For everything there is a season, and a time for every matter under heaven...* dissolved into an inky pool of nonsense hanging out the side of the goat's maw.

Waldemar piped up, "In my field, we begin with documenting ze family history." He cracked open a broad book in his lap. An outline of a tree had been preprinted onto the page. Spidery cursive decorated half of the branches. "We have done *some* work before coming. Herr Pfarrer O'Brien kindly informs me of many family names for *kleines Mädchen* Mary. *Sehen!*" He swept a manicured finger over the right side of the tree, all full of names. "Many, many Finnegans from Tipperary on this side! But—" He held the book for Ailish to see the blank lines on the paternal side of the tree, but she only stared vacantly at the ashes glowing in the hearth. Waldemar said to her, "You can see: Oh, *nein*! No names on Papa's side!" He visually cut Ailish with the emeralds in his eyes. He asked pointedly, "Where is *Vater*, Fräulein Finnegan?"

Ailish produced a bubble of saliva that clung to her bottom lip.

Saro delicately snatched a page from the wall and stuffed it into the pocket of his linen duster. Mary cried, "G'way outta that!"

Waldemar, however, was more interested in his book. He turned to Mary. "Ah, *Mädchen*! *Mutti* seems indisposed. Perhaps you will assist." He gestured to her flour sack, inviting her to sit.

Mary strained against the feeling of becoming a guest in her own home. She declined to sit. "What's a *Mutti*?"

Waldemar showed his incisors. "Mother." Except he said it with a buzz: *Muh-zer*.

"What kind of doctor are you? Mam is sick with fever."

Waldemar sat back and considered her. "It is the field of ancestral heritage *und* eugenics that will be explaining *Mutti's* condition. That is why I have been called to such *ein* hellscape."

"I've never heard of ancestral heritage eugenics."

"And by looking at you, neither have you heard of a damp facecloth."

"Why do you need my history when it's Mam who's sick?"

Waldemar waved away her question. "You are acquainted with your papa?"

"No."

"Ah." Waldemar stuck out his tongue and plucked something distasteful and unseen from its tip. "You can think of no one who visits who might be fitting this description?" He rubbed his fingers together over the fireplace ashes to dislodge the invisible nuisance. "Perhaps Herr Pfarrer O'Brien?"

Mary puckered. "That aul priest couldn't father a fart."

"Astute observance, and scientifically sound, *kleines Mädchen*!" Waldemar pressed, "Perhaps *Papi* is someone coming back every so often with little presents and saying hello to *Mutti*?"

"You mean the Fear Gorta?"

Saro's focus shifted to Mary with a jump of surprise.

Waldemar's spine stiffened. "Now, you are educating me, child." He leaned closer to Mary. She smelled musky aftershave and fruity booze. "Go on."

"He comes in the spring and fall," Mary explained. "Two times a year. He was just here."

Saro detached his focus from Mary, then resumed poking around the cottage, this time more invasively. He pulled books from shelves, ran his fingers along the spines of Ailish's journals, and slid bowls and jars and canisters to feel behind.

Waldemar asked, "When you say *just* here..."

"Ten days ago, maybe more."

Waldemar stood to look out a window. "How did he travel, child? On foot? By cart?"

"In a caravan. He's a Traveller."

Saro rummaged with more urgency.

Mary added, "They're not criminals or ruffians."

"*Ach!*" Waldemar exclaimed. His sweeping glances caught the brass trinkets in the basket. "You are not correct! Travelling people carry diseases! They contribute nothing to society but animal excrement and dirty children. But—some are quite special *und* merit attention." He pulled at the wool of his trousers and sat down again to face Mary. "*Mädchen*, tell me: have you been ill?"

Mary said, "No."

"No fever?"

Mary shook her head.

He flapped his hand next to his head. "No seeing little moths dancing?"

"No."

He flapped again, slower. "Darker creatures?"

Mary thought of the creature in her dreams and said, "No."

Waldemar smacked his lips. "Did Herr Traveller bring anything with him? A present for little Mary, perhaps?"

Mary held herself very still. "Fish."

"Ah hah. I would not eat that. Anything else? Anything...shiny?"

Mary clamped down her vertebrae to prevent movement. She clinched her throat to steady her voice. She would give nothing away. "No."

Immediately, Saro's eyes flicked to the rafters. They landed right on the hiding spot of her world in a box.

Mary let loose the smallest puff. *How did he know?*

Saro inclined his head at her. A small nod.

Mary widened her eyes in confusion. Did this Saro man intend to keep her secret?

Again, he nodded from behind Waldemar. Mary sensed this other man missed far less than the German with the enormous nose.

Waldemar saw none of Saro's gestures. "Pity!" He rose and stretched again. "Waste of valuable petrol to come here. And we all must conserve well. War is coming."

"What?" Mary cried. "Another war?"

Saro stepped forward and smoothly pulled a journal from Ailish's stack. The spine read, *Spring 1937.*

Waldemar held out his hand. Saro slapped the journal into his palm. "Ah!" Waldemar said, riffling through the half-empty book of her mam's writing. "Reading material for my travel!" He held the journal aloft. "You will, of course, not mind if I borrow."

"I *do* mind!"

Waldemar held out the journal for Saro, who clamped the family-tree book and Ailish's notebook together under his arm. Waldemar proclaimed, "We now take our leave of you! As your people say: *slán abhaile!* We shall return frightened Herr Pfarrer O'Brien to his minuscule church and find tolerable lodgings for ourselves for the night. I fear beds without presences of animals will be among most distant hopes." He absently nudged the trinket basket with a lacquered shoe toe. "We shall be close by, *Mädchen*, should you require us."

Mary panicked. "Will you do nothing to help Mam's fever?"

Waldemar made another buzzing noise. "Unfortunately, I am not acquainted with medicines." He held out his hand, and Saro popped gloves into his open palms. "*Einen schönen Tag noch, kleines Mädchen!*" He bowed to Mary. "That means—"

A heavy voice cut through. "Have a nice day."

They all turned to the hearth.

Ailish rose from her chair like a corpse from the dead. She wiped bubbling drool from her lips with a crusty sleeve. "You said, 'Have a nice day,' but you intend anything but. We're poor, not stupid."

Mary rushed to her mam's side. She could cry with relief: her mother had returned to reality, and just in time. These men were overwhelming her, and she suffered the indignant realization that she couldn't handle their intrusions. Ailish's return might last only a moment—a reprieve from the sickness—but Mary clung to those moments of sanity as she would a life raft. Ailish clutched Mary's shoulder for support and aimed an annihilating glance at the men in her home.

"Fräulein!" Waldemar yelped. "Welcome back to land of livings! We have come from Deutschland at the invitation—"

"I know why you're here," Ailish growled. "And you can show yer kraut arses to the door yerselves. I've got nothing to say to yiz."

Waldemar's face collapsed into a thin frown. "Herr Pfarrer O'Brien—"

Ailish's anger cracked like a bullwhip. "Tell that fecking priest to mind his own fecking business." She extended her hand. "I'll have my journal back now."

"Mmmm." Waldemar chewed his initial reply, then reconsidered. "Do not allow my coarse English to fool you. I am nothing if not gentlemanly." Then, he barked, "Saro! We have been *zehr* rude to take what has not been offered! Return Fräulein Finnegan's low-cost and tattered diary!"

Saro held up the notebook like a fugitive surrendering contraband. He placed it on the edge of their wood table and backed away. Waldemar spun to Ailish, beaming. "It is returned!"

"All right, yiz," Ailish said. She wiped her mouth with her sleeve again, then flung her head to the open door. "Out with ya."

Waldemar looked at her a moment, then smiled. He gestured widely to their single room. "It has been pleasurable to visit, Fräulein. Your home is quite charming, though you could use a sunnier attitude and a tissue. Come, Saro!" He strode confidently to the open door.

Saro followed. As he passed Mary, his sapphire linen jacket brushed her.

Time slowed.

Electricity between them sizzled.

A sharp shadow marred her vision, sending her backward. Deep in her head, a bizarre assembly of noises buzzed: a dove calling from the rafters, a spider vibrating its web, a burnt log collapsing in the fireplace, the crackling of embers, the neigh of a pony, the grinding of the water well's pulley. They all gradually coalesced to form two sounds that, when pushed together, pronounced a word: *Danger.*

Mary gasped at the shock of the sounds scraping inside her skull.

When the door slammed, the cacophony of noises stopped.

Mary reeled again, as if she'd been cut loose from a force pulling her off center. She reached out her arms to balance herself. She felt unmoored, adrift. She might have fallen face-first into the dirt floor, but Ailish caught her. "You all right, cherished?" she asked.

"Yes, Mam." Ailish pinched her chin. Mary was grounded again.

"Right," Ailish said to her child. She took in the wrecked cottage: books knocked off her shelves, pots and bowls on the floor, her cedar chest hinged open, and her supply of notebooks scattered. From their bed, the goat held them in a dull, contented stare. The vinyl Bible cover flapped between the goat's wet lips.

Ailish exhaled. "Pet?" she asked. "Why is the goat eating the Word of God?"

Ailish and Mary enjoyed only an hour's reprieve. By nightfall, the fever crept back into Ailish's face, flushing it red. Her eyes burned. Her body ached. Her speech slurred. But her movements became more frantic. She built a fire into a raging inferno. "I shall burn these pages, all of them." She paced in circles around the room, diving at pages tacked to the wall. Each time she came close to tearing one away, she retracted her hand as if the paper were the real source of heat. "You do it, pet," Ailish directed Mary. "Tear them all down."

Mary jerked pages from their nails with a *pop*, stacked them to overflowing, then brought them to her mam. In the flicker of the fire, Mary saw the creatures on the page: the tentacles, the strained eye sockets, the sharp teeth lining gums in rows like sharks, the predatory eyes with double lids and horizontal gashes for pupils. Ailish muttered, "Feed the fire—feed it." But when Mary stepped close with the pages, Ailish shrieked as if she were the one Mary threatened with the flames.

Mary set the pages aside. "Mam, why don't we do this later?"

"Do it now—do it now. Before it returns."

"Before what returns?"

Ailish's eyelids stretched to show the whites of her eyes. "Tower of Babel," she whispered. "We attempt to reach the gods. We can only hope to be met with merciful death."

Mary asked, "Mam, shall I try to find a real doctor this time?" She wasn't sure where to find one, but she would try.

Ailish reached for Mary's collar with a surprisingly strong grip. She blinked away the fever and surfaced for a moment. "The German was right. This is not a medical sickness. An evil has visited me. And we know what brought it."

Mary unpeeled her mother's grasp. "Mam, we shouldn't say such things about—"

"The box."

"No. It's not the box."

Ailish showed her teeth and rattled her head. Greasy hair slapped at her red cheeks. "The box has brought this evil into our home, and I intend to destroy it."

Mary flooded with panic. "No, that is not the answer. The box—"

Ailish dropped to her knees before her daughter, smoothing Mary's hair. "Think about it, love. Our man brought us a fungus not seen before in these bogs. Didn't the sickness begin the very next day?"

"No, no. It was just as likely the fish."

"It was not the fish."

"Neither is it a mushroom closed away in a box, Mam. It makes no sense."

Ailish shrieked, "*Cahf ah nafl! Mglw nafh—*" She slapped a palm over her mouth. "I speak in tongues again!"

Mary patted Mam's hair into a slick ponytail to relieve the heat from her neck. "No matter, Mam. No matter—"

"I'll destroy the box myself."

"No," Mary intoned calmly. "You won't destroy a gift from my people."

Ailish sucked in the air all around them. "Mary. Those are not your people."

"We are poor, Mam. Not stupid."

Her mother let loose a low groan. Then, she clutched at Mary. "Those are *not* your people. You mustn't—"

"They are my people, Mam."

"I AM YOUR PEOPLE."

Mary slicked her mother's hair back again. "Of course, Mam."

"What I did was an abomination. It was against God. It was against everything I'd been taught as a girl to value oneself—"

"No, Mam."

Ailish shook her head so hard, Mary believed it might fly off her neck. "I regret it."

"Please don't say that, Mam."

Ailish cried openly. Mary had never seen her mother so weak. It pricked her eyes and squeezed her gut. "No," Ailish repeated. She gagged on mucus and rattled her words. "I regret allowing him to return. I regret the box."

"The box is a gift." Mary held this fact as steadfastly as a beacon before her. The box would remain. It would remain with *her*.

Ailish clawed at her daughter's arms to raise herself to unsteady feet. She bent to Mary's ear and whispered, "I know where you hid it. I saw."

Mary pulled away with wide eyes.

Ailish looked to the rafters. Mary followed her glance.

In a flash, she found herself on the floor with Ailish leaping over her. She sprang to the table and pushed it to the spot below the rafters. Mary clambered onto her feet. "No, Mam! You'll not take it from me!"

Ailish shoved her hand into the rafters' shadows until she scraped the jeweled box from its hiding place. Then, she turned to Mary. Ember light fired up new shadows on her face. "It'll go into the bog."

A certainty bloomed inside Mary's chest. *No. It will not.* Her voice dropped. "Mam. The box is a gift from my people. It will stay with me."

Ailish shoved the box under her arm and squatted to Mary's face. Mary would not look at her mother's pleading face, only at the box. Ailish said, "They'll not stop, pet. They'll come again for it. They'll come again and again and again. Then, they'll come in greater numbers. They'll come into this house, and they will scatter our things looking for it. There will be no hiding place good enough to stop them. They will obliterate our home for it. They will destroy our land for it. Then—" She turned her child's face to hers. "They will look for *him*!" Mary tried to pull away, but Ailish brought her back. "They will send out men to scour the countryside for him. They will overturn the Traveller camps, innocent camps with nothing to do with this. They will beat them. They will torture them. All to get to *him*. To find *him*. But they will never find him. They have *never* been able to find him." She brought the box to Mary's face. "But they will find *this*."

Mary followed the box from her mother's underarm to her face, then back again. She breathed with patience. She slowed her thinking. *I shall have it,* she thought. *I shall have it.*

Ailish wailed, "I have seen what this box can do, pet, and it is beyond our understanding. It wants—"

In a quick spasm, Mary grabbed at the box, but Ailish was faster. She jumped from the table and sprinted for the door. Mary ratcheted her leg, sprang toward the door, slamming it shut just as her mother pulled at the handle. "Child. No." Ailish slapped a palm to Mary's forehead and shoved her back, pulling the door open in a fluid movement.

Ailish ran into the bog with the box under her arm.

Unlike the Traveller, Ailish slopped through the bog clumsily, missing all the wood planks, plunging ankle-deep into one mud-trap, then calf-deep into another. She crashed into mires as deep as her hips, but she kept pushing through with the strength all her ancestors bequeathed her. Her Grand Mammy's thighs, hardened from childbirth and tending kettles and cauldrons, propelled her through. Her Great-Grand Mammy's ankles, sinewy from walking to town and back, miles and miles in mud and snow and hail and heat, pushed Ailish out of deep mud and onto dry land, then pushed her ahead of her daughter.

Mary raced behind her, using her legs to tilt and launch her forward as the Fear Gorta did. Unlike her mother, Mary's feet landed solely on dry ground, sensing and missing every mud-trap. Ailish huffed and grew red in the face from the extreme exertion. "Mam!" Mary screamed at her. "Stop this! You'll make yourself sick!" Her shouts scoured her throat.

Ailish stared ahead in determination. She twisted her torso—her Great-Great-Grand Mammy's torso, hardened against famine and deprivation—to propel her forward through deep ooze and chilled water, but Mary predicted and cut off every move. Her mind sharpened to her mother, to the box she carried. *I will have it*, she knew. *It remains with me.*

Gradually, Mary immobilized Ailish, circling her on a dry mound, around at the deepest part of the bog, jumping at every move Ailish tried to make, pinning her to one spot. Ailish grunted and panted, panicked at Mary's sudden ability to outmaneuver her. "Evil," Ailish gasped. "Evil."

Mary saw only the box. The embedded jewels flashed once in the moon's bluish spotlight. "It's mine." She pounced.

Ailish's eyes went wide in surprise. She clutched at the box. "Child, let go!"

Mary held tight. She bared her teeth. *I will have it,* the voice inside her insisted. *It remains with me.*

Ailish backed up with her hips, throwing her weight behind her, trying to gain some ground with the box. Mary allowed her this ground. One step. Two steps. Her mother was off her balance now, her momentum pulling her toward the bog pit. "I will have it," Mary said aloud. "It remains with me."

"No, pet!"

Three steps now. Her mother was entirely off balance.

Then, Mary canted her legs and sprang forward. She whipped the box upward, jerking it free of her mother's grasp. She tucked her torso—her father's torso, flexing and contorting—to stop her center of gravity from its forward trajectory. She landed on the mound of dry ground with the box.

Ailish flew backward. Generations of weight and muscle could not escape the momentum. Gravity and physics pulled Ailish along a neat parabola, away from dry ground, and directly into the bog.

"Mam! No!"

What Mary will remember for the rest of her life is her mother's empty hands caught by the pale moonlight as they pinwheeled up and over her head. *Such beautiful hands*, she will think. Like a marble statue with the hardened calluses of a true daughter of Ireland.

Ailish landed bottom-first in the deepest mud pit. The bog inhaled her with a sucking sound, taking her under in one slurp.

Mary did not even see her mother's face as she went down. She would later conjure different possible versions of surprised hurt in her mother's eyes before Ailish went under. Would her expression have accused Mary? Exonerated her? Would it have shown the slightest relief knowing Ailish's pain was about to end? Would it have shown the twisted scowl of fear the pony's mummified carcass had? Mary would never know. She'd only recall the deathlike pale of her mother's hands spiraling helplessly against the laws of gravity and physics and finding no remedy.

Mary set the box down on dry earth.

It was quiet.

She dunked her arm into the bog up to the elbow, grabbing at anything under the surface. She thought she had a clump of hair, but it was a nest of decaying heather. She slung it aside.

"No."

She thought she had an arm, but it was a rotten slat of planking. She slung that aside.

"No. No."

Every time Mary plunged her arm under, the bog delivered something unwanted. Instead of a foot, a skull from another unfortunate animal.

"No no no no no—"

Instead of a nightdress, a handful of reeds. Mary kept pulling at the bog, but it kept saying, *No, no, no. You shall not have her.*

It was all in vain.

"No! Nooo! Noooo!"

Mary raged at the edge of the pit.

Behind her, on dry ground, the box gleamed.

Now, all that she had left in the world was the box.

Its jewels glinted in the cold moonlight, waiting patiently for Mary to exhaust herself, to lie back on dry land, to rest her mud-soaked arms against her chest and howl.

Waldemar squatted before a deep mud-trap in the bog, poking a walking stick to test it. "Ah," he said. "*Zehr* deep." He twisted and bellowed to Mary. "You are saying she went under here?"

Mary stared into the middle distance, catatonic. Her hot breath fogged in the chilled and damp air. Dried sludge caked her sleeves to the shoulders. Her face stretched under drying mud on her cheeks. She had said all she would say to them. Ailish was gone. For several hours now. There weren't any miracles to perform, despite their attempts.

Waldemar grumbled, "Now, *Mädchen* shuts up. Before, is questions, questions, questions. Now, when is important, silence." Then, he resumed submerging the stick and humming a trumpet portion from Wagner's *The Ring of the Nibelung.*

Father O'Brien shifted his weight on the wood platform he improvised for funerary purposes. "Are you certain, Mary?" he had asked many times. "We shan't call the men to pull her out?"

"Yes."

At dawn, after she had spent her rage at the edge of the mud pit, Mary had limped into the village, to the door of the Church, unsure of what to do. She had told the priest when he answered the door, "Mam's gone into the bogs. I saw her go under myself. She's been under for hours now." The priest was about as helpful to Mary then as he had been in managing her mam's sickness. Of course, he asked if he should call the men with the pulleys and ropes, like they had done for the pony that fell in. Mary had said to him, "Do not do that. She will stay where she landed." Those men wouldn't ever be bothered by her mam when she needed help anyway. Not to help with the roof falling in during the storm last winter. Not to help with hauling vegetables to market. They had only derision and nasty names for her, threats to hang her for witchcraft, snide talk from their women. They wouldn't be laying hands on her now that she was beyond helping.

And Mary wasn't saying anything about the jeweled box hidden back at the cottage in the rafters.

Leaning on the church door, the priest had heaved a sigh of relief. "Well, then. We'll call the bog her final resting place."

Waldemar, when told of Ailish's death, sensed something amiss. "An argument, child? Over what?"

Mary had said nothing.

But Waldemar's vast nose sniffed a lie. "Perhaps," he had said, "we should check again for poor *Mutti* to be sure."

Mary had sized up his keen interest in her mother's corpse. *They'll not stop, pet. They'll come again for it.* It was not Mam they were interested in. It never was. It was then Mary knew her mam had been right. *They'll come into this house, and they will scatter our things looking for it. There will be no hiding place good enough to stop them.* Mary's thoughts coalesced around that knowledge, then settled on the same course of action her Grand Mammy and Great Grand Mammy had demonstrated to their daughters: Mary lied to the man. "Of course, we should check again," she had said. "Right this way."

So she had led them into the bogs, away from her home, away from the spot where Ailish had fallen. She pointed to a deep mud pit almost a mile away from where she had last seen her mother's arms work frantically against gravity and fail. And the jeweled box was safe in the rafters before she had even sought help.

Now, Waldemar was up to his shoulder in the mud pit, jabbing at something. He warbled, "Ah! Ahaa!" His stick drilled one spot, slopping mud in all directions. Then, his face fell. "No. This is tree stump."

Mary resettled her gaze to rest in the middle distance. *I will keep it,* she thought. *It remains with me.*

Waldemar scrambled to his feet and wrung the mud from his shirt sleeve. "Ick." He called out to Mary, "You are certain, child? This is the place she met her end?"

Mary dropped her cheeks into a frown. "Yes."

Waldemar flung his head all around the bog. "So difficult to determine directions here. North, south. Who knows?" He asked Mary, "We shall perhaps hire local persons to extract poor *Mutti*?"

"That is against my wishes," Mary stated.

The priest pointed at Mary, a bead of sweat forming on his brow. "Against the child's wishes, thank heaven above. What comes out of the bog is—" He shuddered.

Waldemar locked Mary in a stare. "This is no proper burial."

Mary returned the stare. "It is the burial afforded me."

Waldemar smiled. "Ah! About that."

Father O'Brien interrupted, "Oh, yes! Mary, the greatest luck has befallen us!" He cocked his head. "You, I mean. And me. Us." He continued, "You see, it is law that you, as an orphan with no family, would become a ward of the state of Ireland."

Mary tensed. "What does that—"

The priest waved her question away. "But! Herr Doktor Koltz has agreed to become your ward!"

With the realization of this, Mary spun on the man clomping toward her. "No. I refuse that offer."

Waldemar leaned back and rested his hands on his belly. Mud flaked and dripped from his sleeve. "No need to thank me, *kleines Mädchen*."

"I do not want to live with him."

Waldemar trilled a high laugh. "Ah, *hässlich Mädchen* has misunderstood." He leveled his gaze at Mary again. "You will participate immediately to school in Glasgow. Franciscans!"

Father O'Brien winced. "Franciscans. The best we could do."

Waldemar said, "The best of education only for *mein Mädchen*!"

"I am not *your Mädchen*."

Waldemar said, "You are having little choices with your family in big cities not traceable. The Franciscans offers educations fitting for *Mädchen* Koltz!"

Mary widened her stance. "And if I don't go?"

The priest grabbed Mary's shoulders and spun her to face him. "Mary. Dearest. This is an *opportunity* for you. You will be able to leave here and receive the best education Franciscans can offer. I mean, they're *Franciscans*, but I'm sure they will do their best. Nothing like this would be possible for you here—"

"I won't leave here."

"Mary," the priest lowered his tone, sneaking glances at the German. "It is the Franciscans or the children's home in Limerick." He said to himself, "No doubt a future in the Magdalene Asylum waits." Then to Mary, "One of these choices will give you a life beyond this bog; the other will condemn you to poverty."

Mary squinted at the priest. "What do you get out of this?"

"Me?" He shifted his weight again, creaking the boards. He huffed at Mary. A blast of sour buttermilk hit her. "A considerable donation will of course pave the way for quick processing of the paperwork involved. Your situation has put a burden on the church—"

Mary backed away. "I refuse. I'll live here alone."

Waldemar brushed mud from the front of his white shirt. "Without possessions. Unfortunately."

The bottom fell out of Mary's stomach. "What does that mean?"

Waldemar tipped himself forward on his toes, eager to resettle the weight of the conversation in his favor. "If I am your guardian, then I am deciding what is to be done with cottage's contents. And I am deciding most must return to Germany with me. And Saro."

Saro.

Mary spun quickly, searching in all directions.

No sign of Saro.

Her voice creaked, "Where is Saro?"

"Packing items of importance as we speak," Waldemar said. "Except goat. I will not be accepting livestock. Goat and poultry will remain behind with spineless priest."

Mary snapped her head toward home, invisible behind the dead trees and dense ivy. What *was* visible was a tower of Ailish's books, holding the rusted gate open like a doorstop. Her journals topped the pile. A notebook flapped in a sudden gust. A few pages of her drawings had been unleashed. The goat, tied to a wooden crate caging the chicken, snatched a page from mid-air, and worked it between its lips.

She did not see the jeweled box. Not yet.

Her mam's voice: *They will come again and again and again.*

No.

Mary ratcheted her leg and sprang toward the house.

"Heavens!" Waldemar blurted. *"Mädchen* is speedy! Look at her go!"

Mary covered the distance between herself and the cottage without losing her breath. Bog grasses swept her legs, working free of her long skirt to propel her toward the open gate, toward the front door, wide open now, toward Saro waiting for her inside.

Mary expelled a sharp breath. "Stop."

Saro rose from a seat at the wood table. Tracks etched into the dirt floor showed where he had dragged the Fear Gorta's sturdy chair to the spot below the rafters.

He was waiting for her.

The jeweled box lay at Saro's feet.

"No. That's mine," Mary said.

Saro sized her up, from her reddened and scaly legs visible beneath the hem of her raised skirt to her determined face. He made no move to defend the box. He simply regarded her with the curiosity of her mam inspecting a carrot pulled from the earth. The shape of her, the nature of her. He was *interested* in her.

He breathed a long sigh. It was a sigh of a *very* old man. It was a sigh of one who had seen a lot, and who was now faced with a child who understood nothing of what he knew.

Mary repeated, "That's mine, and you cannot have it."

Saro canted his head. The diamond in his pearl choker glinted, though Mary knew the sun did not reach this far into the cottage.

Mary took a step.

Saro countered with a step toward the box.

"It remains with me," Mary said.

Saro clicked his tongue.

Mary hitched her skirts higher and ratcheted her leg.

Saro smiled. He showed teeth whiter than the pearls lining his neck.

Mary paused. She reevaluated him.

Saro cracked his neck with two quick swishes left and right.

Enough, Mary thought. She canted her leg to jump. "The box stays with me. It is my birthright."

She sprang at it.

Saro lifted the lid of the box.

Then, everything stopped.

28

Saro and the World Box

DUST MITES HOVERING IN the cottage air froze. Animals and insects all around silenced. Approaching footsteps, crunching grass, calls to Mary—they all fell away, as if a tunnel stretched between the two men on the bog and Mary, now suspended six feet above Saro and the open box.

Fog from inside the box flooded the room, blinding Mary. She windmilled her arms, just as her mother had done, but she didn't move. She floated in place. Dense fog clouded everything. She sensed a slipping of her senses. Concrete items—the cottage walls and furniture, the sounds, the aromas, the temperature of the air—disappeared. Without sensory input, she panicked—heart racing and breath galloping. Before now, she had never realized how dependent she was on her senses in this world, how the angle of the sun informed her next chore, how the odor of the bog informed her of the planet's place in its journey around the sun, how the birds' songs informed what vegetable poked from the garden soil, how the cold of the dirt informed the flower buds shriveling. The fog stole both her senses and her place in her world. Her thoughts pushed to the edge of her skull. Where, when, why—nothing made sense. She could not hold on to reality. There was nothing to hold on to. Mary wanted to scream, to call out, but her voice was gone. Her blood had stopped. Her heart had quieted to a sluggish *tick...tick.*

The bog-sod roof and tin dissolved. Opening above her was a brutal emptiness, a cold chasm. Nothing existed there. It pushed down on her, compressing her.

She slipped away, her mind leaving her.

Hold, child.

The words were only a buzzing in her ears tapping out words in breathy syllables with choppy ends. She struggled and flailed. Nothing righted her sense of direction. Nothing anchored her.

Again, the voice: *Hold.*

Mary could not draw breath to still herself. Muscles no longer obeyed. She found no control inside herself, no control over her thoughts racing to the edge, threatening to bring her over.

Hold, child.

To preserve herself, she shut off her vision and forced herself to rest. A spinning sensation dizzied her. Denied perspective and horizon, she could not determine her position in space. She wanted to vomit but had no access to spasming muscles in her stomach.

Hold...

A ground beneath her. Firm but dank.

Was it the bog?

No. Softer. Greener.

Again, the voice: *Open your eyes.*

A shape of someone threaded into place from slender strands of light.

It was Mam.

Mary breathed no air nor controlled any muscles, but she reached her mother with an otherworldly echo. "Mam."

The being before her acknowledged her with a lowering of the chin. A royal nod, majestic. It was far too delicate a movement to belong to any Finnegan woman.

"You are not Mam," Mary said.

The voice replied: *No. This is an illusion. Everything in here is an illusion.*

Mary recognized the voice as the same she had heard from Saro buzzing in her mind.

He said: *You are a strong one. Despite your profound abilities, you must still acclimate to this place.*

"What is this place?" Mary asked.

The figure before her dissolved. Saro's voice came from inside her head. *We have limited time here. It is important that you pay attention, little one.*

A column of light descended from far above. With it, some sensory input returned: an overwhelming odor of earthy mildew. Mary reached out. An arm's width apart, she felt four wooden walls—one with a door. Glowing mushrooms tickled her ankles. Moss undulated all around. "Am I inside the box?" she asked.

Continue, the voice said. *Open the door.*

With nowhere else to go, Mary obeyed. She opened the door and stepped into a corridor, lit only by the soft glow from dangling lanterns and lined with shelves carrying hundreds of books.

Saro's voice was still clear in her mind. *I have seen the books in your dwelling. You and your mother value tales, yes?*

"Mam read to me most nights," Mary replied, examining one of the shelves. She recognized many of the books here as her own. "These are *our* books." A couple had wavy pages from when Mary had spilled water on them. Another had a cracked spine, an accident for which Ailish had scolded Mary. She turned away. "Where is my box?" she asked. "It's my birthright."

The answers to all your questions lie before you. You must travel farther.

Mary passed the bookshelves, making her way to the end of the corridor. There, it veered to the right, revealing an arched entrance to a round room encircled in more bookshelves. Overhead, the room opened to violent, churning clouds. At the center was a marble sculpture of a figure raising a lightning bolt with meaty arms and an open mouth, tensed to hurl the bolt at a giant looming over him. The giant's face was obscured by a wild mane. Its arms were tree trunks, and its fingers were snaking roots. Below the sculpture was a gold plaque: "Zeus in the Titanomachy."

"I know this story," she said to herself. "It's the story of new gods rebelling against old gods. The Titans."

It is also my story.

Above Mary, lightning played among swirling gray clouds.

You are to be commended, Saro spoke. *Few humans can journey this far into another reality. That this has not overwhelmed your mind shows your strength.*

A different room glowed at the end of a connecting corridor.

Farther.

Mary moved on.

Another right turn. A new room.

In this one, there were no shelves. Books were stacked precariously high around another sculpture. This one—crafted from a rougher stone—depicted a man ripped at the chest by the beak of an eagle. Below it was a grate guarding a flickering fire. A gold plaque rested on the grate: "Prometheus and the Stolen Fire."

Saro asked, *Do you know this tale?*

"I do. Against the will of the gods, Prometheus brought fire to humans, saving them from destruction."

It is also my story.

"Will I see the box soon?"

Travel farther.

The third room—yet another right turn. Mary thought, *I'm going in a circle. Clockwise.* This room was lit only by stray embers crawling across the floorboards. Flames licked at handfuls of discarded books, ravaged from empty shelves. The sight shocked her. Setting fire to books was against the Finnegan way. Mary scurried around the room, stomping at fires to save the pages. When the pages were safe, she investigated that room's sculpture: a slick, obsidian figure with feathered wings at razor-sharp angles amid a disorienting fall. She read the gold plaque: "The Fall of the Light Bringer."

Mary added, "Lucifer."

No voice replied.

"Saro?"

She looked around the room, past the heap of half-burned books, and found another door. "How is that possible? The arc of the walls say these rooms are arranged in a circle. Three right turns should take me back to where I started, but there was no door behind me at the start."

Silence.

Mary moved to the door. On it, intricate carvings slithered along the wood, alive.

She moved closer. Figures of all shapes and forms writhed across the door. A knot in the wood glowed like the sun, birthing colossal beings that wandered aimlessly along the door's surface, morphing their shapes every moment. Eyes multiplied into more before closing and opening again as mouths. Many of the creatures attacked one another in violent movements which permanently splintered the door. Smaller creatures scurried inside pits in the wood to hide from the wars around them.

Saro's voice returned. *I have brought you here to bring you comfort. This is a bridge from your world into my memories. These stories you learned are echoes from much older stories, little one. They are reverberations from our story, the story of my family. Open the door to see our story.*

Mary reached out to the brass knob and turned it.

A noiseless cold overwhelmed her. She shook uncontrollably. Beyond, vibrant stars burned in space. Planets collided, spewing their debris among galaxies which swiveled across the cosmos. In front of Mary, a shimmering platform, like a cloud, drifted. Patches of the cloud shone indigo, then violet, then magenta. She cautioned a step forward. The colorful gas held firm. She struggled to ask, "What is this?"

Our story begins here, at the inception of time, the foundation of all beginnings. And in that place, there was only Chaos.

Blinding colors clashed in the distance.

And with Chaos came brutish gods and savage creatures with an endless hunger satisfied only by war.

Streaks of lightning ripped through the cosmos. Some bolts struck planets, shattering them into dust.

This war was so vast, so cataclysmic that the ripples from this conflict created much of what you consider the universe. Indeed, the war was at the center of all creation. Though it would end many things, it was also the beginning of all things.

Other lightning bolts trailed gases and flickering lights, which coalesced into shapeshifting beings. Each of those beings radiated lightning strikes of their own. Glimmers of new stars and shadows of ruptured planets cast the warring figures in silhouette.

Saro narrated: *At the creation of time—in that void of Chaos—a dreadful creature was born. The beast's name has no translation in any human language because you have yet to know such terror. I shall call it The Terror.*

A shadow of tentacles under a bulbous head emerged.

The Terror dreamt countless atrocities, and its wicked lieutenants served its will.

A three-eyed beast with a blunted skull and a hard exoskeleton called to the Terror with a trumpeting shriek. Needlelike legs pierced the ground. Tentacles dragged behind. The Terror responded with a deafening roar.

The Terror broadcast its dreams upon us, and those dreams manipulated us. They set us against each other. It even set his own lieutenants upon themselves, for the Terror cares nothing for any lifeforms. This was its pleasure: to author self-destruction in others. Its only reason for existing was to perpetuate violence. Its hunger for destruction never died. If it continued to roam free, our war would never die.

We fought this Terror—and each other—for eons.

The war had gone on so long that many of us believed that without the energy devoted to this protracted combat, everything would crumble. The entirety of space and time would fade away. Many of us feared this to be true: Our conflict was the fabric of our existence.

The gas cloud under Mary's feet congealed into rock. She now floated on a charred plate, spattered with craters. Dozens of black rocks drifted toward each other. In her periphery—away from the cracking of lightning and the colossal explosions—she noticed a new light born beyond the ridge of the rock she stood on. She turned her back on the celestial conflict to investigate the source.

Saro continued his story: *During this brutal conflict, some began to believe in a different way to live. We were a small faction, a mere fragment of our population. You might call us a family. A pantheon of gods. We wondered if there was peaceful existence away from this war.*

Among our kind, speaking about peace was heresy. Even the act of naming a time without war would have set the Terror upon us, inviting more havoc and pain. Moreover, the others came to believe that talk of peace threatened to fracture reality. We were reduced to a singular function: war. And if we were no longer at war, then who were we?

We had to travel far from the others, in secret, to devise a plan.

So, we opened a door and slipped across untold realities.

We came here. To your world, in its earliest days.

Here, we would bait and trap the Terror, away from its lieutenants, far from the war it fed upon.

Mary saw, over the edge of her drifting plate, a dense core to which the plates gravitated. The charred rocks crashed and shifted into a spinning mass: a new planet.

Saro said, *When we came, this world looked nothing like it does now. It was a field of debris collecting around a rotating, gaseous disc—a remnant of a dead star. We were the only life here.*

Mary's plate smashed against others, pushing the edge to form a cliff, which plummeted into a deep ravine. In that ravine, shadowy figures assembled. Their skin was translucent. Lightning blasted through their veins like an electrified circulatory system. The contours of their form shifted continuously. Quadrupeds merged their limbs to form a single-columned torso, then split to form two legs, then merged again into a shapeless lump.

It did not take long to decide on our plan: we would lure the Terror here to this lifeless planet and imprison it here, far away from our people. We would build a prison for it—a Temple to peace. This prison would seclude the Terror from the others. It would trap it in a dream state. We would guard it here on this outpost, away from our own kind, for our lives are long and our dedication to ending the war steadfast.

But, since we were so few, the construction of our prison required help.

The translucent figures vibrated. With a flicker in their veins, water began to puddle, then rise all around them, in the ravine.

So, we did what pantheons do. We created children. Children like your father.

Mary noticed a new vibration in that accumulating water. Oversized tadpoles flailed at first, then swam through the water with ease. Shells hardened on their backs, which pushed a hunch into their spine. They sprouted scaly legs, which canted backwards under double-jointed knees.

Mary recognized them. "The Travellers," she said aloud. "Fear Gorta."

Saro said: *Yes. And others—ones you have yet to meet. Humans who have met them call them Light Ones. They were tasked to create the building blocks of our design.*

Sparks of electricity shot from the water, then arced into white-hot streaks shooting about the Travellers. After circling the scaly beings, the Light Ones fizzled in place, forming into humanoid figures that glowed. Each paired off, finding a Traveller as a partner. Then, the Light Ones dipped their stark-white hands inside the Travellers' shells as if dipping into wells of energy. Their fingers ignited with red heat, which they pressed into charred rock, liquefying it. The magma evaporated into a gas, which the Light Ones kneaded into blocks of an iridescent material.

Mary said, "I know this relationship from science books. They're symbiotic."

Saro said: *Yes. We liken our children to gardeners and masons.*

The Travellers took up the iridescent blocks and carried them to the center of the ravine, carving glyphs on their surfaces before stacking them in intricate designs. An incomplete building in the center sprouted vast spires of morphing sizes and positions. The spire walls pulsed like breaths, sending waves in hypnotic circles about the ravine's floor.

Saro said: *The Travellers provided the labor to execute our design, but they also carried the spores from our home, the spores that could create life.*

Between the cracks of the Travellers' shells, a fungus grew. It was shed as they swam.

If you look closely within the cracks of their scaly skin, verdant valleys grow these life-giving spores.

Spores rose off the fungus and sparked in proximity as if greeting one another. The floating fungus expanded and crawled up the side walls of the ravine. Fruiting bodies—mushrooms—multiplied by the thousands. Spores rose from these mushrooms and sparked in the air. A cloud of drifting spores became millions within seconds. Soon the ravine was lit entirely by the spores in hues of yellow, purple, green, and red.

On this far outpost away from the war, we needed a way to lure the Terror here. The spores would serve as bait. They were pure life, untouched by malice, the kind of life that the beast hungers for. The Terror would not be able to resist them.

The spores drifted toward the central building's spires, calcifying when they made contact. The ever-shifting spires kneaded the spores into the architecture's iridescent skin. Soon, rivers of the calcified spores could be seen glowing from within the entire construction.

We never intended for our children to remain here with us. The Terror was coming. When it arrived, it would set them upon each other, goading them into acts of destruction. We had known this violence for so long in our home world and could not bear the thought of our children suffering the same way.

What we did next, we did out of love.

The earth below Mary's feet cracked.

She clawed at the ground for stability, but when the entire cliffside disengaged Mary was suddenly falling into the ravine of spores. Flashes of light zipped past Mary as she accelerated. The spores multiplied further. Millions. Billions. Spores crowded the air, jostling each other, glowing with energy. Mary was blinded by them.

Then Mary hit water.

For a moment, everything was black. Then she breached the water's surface and filled her lungs with air. The translucent, shapeshifting figures—the first in the ravine—now searched it from the cliffs above. Travellers and Light Ones scuttled around the bottom in outcrops and caves in the ravine walls.

A ray of light broke through the vast space above Earth.

Saro said: *Our pure lifeforms did the job; the bait worked. The Terror found us quickly.*

A shattering howl crumbled rocks and vibrated plates.

Saro said: *We were out of time. We had one final task.*

We had to kill our children.

The translucent figures chased down a handful of Travellers and Light Ones. The figures ripped them from their caves and hauled them to the crest of the ravine. There, hundreds of eyes opened all over the translucent figures' morphing bodies. The cosmic lightning in their veins extended, spilling out of the open sockets, and charring the Travellers and Light Ones. They shrieked with agony, withering and sliding into the ravine where their corpses simmered.

Only a few survived our great culling.

"You murdered your children?"

Saro said: *In their pure innocence, they would have never survived the beast. The Terror never kills quickly, not as we did. It was a kindness.*

Mary gasped. "You're no gods. You're monsters."

Saro said: *They are one and the same. I have lived a long life, little one, and have pondered my nature billions of times over. Ours was a necessary cruelty. Yet, it was out of the rebellion of our children to our cruelty that Earth flourished.*

A surviving Traveller, shaking and whimpering, pried scales off its own shell. A surviving Light One assisted, clawing open the Traveller's backside to reveal a shimmering pool which spores multiplied inside. The Light One plunged its hands inside, igniting its arms like flares. Flames sputtered in the surrounding air. The blinding liquid dripped from the Light One's hands as it buried them into the earth. Dry rock moistened into fertile soil. Grass radiated from the site, and the wind played with the grass. Trees rose from the ground, and singing birds escaped from their bushy leaves.

A translucent figure killed the Traveller and the Light One and tossed them into the ravine with the other corpses.

The rest of our children escaped us, just as we once fled our own kind. They are strangers to each other now, never crossing paths. They elude us to this day.

The remaining Travellers and Light Ones cowered in their caves and alcoves, hunkering down in the darkness. Life and light continued to blossom in the world while they secluded themselves. The beast bellowed again from far out in space, which could only be felt by tremendous shock waves impacting the planet.

There was no time to eradicate the remainder of our children. The Terror was here. And we hoped it was alone.

A deep blackness separated the warring colors and lightning bolts. A winged beast tumbled uncontrollably through the cosmos. All color faded. Soon, a black void drained the sky of light. The cosmic lightning bolts retreated to their origins, leaving pinpricks of white stars behind.

Our dream to end the war was coming true.

The creature screamed, but the bleak cosmos drained the sound, rendering the Leviathan mute. White stars revolved at a dizzying speed.

The Temple City crawling with life stood ready. The translucent figures gathered around.

Mary's intestines slithered around her stomach. Her heart froze and plummeted to cool the friction burning her insides.

The creature entered the atmosphere. Any remaining color drained from the planet. The translucent figures grasped each other in fear.

Saro said: *It came alone. As afraid as we were, we were relieved it had left its lieutenants behind. So hungry for new life, it was not its nature to share.*

The Terror barreled toward them with wings stretched. Dark veins pulsed in the wing membranes. Tentacles whipped from its chin like a beard. Muscled arms ending in luminescent claws dug into rock, catapulting it into the air. Red eyes narrowed in hate, focusing on the translucent ones.

The Terror stopped, its attention diverted. It swiveled its rounded head to the Temple.

As planned, the spores planted within the Temple baited the dreadful Terror. It could not resist a network of life yet to be seduced by its dreams of malice.

Its red eyes dilated. It twitched.

It took the bait.

The Earth shook under the pressure of the Terror's footfalls. It launched itself airborne, spraying rock behind it.

The translucent ones gripped each other but held their ground.

The Temple structure flexed. The central structure yawned, ready to swallow the beast.

As the Terror took flight, the glowing spores on the Temple walls faded to a gray ash. The carved glyphs on the bricks jittered and blended.

The spores shot toward the Terror, encasing it in black slime. The beast stretched its arms, but the slime held them taut. Tentacles slashed around, but the slime oozed between, gluing them together. Slime encased the wings, weighing them and immobilizing them.

The Terror fell to the Earth in a pulsating black sludge.

The creature bellowed its siren call, which shook Mary to her bones.

The roof of the Temple reassembled before the dust from the impact had clouded Mary's vision. The winged creature thrashed inside the Temple with a thunderous barrage of noise.

The crash had weakened the creature. Still, it was a formidable opponent. So, we weaved a net of slumber to immobilize it, then clamped its jaws shut.

The light of the translucent figures zipped inside the building as its walls rapidly shifted.

We trapped the Terror in an indefinite fit of dreaming and restricted its reach to that of the dreamlands. It could not call to its lieutenants. It could not wake itself.

The noise from the creature died. Earth settled.

Then, we sank that prison into the depths of this world.

Mary noticed the waters from the ravine rising. She rose, with the water, to the brim of the ravine and beyond. Soon, most of the planet was shrouded in water—the beast's Temple City lost somewhere deep below. But Mary kept rising. She left the water and took to the air.

Saro said: *Against all odds, the war, which had begun at the inception of time, faltered and died.*

And the fruits of our rebellious children changed this planet into a life-giving source.

Seeds from their bodies had planted here. And they grew.

This was a failure in our plan, little one.

As our children's life network grew, cells formed, and algae coated the sea and organisms bubbled with life. Yet, this life, born outside our power and influence, was capable of the same kind of manipulation the Terror had used to turn us against ourselves. Life was vulnerable to the Terror's will, the will to unravel the binds we placed upon it.

This is Earth's life network. Everything that lives here began with our children. Everything that lives here began with the innocent seeds our children spawned at the Temple. But the Temple is corrupted by its occupant, wrecked by the proximity of the beast. From there, sequestered to the dreamlands, it pulled the strings of evolution.

It wants to be found. It wants to wake.

What has evolved here on Earth has evolved to do the bidding of the Terror.

Oh, little one. Your kind is so vulnerable to its will.

Mary had risen into the atmosphere. Hers was now an incomparable view of the entire planet. She asked, "What of the rest of your kind? Are they still here?"

Saro said: *No. After the Terror was imprisoned, we lost grip on reality. We lost much of our power. We doubted our actions. And one by one, we faded away.*

Mary asked, "You are alone?"

For eons.

Saro added: *Yet, I have doggedly persisted and watched. I kept the Terror hidden. I am the underwater prisoner's final guard.*

I have witnessed its lieutenants come here, seeking to free the Terror. They always fail.

Others have come, too. They are far more powerful than I, and they, too, want to revive the war. Still, the prison holds.

Yet, the greatest threat to our plan thus far has been humanity. Your intelligence was not planned for. Your connection to the Temple's life force was a mistake.

And every day I grow weaker. One day I shall join my family: extinguished on this plane of reality.

When my existence comes to an end, there will be nothing left to protect you from the neverending darkness brought by the Terror. Nothing left to protect my people, so far away.

And so, I have developed a new plan.

I need a successor.

Because I am weak, I require help for an act of creation.

My children are the only ones who can do this.

Time advanced rapidly. Continents separated and froze before returning to their green state. The world Mary recognized took shape. The dense fog returned, surrounding Mary and the Earth. Light bent, and Mary could not tell if she was growing or if the world was shrinking. But soon, she held it in her cupped hands.

My children have long since abandoned me. I have tried to make other children. But, in my frailty, I was unsuccessful. The results were...hideous.

Imagine my shock to find you, little one. A child of both realities: cosmic and terrestrial. One half, a pure form of life; the other, deeply connected to the earthly network.

It is a miracle even I do not fully understand.

You, child, are a miracle.

Your father was able to accomplish what I could not: a child in his image. The earthly wisdom is true, that if you live long enough your children will surpass you.

Your existence causes me to rethink: were my children a flaw in the plan or a necessity?

Mary felt the weight of the miniature world in her hands, comparing it to the infinite space around her. Then, a mushroom sprouted in Africa. Another in Australia, then one in South America. Spores rose like steam from the oceans. The ice in the poles produced a thick sludge which congealed into walls surrounding the world. Then the world was gone. A box full of glowing mushrooms had taken its place.

This was not a power Mary desired. She released the box. It floated away into the void.

Your birthright, little one, is a glorious achievement. If my family could have made one like it, we would have. But it was far beyond us.

And now it has come to you. The box, which holds the power of your father's creation.

A seed like one that made all the life on Earth. It holds the promise of another world.

In your hands, it is a wonder. Nothing more.

In mine, it is a chance at the continuation of a legacy of peace: a cosmos without the Terror.

Fog rushed toward Mary. Her vision brightened then expanded. She saw her cottage, but from different angles. Above, below, from all sides. Saro still stood inside, the jeweled box at his feet.

Lend me your birthright, little one. Lend me the ability to create once more.

I will create new children. More than just two species. A strong gene pool for the future.

Some will be born of exposure to your father's gift.

One will be born of me. Upon this child, much hope will be placed.

From you, I have learned the benefit of connecting the children to the Earth network. So, my new children will share your humanity.

I ask you, child: will you guide them? Encourage their intuitions. Ensure their safekeeping. Encourage the best parts of their humanity. With your protection, they will know what to do.

Mary's body lay slumped on the cottage floor before Saro. His eyes followed Mary in her new reality as she shifted perspectives in the other realm. He was aware of her in the nothingness. Mary tilted about the cottage, circling Saro, then settling into her own body.

If so, I will let you know of their arrival, but you must arrange for them to be where I need them to be.

If you do not, we will fail.

Mary felt her blood flow return. Her breathing restored. Lungs inflated and deflated.

Mary moved her fingers. Her eyes. Her toes.

With this done, your box will be returned to you. Your birthright will be restored. All hope is with you now.

Mary opened her mouth and unleashed a ragged scream.

"*Ach! Kleines Mädchen* is as deafening as is quick!"

Above her, Waldemar and the priest hovered.

The priest fanned her with the edge of his tunic. "Mother Mary! Her hair's gone white!"

Mary pulled a strand of hair in front of her face. The red color had drained. Alabaster strands reflected a weak ray of sunlight let in at the open front door.

"She experiences shock," Waldemar noted. "Mutti's mud death perhaps weighs heavily. Saro! Bring schnapps!"

Saro.

Mary bolted upright, throwing the men aside with a strength that surprised them. She looked around the cottage for Saro and found him holding the jeweled box.

Mary gnashed her teeth. The words were difficult to utter. She grimaced and growled.

All hope is with you, child.

"Take it," she said.

Saro nodded. He loaded the jeweled box into a heavier box painted with ecru enamel. A label was already affixed to the exterior: *Domhan*. Irish for "world box."

Mary's eyes rolled back in her head. The last thing she said: "Until everything is in place..."

"Stand back," Father O'Brien said to Waldemar. "The poor dear might faint again—"

29

Hija

Mexico City, November 1, 1993

LucíA took up a plastic hotel-room trash bin and vomited into it.

Mary said, "Breathe, pet." The nun pried the flask from Lucía's grasp and shook it. "Emptied that in no time, didn't ya?"

Lucía reared up. "Breathe? *Breathe?* I've been asking you for details about your life for *years,* and when you finally give them to me, you say you are the daughter of a delusional fringe-religion prophet and a traveling Irish merman—AND that you were adopted by a Nazi and an interdimensional being with a taste for expensive jewelry—"

The nun inclined her head. "Eh. I wouldn't say *interdimensional*—"

"—AND who was told by said being that he intends to save the world by making himself some children using a mushroom in a box!"

"You're generalizing. Exposure to the fungus is a part of the method. There have been different types of humans involved—"

Lucía cut her off. "How many are there?"

"Saro's new children?" Mary said, "The early versions were not as successful in establishing themselves."

"Meaning?"

"There were some ineffective hybrids. Genetically unsound. It took decades for him to get it right."

"Am I involved in this?"

"I believe you are the one he considers 'born of him'—the most powerful of his progeny."

Lucía held her breath and rocked. Mary waited. Eventually, Lucía blew out in a long whistle like a kettle approaching the boiling point, then screamed. "I'm part alien!"

Mary scoffed. "Don't let it go to your head. Your human mother was likely a destitute sex worker from the brothel by the marina. Not the brightest crayon in the box."

"You know who my mother was?"

"All the nuns did. We didn't want to upset you."

"All this time—" Lucía's thoughts wandered. "I'm gonna barf again." She retched into the trash bin.

Mary folded her hands, "I'd been looking for you for decades by the time you washed up in the Veracruz harbor."

Lucía's voice echoed in the bin. "I'm not finished breaking down this story!"

The nun swept a flat hand before Lucía.

"And—and—"

"Pet, do try to breathe. Your face is red."

"I'm supposed to know what to do to save the world from the Sleeping One? That's what Saro's talking about, right? He imprisoned that Terror thing, and he's afraid it will get out because it will destroy universes—" Lucía retched.

Mary said, "He did say his progeny would know how to apply their talents. Do you?"

Lucía brought her head up. "DO I LOOK LIKE I KNOW WHAT THE FUCK I'M DOING?"

"That's a no from me. But the fate of our world is at stake, so I thought I would check."

Lucía threw the trash bin. "*Pinche culero!*" she shrieked. The trash bin landed on the upholstered headboard with a *thunk*. "My life is a fucking lie! How about that?"

"You've summed it up with your usual flair." She removed the trash bin from the bed and set it upright on the floor.

Lucía kicked the bed repeatedly. "Are you even Catholic?"

"I used to be. My heart's not been in it for a while. I was already thinking of leaving the Church when your skills became evident."

"Skills?"

"Tulip, you were weird."

"FUCK." She spared a thought for Daas, who was right about her weirdness, whose words now echoed with a kindness she had missed in the heat of the moment. She felt shame mixed with an odd relief. She'd been diagnosed, categorized. She *was* weird.

The nun continued, "I connect with Providence Group on matters important to the mission. Documenting the presence of cosmic life on Earth has yielded some helpful artifacts. Who knows what might be of use? Along with keeping you in line, it has been more than a full time job." Mary pressed her tunic under her wrinkled hands. "I keep the nun's habit, though. I earned it. And it's good cover for my scaly legs. Even better for free booze."

Lucía shot a look at Mary's legs and backed away. "Your leg—"

The nun cracked a smile. "It isn't what it used to be. It's been a long time since I went bog hopping."

Lucía's voice darkened. "I don't believe a word of it. Not one word of your story."

"All right." The nun scooted toward her. "Tell me what point I've referenced that feels like a lie to you." Mary rearranged her tunic. "Anything at all sound out of place? Anything amiss?"

Lucía shot up, paced, and pulled her hair.

"Well? Let's have it, pet."

Lucía unleashed a low gurgle in the back of her throat. "Fuck you!"

"I'll give you a minute to yourself." The nun pulled the headdress from the bed, unfolded it, and replaced it on her head. She tucked her dandelion frizz into the sides.

Lucía collapsed against the wall into a defeated slouch. She wiped her mouth with her sleeve.

"Use a towel, pigeon."

Lucía asked in a whisper, "Is the Nazi a cosmic being?"

"I do not think so. He was exposed to the box, so he had some special insights. But he's not cosmic. He has since died."

"He's dead?"

"Recently."

"I will decline that story today, thanks." Lucía thought a moment, then asked, "Did you ever see Saro again?"

"That one, yes."

"Why do you call him 'that one'?"

"He's a shapeshifter. Lately, he sticks with the disguise of an African with a white Afro and black fringe, the disguise he used with me and Dr. Koltz. It's his favorite, I suppose. Or, because he's dying, he hasn't the strength to shift his appearance anymore. I'm not sure. Once, I saw him in what I think is his real form. Tentacled mess."

"How many times have you met Saro?"

Mary searched the ceiling for her answer. "Not many. He'd show up every now and then to scare the shite out of me."

"Why?"

"I'm as stubborn as you are, pet. He has his ways of letting me know when I am off track. Sometimes, he'd show me what I needed at the time to keep me motivated."

"Now, I know where you get it from."

Mary raised her eyebrows. "At least I only ever *kidnapped* you. Whipping you off to another dimension wasn't within my abilities." She patted her headpiece. "It's hell on the hair follicles, too. That trip through the world box, enlightening as it was, ruined my beautiful red hair."

Lucía mulled over another terrifying option. "Is Daas a part of this plan? Is his father a mushroom spore from a box, too?"

"He's human."

Lucía ran her hands through her hair. It needed washing. "Daas said he met you before."

The nun waggled her head. "At the conference? We never met. He saw me. I was scouting. Scouting him, actually."

"So, Daas is just in the right place at the right time?"

"A little more than that. His advances in the field of artificial life, when compared to others, are abnormally fast. No one else has come close to what he can do. I attribute most of that to you."

Lucía choked on her words. "I'm helping him with my...cosmic abilities?"

"Besides drugs, I don't know what you do in that lab."

"I meant help from Saro. Has Daas met him?" She held her mouth. "Oh my god. I think he has. A disk arrived at the lab, and he couldn't account for who sent it, except that he had amazing abilities, and after we loaded it—"

"Unexplained advances? Sounds right. And Saro did vet Daas, yes, so they did know each other."

"Why involve Daas?"

Mary threw up her hands. "Who knows. Saro has been known to interfere with human development to advance his agenda."

"And his agenda is limited to keeping the Sleeping One asleep and in his little underwater tower? Forever sending out its dreams along our DNA like SOS radio calls?"

Mary flexed her fingers to flex her mind. "Listen, tulip. These beings operate on a different scale of time. What's a year to them? Nothing. A hundred years? A blink. If they do use humans to further their agenda, we likely don't have the brain power to understand what that agenda is."

Lucía pondered that. "So, we aren't dealing with friendly aliens helping us out of a tight spot?"

Mary readjusted her headpiece. "I'd venture that they consider us as we might consider an anthill. Some of us might go out of our way to step on it. Some might express a passing interest in preserving it. But we won't lose sleep over its fate in the grand scheme of things."

Lucía twitched. "He killed his own children."

"And he told me about it, so there might be some regret there. I believe part of his plan is a second try at ushering along his creations. I believe he used the Nazi to try to track his first children. Saro is interested in power, yes, and possibly reconciliation. The Nazi was the key to that. That man was a good hunter. He came close to finding my father. And he kept me shadowed for years to see if my father would return, but he never did. Did not stop Waldemar from using me as bait though."

"No," Lucía shook her head. "I'm sick of being a plaything for bad fathers. I refuse to participate. Humans don't give murderous parents second tries. Especially ones who hang out with Nazis."

"No. But we are not 100 percent human, are we, pet?"

Lucía scrunched her face to shield her against that statement. "How do we know we aren't being led down a path that will destroy us?"

The nun tilted her head, allowing her thoughts to flow. "I spent my first year in the Scottish convent thinking about that one. What I kept returning to was that Saro took enough interest in recruiting me to guide you. There is an investment of time and some trust on his part."

"Because you're half of his race?"

"A quarter. I descend from his children, a race he considers slave labor for his prison project. *You* are half. A direct descendant."

"Well, shit, Mary. I should have insisted on a nanny befitting my station."

Mary tipped her chin up and laughed. "Good. A sense of humor will go a long way now that this is out."

Lucía kept pacing, her thoughts running wild. "How many of the other types of children are there?"

"I'm not even sure I know. Anyway, there are things about my work you shouldn't know. That will serve as our system of checks and balances, since we are running blind, you and I. The others I've recruited—the ones vetted by me—will come to you in time. And in the end, they'll possibly become apparent to you. But for now, you must judge everyone who comes to your project with the best of your abilities. Let no one near it who doesn't pass your sniff test." Mary pointed to her. "You are very protective about your project. That is your sign that the Artificial Lifeforms are of use to Saro's plan."

"Saro. The one who killed *his* children."

Mary turned Lucía by her elbows to look in her eyes. "You see now why you must go back. You must protect Daas from his own fears and continue what Saro helped you accomplish. And if you sense that anyone—Howard Winfield or even Oliver Daas—has the capability to diminish or destroy what you've created, then you must obey that instinct and react as if your life depended on it."

"Does it?"

"I believe all of our lives depend on it, yes."

Lucía backed against the wall and slid downward to the floor. "Great."

"Now," the nun chirped, "go clean yourself up."

Lucía didn't move. "You could always read my thoughts. Is that an ability of yours?"

Mary said, "It comes and goes. Children are easiest, especially when they're hiding something. They often focus on the exact thing they don't want me to know, and I can see what they hide as clear as their lying faces. Adults are more difficult to read. They lie to themselves on so many topics that it all comes at me in a muddle."

Lucía scuffed the carpet. "Providence. Half alien. Suspect mushrooms." She raised one eyebrow. "It all makes sense." She zoned out. "All makes sense." Lucía remembered, "The box! Did Saro ever return it?"

"He did."

"Does that mean your purpose in his agenda has been complete?"

"I don't know." Mary twisted her lips, hesitating. "I used to think the return of that box was all I wanted. My birthright, I called it. But many times now I have been in Saro's position, taking cosmic items away from grieving children—who always seem to end up with them—items they believed they wanted desperately but would end up destroying them if they held on to those items. I was that child once, so I know that Saro meant well. Removing the box from me *was* for my own good. It was not my fortune to wield it to help humanity, nor was it best for those children to keep their discoveries. Not according to Saro's plan, and not yet anyway. May it all come to them when they reach their full power."

"What's your real birthright, then?"

Mary said nothing. She was very still.

"Well," Lucía chuckled. "Better figure it out before Saro cuts your puppet strings. When you are past your usefulness, *snip, snip,* down you go."

Mary shrugged.

Lucía stood. "If he has no more consideration for humans than we do for an anthill, what's to stop him from offing you when you've served your purpose? He'll kill you. Cut your puppet strings. *Snip—*"

"I understood the metaphor, Lucía."

"What, then?"

Mary replied, "If he feels like killing me, I won't have much say in the matter."

"Unless you have the power to stop him."

"I don't."

A moment passed when neither spoke.

Then, Lucía leaned in close. "What did you do with the box?"

Mary laughed. "No way am I telling you that."

Lucía suggested, "You can use the box against him."

"It doesn't work that way."

"Where is it?" Lucía asked.

"You can't see it. Don't ask."

"I'm just curious. I thought you were in a sharing mood."

The nun closed her eyes, weary. "When it came back to me, I used to carry it around with me. I did it to keep a part of my family with me. It does come with nasty side effects, even for me. But what to *do* with it? I wouldn't know. And I'm afraid of it falling into the wrong hands. After all I've seen, after what I know about the stupidity of humanity, how often people choose to shoot themselves in the foot when given the opportunity, I hid it away somewhere safe. One day, it might play a different role."

"What kind of role?"

"It was made by my father, a child of Saro, an innocent creator of the Terror's prison. It could have value," Mary said. "It's an ace up humanity's sleeve if Saro gets nasty. Until then, it stays away from self-destructive humans."

"I didn't know you were such a fatalist about humanity."

"Am I wrong?"

"No."

The nun slapped her lap and stood. "We'll end on that note." She lifted a phone receiver on a nightstand and pressed a button. To Lucía she said, "We must get you back to the States, and I've got to get back to work. To make myself useful, as you say. I've been busy since that game-show host made an idiot of humanity. Places to go, people to see, sports cars to rent." She said into the receiver, "Pick up out front in two minutes. Private plane to Boston, departing immediately. No drugs for the passenger." She moved to hang up, but quickly added, "And bring me up some schnapps. I have a long night ahead." She slammed the phone down.

"What do you have going on that's so urgent?" Lucía asked.

"Enough questions. Your ride is downstairs." Mary swished over to the door and opened it. "Out with ya."

Lucía picked herself up from the floor. She mumbled, "Nice seeing you, too, *Fantasma*."

"Don't start with the names. I'll chase your arse down and throw you in a mud pit."

"I always had the feeling I was courting death by talking back to you." She limped to the door, stiff from sitting on the floor. "I hope Daas takes me back."

"He will."

"I wasn't exactly easy to work with."

"Perhaps if you ceased the illicit drugs—"

"I'm half cosmic being. Maybe it's what they eat for sustenance." Lucía passed the nun into the dark hallway. She turned back. "The photos. From the dig under the cathedral. Zumaa's room?"

The nun looked at her.

"I can read the writing. You can't. That was a hell of a long way around the barn to ask me to translate cosmic speak."

"Well?"

"The engravings say, 'I am the harbinger of the Great One. I am the singer of Earth's final rites.' Roughly."

Mary nodded. "That's what I was afraid of."

Lucía slapped the nun's arm. "I'd give you a hug, but we never hugged but once before. When I left for Boston the first time. Remember?"

"Salad days, pet." The nun swung the door closed. "Say hello to Claire for me."

The door thumped against Lucía's outstretched hand. She pushed the door back open. "I never told you about Claire."

The nun gave a blank stare.

"How did you know our ArLiF prototype was named Claire? Did you read my thoughts?"

"Yes." Mary showed her teeth in a broad grin. "She's been on your mind since you walked in the door. *Claire, Claire, Claire*. You are hyper-focused on her. You need to be with her. Trust that instinct."

"Did Saro tell you anything about Claire?"

"He's pleased with her. That's all I know."

"But—"

"You know, pet, at first, I thought the ArLiFs were an *alternate* plan for Saro, in case humans couldn't pull off a miracle and keep the creature under wraps. But now that I've spent my whole life on this work, I realize I would never live long enough to complete his plan. A human lifetime would never be enough to prepare anyone to lead humanity to a peaceful coexistence with that creature. But Claire shows promise, doesn't she?"

Lucía's heart hammered. "What?"

Mary peeled Lucía's fingers from the door jamb. "Time to go. Don't keep the cartel waiting. You have worn their patience to the limit on that trip from Veracruz."

Lucía backed away.

"Pet?" The nun said as she closed the door. "Don't let Howard get his hands on Claire. Nothing could be more dangerous."

Lucía laughed. "Not even the Sleeping One?"

Mary said darkly, "Nothing."

Entr'acte IV:
The Diaries of Oliver Daas

Ascent

Boston
November 1993 to January 1995

November 3, 1993

Pythia Lab

I ARRIVED EARLY THIS morning to discover a missing Lucía Santamaría sleeping in the lab. She was in quite a state of shock. I asked her many times if there was someone I could call, or if she needed a doctor. The answer was always no. Then, she asked for her job back. What a ridiculous question!

My relief knows no bounds. I called Nessa. She was impressed that Lucía had returned. I did not dispel Nessa's notion that I had anything to do with this miracle.

Lucía did not want to talk about wherever she went. "Do not say a word," she told me.

"Where were you?" I asked.

"That's three words." She slumped in front of the ArLiFs and stared at them for hours. Then, she began to eat some fruit I brought her.

Today she has been quiet and vacant. Shell-shocked. She did admit that she went to Mexico, to the orphanage where she was raised. She spoke nothing of what happened there. But *something* happened.

By the afternoon, some things had returned to normal. We were working side-by-side. We had planned to share a drink on the roof. Lucía had taped a printout of an ArLiF achievement to our lab's miniature fridge. Still, something is different with her now. Several times today, I caught her sitting motionless and staring at the ArLiFs—especially Claire. Lucía is miles away.

This evening, she is programming more ArLiFs as if her life depended on it. She's designing better firewalls, requesting more security. And she told me she wants to accelerate the move off-campus.

Her behavior is...Well, I will keep that opinion to myself. Let it not be said I cannot learn from my mistakes, even if I feel bruised about them. Whether I'm an absent parent or a fully present, albeit opinionated one, I cannot win with the younger female audience.

Current ArLiF population count: 102 and rising fast.

January 1, 1994

Pythia Lab

HAPPY NEW YEAR! WE have a world government!

UNITED EARTH ALLIANCE CHARTER SIGNED; UNITED NATIONS DISBANDS

Jan 1, 1994

SAN FRANCISCO (AP)—On this day, 190 sovereign states signed the United Earth Alliance, or UEA, Charter in San Francisco.

The UEA began in 1993 with a formal declaration from Lelee Stern stating the need for an international organization to replace the United Nations. The late Stern, with her spouse Pinchas, made the statement on behalf of South Africa at the Montclair Conference. She said at the time, "In our new world, a replacement organization with more teeth than the UN, one with more wide-ranging judicial and legislative powers to maintain global security, is required. The dangers of an ineffective international government are fully obvious with the Discovery of the Sleeping One."

Further meetings outlined the framework and structure of the UEA. Three main bodies—executive, judicial, and legislative—are led by Danish activist Per Paske. A military body, led by a governing Security Chamber, will be responsible for global peace. "World peace is a tall order," Paske said. "But a divided globe cannot represent itself, nor defend itself, in the event of alien contact."

The UEA tested its mettle as a peacemaker a few months ago, when they negotiated an end to a civil war that had been plaguing Somalia since the early 1980s. By extracting the warring militias, empowering the Islamic elders, and redrawing the country's colonial boundaries, Somalia knows peace for the first time in decades. And with that success, the UEA made a formal call for all global conflicts to end. Paske said, "We will give warring nations six months to achieve a full-stop on all conflicts. We are watching."

The UEA will keep the UN's humanitarian agencies intact. Health, education, science, and culture will be represented in—

Lucía and I had a good chuckle at the UEA wanting world peace like some air-headed response at a beauty pageant. She was up to her old antics again when she collected some stray cables in the lab, stood on a table, and held the cables like a bouquet of roses. Lucía imitated Per Paske's garbled accent perfectly. "We want *warld peez*. We are *witching*." Our interns loved it. Lucía said, "Paske sounds like he wears a retainer in his mouth."

I can still see a difference in her, even in these lighter moments. She doesn't laugh as long or as openly as she used to. Something weighs on her.

To my surprise, Lucía will apply for the UEA's new Continental Citizenship program, which will expand her citizenship rights into the United States. She's proud of her country and has never spoken before of US citizenship. She even asked Nessa to support her application with a letter from the Griff Tran Foundation. Lucía was shocked and slightly angry to hear that *Howard* was the one who provided the letter of recommendation, and that her application was fast-tracked because of it. "I don't want to owe that asshat a thing," she said to me.

March 10, 1994

Pythia Institute, Downtown Boston

OUR MOVE IS COMPLETE! We are now residents of downtown Boston!

Also, Lucía and I formalized the Pythia Institute as a business separate from the University. I serve as its President, and she serves as its Director.

We will still work with University students to provide internships and practicum experiences. It's strange not to be inside of a classroom full-time. No more students to advise. No more curriculum planning and grading. (Though, since Discovery these activities have been things of the past.) But the ArLiF program is where my heart has always been, and I can finally devote full-time focus to it.

A major concession: Howard Winfield sits on the Pythia Institute Board.

This is not what Lucía or I wanted, but his presence on paper increases our fiscal reputation and appeases some University administrative suits who require assurances of our business acumen. It was the only way to continue an educational programming partnership. I assured Lucía she wouldn't have to work with Howard, but she's not comforted. Likewise, I only have to remember Ahmadi's warnings and Howard's timely backing of Per Paske leading up to the Stern assassination to dispel the dazzling spell Howard can cast. I am not immune to his charm, his money, his power...

More good news: Lucía has entered the teaching component of her PhD studies. She's holding lectures for students in the new Amphitheater. She even holds public forums, though nowhere near the Amphitheater, which is too close to the ArLiF servers for general public admission. (The specter of Dennis Beggan is still with us.) With the press frenzy her forums can create, I doubt she will continue them for long. The Mother of ArLiFs has lost her patience for the public fervor for our creations.

We hear occasional news of the Apostles of the Singularity. We try not to pay attention to them, but I worry they will try to break in again. I've been advised by WINmedia's security team once or twice of some serious security lapses in the lab and had to address them on the spot. Howard's security detail has been very involved. They send me occasional alerts about potential terrorist plans. Terrorism! In Claire's name! It makes me ill. If anyone did get in though, I don't know how they would access the servers. Lucía has them locked down so tightly that even I have problems getting in. But if the Dennis Beggan Apostles have bombs now (!) I hardly see how Lucía can stop them.

Nessa has been prodding lately. She wants to know if Lucía and I would be interested in special funding opportunities for military solutions connected to our neural network. I remind her of her upbringing and how her grandmother would be ashamed of her even asking. She says, "Dad, calm down. I'm only making you aware of funding opportunities."

Is she?

Lucía says, "Evolution is power. *Howard* is power. He's not going to stop."

I see on the news how the UEA has strong-armed more signatories to their charter. Rumors of atrocities by their new army boggle the mind. Summary executions! Regime changes! Secret prison sites! How can one slaughter in the name of peace? Yet, Per Paske appears on camera to support exactly that notion! And Howard supports him, and my daughter works for him and calls me for "funding opportunities!"

I have never in my life feared so deeply the consequences of associating with powerful people.

June 23, 1994

Pythia Institute

THE APOSTLES OF THE Singularity have set off a series of car bombs in Europe to oppose the UEA. They say that Claire is the one true leader of our reality.

Nessa called me for a quote to add to the WINmedia press release. She said that Howard wanted to address this situation head-on. I screamed at her, "He is the one who encouraged them! Why did he give them coverage at all? And a book contract!" I sputtered and raged. Nessa calmly informed me about the public's right to know, and Dennis Beggan, in Howard's view, had information the public wanted to know.

I seethed at my daughter. "Just like the Discovery! The public had a right to know? Look at us! Look at what you've done!"

She hung up on me.

Lucía was watching. She said, "If I were nosy, I'd say something like, 'I told you so.' But I won't."

I threw a mouse pad at her.

And then there is this bullshit:

PROVIDENCE GROUP CLAIMS UEA BLACK OPS HOLDING ITS MEMBERS

Jun 23, 1994

PROVIDENCE, RI (AP)—The Providence Group has denounced the United Earth Alliance's broadening military powers with accusations of kidnapping and imprisonment in clandestine, extrajudicial prison sites around the world.

Cosmo Donato, Chief Evangelist of the Providence Group, says, "We know of at least six prison sites in Eastern Europe, the Middle East, and Asia. We also know the UEA Security Chamber employs a black-ops military to keep its dirty secrets and to protect its power. Right now, those guys are holding 12 of our members without charges or legal representation. The Providence Group demands the safe return of our members immediately, as well as the disbanding of this undemocratic black-ops group."

UEA President Per Paske denied these charges. "The Providence Group has no proof of their claims. If they do, I invite them to submit that proof to the UEA Security Chamber for a thorough investigation."

Paske added that Donato's claims are a public-relations stunt. Paske said, "What I do know is that the Providence Group is alarmed at the decline in public interest in their churches since the UEA began its push for scientific understanding of world events. We have expelled dozens of Providence members from our staff for theft of sensitive scientific documents. So, I view these accusations as nothing more than sour grapes. They need to stop wasting everyone's valuable time with their fabrications."

In another claim, Donato said that the UEA is holding a substance of religious value, to which the greater public has rights. Donato said, "We suspect the UEA has been holding a black fungus taken from Yuna II. We also suspect they have been hiding that damaged camera unit to prevent others from accessing it. Further, we suspect the UEA are experimenting on the black fungus now, a claim easily supported by Griff Tran's letter and the mycology reports hidden within. This fungal substance does not belong to the UEA. Manny's footage and Griff's letter tell us that human consumption of that fungus leads to prophecies and visions, sometimes of creatures like the Sleeping One. We demand a sustainable source of the black fungus to enrich our religious life."

Paske replied, "What will Providence Group want next? Samples of nuclear reactor fuel? Nerve-agent freebies? Ridiculous! Some substances should not be made public. This is not a new concept, but one on which law-abiding citizens agree!"

No! The fungus is not *anyone's* property! Why isn't anyone refuting this point? What kind of news coverage is this? Howard's type, that's what! The point of an international scientific consortium, which we already proposed by petition after Discovery, is that not one government or entity can benefit from scientific findings! Now, the UEA has wedged itself into any and all scientific exploration having to do with the Sleeping One, and the rest of us are beholden to the UEA to tell us what they have and whether it's of value!

Lucía says we are teetering toward world authoritarianism. I said we are already there. She shrugged it off. I raged at her, "Why are you so calm?"

She stood and shook me by the shoulders. "Focus, dammit!" Then she pointed at the monitors, at our ArLiFs building and communicating and worshipping. "Focus on them! Focus on 577 of them, building something better!"

"But are we too late?" I fretted.

She looked down at her feet. "I certainly fucking hope not." After a moment, she added, "I'm changing security protocols again. Providence. Apostles. Howard. Too many people want Claire."

"You mean the ArLiFs? They want the *ArLiFs*."

She walked away. "I meant what I said."

September 1, 1994

Pythia Institute

Stressors keep coming.

UEA PRIORITY: ELIMINATION OF GLOBAL CONFLICT
Sep 1, 1994

SARAJEVO (AP)—Peace has finally come to the Balkan nations, thanks to the United Earth Alliance.

In October 1993, before the UEA Charter was even signed, the fledgling UEA tested its authority by successfully negotiating an end to the civil war in Somalia. After that, the UEA called for the end of global conflict altogether. With help, Chechnya, Sudan, and Algeria ended their wars. Yet, in the former Yugoslavia, war raged on. The chief aggressor, Serbia, responded to UEA calls for peace with more sieges against majority-Bosniak cities and increased cases of crimes against humanity. But today, all parties in that war, even Serbia, have submitted to a ceasefire.

The road to peace has been a strange one.

At first, the Serbian government promised compliance to a UEA-negotiated treaty, but a month afterward reneged. That is when the Serbian Army unleashed their Scorpion Unit to conduct a surprise-genocidal campaign along Serbia's border with Bosnia and Herzegovina. Muslim civilians, over 10,000 Bosnian men and boys, found themselves at the edges of mass graves with Serbian military pulling the triggers. Over 20,000 women and children were victims of rape, murder, torture, and forced resettlement. A Serbian general sent a telegram to the UEA: "To the United Nations baby-pretenders: go [expletive] yourselves."

The UEA responded with an unusual military tactic.

President Per Paske explained the UEA's methods. He said, "The UEA Security Chamber recognizes that militaries around the world provide food, safety, and stable jobs in countries where those things are in short supply. Asking civilians to end conflicts and reduce their military influences could economically destabilize some areas."

Algeria, Chechnya, Somalia, and Sudan were four such areas of concern. The UEA Security Chamber addressed those concerns by enfolding former high-need militia members into a new global unit, retraining those in need for UEA-peacemaking missions. Removed from their home countries and offered extensive drug rehabilitation, counseling, and nutrition, these UEA soldiers found a new life in Japan while training in the ancient arts of infiltration, reconnaissance, ambush, espionage, and siege. "Currently," Paske said, "we are building the most unique, loyal, and ethical peacekeeping force the world has ever seen. And we pay very well."

And so, in response to Serbian recalcitrance to the UEA treaty, the UEA airdropped 30,000 Chechen, Somali, and Sudanese ninjas into greater Bosnia and Herzegovina, Croatia, Kosovo, and Serbia. In under three hours, the UEA soldiers had assassinated eight top generals, 42 officers, 15 politicians, 123 regional security police captains, and one telephone clerk.

"Our first surgical strike intends to decapitate the military machine," Paske said.

Politicians in the highest offices fled. Chechen and Algerian operatives in rural areas of the Balkans scooped up top brass for war-crimes trials, to be televised at a later date.

"These are offenders of global peace," Paske said, "and the world will know their names and their punishments—"

"Somali ninjas," Lucía said. "That's funny."

I took the paper away from her. "It's not."

"Yes. It is. Speaking of funny," she told me, "I heard that Providence wants the black fungus because they want a Modern Prophet Program."

"Where did you hear this?"

"Students." A few interns looked over at us.

I bit. "What's a Modern Prophet Program?"

"Supposedly when people eat that fungus, they can hear and see things," Lucía said. "I also heard that they want to resurrect Manny di Martini with it."

I had to laugh at that. "But he's not dead!"

"He's dating Céline Dion! I read it in a magazine! It must be true!"

We laughed so hard that the interns rolled their eyes.

October 10, 1994

Pythia Institute

Is THIS THE BRIGHT and shining moment we have all wished for? Or are we playing into the hands of the powerful yet again?

UEA ANNOUNCES SCIENCE CONFERENCE, EXPO FOR THIRD ANNIVERSARY OF DISCOVERY

Oct 10, 1994

NEW YORK CITY (AP)—The United Earth Alliance has announced its first annual International Science Conference and Expo scheduled for April 7-9, 1995, in Boston, with a Discovery Commemoration and Parade on Wednesday, April 12. The theme is "Three Years of Discovery" and will feature new products and technologies, educational activities, and networking opportunities. The keynote speaker will be Dr. William Ahmadi, Director of the Center for Neuroimaging in Berkeley, C.A. Ahmadi will unveil to the public for the first time the full design plans for the Constellation System, scheduled to begin construction in the South Pacific next year—

I called Will Ahmadi to congratulate him on top billing for the world's most sought-after keynote engagement, but he was oddly cagey. He told me nothing I didn't already know. When I pressed him for some progress on the Sleeping One dream research, he said, "Well, that's classified now, my friend." *Classified?* I was indignant. But then, I thought, is it for the best? Am I becoming like Nessa, pushing for public information when it's not advisable to be spouting off about every little thing, lest the public barrel toward Collapse once more?

I asked Lucía what she thought, and she asked why she and I hadn't been asked to present on the ArLiFs. Practical as ever. I would have thought her own increasing guardedness about Claire would stifle her drive to present at a conference, but no. "I haven't been able to present once since the Collapse," she said. "Or like, *ever*, really."

"But the UEA is using science to whitewash their image," I pointed out.

"Yeah, but I want to *play*," she whined. "We can present *and* be cagey. I can top Will Ahmadi for cagey. Let me *try*."

"Who are you? You spend most of your time excluding people from the ArLiFs, building firewalls and designing ingenious locks on doors requiring blood samples and deposits of firstborn babies to even *look* at Claire. And now you want to present? In public?"

Lucía's lips flattened into a straight line. "You say that play is the purest form of evolution. Maybe I want to evolve, too."

What could I say to that? Lord. She is the most mercurial person I have ever met.

So, for Lucía, I called Nessa for advice on getting onto the conference agenda. Nessa made an appointment to see us in the new year. "It's time to renegotiate your grant contract anyway," she said. "You're almost due."

Lucía seemed pleased.

My nightmares are back. It's the stress, I know.

I can feel the splinters in my hand from the dream-attic as floodwaters rise, as old photos and antique junk swirl around me. I can feel the girl clawing at my waist. I think, *Don't look at me with your awful face like the center of the Earth.* Then the train with the white-robed people speeds underneath, ripping through the floodwaters. My mother's voice says, "Don't look, Ollie."

I never see the Sikh Jathas in the dreams, but I know they are there. They are approaching the train with their swords. If I do not wake up in time, I might see them.

Last night, I had turned to my mother to speak. But it was not my mother. It was Claire. She said, "Don't look, Dr. Daas." She was growing human features, lifelike. She reached for me. I was confused, frightened. Terrified.

I woke on the floor, my sheets twisted in knots.

My therapist is not taking appointments. No openings—try again later.

November 16, 1994

Pythia Institute

HAPPY BIRTHDAY TO LUCÍA!

She's never had a party, so I arranged one. Staff and interns contributed gifts from the vending machine. Lucía had a big pile of chips and cookies greeting her when she showed up for work. And a cake. One of the intern programmers baked her a traditional dulce de tres leches. I gave Lucía coffee shipped in from Veracruz.

She exuded tension as we sang to her. "I've never had a party for myself," she said. "I don't know my real birthday, you know."

"Yes, I know," I said. "But you told me before that you were found in the harbor in November. So, I made a day for you. It's today. This is your day now."

A darkness curtained over her, and she backed away from us. "I'm sorry," she said. "I need a minute."

I left the staff to devour the cake and went to her. She was with Claire in the Amphitheater. It's where she goes now, to center herself.

"Come on," I said to her. "Let's go to the roof."

She shook her head. "You go."

"Without my colleague? Where is the fun in that?"

"Not in the mood."

I slid a pack of snack cakes down the table. It skidded to a stop in front of her. "I brought Ho Hos. And there's more where that came from." I waggled my eyebrows.

She tried to hold in a laugh but snorted.

"Come on, kid," I said. "Let's dust off those chairs on the roof and see which car dealership is on fire today."

"But Claire—"

"Claire can wait. Time to be human."

January 4, 1995

Pythia Institute

MY HANDS ARE SHAKING as I write this.

Today was our scheduled appointment with Nessa at our new Pythia facility to discuss Lucía and I being a part of the UEA conference. We were also supposed to negotiate a new grant contract. To prepare for Nessa's visit, Lucía had lined up students and apprentice programmers to give Foundation staff a tour of the Amphitheater. Lucía had brushed her hair and put on a shirt with a collar. She had promised not to curse in any language. But, to our surprise, Nessa brought Howard and his entourage.

When they arrived, Howard politely acknowledged our staff ("How kind! Pleasure to meet you!"). The rose usually present in his buttonhole was a sweet pink today. He still walked with a cane, but some life had revitalized him. Perhaps it was the global government, or the media successes. But he quickly dismissed our dog-and-pony show without going on the planned tour. He wanted to speak with us behind closed doors. Us, a few security guards, and Nessa, that is.

Nessa looked pale and worried, like she did when she was a child and had done something wrong. Only this time, I felt, something was about to go wrong for me.

It was Nessa who started the conversation, as Howard leaned against a desk. She said, "The Griff Tran Foundation is shifting focus."

I hit the roof. "We *just* moved into this space," I said. "Why would you do this? The ArLiFs are a valuable commodity to you. What—"

Nessa put up a hand to stop my rant. "You are not the only grantee who is disappointed at this news." Nessa explained how the UEA's primary focus is planetary peace. "Mr. Winfield wants all the Foundation's projects to align with that same goal. Without a program that fully supports that goal, the Pythia Institute's three-year contract for funding will expire after the current term."

I couldn't believe what I was hearing.

Yet, Nessa added—and I detected a stomach-churning manipulation coming—she felt certain we could support the military objective.

"Absolutely not," I said.

Nessa did not look relieved at that. Lucía, however, was overjoyed. "Welp!" She shook Nessa's hand, then Howard's (probably boiled her skin afterward), and reiterated how the ArLiFs' utopian core values were set in stone. "No guns! No boom-boom sticks," as Lucía put it. "It will be a pain to patch together our expense budget without the Tran Foundation, but with the generous press attention and the shit-show (so much for her non-cursing promise) that is the Apostles of Singularity, we will manage." She flashed a huge smile.

"You don't understand," Nessa said. I could have sworn Howard smirked. "Without a grant contract with us," Nessa said, "you lose all of this." She gestured all around at our new office digs. "The computers. The facility. The ArLiFs. It's *you* who will go."

Lucía plopped down. I sat. "No," we both said.

At this point, Howard stepped in. "Afraid so. I would hate to lose the founding programmers of this project, but I imagine my requests for cooperation from Pythia staff regarding any military plans will run much more smoothly without you."

"How is this possible?" I asked.

Nessa explained that the agreement we signed at the outset dictated a forfeiture of equipment and intellectual property should we default on our responsibilities.

Lucía leapt at that. "We are *not* in default. We submitted all the financial reports. On time. In detail. As outlined in the agreement—"

"Ms. Santamaría." Howard held his chin above us. "Have you met my lawyer, Fritz?"

Lucía looked confused. "No."

Nessa settled her face into a glare that could dissolve stone.

Howard found something interesting under his fingernails and focused there. "Had my back, Fritz did, at the moment of Discovery. That was a harrowing moment, was it not, Nessa?"

My daughter didn't so much as twitch an eyelid.

Howard continued, "Looking at that monster, at those fluttering pulses under that unearthly white skin, I had to decide, What are my obligations here?"

Lucía and I were quiet. Where was he going with this?

He continued, "What are my obligations to humanity at this moment? I knew we were looking at an alien. Nothing else was possible. My news team and I were meeting humanity's next great foe, and do you know what happened?"

"A fucking heart attack," Lucía said.

Howard lurched forward. His hands never seemed so large, his height never so imposing. Both Lucía and I flinched. Howard was in our faces. "Fritz backed me," he said. "Nessa championed me. While the rest of my team hemmed and hawed over what to do, pussyfooting around my heart symptoms, Nessa and Fritz had my back. They knew what we might have. And they knew we had to investigate it." He brought down a fist hard on a table. "THESE ARE THE PEOPLE ON MY SIDE. They look down the barrel of humanity's greatest find, and they *do not* flinch. And when we did air the tapes, they *kept* protecting me—with legal defenses for our actions and plans of charitable giving to offset the damages. We built an airtight empire upon this Discovery, and we do not intend to let it go."

I looked to Nessa, but she gave me nothing. I had heard stories of Howard's bullying, but never had it extended to Lucía and me with such an immediate threat. I felt pins and needles in my hands and feet. I felt humiliated and submissive. Then, angry. Yet, I could do nothing. His security detail did nothing. Nessa looked bored, as if expecting this. Lucía looked as though she would bore through him and eat his heart. Sweat lined her lip. Her legs tensed as if to pounce. She nearly snarled.

Howard leaned in closer. He was spitting on our faces now. "Fritz has my back. That fucking kraut always has my back. Griff used to have my back, but now it's Fritz. *And* your daughter, Dr. Daas. Your daughter is more loyal to me than any child of mine ever was."

I lunged, but Lucía grabbed my arm. I didn't know who better deserved my ire. How dare he! How dare my daughter seek leadership from this man!

Howard kept ranting. "And I deserve safety. I deserve loyalty. I deserve the kind of protection Fritz offers. I deserve the kind of loyalty your daughter offers. Safety, Ms. Santamaría, is paramount. As is loyalty, Dr. Daas. And *vision*. Without these, the money to fuel your little computer project does not exist. So, if we say we own you, we own you. If we say you are no longer relevant, you are no longer Mother or Father of anything here."

Howard leaned back, allowing his words to sink in.

Lucía looked at me with an open mouth, like she couldn't believe what she was hearing.

Then, Howard shifted his tone to light detachment. "Actually, the equipment and the intellectual property are mine because I say they are. And because I say they are, Fritz says they are. He says it in Latin, in loopholes, and in clauses. He says it so you can't see it, but it's there. Take it to court. Take anything you signed to court. The contract says nothing but what I want it to say because I am Howard Winfield, and you are nothing."

Lucía's skin had turned a shade of bioluminescence I had never seen before. She wore her anger like a sheath. I feared she would bring out her verbal sword and we would lose everything.

"Be calm," I said under my breath to her.

She did not seem to hear me. Her eyes were on Howard. "That's right," Howard said to me. "Keep your dog on a leash."

"Call me a dog again," Lucía said to him. Her voice came out in a growl.

"Lucía!" I said. "Please." I was having a hard time fighting back tears.

Howard wasn't finished taunting her. "Oh, yes. I'll take your children today, Mother of ArLiFs. I'll move your mainframe out of here within minutes. I'll cart your babies away and sell them off to the highest bidder. I'll sell them to the UEA military—"

Nessa still did nothing. Was this the girl I raised? To witness such bullying and do nothing? The *shame* of it.

Could I stop this?

Yes. There was something I could do. I could stop it.

I turned to Howard. "Enough. This ends now."

"What ends—?" Howard started.

I interrupted, "I can do what you say you want."

Even Nessa perked up.

This was news to Lucía. "We can?"

I said to her, "*I* can. You will stay right here."

She struggled to compute my logic. "What?"

Howard exhaled. "Delighted to hear this." He reclined himself against the edge of the desk again and crossed his ankles. His energy dissipated into the casual talk of a business deal. "What do you have for me today, Father of ArLiFs?"

Nessa took out a pen. Now, all of this seemed like standard operating procedure. Is this how it worked? Put the screws to someone and stand back to take notes about what happened next? How many times had she seen this before?

Lucía leaned back and slowed her breath. "Yeah, what do you have, Dr. Daas?"

I began with a flight by the seat of my pants, with ideas that were so half-baked that I hadn't even journaled them.

I said, "If I use a copy of our neural network to translate the dream data from the Sleeping One, data currently being collected by Will Ahmadi, what would that be worth to you?"

Howard dropped the arms crossed at his chest. Nessa looked up from her notepad. Lucía's wild eyebrows shot skyward.

Nessa said, "You shouldn't know about Ahmadi's work. It's classified—"

"I'm listening," Howard interrupted.

Then, I launched into the world of my new vision.

I told them I knew Ahmadi had been working on a human dream database before the Collapse, that with his neurosurgical talents, he had devised a way to map the human brain's electricity during thematic dreams that we all have. Common themes like running from a threat, coming to class naked, losing one's teeth, or engaging in sexual fantasies. All those standard dreams light up specific areas of our brains, and Ahmadi now knows how to predict a human dream's content just by looking at brain scans, no self-reporting required.

"But how do you know what Ahmadi is doing?" Nessa asked.

"I don't. But I can guess." I laid out my logic. "When Ahmadi wouldn't talk about his new work with the UEA, I knew he had found a way to access the creature's dreams. It's in line with his previous work, and it's big enough to shut up the most gossipy man in the industry. The creature, of course, isn't accessible for brain scans, not even if conducted by robotics. The radiation is much too intense for us to approach it with any equipment. However, the UEA's intense guarding of the black fungus gave me a clue as to how you intend to get to its dreams. That, and Griff Tran's letter. You intend to—or are already—feeding humans the fungus in an experimental setting, then mapping new electrical circuits in their brains. You are tapping into what the creature sees when it dreams, then matching our brain waves with the Pulses the creature continually puts out."

Howard said, "Even if we are conducting highly illegal human experiments, which would be speculation on your part and I won't acknowledge that, how is that relevant to *your* project?"

"Illegal or not," I said, "it's an experiment that should be done. If it's true that humans can see and understand visions after ingesting the fungus, we have to consider that the fungus acts as a psychotropic bridge of some sort. It's evident from the Manny tapes and the Griff letter that humans can merge with the creature's thoughts or dreams. Griff wrote on the boat as he approached the site, *Whose dreams were these? Not mine. These were not wars I knew. They were fought by amorphous creatures in cloudy landscapes I did not recognize.* We all know that, thanks to your broadcasts, Mr. Winfield. And we know that the closer Griff got, the worse the reactions became. So, whether Ahmadi is unlocking the creature's Pulse, or whether he is tapping into some kind of call for help the creature is releasing, or whether humans are seeing the creature's deepest fears playing out in its brain waves, we have to consider how this information can give us an advantage if or when that thing ever wakes."

Howard was almost smiling. "And how do you fit in?"

"Yeah!" Lucía blurted. "How the fuck do you fit in?"

"The military response," I said.

Lucía turned away.

I grabbed her arm and made her hear me. "I will create a new Hold of ArLiFs that will run military simulations based on the key findings within the dream data. Is the creature afraid of something? Does it fear sharks or algae or guns or grapefruit? We should find out, then develop a plan with that information. I can program the digital beings to enact those plans and see which ones work best. We would be able to see what military personnel are required to enact those plans. We could see how human communities can support those plans logistically. Is there need for staging for an invasion of Temple City? If so, let's see what the casualty rate might be—"

"You're sacrificing ArLiFs to save humans," Lucía said, shaking her head.

"Not Keyhole's ArLiFs," I explained. "A new set of ArLiFs. Ones designed NOT to evolve. They would carry enough human qualities to mimic human behavior, but that would be all. Only as much as needed to run if/when scenarios."

"A new Hold?" Lucía asked.

"Geographically separated from Keyhole and its servers," I said. "On the other coast. Close to Ahmadi, so I can work with him."

"Sharing Keyhole's assets?" she asked.

"A copy," I said. "Or, cloud-based assets. That technology is new, I'll have to investigate it. But a one-way channeling of assets from Keyhole to the new Hold. The new Hold takes, but it leaves nothing behind inside Keyhole."

Lucía shook her head. "The Bob incident tells us that ArLiFs leave traces that are difficult to detect."

"*Bob* incident?" Nessa asked.

I countered, "Then, use your engineering math for a better firewall. This is the plan, Lucía."

Howard jumped in. "And where will this—uh—new Hold be built?"

"San Francisco," I said.

"City of peace and love," Lucía mumbled.

"It sounds flimsy," Nessa said.

Lucía said to her, "He's making it possible to prevail over the beast without endangering humans on a massive scale. Don't you get it?"

I asked them all, "Ever had a nightmare that nearly killed you? Heart rate too high? Acting out your dream in dangerous ways, like running in your sleep or punching a wall?"

Nessa looked at me with narrowed eyes.

I said, "Ahmadi knows that there are ways to kill the one who is dreaming. With a big enough nightmare, and without the ability to wake up—"

"Heart attack," Howard said.

"If it has a heart," Nessa said.

"If the beast dreams, we will find a way to link its physiology to its mental images," I said. "We *will* find a way."

"The ArLiFs," Lucía added, "can be quite creative in that respect."

There was a long silence in which Howard said nothing, but Nessa scribbled. I held my breath. I believe Lucía did as well.

"One thing," I added. "Keyhole remains untouched but fully funded."

"Why?" Howard asked.

"A control group," Lucía said, getting in on the game. "And a pristine backup copy of the neural network in case something goes wrong. Then, we won't be reinventing the wheel to get back on track." She winked at me. She was getting the idea. We were luring Howard away from the Keyhole ArLiFs. Possibly into a larger mess, but we could only deal with one threat at a time.

Nessa had reached the end of her notes. Howard was still staring at us.

Suddenly, he spoke. "Safety is my first concern. I don't want another agency or government to run with this idea. The UEA will need to hear this. So, I'm keeping you close, Dr. Daas."

I nodded. So. The idea was too big to let go, even if he didn't fully see the plan yet.

Howard said, "A full proposal from you and Dr. Ahmadi, then." He leaned on his cane and stood. "And a *reasonable* budget to keep the Keyhole ArLiFs advancing on their evolutionary track."

"And Lucía Santamaría runs Boston," I said.

Lucía blinked.

Nessa said, "That goes without saying. But she will consult on San Francisco."

"Try to stop me," she said. "But we need more staff. Geniuses."

"Naturally." Howard nodded to both of us. "This meeting has been quite productive." He sighed and slumped slightly, almost speaking exclusively to Nessa. "I do wish people would give their best without the coercion. It raises my blood pressure. At my age and condition, I could do without it." He turned to us. "In the future, Dr. Daas—and you Ms. Santamaría—consider your feet to the fire at every moment. Give me your best without the torture." Howard tapped his cane on the nice carpet, which he paid for. "If you heard some of the things I have heard at these UEA security meetings, you'd agree: humanity's feet are not only to the fire, but our flesh is burning."

"Jesus," Lucía mumbled.

Howard chirped, "Good work! It's a good day!"

He and his team made for the door.

Nessa gave me a look I couldn't read upon exiting. It was a raised eyebrow combined with a headshake. It might have been respect. Or disbelief at my stupidity.

Before Howard reached the hall, he backtracked and knocked on the doorframe. "Oh, the original point of the meeting: you are invited to present at the UEA conference, though what was said here today is off-limits. New Hold, Ahmadi, and all that. Fritz will be delivering non-disclosure agreements within the hour. I expect them signed in his presence."

"Can't wait to meet him," Lucía said. "Sounds like a great guy."

And then they were gone.

Lucía nearly lost her balance in finding a chair. "What the fuck just happened?"

I stood with my knees locked. "I'm not sure."

"Does Ahmadi know about this?"

"No."

"Better call him. Like now." After a long silence, she said, "You deserve to know something."

I shooed away that offer. "No, I—"

"Someone in Mexico told me Claire would be important, and I believe her."

"Important to what?"

"Saving humanity."

"I see."

I did *not* want to know more. Another lunatic with an opinion about Claire. So many people think Claire is important—and none of them for the reasons I see. Perhaps that is her magic. Everyone sees the hope in her in different ways.

"You sacrificed your life's work," Lucía said, looking at her hands. "For me."

"It's not a sacrifice," I said. "I have wanted to create a sustainable source of consistent electricity to power the ArLiFs in the event of power-grid failure. I've long held that Ahmadi knew how to do it, if properly motivated."

"What? What is your power source?"

"Brains," I said, "are batteries."

Lucía's lips flattened. "You intend to use human energy to power ArLiFs?"

"Brain-computer interface."

Lucía did not speak.

"Not your concern," I said.

"Ethically—"

"We are living in a new era," I said. "Ethics are out the window."

Lucía looked in every direction, processing that. "As long as you know what you're doing."

"Worry about the conference," I said. "It's only a few months away. And protect Claire. I have your back, Mother of ArLiFs."

Act V

Chaos

———————

Boston
April 7, 1995

30

Saro

Three Years Since Discovery

IN THE AMPHITHEATER AT the Pythia Institute in downtown Boston, the lights were out. Tiered tables rose from the center in curved rows, inclining to a top row and ending in double doors. Monitors at each desk area were dark. Dozens of rolling chairs were empty.

Before the half-ring of ascending tables, a wall of 24 monitors exploded with color and movement. Behind that wall, servers, switches, and routers hummed. Electric impulses zipped through circuitry, broadcasting source code through a web of cables. The 24 monitors translated that code into vectors, colors, and coordinates, which formed animated imagery recognizable to the human eye. The animated imagery personified individual neural agents—ArLiFs of Keyhole Island.

ArLiFs heaved ropes that brought in nets full of fish.

ArLiFs delivered coffee orders to ArLiFs chatting at cafe tables.

ArLiFs assembled in classrooms to sing songs about animal sounds.

ArLiFs dragged planters behind tractors, seeding lettuces and green beans and tomatoes.

ArLiFs drove sledgehammers into the walls of a church to open a sanctuary to the ocean wind.

ArLiFs weaved grasses and ribbons into equilateral crosses that spiraled into three dimensions.

ArLiFs tied bells to tree branches to bless the fishes and crops.

Exactly 1,015 ArLiFs populated the 24 monitors. Keyhole Island could handle no more.

A new era was coming for the ArLiFs. It was time for growth in intelligence, emotion, and awareness.

From the center of the Amphitheater, seated alone with crossed legs and a twitching foot, Saro examined the monitors teeming with life. He observed the digital imagery, reading the code behind their actions. He could envision inside the processors, where atoms pushed electrons away from the nuclei, shifting into new orbits. He saw the charge from that orbital shift igniting life.

The ruby and diamond choker at his neck emitted a flicker in the dazzle of the monitors. His foot twitched faster as he contemplated all he witnessed. Was this enough to counter the threat?

It was a start.

His own pulse ran slower with the latest orbit around the sun. He would have enough life force, he estimated, for some final acts of creation before he expired. He would hold that energy in reserve, until he judged it to be most advantageous.

When would that be? It would depend on the humans. They were difficult to predict. Humans made decisions independent of logic. Still, the child of the Traveller had done well assembling a talented human retinue. They could do the work required and guard the contingencies, now and in the future. Further, his own offspring-hybrid had yet to reach her fullest potential.

It was, he judged, more than a start. It was an *auspicious* start.

Behind him, a door opened.

A ray briefly lit the Amphitheater. Light refracted inside the gems in Saro's choker.

A man entered, pushing a trash bin ringed with a caddy of paper towel rolls and spray bottles. A bucket and mop rode a platform at the front. The hulking contraption careened into a table.

The pneumatic door wheezed to a close.

The man checked the room, sensing another occupant. He squatted and squinted. "Who's in dere?" He cast a long shadow onto the downward rake of empty tables. His skin was darker than the room, reflecting no light. His Afro jiggled. He pressed the edge of a flat hand to his brows and squinted until wrinkles creased his eyes. "No one supposed to be in dis place when Miss Lucía gone!" His accent soared like rhythms of West African heat waves.

Saro stopped twitching his foot. He didn't move. He didn't make a sound.

The trash-bin caddy rolled and clattered deeper into the Amphitheater. The man called out again, "Eh! You gonna see trouble for being here, mistah! I call security now!" Bouncing on his chest: a yellowed chicken claw dangling from a cord.

Saro was as still as a hunted animal.

The man slapped his thighs. "Ohhhhh kaaaay!" he sang out. His chicken foot *thump thumped* against his dirty t-shirt as he moved farther into the Amphitheater. He picked up the chicken foot and held it by the leg. "Scratch, scratch, my enemy! Last chance!" He ducked between aisles, searching. "I be calling human police officer peoples here to kill you with guns and lasers!" He tiptoed along the carpeted rows. "*Bang bang, pew pew!*" He straightened to his full height to amplify his voice. "Then you be dead! Down goes Senhor Mister Saro or whatever you call yourself to humans deez days!" The man held back a raspy snicker. "Come out, come out, goody two-shoes booger eater!" His laugh spilled over into cackles.

Saro summoned sound from the thrumming of electrical circuits, from the artificial voice files of the ArLiFs, from the whirr of fans cooling the servers. *I've been expecting you.*

The man yipped, then jumped in place with fists pumping. He tossed aside a desk chair and leapt onto a table. "Ta-da! It's me! I fooled you!" He deftly sprang from one row of tables to another until he reached Saro, then dropped down into a rolling chair in front of him. "Here you are!"

Saro still did not move.

"Still haven't gotten de hang of mimicking dat human voice box? Still gotta pull your voice from deez surroundings?" The man reached over to touch Saro's ruby choker. "Dis is fancy."

Saro flinched.

"It's been a *loooooong* time, Senhorrrrrr Mister Saro." The man retreated and settled low into his chair. "I need a name, by de way. *You* have a name. Sr. Mr. Saro. I want name like you."

You already have a name.

"I want a new name."

Your name is Chaos, First Child of the Cosmos, God of Infinite Faces.

"Doesn't roll off de tongue, does it?"

That is all you have ever been.

Chaos pouted. "No new name?" He brightened. "Can I be Ricardo? I like dat name! I like how it sounds." He chewed on the name. "Reeee-CAR-doeeee."

Saro said nothing.

"Awwwww. You won't play fun game with me? Been so long."

Saro did not even uncross his legs. *Drop that accent. It's childish.*

"I am a child."

You are an abomination.

Chaos stretched his eyelids wide, showing the whites. Jewel-toned veins cracked his irises. A dizzying depth telescoped beyond his pupils into a nebula cloud. "And what does dat make you?" he taunted. "A lame bag of farts with a poopy hairstyle?" He drew his knees in and rocked, cackling.

Saro shot his fingers outward. Carpal bones snapped. Tendons extended from the skin, transforming into tentacles. Ten of them snaked toward the man, whipping and slashing at the air.

Chaos pointed and laughed harder. "I made you mad!"

Saro's tentacles thrashed at air, threatening the man's neck.

"Mmmmm," Chaos hummed. He dropped his shoulders. "Let's not fight. If we fight, I will win. If we *know* I will win, then it's no longer fun. So put those away and let's just talk—There. I dropped the accent. Happy?"

Saro's tentacles retracted in a slick *zip*. Tendons and joints realigned. He flexed his phalanges back into place.

"Yay." Chaos crossed his legs, mimicking Saro. He canted his head. "So. How have you been?" He prodded Saro's skin. "You look sick? How's your health? You're not dying, are you?"

Saro grimaced.

"I mean today. Not dying today. I know you're *dying*, but don't do it today. That would be no fun. I'm not looking for a sad time today. Fun only." Chaos spun and gazed at the monitors full of working ArLiFs. "Ooooh. These are new."

Why have you come?

Chaos smiled from one side of his mouth. "You said you were expecting me. You tell me."

I only knew you were coming. I did not know the reason.

"I have reasons?" Chaos scooted to the edge of his chair and bobbed up and down to roll closer to Saro. "Your small-talk skills need work. It is not fun to determine the intention of a visit so quickly. Try again." He pushed himself away and recrossed his legs. He held Saro back with outstretched fingers to indicate he should speak first. "So," Chaos repeated, louder. "How have you been?"

Saro said nothing.

Chaos's face wilted. "Poop! Snot!" He kicked the metal leg of a table. "Since you won't ask, I will tell you how I've been. BORED! Since you locked up the Terror, it's been BORING out there. So, I thought to myself, 'Ricardo?'" He smacked his lips. "Such a good name." He continued, "So, I thought to myself, 'Ricardo? Why does Sr. Mr. Saro have all the fun?' Because here you are, Mr. Poop, playing prison guard to a weapon of mass destruction! Fun job for you, but not so fun for us out here in the cosmos. Sr. Mr. Killjoy should be your name." He tapped his fingers along his lips. "This whole situation has been enticing me, I tell you. I just *have* to attempt a jailbreak to liven things up." He lit up. "By the way!" He leaned over to Saro for a confidential aside. "The Terror's prison is incredibly effective. Can't get in there, and I've tried. It's a class-act layering of goop and magic, and I cannot figure it out for the life of me! I salute you! Rather, I salute your slave children who did all the work!"

Saro interjected, *You have it in your power to destroy whatever you wish without the help of the Terror.*

Chaos twisted a dial on the side of the chair. "Hey, this chair has lumbar support!"

Releasing the Terror does not serve you. Let it be.

Chaos hopped up and down on the chair, which whooshed under his weight. "AND a gas lift!"

Why don't you find another galaxy to menace?

Chaos froze in his chair. "Another galaxy?" He ratcheted his voice upward. "I can't *possibly* go anywhere else!" He ejected himself from the chair and paced while he babbled. "You know what you've done, right? You captured the major opposing force of all of Creation—the High Priest of Destruction and Decay, and—" He cramped his hands to illustrate. "—withheld him! You stole the one who pushes us all forward, the one who makes everything matter, the yin to our yang, the one who makes it all *go go go*—and SHUT HIM AWAY! It's like you captured the theory of relativity itself and sent it to its bedroom without dinner! I *could* go somewhere else, but for what reason? Nothing else is going on!" He flung an arm toward the heavens. "It's like watching paint dry out there! Do you know how boring it is to play with rocks?" He dove onto a tabletop, sending a cup of pens flying. "This is where the show is." He knocked on the tabletop. "Right here. It's an explosion of fun waiting to happen. A show like none other. Top-notch entertainment that pumps the blood—if I had any." He leaned in. "Want to know the sad part? Ready?" He whispered. Then, coming to a crescendo: "Ladies and gentlemen we regret to inform you, due to Sr. Mr. Poop Pants, the Terror Show is—" He yelled, "CLOSED." He pulled at his Afro and paced again. "The Terror Show never travels. The Terror Show never opens. The Terror Show never puts on one single performance, not even a Sunday matinee. But now? Now, I have a front-row seat to the Show's grand opening! No rehearsals, no previews, straight to opening night, baby!" He leapt up and performed side kicks and karate chops. "Ha! HA HA! Why would I leave? The entire cosmos deserves this show. It needs it! It is begging for it! Like the dark needs the light! Like the sound needs the fury! Like a scissor blade needs...the other scissor blade!" He collapsed onto the table. "So, you see? Nothing else in the entire cosmos is working for me because you have the Lord of Carnage trapped here!" He scooted forward and wriggled his fingers. "Tell me, Sr. Mr. Smarty Pants. You've been here for an eon or three; why do you think it's so entertaining on this planet, even with the Grand Sire of Rot and Ruin locked away? Hmm? Why do you think these quasi-intelligent monkeys even stretched their little arms out of the muck, evolving out of microbes and bacteria and lipids, skittering toward sentience with the one goal of making each other miserable? Why do you think it's in the genetic makeup of these apes dragging their knuckles in the dirt to piss a circle around what's theirs—*mine mine mine*—and torture and maim and kill everything outside their territory?" He tapped Saro's temple. "Does this sound vaguely familiar to you?" He smiled with sharp teeth. "Yes! And

I'll tell you why! It's because you trapped the Terror here on this planet! You threw the Arch-Demon of Destruction into the same primordial soup as the evolving microbes on this planet, connected them all with a spiderweb of fungal roots that pulses out messages of 'Find me, free me, you special snowflakes!'—and 4 billion years later: VOILA! GENOCIDAL, HAIRLESS CHIMPS!" He stretched out his arms and stomped. "Time to take this show on the road. I need it out of here. On tour to 70 million galaxies. The Terror Show needs a performance date on every planet, every star, every pit of noxious gas. And until that happens—" He stabbed the table with a long finger. "—this is where I'll be." He shouted in Saro's face. "Because there's NOWHERE ELSE TO GO!" He collapsed into the desk chair. He fiddled with the armrests and mumbled, "Adjustable armrests. This chair has everything."

Saro settled back into a seething roil.

Chaos lifted both feet into the chair and spun himself. "Be mad all you want, poop-face. I'm here to stay. Nonnegotiable. The least you could do is be more companionable."

Saro tried again. *The Terror's imprisonment is not a game. It slaughtered untold numbers—*

Chaos exploded, hammering the armrests. "It is very much a game! And it should be a fun one!"

Saro took a deep breath. *Why make an appearance here today?*

Chaos lolled his head back and forth. "Blah, blah, blah. All questions, no talk. The interrogation has begun!" He chirped, "Well! Two can play that game."

Saro released his breath in a long, slow stream. Patience. Dealing with Chaos required patience.

Chaos rolled his eyes to the back of his head. Pupils and irises clouded into a deep void. Nebulae swirled. "Tell me, Sr. Mr. Fart Bag: Wasn't it enjoyable to suspend yourself in the anticipation of what I would say when I arrived? I'm a cosmic! You can't predict me! Didn't you enjoy *not* knowing what would happen? For once, whatever happened today would not be foreseeable to you. It would be a *surprise*." He raised a finger. A long nail shone in the darkness. "Answer me, and I will tell you why I've come." His teeth extended into knife points. "How long did you wait for me? In days, hours, or minutes—whatever works for you. I'm here for your needs, too."

Saro paused before answering. Chaos waited.

Two hours and twelve minutes.

"Whoa! That's a LOT of time!" He leaned in to Saro and whispered, "Is that a lot of time? It *sounds* like a lot of time. Is it?"

Saro blinked slowly.

Chaos clapped and giggled. "My time! Time for *me*! Time *all* for me! You're the parent I never had! Me-Time is great time!" He dove back into Saro's face. "And *how* did you know I would come?"

Saro crossed arms in front of his chest.

Chaos smacked the table. Pencils and pens and computer mice bounced. "ANSWER! HOW DID YOU KNOW—?"

Because my plans were nearly in place.

Chaos tilted his chin to the ceiling and belly laughed. "You count on me to wreck your plans? How sweet!"

You are inevitable.

"And here I am!" Chaos pushed away from the table and spun wildly in the chair. He rounded his lips. "Ohhhh. These are fun!" He pushed away from the table again, relaunching himself into a rotational frenzy. "Fun! Fun! Almost as fun as—" He slammed a hand down to stop his spinning and leaned far forward to point at the wall of monitors. His clawed fingernail glowed. "Those!"

He sat back, frowning at the ArLiFs.

Then, he blew a raspberry. "Not those. I didn't mean those. Those are boring." He winked. "Right *now* they are. But later, when they grow up, woooo boy! But right now, yawn."

Chaos climbed on the table and spread his arms wide, jutting his chest out. Sucking in a noisy breath, he bulged out his eyes and held in the air for a moment. He glanced down at Saro.

Saro watched him carefully.

Then, Chaos faced the wall of monitors and blew.

The scenes of ArLiFs fishing, drinking coffee, schooling, demolition, building, all cartwheeled to the monitors' edges and disappeared.

Chaos rubbed his hands together. "If we're going to watch the children play, let's watch the fun ones!" He scratched his head in a show of puzzlement. "And where are they today? Any ideas?"

He looked to Saro, who was watching without emotion.

Chaos hummed. "Mmmmm—I know!"

He smacked his hands together. Thousands of new images populated the monitors. Humans. They milled about on the floor of a conference hall, talking and laughing.

Chaos stretched his arms wider. More images extended beyond the monitors, covering the walls and ceiling, all focused on the humans at the conference center.

He stretched his arms until they met behind his back. Images now surrounded them: all four walls, ceiling, floor, tables, chairs.

Then, Chaos plopped into his chair and plunked both feet onto the table. "That's better."

He took in the scene, eyes swirling with galaxies and black holes. He tutted, "What do we have here?" He mumbled to himself, "A gathering of some sort? Is it a conferring and a congratulating festival? I love a festival." He smacked his lips. "Spectacle. Show. Yippee."

The largest banner hanging above the humans who were milling about onscreen read, *Three Years of Discovery: United Earth Alliance Science Conference and Expo*.

"Hmph. I did *not* receive my invitation." Chaos asked Saro, "This is happening now? And just down the street? Right NOW?"

Saro said nothing.

Chaos called out, "It is!" Then he said to himself. "I knew that. I was just seeing if you knew that." He took in the vast numbers of humans. "United *Earth* Alliance? Quaint, quaint. Charming." He clicked his tongue and scanned the people roaming the conference floor. "Where to begin...where to begin..."

Saro waited. He would have to keep waiting. Time was no longer his. He did not have the upper hand. This was a being whose motives adhered only to the laws of chaos. And Chaos was far more powerful. He was the first created, the first to roam the cosmos, the first to understand its realities were flimsy. He could destroy the fabric of Saro's reality with a blink. The reason, he suspected, that Chaos *didn't* was that the void of space was maddeningly monotonous.

Chaos hummed again, then tapped a sharp nail against his pursed lips. "Who shall we watch? Who would be *fun* to watch? Whoooooo? Who who?" He jumped up, pushed the images away, then pulled one tiny corner of the larger image into the center.

A single human magnified onto the wall of monitors.

31

Tony

THE YOUNG MAN BLEW through the doors into the Boston Conference Center wearing a University of São Paulo sweatshirt and the confidence of his great-grandfather. *"Olá, Americanos!* Point me toward the ArLiFs!" A duffel bag swung from his back. Inside was a full album set of Wagner's *Der Ring des Nibelungen* and several odd rings. He smacked a laminated folder in his hands. He was here to put his résumé into the hands of the Mother of ArLiFs.

With encouragement from the nun, Tony had written to Dr. Oliver Daas during his first semester at University of São Paulo to find out exactly what courses he needed to align his credits for a transfer to Boston. Daas responded with enthusiasm. Eventually, their casual correspondence led to an interview with Lucía Santamaría, Director of the Pythia Institute, for an internship.

"ArLiFs?" Tony asked a frowning security guard. The guard gestured to a banner picturing Oliver Daas and Lucía Santamaría. It appeared that Daas fully embraced the appearance of the nutty professor, sporting round-framed glasses, a rumpled coat, and flyaway hair. With an open mouth in mid-sentence, the man looked slightly surprised that anyone wanted to photograph him at all. Lucía, however, knew how to take a photo. She held her chin out, her hands on her hips. Her wry smile said she knew who she was and exactly what she was doing. A sign beneath the photo read: *Keynote Speakers. Exhibit Hall B.*

Tony nodded to the security guard. *"Muito obrigado,* my man."

The front hall was packed, shoulder to shoulder. Young people, older people, all skin colors and accents. It was a global melting pot of chatter and action. Tony dove in.

Tables lined up before him. They exploded with colorful logos and pamphlets designed to ensnare young academics like himself. Universities from all over the world were hawking new programs, all promising a pipeline to UEA careers: oceanography, planetary protection and defense, astrobiology, Temple radiology, Temple architecture, astrophysics, astronomy, geological sciences.

Tony ticked off the disciplines present in the lobby and noted an appalling lack of computer science. "Mistaaake," he warbled. Digital processors would run this new world. They would translate and extrapolate and collate information, show humans how to navigate the uncertainties, guide them to a new understanding of their place in the universe. Tony sang again from the gut, "Where are compuuuuuters?" A few people looked at him. He gave a thumbs up.

After a push from behind, Tony lunged forward. His duffel swayed backward and nearly dragged him off his feet. "Sorry," a female voice said. A woman with stringy blonde hair and black roots had bent forward to collect something that had fallen. Eastern European, Tony guessed her accent to be.

She reached for a rolled-up notebook that had landed at Tony's feet. But he grabbed it first and held it out to her. "No harm—" Tony said.

The reverse side of her notebook was covered in drawings. He had seen those images before. They lived in a dark corner of his mind too frightening to visit. Creatures, symbols, a dark split in the sky. "Heeeyyy," Tony said, upon seeing them.

The woman snatched at the notebook and plunged it back into her furry jacket. "*Odjebi,*" she said before she hurried away.

"Nice to meet you, too." Russian, Tony guessed. And her jacket was either faux fur or roadkill. If Ignácio Cavalcante were alive today, it was only in Tony's judgment in fashion.

He pressed deeper into the conference center.

Amid the tables belonging to the academics, the UEA had staked out their territory with a career booth, promising jobs at the new science center in the South Pacific. Cutting-edge science! Food service! Janitorial! Another UEA booth touted the benefits of joining the world's premier military force, dedicated to planetary peace. "Nooooo, thank you," Tony said to himself. He shifted the duffel bag on his shoulder. *My stuffs,* a voice echoed.

Tony ignored that.

He fanned the folder he was carrying. "Pythia, Pythia, where are you?" He spied, and then followed another sign pointed to Exhibit Hall B.

Standing in his way was a maze of human-sized photos depicting the signing of the United Earth Alliance Charter. World leaders had assembled in San Francisco to pledge funding and staff toward a united response to whatever was "out there." The UEA would accelerate scientific study of the Sleeping One and the undersea city that housed it. Billions toward new floating science labs. Billions more for technological advances to ensure our planet was prepared for anything—especially for if the creature woke.

Tony was here to get in on the action. Not even 20 years old, he already had a résumé packed with accomplishments in the computer sciences. Photorealistic graphics were his specialty, but he also dabbled in hardware. Processors had difficulty keeping up with what he designed, so he had engineered a directory to pull assets from a larger mainframe to deliver to smaller computers on demand.

This was what he knew Dr. Daas and Lucía Santamaría would want. Tony knew he held the key to expanding the ArLiFs.

Uh-oh. Bürschchen *forgets flaws in his work.*

Tony swatted away the voice. He had learned to live with it, to maneuver around its rude interruptions in his life.

Ever since he left the plantation, the old man's obnoxious voice had clung to him like a lingering flu. Sometimes Tony chatted with Waldemar. And Waldemar spoke back, told Tony things about the world, what kind of choices to make, what would benefit Tony best in the long run. At first, the persistent voice had alarmed Tony, and he got evaluated for a psychotic break. Who wouldn't have a psychotic break after finding Ignácio hacked to death in the villa, the same way Lotte had been, upon returning to São Paulo that summer? Tony learned, through therapy, that he had a nasty case of post-traumatic stress disorder, a psychological trauma best treated with persistent exposure to the triggering events. It was the therapist's view that Waldemar's voice was a stabilizing sliver of personality Tony had conjured to guide him through his torn psyche. Tony knew it was more than that, but he was happy for some meds to shut off the voice when it got too loud. Today, it was passably dull.

In addition to Waldemar's voice, Tony still experienced terrifying visions of roots and branches reaching into the earth and tapping into an infinite well of human creativity. It's like the collective wisdom of humanity spoke to him, but he had to put up with the voice of a Nazi as the entry price. The results were hard to dispute. His professors called Tony a genius. If he were a genius, he told himself, why couldn't he rid his game designs of the graphic crevice that had appeared in each one? It looked like a scar had blemished each of his beautiful graphic scenes, and that scar opened onto a bleak universe of swirling stars and gaseous clouds. No one else seemed to mind it, or they thought it was an unobtrusive graphic signature of his, placed there on purpose. But its insistent presence vexed him. He worked to get rid of it, and sometimes Tony could banish it temporarily by deleting random code he discovered and had no memory of writing. However, the crevice reappeared soon after. Perhaps the Pythia people would know what was happening. Perhaps Lucía Santamaría would know how to work with it. Or perhaps Oliver Daas would tell Tony how to incorporate the crevice into his designs. All Tony knew was that he was out of options in Brazil. America was the land of opportunity for Tony Cavalcante. If he could only find Exhibit Hall B.

He ran into a UEA photo maze, a memorial to Manny di Martini: "the hero in our planet's history." Tony had to laugh at that. The UEA saw fit to include a photo of Manny with the *Rosie* crew. It was the islanders, Tony felt, who deserved the respect. The islanders had no choice in the Discovery.

Just then, Tony noticed the nun moving through the crowd. She was followed by students in matching jackets. That woman was difficult to miss. Tony called out, "What up, Sister!" She did not hear him over the racket. He might find her later to say hello, perhaps share a drink. They had become friends of a sort. Over the years, Sister Mary had shown up to campus to ask about Tony's courses and to pry with other questions about his mental state. For a while after the plantation, he wasn't right in the head at all. Sister Mary was the only one who knew what Tony had been through with Waldemar and Saro, then Ignácio.

An intrusive image of Ignácio. Blood everywhere. Flies feasting. Axe left inside the chest cavity.

Tony said to the image, *No.*

Very good, great-grandson.

Right after Tony met the nun, Tony had returned to the villa in São Paulo to discover Ignácio hacked to death in his bed. It had happened within days of returning from dropping Tony at the plantation, just as Waldemar had predicted. A break-and-enter job gone wrong, the police had told him. Tony knew they were wrong. It was Sr. Rocha. "What can we do?" the police had asked Tony. The crime scene was four months old, and the Collapse crime rate was still high. They had bigger fish to fry. So, Tony advertised a reward for information about their driver, but no one responded. Sr. Rocha had disappeared off the face of the earth.

After that grim discovery, Tony refused to return to the villa. He sold it. But, as Ignácio had wanted, Tony kept the plantation. He was in no position to run it, so he made a deal—not with his cousins, but rather with the workers, a minority-shareholding plan for those who agreed to stay on and cultivate the land in Tony's absence. It was a decent passive income for Tony and a bargain for poor families who now subdivided the casa grande into more practical, modern living spaces. The workers even agreed to the upkeep of the Koltz mausoleum. An engraved stone for Lotte was installed, and Waldemar rested there now.

The old man *should* have been quiet. But he was not. His voice crooned:

> *I am so proud*
> *If I allowed*
> *My family pride*
> *To be my guide...*

Tony knew it wouldn't make a good first impression at the conference to respond to him. Talking to Waldemar sounded like Tony was talking to himself. So, Tony let the old man have his Gilbert and Sullivan song for the time it would take Tony to locate Exhibit Hall B— "Where the FUCK is it?"

A few people at Howard Winfield's booth for the Griff Tran Memorial Foundation looked over at him. "ArLiFs?" Tony asked them. A woman with a severe slicked-back bun pointed to Oliver Daas, the man himself. He was locked into an intimate conversation in a side hallway. A security guard stood closeby.

Tony was taken aback. Daas was much taller than he expected. His hands were stuffed deep into his pockets. He looked a little green in the face, but that might be the shade of American skin. So white it glowed.

Tony couldn't hear what Daas was saying, but the man with him—Tony knew him to be Dr. William Ahmadi, an accomplished neurosurgeon and the UEA's public face—spoke louder. Tony heard Ahmadi say, "Singularity."

That stopped Tony's heart for a second.

The technological singularity.

That was a subject no one at his university would touch. It was not an academic subject, more like science fiction, when computers would evolve beyond human intelligence.

Suddenly Tony wondered if his résumé was good enough to recommend him to Pythia. If Daas was casually chatting about a taboo subject like the singularity, would Tony appear provincial to him?

Daas noticed Tony staring and signaled. "Mr. Cavalcante," he called out. "Nice to see you at last! Ms. Santamaría is rehearsing her speech in here." He pointed to a door closeby. "Go on in."

Ahmadi flashed a photogenic smile at Tony. The man looked every inch the part of a Hollywood scientist. "How are you today, young man?" he asked. Tony didn't respond. Americans were creepily tall and took up a lot of space. Tony would have to up his game.

Pants-shitter taken down a few pegs, Waldemar tittered.

Ahmadi returned to his chat with Daas. Ahmadi said, "Give the Constellation a chance for advancements that might contribute to—" His gelled hair swooped an easy six inches away from his smooth forehead.

Tony ran a hand through his unstyled hair pointing in all directions. He slid past the conversing duo and faced the door before him.

Inside he heard a woman in heavily accented English rehearsing a speech. "—asset placements inside the Keyhole Hold have been the key to Claire's neural network growth—"

Tony smacked the laminated folder against his palm.

Waldemar struck up a jazzy cadence:

Und der shark fish, he has teeths, big
Und he wears zem on his face

Inside, Lucía rehearsed. "—a central computer design that allows ArLiFs to select their own assets removes humans from decision making, increasing intelligence—"

Und MacHeath he has übel knife
But das knife, you cannot see!

Tony shed the duffel bag. He reached for the doorknob. He turned it and stepped inside.

He said, with volume, "Lucía Santamaría?"

The woman did not look up from her notes. "Who the fuck are you?"

Tony pushed forward into the room despite his fear. "Dr. Daas invited me here today. My name is Pascual Antonio Aurea Leoncio Cavalcante." He extended the folder to Lucía, who had stopped pacing. "But you can call me Tony."

32

Saro

"Touchdown for Sr. Mr. Saro!"

Chaos scampered onto a table, the dried chicken foot banging against his chest. He stuck out his rear end and gyrated. "Score 1 billion points for the god with the craptastic hairdo!"

Saro held back any thoughts of victory. When Chaos was present, nothing was as it seemed.

Chaos jumped in place. "Did you see the cameo by your bambino? Of course, you did. You must be a proud papa! By far, Lucía represents the most flattering arrangement of your genetic code. Not that your other swamp-dwelling kiddos offered much in the way of competition. Inbred frogs and murderous-plasma lightning? Way to step it up a notch with this human hybrid! Hope she doesn't end up hating your guts like the others did."

Saro recrossed his legs and twitched his foot.

"This calls for a costume change!" Chaos took a wide stance, then shook himself like a wet dog. A dozen faces and hairstyles and outfits and skin colors flickered over his body. When he gave one final shiver, his skin sloughed off a shade of darkness. His hair straightened; the Afro shrank to form a flat driver's cap on top of his head. A sticker on his chest read, *Hello! My name is RICARDO ROCHA.*

He turned to Saro. "You remember this one?" He pulled at the bill of the hat. "You almost gave me away in that plantation driveway. I *let* you have the Cavalcante kid. You remember that. I *delivered* him to you."

Saro spoke up. *There remains a scar in his psyche. A crevice now plagues his computer designs. He was of no use to you.*

Chaos clutched his collar. "My oh my, fancy pants! Are you pulling a fast one? The crack in his psyche was my fault? Oh, hahaha, no! You caged him in a house all summer with your cosmic mind games and expected him to come out smelling like dozens of roses? We both know pure-blooded humans can't hang out with us without losing their marbles. Case in point: Nazi." He gripped his hips and cocked one outward. "No, no. The crack in the boy's psyche was your plan. I haven't figured out how it fits in yet, but it's fun to think about. And what really juiced the kid up was when he opened the box! You practically painted arrows to it and begged him not to open it. He was told not to go into the room, and what does he do? Goes into the room! Opens the box!" He dropped down to sit. Monitors and mice bounced off the table. Chaos dangled his legs off the end. "Seriously, Sr. Mr. Saro. It's *your* dirty fungal children making people-killing boxes of precious network-starter 'shrooms and passing them out like candy. Don't blame *me* for that." He tap-danced on the table. "Besides! The Cavalcante kid is more valuable now that he's broken. Did you see how he can access the Earth network? His dead great-grand-oom-pah-pah is coming in loud and clear. That's a bonus—"

Saro seethed. *It's a vulnerability.*

Chaos frowned. "That kid is staying in touch with his roots. It can't be all bad. *You* must have thought the Nazi helpful. You spent half a century with him."

He excelled at collecting stray artifacts necessary for my work.

Chaos tipped his cap at Saro. "That's not why the Nazi interested you." He shook a finger. "Do not lie to me, Mister. Waldemar had *quite* the missing-children project going on. Your kids had evaded you for eons, but not Waldemar! He had a nose for those rugrats. Speaking of, how *are* the kiddos? Still hating you, I imagine. Built the prison for you, then—" He kissed his fingertips. "—buggered off into the muddiest deathtraps on the planet's surface."

Involving the humans was a necessity.

"Do you *have* to involve them, though? Is it because you're a shadow of what you once were? Losing your vitality by the minute?"

Saro did not reply.

"Sore subject?"

Silence.

"I wouldn't know. I'm immortal." Chaos frisbeed the cap toward the wall of monitors. "Okaaaaaay!" The cap dinged against a monitor rail. The entire room exploded with images from the conference. "Next at bat!" Chaos swayed his head until he found his mark. "Well, well, lookie here! It's the little lady from the land of dried chicken-feet necklaces! The rook in Sr. Mr. Saro's long game! The champion in the religious corner..." Chaos swatted away the images one by one until only a close-up remained.

33

Ashanti

Providence Group protesters ringed the conference center with signs reading, *Faith, not science* and *We don't fear the Sleeping One* and *Prophets before ArLiFs*.

The Apostles of the Singularity also milled about. They dressed in black and white and sang songs about Claire's righteous place as the monarch of reality.

From an inside window, a young woman inspected all of them. She had slipped her jacket off her shoulders to hide the stitching on the back: *Providence Academy, Ingolstadt, Germany*. The dull maroon and silver colors did nothing for her skin coloring, she thought. Besides, she did not like to advertise her school. The people at this conference might have the wrong idea about Providence's dedication to science, thanks to the crowd outside. The protesters were a noisy minority, here for the cameras more than their convictions.

Just then, a man stepped from the Providence Group protesters with a bullhorn. He clinched it between his knees to retighten his strawberry-blonde ponytail and to push blue-tinted spectacles up the bridge of his nose. He was about to get to the business of leading crowd chants. "We are here to show our strength!" he said into the bullhorn. "Twelve united churches of 12 prophets across the globe! A unified faith in the cosmic—"

She disapproved of this performative publicity. Nothing about an aversion to science fit with their beliefs.

A piercing whistle from behind her interrupted her reverie. "Ashanti Oko! Stop straying from the group!"

Ashanti pulled herself away from the window to trudge back toward the students lined up behind the nun.

"Miss Oko," Sister Mary said, "never was it my dream to chaperone a high-school group to a science conference. I'll thank you for not running off like a skittish poodle at every opportunity."

Ashanti shuffled back to the line of students, all with the same jackets with the same stitching on the back. They poked their heads around Sister Mary to goggle at the protesters outside.

"For the sake of—" the nun barked, "Miss Oko! Come here."

Ashanti's hair bounced in time to her footfalls—hers was a light, free-flowing Afro that she had let grow since she left Ghana. If she were going to live among white people in Europe, she wasn't going to hide who she was. She would grow the broadest Afro in all of Bavaria.

Sister Mary grabbed Ashanti's lapels to straighten the girl's jacket. Mary whispered, "Did you recognize anyone out there?"

Ashanti tugged at her sleeves and murmured, "The new American with the red ponytail. His name is Cosmo Donato."

"Anyone else?"

"No." She added, "A church shouldn't be divided like this."

Sister Mary patted her arms. "Every good church is divided. Disagreement is healthy. Return to the line, please."

Ashanti persisted, "The things they're saying about science—"

"And what do *you* think about science?"

Ashanti looked to the four corners of the room. She was certain of her convictions, but the protesters unsettled her.

"Allow me to advise." Mary tweaked the girl's chin to bring her close to her face. "*Never* trust anyone who devalues education. Anyone who wants you dumb and compliant isn't worth following." Mary pulled her even closer. "Use your brain." She let go, then whipped a conference brochure from her tunic. "All right, my precious lambs," she called out to the line of students, eyes roving the conference map. "We are due *in our seats* for Dr. Ahmadi's presentation in 15 minutes. That gives us just enough time to tour the media exhibit. Briefly!" Mary accordioned the brochure and tucked it away. "If anyone sees a full bar, preferably with Irish whiskey, not that Proddie rubbish, then give us a shout. Otherwise, lips closed and follow me."

Just then, a crowd of women in hijabs nearly separated the line of students from the nun, who had already launched toward the media hall. A breakout panel had just been released: *Did the Sleeping One Receive One of the 124,000 Prophets from God?: Islam as a Model Religious Response*. This panel upset Ashanti. Providence should have had a presence here, she thought, *inside* the conference hall, not out there. She noted that no one from Islam had protested the conference, but then again, the Muslims seemed to be processing the cosmic presence with grace.

The students darted after Sister Mary, and Ashanti followed. Mary scampered through the crowd, dashing between gawking tourists and debating scientists, zooming past tables set up to entice young people to new academic programs at universities.

Ashanti noticed an overhead banner reading, *Today's proud sponsor: WINmedia*. Ashanti wondered if Providence would elevate Howard Winfield or Manny di Martini to prophethood. Credit for Discovery had all gone to Manny, but Ashanti reasoned that without Howard, no one would have known about it. She guessed that Providence was likely to choose Manny as their thirteenth prophet because he was so well known. And Howard was still alive. There had never been a living prophet in the Providence Group.

Ashanti could ask her father about how the debate was coming along in the new Providence Senate, where he took up a representative post for the Church of Reverend Lazarus Bethlehem Grieves but she did not want to reopen those lines of communication. Recently, he had moved from Accra to Providence, Rhode Island, to serve on the Senate, leaving Adom in charge of the mega-institution that the Grieves Church had become in Accra. Nkrumah left monthly voicemails for Ashanti, prattling on about how her future was in the Church. She never called him back, not even to find out how much Adom was embezzling from Church funds to fund his cocaine habit. She did not want to explain to her father her work in studying the powder that Ama had brought back from the Great Dismal Swamp. The future, Ashanti came to believe, was in that powder.

As soon as Ashanti had arrived at the Providence Academy in Bavaria, she had coordinated with Sister Mary to access a sample of the powder, then sought permission to use it in the school's biology lab. So far, she was able to confirm that Ama's powder was loaded with fungal spores. Ashanti read books on how to grow them properly. She fashioned a small tent out of a clean plastic bag, then sprinkled a sample of powder on a pan of warm soil. At first, the spores would not root at all. Then, Ashanti thought to mimic the conditions of the Great Dismal Swamp—organic soil mixed with muddy peat, and water with a low pH. That method produced results: at first, white roots that shot out all over the soil, then dozens of bioluminescent fruiting bodies.

Although Ashanti kept the experiment under lock and key, another biology student accidentally found it. The poor girl thought Ashanti was growing psychedelics, so she consumed one of the mushrooms. That stunt bought the biology student a two-month stay at a psychiatric hospital until she stopped speaking with her dead uncle Günter. Administrators demanded that Ashanti destroy the entire crop of mushrooms and discontinue the experiments. No one ever saw the biology student again.

The nun had intervened before the experiment could be trashed. Ashanti's work was, Mary insisted, a matter of international importance. The school decided that Ashanti could retry the experiments after the whole Günter incident had calmed down. In the meantime, Mary convinced Ashanti to sign up for the UEA Conference Field Trip. "Let's air you out," Mary had said. "It will be good for you to see the outside of a library or a lab. You have more academic journal subscriptions than friends, tulip."

Ashanti had agreed to anything that might get her back into the lab faster.

"Fifteen minutes!" Mary had posted herself at the entrance to the media exhibit, tapping each passing student on the head. "I mean it. Fifteen! Not your idea of 15! I am looking at you, Helmut!" A pudgy boy in the middle of the line suddenly found his shoes fascinating.

Inside the media exhibit, Ashanti was surprised to be greeted by Howard Winfield himself in poster-board medium. He was larger than life in the center of the room, raising his arms like a Christ figure bearing gifts for the world. His silver hair was almost as sleek as his shiny suit. He looked just like he did on television, down to the flower in his buttonhole. This poster-board Howard promoted a new 24-hour news network at the Temple Site, offering monitoring of the creature and news analysis on scientific breakthroughs. A few interactive panels nearby promised educational content for classrooms and discerning family viewers. Other panels showed military men and women monitoring screens with the Temple City's spiraling architecture. All this funded, in part, by Howard. *The man has bottomless pits of money*, Ashanti thought, *and won't solve world hunger. What a dick.*

Still, the display of media projects in progress impressed her. These offerings would have induced euphoria in her a few years ago, but now Ashanti viewed them through the lens of how they could help her own work. If the spores Ama had brought back from the Great Dismal Swamp had swiftly killed the tourists she had guided and had caused her own insanity, was it logical to hypothesize that *all* fungi accompanying cosmic beings would have an adverse effect on humans? What of the hallucinations of ancestors reported by Ama and the biology student? Ashanti knew that the fungi coating the *Yuna II* when it had been brought back to the boat was radioactive and extremely dangerous, likely responsible for the gory deaths of the *Rosie* crew and the news reporters. How were the construction crews of the new science labs—and now, it seemed, television crews—near the Sleeping One protected against this danger? Or were they being sent to a gruesome slaughter, a sacrifice for human knowledge like the early chimps shot into space? These were the questions Ashanti wanted answered.

The rest of the media exhibit featured the new WINmedia Movie Studio promotions. A documentary about Discovery Day. An action flick about defeating the Sleeping One in the deep ocean. Those didn't interest her.

Another panel promised Temple Site tourism. *That* interested Ashanti. She read further. *Effective vaccine pending.*

She startled. *Is there a vaccine against the effects of the Temple City in progress?* She withdrew a small notebook from her jacket to document this. These days, she carried a plain notebook like Sister Mary did, no cartoonish white girls on the cover. In it, she kept all her notes about scientific advancements she wanted addressed. She would ask about this vaccine later if no one addressed it in the keynote today.

A sudden noise in the hallway drew her attention. A small crowd had formed near a back entrance.

Ashanti sucked in her breath.

In the center of the crowd was the real Howard Winfield, tall and commanding, flanked by three armed men. The men held back the people seeking handshakes and conversation, but Howard beamed at his followers.

Ashanti wandered closer. She had never seen a celebrity before.

Howard was thinner than she expected. Dark circles under his eyes couldn't be hidden with caked concealer one shade too dark. *Doesn't he have people to help him look right? Or is he such a jerk they let him walk into public like that?* Howard spoke with an authoritarian volume, a deep voice that rattled the bones. He rumbled at his admirers, "How are you? Thank you for coming." Ashanti could tell that his was a voice that triggered an electric response to jump and obey. She ground her teeth at her muscles aching now to do that man's bidding.

The rose in his lapel was a deep champagne, as if stolen from a sepia-toned photo.

Someone in the crowd asked Howard, "What do you say to the Providence Group calling your Artificial Lifeforms a distraction from what should be worshipped? That the cult forming around the ArLiFs is nothing but a bunch of zealots pushing a brand of escapism?"

Howard laughed at that. Ashanti felt that roar of noise in her chest. Howard replied, "I'm delighted that the world is just as enchanted by the ArLiFs as I was when I first met them, but I assure you that I have no control over these cults or these zealots, as you say. They are independent actors who will answer for all their nefarious deeds." He passed a hand before him, as if blessing the questioner. "I thank you for the flattery that I might have that much control over people. If I did, I should cast a spell to make everyone see our new movie: *Polaris II: Return to Temple City!*" The crowd chuckled. Howard pressed his silk tie into place. "Now, won't you join me for Dr. Ahmadi's presentation? The Constellation System is the true star of today's show!"

Ashanti felt the nun's hand on her shoulder. "Would it kill you to stay with the group, pet?"

"Sorry."

Sister Mary tossed a passing glance at Howard. "Why does that man interest anyone?"

Ashanti shrugged. "He kinda changed the world."

"He took a big shite on it, you mean."

Count on Sister Mary for a concise summary. The nun's initial assessment about Ashanti had been right, though: Ashanti did thrive at the new school in Bavaria, and they did eventually develop a friendship. Ashanti had even come to look forward to Mary's sporadic visits to check on her studies. "Extraterrestrial mycology" was what Ashanti told her when Mary asked about her interests.

Sister Mary had raised an eyebrow at that. "Excellent choice, dearest."

Now, Mary was ushering them into a larger hall where hundreds had assembled to hear Dr. William Ahmadi unveil the floating science lab in the South Pacific. The Constellation System, they called it. Built and run by the UEA, with funds from Howard Winfield.

It was where Ashanti wanted to work.

She followed her school group to their row of reserved seats near the front. Other school groups occupied other rows in jackets with better color combinations.

Ashanti felt the heat of their stares. Apparently, it wasn't well known that some in the Providence Group wanted to be involved in the UEA's science mission. Ashanti tried to appear indifferent, but she knew she was attracting the most attention. Her classmates were all white. Being a cultural ambassador for her religion *and* her race sucked.

One of the students from Korea tried to get Ashanti's attention with small waves. His stare didn't convey judgment, but instead, fascination. Ashanti ignored him.

The lights dimmed.

Dr. Ahmadi took the stage to thunderous applause. His straight white teeth in the spotlight nearly blinded her. Americans' teeth looked unnatural. Still, Ahmadi had a charisma about him. The way he nodded sagely to his audience. The way he tilted his head thoughtfully as he held for applause. She heard a titter among the girls in all the rows behind her.

As if reading her thoughts, Sister Mary said to her, "Whatever works, pet."

Ashanti frowned. She hated it when she did that.

Dr. Ahmadi held out his hand to quiet the crowd, then boomed, "Welcome to the United Earth Alliance's Age of Science!"

34

Saro

CHAOS CRAMMED A HANDFUL of popcorn into his mouth, most of which cascaded down his chin and onto the floor. "I spy with my little eye another victory for Sr. Mr. Saro! Now, things are getting good!"

Saro cracked his neck. *This is getting tedious.*

Chaos tossed the box, raining popcorn over his shoulder. "Are you not having fun?"

No.

Chaos dove onto the table, sending a monitor and another pen cup flying. He landed with a skid in front of Saro. "Sr. Mr. Saro would like to see the point of all this? Approaching three hours of waiting has him cranky?" Chaos toyed with Saro's ruby choker. "Okay. I'll get to the point if you say 'please.'"

Saro narrowed his eyes. *Please.*

"Say *pretty* please."

Saro shot a handful of tentacles into Chaos's face, sending him backward.

Chaos bounced up. He flicked a finger.

Every ray of light in the room arced. Sound reversed into an incomprehensible muddle.

Chaos's skin radiated a bioluminescent aquamarine. His body flung itself backward onto the table.

More light focused onto Saro's hands. His tentacles sucked back into his fingers.

Sound realigned. Lights returned to normal.

The scene had reset itself.

Saro hissed through gritted teeth. A time reset like that was not easy on his dwindling life force. Only those as powerful as Chaos could do them.

Chaos casually lay on his side. "I thought we had agreed not to fight. You are in no condition to take on a baby hamster, much less a god of chaos."

Saro's ruby choker flashed. Color pulsed beneath his skin. He slowed his breathing.

Chaos quickly bounded onto his feet. "Showtime!" He anchored himself and shook himself all over. Faces and costumes flickered by the hundreds. When he righted himself, he was a bulky man dressed all in black with a balaclava pulled over his head. "Boo, *amigo!*"

He flopped onto another rolling chair, adjusting the armrests and lumbar support. "Did you know I spent five hours trapped in a car with your daughter in Mexico? They were among the most trying hours in my existence, and that's saying something. I wanted so badly to show her what I really was, but she wouldn't have taken it well." Chaos hopped in place in the chair, testing its cushion. "You should have seen her after she got the word about who dear old Daddy was! There wasn't a bag of drugs big enough to handle *that* news. Little did she know how ugly you were. It might have killed her right then and there."

Saro collected himself. The time reset had drained him. He would need to be still for a moment. Jeweled colors glimmered under his skin. The ruby choker fed the color stream in pulses of energy.

Chaos spun around to take in the walls of images. He pulled at the mask and spat out fuzz. "*Pft pft pft.* Look at all the humans, assembling to hear the great news about the island in the sea!" He pointed to the edge of the images. Lucía had slipped into the exhibit hall and leaned on the wall. "There's your offspring, sneaking in the back." He pointed to the other side. Daas kneeled before a toilet. "There's her partner, Dr. Daas, barfing in the gentleman's room. So nervous about that presentation. What will happen?"

Saro felt a catch in his throat.

"I see the Cavalcante kid in the audience. He looks happy. Got himself an internship with Pythia, I'd say. And I see the Oko kid. She's got her guard dog, the nun right next to her. Everyone's in place." Chaos bit at his long nails, eyes racing over the images. "You're right. This is getting tedious. It's time to move this show along." He leaned back and grinned at Saro.

Saro steadied himself. He had no idea what to expect.

Chaos held him in a tender gaze. The eyeholes in his mask revealed nothing but a bleak void swirling with space rocks and gasses. "I never like to predict how things will go, but this?" With long fingers, he pulled at the images until he found what he wanted. "This might be the best one yet."

35

Mary

LATELY, MARY HAD BEEN thinking about Ireland. She missed the wind that took the top of her head off with its bracing chill. She missed her mother. She missed the simple life of tending the animals and the garden. She missed the reading and learning. She missed the cottage on the bog, passed on to her by the Nazi after his death, bless him.

Mary had returned to the cottage few times in the two years since ownership reverted to her. Waldemar hadn't touched it since that spring day in 1937. So, Mary paid for some basic upkeeping. She had the weeds and the wildlife cleared. She added electricity. Climate control. Plumbing. She had even hired a few locals to keep the place secure from the vandals and the morbidly curious. Many still wanted to see the sight where Ailish Finnegan, Providence Prophet of Suicidal Madness, had lived and died. A myth is a strong force among intelligent life, Mary knew. People needed their stories.

Mary decided she would visit there after she deposited these high schoolers back in Bavaria. She would check in on the recent improvements. Check on the box. It should be secure in the rafters. Until it was needed.

Her birthright, she remembered calling it. Since it came back into her possession, she hadn't called it that. Tony had believed the same about it. Mary had watched him grow into a man to prepare to take his place in the world. His talents have blossomed. Same for Lucía. And Ashanti. And the others. Each had their mistaken ideas of what would make them whole. Mary had tried to help them see otherwise. It was her journey as well.

Humans. Funny creatures. Possessive about all the wrong things.

She patted Ashanti Oko on the knee. The kid's face had been in a perpetual frown since the Providence protesters had shown up outside the conference hall. But Mary had wanted her to see this presentation today. She wanted the child to see what she had been working for since the kid left Ghana.

Dr. Ahmadi paced the stage. He began, "First, an introduction!" He held for minor applause. "The UEA has undertaken an extraordinary process to decide who will be the first scientists to take up residence at the new Constellation System's undersea lab over the Temple Site. Competition was fierce! Over 1,000 applications! Today we will meet the first *two* scientists who will live at the station. Let's see who our selection committee chose!" He flashed a smile which, Sister Mary felt, failed to mask his disappointment that one of the finalists wasn't him. "Our first finalist is a 3D model expert out of New Delhi. He's designed an impressive new software system that intends to map the Temple City in all its intricacies. Ladies and gentlemen, I'm happy to present the first resident of the UEA Constellation System: Dr. Krishna Rai!"

A slight man on the front row briefly stood for applause. He gave a quick wave to the crowd and planted himself back out of sight. *Shy one*, Sister Mary thought. They only met for a moment years ago. He hadn't needed much guidance from her. He was singularly focused and wise to the unpredictability of cosmic elements, unlike the others in that regard.

Ahmadi continued, "Our second finalist comes from the University of South Wales in Sydney! She's a doctoral candidate in mycology—"

Ashanti perked up.

"—with a proposal to study the fungus collected by drones from the Temple City—"

Ashanti couldn't contain herself. "Oh. Oh."

Sister Mary smiled. It was really this moment she wanted Ashanti to see.

"Ladies and gentlemen, please give a round of applause to Dr. Kiri Mahuta!"

A giant woman from the Pacific Islands cast a long shadow on the stage. A few in the audience murmured. She wore the traditional face tattoo, the *moko kauae* that denoted her ancestral powers, under her lips.

Kiri frowned at the audience reaction.

Stiff upper lip, pet, Mary thought. *Show them what you have.*

Kiri settled into a coy smile.

Never let them degrade your confidence.

Ashanti blurted, "Can I meet her? Do you know her? What do you know? Is there time afterward? How long can I talk with her?"

"Ashanti Oko, I am pleased to hear your enthusiasm, but we have an entire presentation to get through, so settle yourself—"

Just then, a student behind Ashanti tapped her shoulder to pass a note written on a scrap of a conference map. Ashanti unfolded it. It read: *Meet me after?*

Both Ashanti and Mary turned. The boy from Korea waved again. Ashanti made a sour face and flipped the note into Mary's lap. The nun pinched the note and stood. The ends of her headpiece splayed wide on her shoulders like a cobra hood. The kid ducked. *He better*, she thought. She crumpled the note and tossed it into the aisle so he could see where it landed.

Before Mary sat, she noticed where Lucía was camped out in the back. When they made eye contact, Lucía shuffled her feet and lowered her gaze. *She's nervous*, Mary thought. *I hope she's sober.*

Mary scanned the room before reseating herself. Tony was in the audience somewhere, she knew. Oliver Daas had to be close. All her chickens together.

Howard Winfield lingered in a side door, backlit to disguise his identity. *Here to see what his money bought him*, Mary supposed.

Lucía set her jaw and pointedly looked away from Howard's shadow. *That one sure can hold a grudge*, Mary remembered.

A mousy woman approached Howard and whispered something to him. He nodded, then whispered something in return. Mary felt a shock of electricity at the sight of the woman, a lightning flash that burned a path all the way to Griff Tran in a hospital bed.

—a parting gift, from me to you—you will see what I see—

The woman nodded at Howard and walked away. The thread fizzled.

Interesting, the nun thought. *I haven't seen a network thread that strong in ages.*

From the stage, Ahmadi announced, "I know you haven't assembled here today to see my shining face." Many girls in the audience chattered. Sister Mary rolled her eyes. "So, shall we get to the presentation?"

An overhead animation began. Ahmadi said, "First, let's take a quick look at the object of study: The Temple City and its infamous resident: The Sleeping One."

On the screen, schematics rotated to show the Temple City on the floor of the Pacific. The animation flew through the site to show its walls and buildings. Ahmadi supplied the narrative. "On the ocean floor, at just over 3,000 meters below the surface, the Temple City is laid out in a precise rectangle that measures roughly two square kilometers."

At the center of the city, a temple spiraled up from the ocean floor. Ahmadi said, "Rising about 830 meters high, among a variety of structures, is what we call the Temple, due to some early clues that the structure was the object of some ceremonial meaning to the builders." The animation showed a transparent shape inside the temple: The Sleeping One. "Here is our resident," Ahmadi said. "An approximate rendering of its position and size, though we can't know for certain." It showed the figure sitting on a throne, tentacles dangling from its head, heaped about on the temple floor.

"Now," Ahmadi said. "We've determined that the crash of the *Yuna II* possibly broke a seal on the Temple, releasing a toxin that has now been contained to within 500 meters of the Temple City's borders." A new diagram appeared, marking a boundary on the ocean floor and overhead. "The UEA has forbidden any human or mechanical presence within that 500-meter zone," Ahmadi said. "We call it the Exclusion Zone: nothing in or out."

The animation overhead vanished.

"With that in mind," Ahmadi said, "let's get a look at the labs!"

The crowd applauded. "Ladies and gentlemen," Ahmadi announced, "the United Earth Alliance is proud to present the Constellation System! Funded by generous corporate support from Lelee and Pinchas Stern, WINmedia, the Griff Tran Foundation, and many others—"

On several overhead screens, new schematics appeared. The press at the side of the stage surged closer. Ashanti scooted forward in her seat. The audience was rumbling. Ashanti whispered, "How will they address the radiation?"

Mary tapped her knee for patience.

"As you can see, the Constellation System is comprised of three levels suspended vertically above the Temple City," Ahmadi said. Animation blinked along with his narrative. "The surface level: Temple Star." This was a sphere with radiating arms. "The mid-level: the Polaris Lab." This was a disc-shaped level suspended by cables from the surface-level sphere. "And the deepest level: Equinox Deep." This was a small box suspended above the Temple, just outside the Exclusion Zone. "The entire site," Ahmadi said, "is a human-made system for study, learning, and long-term residence at the isolated site of the Temple City in the South Pacific."

Mary glanced back at Lucía. She was chewing on her lips and hugging herself with crossed arms.

Animation zoomed in on the surface sphere. It looked to Mary like a giant, floating ball bobbing in the ocean with metal arms radiating outward. "This is a state-of-the-art biosphere," Ahmadi continued. "At 330 meters in diameter, it's the height and width of the Eiffel Tower. Ten stories will rise above the ocean's surface, and ten stories will be submerged. Residencies are planned for 100 scientists in this sphere. Tourists and educational groups will be permitted with UEA approval."

Ashanti shifted in her seat.

Mary zoned out as Ahmadi described the sphere's construction, but she caught the gist. A prefabricated sphere would be shipped to the site in halves, then assembled and welded on site. She watched the animated boats and planes docking and landing on the radial arms. "It's a clean-energy site," Ahmadi said, "powered by solar panels and underwater turbines. Fresh water is available to residents via the rain-capture system at the top of the sphere and desalination devices at the base. Two state-of-the-art energy islands, named Venus and Mars, provide the real power. It's also where our support staff will live year-round!"

The animations dove inside the sphere. "Inside Temple Star, hydroponic crops will be grown on site, and an off-site aquaculture farm will provide residents fresh seafood," Ahmadi said. "When complete, Temple Star would provide guests with fresh air and water, self-grown food, electricity, video conferencing, internet, and phone."

Sister Mary's brain throbbed. At the back, Lucía studied the schematics, nodding slightly. At the side door, Howard was gone. Lucía seemed to breathe easier without him in the room.

Ashanti was holding her breath as she took in the design. Mary whispered, "Breathe, pet." The kid was beside herself with excitement. *Well,* Mary thought, *good. She's worked hard for it.*

The overhead animations shifted to the labs suspended underneath the sphere. "The Temple Star and the two below-surface labs are all supported by ballast spheres and cables. These ballasts also serve as beacons and emergency ports for deep-sea submersibles exploring the site." Animated minisubs launched from the bottom of the sphere. "Let's visit the second level: the Polaris Lab."

The animated minisub traveled into the dark ocean. "The Polaris Lab is suspended by cables from the sphere at a depth of 1,250 meters. That's halfway to the Temple City. A journey by minisub will take a little over two hours." Ahmadi turned to the audience. "Hey, everyone! This is where Dr. Rai and Dr. Mahuta are headed!"

Rai sunk in his seat. Kiri stared blankly.

Ahmadi continued, "The Polaris Lab is disc-shaped, offering almost 1,400 square meters of labs, dorms, and human support facilities. Only trained scientists will be permitted at this level."

Sister Mary imagined Dr. Rai down there all alone until the program opened to support more staff. Dr. Mahuta would be first. Hardly a chatterbox. It would be enough to drive anyone insane. She hoped Rai had prepared for that.

These visions of the future were abnormal for her. Her abilities lay in the mental trick of seeing what humans held back from her. But lately, she had failed to find herself in any of these visions. She had assembled the best team she could, assured they were educated and as aware of the larger picture as their minds could tolerate. Lucía could tolerate the most information. Of course. Her Lucía. What was there for Mary to do now but enjoy the fruits of her labor? And if Saro was done with her, content to snip her strings and allow her to fall away from this life? She held the box in reserve. Her real birthright, her team—they would not remain defenseless against him or whatever he may have planned for them.

The animation now showed the interior of the Polaris Lab. The three stories seemed to travel on a continuous loop. Sister recognized it as a Lucía signature design. This was the MC Escher quality to her work: how humans move through a representation of infinite space.

"This is special!" Ahmadi noted. "Have you ever seen an impossible staircase in art? It forever extends upward but runs in a closed loop. Well, this is a variation on that theme: a closed loop of three floors. Imagine living at the Polaris Lab! You could go for a jog in the hallways, travel all three floors without climbing one step, and end up back where you started by only going forward!" The audience clapped. "This design really caters to the human occupants, who might go stir crazy from living in a lab the size of a warehouse for three months. Such an advancement will allow more time for the scientists to stay safely at the lab, more time to focus on their work, more access to the Temple Site's samples and visuals. And this idea was submitted by an anonymous civilian! Brilliant!"

Sister noticed Lucía wasn't receiving any credit for this design. Was that intentional? If so, whose intention was it? Had Lucía had enough attention with the ArLiFs?

Ashanti leaned back and crossed her arms. "What about the radiation?"

"Let the pretty boy finish, tulip."

Ahmadi asked, "And how will scientists safely access the Temple Site? Let's travel to the third level to find out!"

Animations again showed a minisub launching from the base of the second level, following cables even deeper into the ocean. "You'll notice," Ahmadi said, "from the surface to the bottom, humans will travel in a closed system of pressurized environments. At no time is there a requirement to pause for the body to acclimate to the new environment. At these levels human life normally cannot be sustained."

The animated minisub docked at the deepest lab in the Constellation System, a box suspended above the spire of the Temple. "Equinox Deep," Ahmadi announced. "Another hour's journey takes our scientists 2,500 meters below the surface of the ocean. This third level hangs right over the Temple, just outside the Exclusion Zone."

Ashanti leaned in again. "They can't possibly understand the effects on the human body at those levels. Not yet. It's not safe."

"Is that your opinion after completing high-school oceanography?" Mary asked.

Ashanti sat back with a sour look.

"Equinox Deep," Ahmadi continued, "would be the smallest level in the system at only 130 square meters and no overnight facilities. At that depth, only eight-hour stays would be safe. No sleepovers, Dr. Rai! Dr. Mahuta!"

Both smiled halfheartedly.

Ahmadi said, "Now, this lab will house mostly computers, scanners, and cameras for data collection and monitoring. Notice the lights and cameras welded to the bottom? That's the source for Howard Winfield's new 24-hour Sleeping One news channel!"

The audience erupted into applause. They looked around for Howard, but he wasn't in the room.

"The lab," Ahmadi said, "will have two airlocks for submersible travel to collect samples. Pilots would be required to carry a license to navigate deep water and be trained in Temple City safety regulations."

The audience fidgeted, murmuring.

"Upon seeing these schematics, myself," Ahmadi said, "I had two serious questions." He held up two fingers to the audience. "One: how would this site be secured? Two: how would we ensure the safety of our scientists against the known effects of the Temple City?"

"Finally," Ashanti said.

Another image replaced the Constellation site schematics: a sea wall extending all the way around the Temple Star at a distance. "Perhaps you've heard of the new UEA military?" Ahmadi asked.

The audience burst into applause.

"Here, they will patrol the Temple Star with helicopters, high-speed boats, high-speed subs, underwater radar, and a perimeter detection unit," Ahmadi said. "The UEA will have the authority to fire upon trespassers, stun pilots, and tow the craft to safety."

Mary raised her brows. Her headpiece wrinkled.

Onscreen, a second image appeared: an inoculation schedule and a digital passport.

Ahmadi continued, "Further, the UEA's research teams are now working on a vaccine against the most egregious effects of the Temple Site. We call them 'counteragents.' They are in human trials now."

The image shifted to a scientist in a UEA jumpsuit seated at a vaccine kiosk. "A UEA passport will be required for all visitors to the Constellation System, which also requires registry to a database to monitor health effects and counteragent boosters. In addition, scientists will be required to pass a background test and a psychiatric evaluation—"

36

Saro

CHAOS BREATHED IN SARO'S ear. Cosmic dust sprayed from his mouth as he spoke. "The players are all on the board. Do you see them?"

Saro slowed his breathing. This was it. Chaos was ready to make a move.

"I know you see them," Chaos continued. "You've been working for many, many revolutions around the sun to mark the occasion when they would all come together like this. Working, working, working. All to do your bidding." Chaos poked Saro's ear. "Did you believe I would let you have your fun all alone?"

Saro twitched his foot. His ruby choker glowed. His skin shivered with iridescent color.

Chaos breathed, "Did you see *my* player on the board?"

Saro stopped twitching.

"That player will remain hidden. For now." Chaos giggled. "I've been busy, too. Oh, pleeeeease. Tell me you've noticed."

Saro focused on the images. Had he noticed? No. He was too focused on his own humans, their placement, their objectives, their preparation—

"Ohhhh," Chaos whispered. "You *hadn't* noticed." He patted his hands together. "What a surprise! I love surprises!"

Chaos assumed another wide stance and shook all over. Faces and outfits flickered like cards shuffling. They landed on an islander with a wide face and magenta-painted lips. A tropical flower was tucked behind his ear. His outfit was an eye-aching fuchsia, and his sarong was knotted at the waist. His eyes enlarged and clouded, then went completely black. He spoke with a breathy whisper. "This costume was from the first day on the sandbar with Manny di Martini, hours from revealing the truth of the snoozing beast on the ocean floor." Chaos twirled. "This one might be my favorite. I just *had* to show you." He curtsied. "When I showed up, Manny was so desperate. He *believed*. He just needed a little *direction*." He twiddled his fingers under his chin.

Saro scooted back.

Chaos bent over to look him in the eyes with the swirling voids in his sockets. "I've been there since day one. And now, I'm ready for my first move." Chaos smiled a row of sharp teeth. "Are *you* ready?"

Saro flexed his fingers. He tensed his legs.

Chaos's eyes rotated like black holes, pulling light from the room, darkening it like an oncoming storm. His eyes shone with stars from deep space. He turned to the images of the humans before them and spread his arms wide.

Then, Chaos screeched, "I TAKE YOUR QUEEN!"

37

Lucía

THIS WAS WHAT SHE saw from the back of the conference hall.

Dr. Ahmadi onstage, the lights bright.

The shadow of the nun in the audience, near the front, struggling to stand.

For a moment, tension and confusion.

Then, the nun fell into the aisle.

One of the kids seated next to her cried out and reached for her.

Mary got up, hunched over. She reeled about, blind. People flew out of their seats.

A few overhead lights flickered on. The brightness caused the audience to blink.

Now, Lucía could see the blood streaming from Mary's eye sockets. The nun turned in her direction. "Lucía," she murmured.

Lucía could hear Mary as if they were connected with a taut, vibrating wire. Lucía felt the word in her bones, vibrating there.

Several of the girls behind the nun started screaming. A boy from Korea jumped forward to scoop Mary under the arms, to help her stand, but Mary pushed him aside. "Lucía," the nun repeated.

Again, a shock fried Lucía's nerves. She was feeling each of the nun's words like an electric prod.

Blood filled Mary's mouth and flowed down her chin. She coughed. Blood sprayed.

An African girl called out, "What's happening?" She was braver than the others. She stepped over another girl who had fainted.

The nun weaved down the aisle toward Lucía. People scattered everywhere, overturning chairs and tossing programs. Mary reached out blindly, feeling her way forward. "Lucía," she gurgled.

That shock again.

Blood trickled from Mary's ears, soaking her headpiece.

A humming in Lucía's blood.

Lucía ran to her.

By now, audience members were pushing each other over to back away from the nun.

The giant Māori woman pulled smaller kids from the ground who were in danger of being trampled.

The new Pythia intern, Tony, leapt over the back of his chair and scooped Mary's elbows from behind to support her. He spoke to her in her ear.

Lucía kept running. *Why was this aisle so long?*

Krishna Rai scooted alongside the edge of the stage to get around a tangled mess of people. He asked Tony, "Is there something I can do?"

The African girl sobbed, "What's happening?"

From the stage, Ahmadi called out, "Is there a medical doctor in the audience? Jesus!"

Blood soaked the front of Mary's tunic. "Lucía," she repeated. She tripped over her scapular and collapsed to the carpet. "Lucía."

Buzz buzzzzz. We are connected.

"I'm here."

Lucía's warm hand under Mary's cold neck. Another hand reached out for Mary's bloody one.

Mary cried out through blood in her mouth, "Puppet strings cut!"

Lucía's hand was hot now, shaking. In a low voice she asked, "Saro?"

The nun searched the room wildly with blind eyes.

The African kid was at Mary's ear. "What's happening? What's happening?"

Lucía offered a solid voice. "Mary? Mary. What do I do?"

The nun said, "Return to the beginning." She seized and spasmed. It was difficult to hear her now. "Return to the bog. The cottage. The world—"

Lucía arranged Mary's tunic to cover her feet.

The nun strained with reddened teeth and black gums. "Tipperary County." She struggled to breathe. "Back to the bog. The world. It's there."

"I understand, Mary. I will get it. It will be safe."

Mary's grip loosened. Her eyes unfocused. "It was you, pet. It was you."

"What, Mary? What was me?"

Mary coughed. Blood sprayed. Her breath rattled. "My real birthright—It was you."

Mary's hand fell away.

38

Saro

SARO SUMMONED THE HIGH-PITCHED noise from a grinding fan with an overworked motor and blasted it at Chaos. *SKREEEEEEEEEE.*

Chaos roared, "I took your queen! I took—"

Saro levitated, shooting tentacles from fingers and feet.

"Ooooh! I knew you cared! I *knew* it! You've gone *native*! You got attached to the nun! Look at you! You're *angry*!" Chaos got in Saro's face. "How far gone are you, Sr. Mr. Saro? I knew you were far gone enough to take a human name. Saro. What a laugh! Have you forgotten your real name? God of Light, Spawn of Stars, the Elder—"

Bright colors swarmed in angry patterns under Saro's skin. His choker fired streams of radiation in all directions.

"Careful with that!" Chaos said, waving his arms. "These computers cost an arm and a—"

Twenty tentacles flew at Chaos. Ten wrapped around his torso. Ten more encased his head.

Saro grunted and twisted, separating Chaos's head from his body. Saro slung the head with the magenta lips at the wall of monitors, where it bounced and landed at the base of the wall with a *thunk*.

Saro wheezed. Tentacles retracted.

A single spark ejected from an overhead light, which swung by a frayed cable.

Saro looked all around.

Behind him, a door opened.

A ray of light briefly lit the Amphitheater. Light bounced and refracted inside the gems in Saro's choker.

A man entered, pushing a trash bin ringed with a caddy full of paper towel rolls and spray bottles. A bucket and mop rode a platform at the front. The hulking contraption careened into a table.

The door wheezed to a close.

The man checked the room. He squatted and squinted. "Who's in dere?" He guffawed.

Saro growled and sent the tentacles after him.

Chaos shoved the cart down the steps toward Saro, then climbed the walls like a spider, cartwheeling on the tables and kicking away monitors and desk supplies. "Whee! Now, we're having fun!"

Saro shot tentacles at him, snatched him, flipped him upside down, then stuffed him into the rolling trash bin. Then, Saro hurled the trash bin against the wall. The wall exploded. Behind it was deep space—colorful planets ringed with deadly gases. The trash bin sailed into the void. Chaos howled with delight.

Saro sealed the wall.

Silence.

Behind him, the door opened again.

Two parallel beams of light briefly lit the Amphitheater. Ignácio Cavalcante's Mercedes crashed through the doors, roaring over the tables, grinding its gears. Dust and debris rained down. Sparks lit the Amphitheater.

The wrecked car honked twice. The driver's door groaned open. Chaos stepped out and tipped his driver's cap. "Guess who!"

Saro grabbed at the floor. He whipped the concrete like a rug. The floor rippled. The edge extended outward then curled into a loop, with the desks, chairs, and computer monitors arcing overhead.

The walls bulged outward, and the ceiling rounded. The air collapsed, producing a thrumming sound.

"Now, we're talking!" Chaos cheered. He rode a ripple in the floor like a wave, surfing into the underside of its crest. He batted more tables and monitors into the suspended gravity, sending them all reeling and crashing into each other and the bulging walls.

Saro pulled monitors from the front wall and flung them at Chaos. Each of them sliced Chaos into a smaller segment. Two dozen versions of Chaos rode the wave of office furniture, tumbling and spinning. "Wheee!"

Saro flipped the scene, turning the room like a snow globe, sending Chaos on another ride. Then, Saro punched the floor. Iron beams collapsed, squaring off in a downward ramp.

Chaos rode down, hollering all the way.

Saro piled concrete and iron beams on top of him, pressing him down into the earth.

Another silence.

Saro retracted his tentacles. His choker glowed weakly.

He breathed. He grasped a table for support.

The room was a mess of drywall and fried computer monitors. Electricity sparked from the ceiling lights. Water sprayed from the fire-suppression system.

The quality of light shifted.

Every ray of light in the room arced. Sound reversed. The floor opened back up. Iron beams stretched back into place. The floor whipped and curled, then straightened. Tables and monitors righted themselves. Ignácio's car reversed out of the room. The wall sealed behind it. The side wall opened. A trash bin cruised from deep space and landed at the door.

"This has been a significant improvement over playing with rocks, and I thank you."

By the door, Chaos held a mop upright. The trash bin skittered backward and stopped by his feet. He plunged the mop into the caddy. He shook all over, changing back into the Ghanaian fisherman. The dried chicken foot thumped against his chest.

Saro crumbled to the floor.

Chaos strode over to him. He knelt, then slapped him across the face. Hard. Once, twice. Teeth fragments flew out of Saro's mouth. "That's for putting me in a trash can."

Saro shot a handful of tentacles around Chaos's throat.

Chaos raised an arm. Skin melted from his hand. Bones sharpened into a sleek edge of hot metal. He sliced off Saro's tentacles. *THWAP!*

Saro flipped over and shot tentacles from his other hand.

"No, no," Chaos said. "We're done here." He bent the light again. Sound muffled and congealed.

Saro's tentacles reflected backward, wrapping around his own throat.

"Stay down," Chaos said. "You're weak." He knelt and spoke into Saro's face. "You've gone native with these monkeys, and you forget who you are. You're *better* than this. You got attached to your work and forgot some basics. This was just an opening move, a taste of my game before things really get going. Be a good sport."

Saro gasped for air.

Chaos slapped him again. Saro spat another tooth. "Stop that," Chaos said. "You don't need air."

Saro flailed his arms, suffocating.

"Oh, please. This is pathetic." Chaos let go. Tentacles fell away from Saro's throat in a limp pile. "You're tired and need a nap. Want a juice box?"

Chaos summoned a heap of juice boxes. They rained down onto Saro and buried him.

Chaos bounded up. "What a mess." He dug his hands into his hips and looked around. The West African accent returned. "What will Miss Lucía say?"

Saro shivered. Juice boxes tumbled.

"Only one thing left to do." Chaos clapped. "Clean it up! Clean it up!" he sang. "And I'll turn your television show back on, Sr. Mr. Pansy Pants." He flexed his fingers. Monitors flew to the wall and refastened. A spark ignited and all 24 blinked back to life. ArLiFs repopulated the screens.

Chaos looked around and huffed. "Welp!" He flapped his arms to his thighs. "It looks like this game done tuckered you out." He plodded over to where Saro lay under the mountain of juice boxes. He flicked a finger, and they tumbled away.

Chaos climbed down next to Saro and pulled a fleck of drywall from his Afro. "Are we friends? I hope so. Did I say it was nice to see you? It is." He touched Saro's choker. "So ingenious to power yourself by using the precious gems of the planet. Formed deep in the earth by the lava pit your children robbed to make those prison rocks. What *power* is in those things!" Chaos tapped the ruby. "Creative. Just like your kind to be inventive." He flipped to his belly, interlacing his fingers under his chin and kicking his legs behind him. "I always admired your race. Such an industrious tribe." He smoothed Saro's white Afro and arranged his black fringe. "This really is a repellent hairstyle. Even so, I hope you know that I respect you." Chaos kissed Saro on the forehead with a loud smack. "Gotta run. My game pieces are already in motion." He touched Saro's nose with a bioluminescent fingertip. "Rest up. I don't want you to miss it."

Saro watched Chaos skip up the steps to the exit. At the top, he paused; then turned around.

He tramped back to Saro. "I'm taking this." He yanked a desk chair by the armrest and clunked it up the stairs. *Ka-chunk. Ka-chunk.* "Nighty night!"

Chaos closed the door behind him.

Onscreen, at the front of the room, the ArLiFs went about their tasks.

Saro rolled over and collected his severed tentacles. Oily black liquid oozed from an amputated limb. He held it to his chest and slowed his breathing. He spat drywall and car-tire rubber. Every part of him ached.

Onscreen, inside the open air church on Keyhole Island, Claire instructed a group about how riddles work. "A riddle is a question intended to cause confusion. The answer could have a double meaning, and it's good for a chuckle. Let's try one!" She called out, "I can fly but have no wings. I can cry but have no eyes. Wherever I go, darkness follows. What am I?"

An ArLiF replied, "A cloud!"

"Good!" Claire said. "You have it!"

Saro rested. He pulled his energy inward. Chaos had dealt significant damage, as expected. Saro would have to heal himself. And new plans were needed.

Onscreen, Claire called out, "Here's another! I'm a seed with three letters in my name. Take away two, and I still sound the same. What am I?"

"A pea!" A few ArLiFs giggled.

Saro spat more drywall. He replayed Chaos's words in his mind, checking and double-checking everything he had said.

Onscreen, Claire announced, "Here's a harder one! I may seem real, yet I am not. Once you're gone, I'm often forgot."

The ArLiFs mouthed her question to themselves but had no answer.

Claire added, "Here's a hint! Time in here stretches and shrinks. It all depends on how you think."

The ArLiFs talked among themselves. They were stumped.

Saro smiled with broken teeth.

Claire said, "Dreams! The answer is: dreams!"

The ArLiFs stared at her and blinked.

Claire added to herself, "Not ready for that one yet." She laughed. "Oh well."

The ArLiFs laughed but looked around as if trying to understand what was funny.

My granddaughter. My Claire. My best one yet.

Saro summoned Claire's laugh, which filled the Amphitheater. Sister Mary was a loss, yes. But the game was not over.

There was one piece Chaos should have taken off the board, one that would have dealt irrecoverable damage, one that would have ended the game and guaranteed freedom for the Terror. But he didn't. He missed her.

The piece Chaos should have taken out was Claire.

Entr'acte V:
The Diaries of Oliver Daas

Resurrection

Boston
April to July 1995

April 13, 1995

Pythia Institute

IN THE WORDS OF Lucía Santamaría, that keynote was a shit show.

DEATH DURING KEYNOTE: PUBLIC PANIC SPURS UEA TO DELAY REMAINDER OF SCIENCE CONFERENCE

Apr 8, 1995

BOSTON (AP)—The remainder of the inaugural United Earth Alliance international science conference has been delayed due to the "dramatic" death of a woman in attendance. Dr. William Ahmadi's keynote address revealing the schematics of the much-awaited Constellation Labs in the South Pacific was interrupted by a nun-in-distress. One bystander commented, "It looked like she had some kind of tropical disease or something. Security had to quarantine some of us. It was awful—"

All the press about the conference has been like this: focused on the death of the nun instead of the science advances. It's nearly threatening another Collapse. Was it murder? If so, who did it? Was it an assassin? Why? Everyone was looking at the Apostles and Providence, but they said, "Not us."

Worse yet, the nun was known to Lucía. A caretaker from the orphanage. She had come all this way to see her. Lucía is bereft and angry. She senses someone is to blame, but she won't say who. If she thought it was either Dennis Beggan's group or Providence, she would have said, but she's tightlipped.

She leaves tomorrow to take the nun's ashes to Ireland. It was her wish, Lucía told me. "It's something I have to do," she said. I know better than to ask for details. By the time she returns, I'll be in San Francisco. The staff to support her here in Boston is in place. I am to meet Ahmadi at Pythia's new facility near Fisherman's Wharf. (I was pleased at how easily he agreed to our partnership, though now that I think about it, our working together might have been dictated from on high. I sense his ego will require massaging. Nothing I can't handle.) Lucía and I have already said our goodbyes. I'll even miss her dissertation defense in May. But she will be flying out to San Francisco when we have all the new equipment moved in. It won't be the same. Nevertheless, I meant what I said: the singularity is the priority.

Me, I saw none of the conference panic. I was in the restroom revisiting my breakfast due to terrible stage fright. I did, however, see my daughter.

The gentleman's room was a lonely place during the Constellation presentation. Just me and the sounds of my vomiting.

Vanessa Daas, now known as Nessa Decker, walked in just as I was putting myself together to head toward our presentation stage.

It was just her. No security. No Howard.

Her hair was slicked back, so unlike her. Her suit pressed. Her shoes immaculate. She had gained new life from something. Power? Control? She fed on it. It made her glow.

"Hello—" I started, but she held up a hand.

"About this San Francisco project," she said to me. No introduction, just right to the point. And how did she know to find me here?

"It's Lucía you want," I said. "She's overseeing the new budget—"

"No," she said. "It's you." The way she said it sounded as if she had bad news to break, but she went in a different direction. "Dad, I'm proud of you."

After the word "proud" stopped ringing in my ears, I asked, "Why?"

"You joined the human race. You made a significant sacrifice."

I said, "You mean giving up control of my work?"

She nodded. "And your rigid ethics. It's the right thing to do."

I had nothing to say about that. I wasn't so certain. What I did say was, "It must have been hell being my daughter. But I do hope one day you will see it was all worth it."

"I will always choose a better father over the singularity. It could have been someone else who pursued that."

I said, "That's selfish of you."

"I know. Not what Nani Lily taught us. How is she?"

"Good days and bad," I reported from my sister Iris's most recent call. "Mostly bad now. A matter of time."

Nessa pressed her lips together. "Interesting. Of the two of you, she came away with no trauma from that sad event."

I craned my neck at her. "What are you talking about?"

"I just mean—and I know you never talk about it—but there are some things I know. Things Mom told me. That you are a traumatized man, and Nani Lily was there, too."

I said, "No, sweetheart. Nani Lily was not there when the Chapman girl drowned."

It was Nessa's turn to strain for my meaning. "Dad. I don't mean that."

Confusion. "You don't mean—?"

"I don't mean the attic. Not the drowning. I know Nani wasn't there for that. I mean the other thing. The *much* older thing. In India—"

I cut her off. "I know which one you're talking about." Bile rose in my throat. My jawline warmed. I wanted to throw up again.

Nessa backed away. "I see I've upset you."

"No—" But it was out of my control. I was shaking. *Please no. Please. Not now.*

"Yes. I have," she said.

"It's just stage fright. I'll just duck back into this stall." I closed my eyes. The train barged into my mind, white-robed passengers clinging to roof and falling out windows. The soldiers boarding. My mother, "Don't look, Ollie."

A sweaty handprint on the stall door. "I'll be fine. Why don't I call you tomorrow to check in?"

"I'm sorry, Dad."

"I just need a moment. It will pass." Bodies along the tracks. Blood spattered on white robes. And my grandmother Nourin. *She's on board. She's...*

"Before I go—" She assessed my ability to hear something else. I must have winced. "I'll be quick. We found a new partner for you in San Francisco."

"Ahmadi is not a programmer."

"Yeah. We know Ahmadi is a neurosurgeon. Are you sure you're okay?"

"You want to recommend a programmer for the new Hold? That is outside of your job description, isn't it?"

Nessa shook her head. "I'm afraid it's a condition. We have already hired her. Sonja Blažić. But she's changing her last name to Black with her American citizenship, which we are processing on a fast track. She's an ethnic Serbian from Bosnia. Really helped the UEA with the Balkan invasion, so she's got high-security clearance. You'll like her." Nessa raised her brows and shook her head. "Even more messed up than Lucía. You two should be a match made in heaven."

I laughed weakly. "Another lunatic foisted upon me by outside forces. If her skills are not—"

Nessa interrupted. "Her skills are—quite something. You'll see." After an awkward moment, she said, "If there's nothing else I can do—"

I waved her off. "I will call."

"All right. Call. Tomorrow, okay? My house. Not work. You have the number."

I do. I have it on speed dial.

My Vanessa.

July 20, 1995

Cambridgeport Yellow House

THE FACELESS GIRL NO longer haunts my dreams. Now, it is Nourin. I know her name, but I have forgotten her face. She was my grandmother who died in India in August 1947.

The British Partition. Such a cold phrase to denote the mass rioting, migration, and killing that followed the redrawing of political borders in India. The British Raj split our nation into districts meant to, as they claimed, preserve the identities of Muslim, Hindu, and Sikh peoples. The British did not care about everyone living in the wrong district who was suddenly out of a home. The result was hysteria and chaos. Fifteen million displaced, more than a million killed. Trains full-to-bursting, carrying the suddenly displaced into parts of India they may have never seen before. My grandmother was one of them.

Just as our blended neighborhood in Delhi was, ours was a family of mixed marriages living in harmony for centuries. My grandfather was Hindu. My grandmother, Nourin, Muslim. My father was raised to respect both religions. My mother was a British Quaker, an aid worker. That August, our family was shocked at the violence our neighborhood experienced. Formerly peaceful people panicked that their way of life might be destroyed if blood did not run in the streets. It made no sense. My grandmother was threatened with harm and warned to leave. For her safety, she had to go away. A train ride to Punjab, it was decided, where her relatives would house her. Where she would be safe until the madness died down. Then she could return to us.

The station in Delhi was a madhouse. Screaming people, bereft families, cries of agony at separation. My mother and I saw Nourin off. My mother and I could not approach the station. Protected as we were with our white skin, we still heard the threats on the streets. "Quit India!" they yelled at my mother. But nothing could rankle her. "Let us go to the hilltop," she said to me. "We will wave at Nani's train from there."

A clearing on a hill. We could see the train glide out of the station toward the north. The white-robed passengers on the roof. Overflow. People hanging out the windows. Desperation to get out had filled every space in every carriage. The train cars were riding low on the tracks under such weight.

The turbaned Sikh Jathas came on foot, around the refugee camp that framed the tracks. The Jathas' swords were unsheathed. Some carried clubs. They stopped the train. They boarded.

"Don't look, Ollie!"

I turned away. I only *heard*.

What made my mother stay, holding me close to her and shielding my eyes? To witness? Perhaps. She was helpless, but she witnessed. It was a slaughter of innocents. Blood ran from the train. And when the rooftops of carriages were clear of people and the windows free from living bodies clamoring for escape, the train rolled north. That was the command: to send the train to Punjab with carriages packed with the Muslim dead. It was terrorism. It was genocide.

My mother and I left India by boat soon after. My father joined later.

But that was long ago.

Here is a space in which I can breathe.

No, Vanessa. You are wrong. This has not been about India. This has been about *all* my clinging dead.

Years ago, when Lucía insisted on taking over the design for Claire, the first ArLiF—I knew I was putting a face on the dead ones who had lost their souls in their abrupt departures. They no longer lived concretely in my memories. Their faces were gone.

Perhaps Ahmadi could have found them in my brain with his electrical prodder, deep in those cerebral folds. Perhaps those memories have been alive in there this whole time.

It was Lucía who insisted on completing Claire's image with the determination that the ArLiF girl be *finished*, that her face be *concrete*.

But when Lucía submitted drafts of Claire's design to me, didn't I tell her to elongate her face a little bit more? Didn't I ask Lucía to darken Claire's hair? To place a slight cowlick at her temple? To shorten her stature so that she would stand slightly below the height of the lowest branch of the tree in her side yard?

Wasn't it I who requested that Lucía instill the irksome habit of Claire chewing on the ends of her hair—like she might gnaw on the dress of her doll like the Chapman girl did, the edge of her collar like my little Vanessa did, the ends of her hijab like my Nana Nourin did?

Where did the name Claire come from? Lucía and I each had a hand in naming so many things in Pythia. Like gods we were, naming our creations.

ArLiFs. The Hold. Pythia. Keyhole Island.

Was it me, or was it Lucía who named Claire?

In my mind, it is all one.

Claire is a haunting from the deepest recesses of my mind. She is the faceless girl. She is Nourin. She is Vanessa Decker Daas. She is even Lucía.

She is the best of us.

And now I must let her go.

Encore

Planet Earth

1992-1995

Do not panic—
Focus.

First, see...
Pull yourself together!

See the island: mountains of calcified sea skeletons latching onto an underwater volcanic peak then latching upon each other, layer upon layer, eon after eon, until the cadaverous mass rises from the ocean.

This scene is a million years in the making—

Stop.

I am weak, incapable of retaliation. I have looked at these stories, searching them for clues. I tug at time like pulling threads. All my players on the board. Lined up like soldiers. A brilliant line of defense. Minus one.

Chaos said to me, "Do you see my player on the board?"

That player is orbiting closer to my soldiers now—readying to begin a game that could rip the fabric of the cosmos apart.

Until I am ready to rejoin the game, I will watch over my players.

Now, I summon my leads:

Tony.

His Pythia internship in Boston places him in the realm of the ArLiFs at last. He has earned a place of tenuous trust with Lucía. Yet, the fissure in his psyche begins to reflect in the Keyhole Hold's graphics. A dangerous gambit on my part. Sacrifice will be necessary. But I expect the compensation will be worth the risk.

Ashanti.

She has taken a call from her brother, Adom, on her high-school graduation. She refused again to take part in the church in Accra, to work under his command. But his connections inside Providence have been watching her. Those connections told him of Ashanti's fungus experiments at school, proceeding under the orders of the nun. "Where did you get that?" Adom had demanded. Ashanti will never tell. "I need it," he tells her. She disagrees. "For a new pantheon of prophets," he says to her. She is quiet. And now a hunger for power grows in her. I am counting on her to obey it, and she does. "No," she tells him. "I will not return to the church." Adom is livid. He promises to ruin her. "You will never work for Providence!" Ashanti promises him, "I have no intention of working for Providence. I intend to lead it." My new queen.

Lucía.

My child is furious with me. Chaos planned that rather well. Perhaps Lucía's anger will work to my advantage, but right now she has the potential to unsettle the whole game. As she stands at the edge of the bog with Mary's ashes, Lucía has a notion to check the cottage outside the village on her return trip. She saw it while driving in. It looked like a cottage you have to fight your way into. She knows that when she looks up in the rafters, she will find an ace to place inside humanity's sleeve. Perhaps that will also work to my advantage.

There are others, all heading to their places on the board. Dr. Rai and Dr. Mahuta into the Constellation System labs. Dr. Ahmadi and Dr. Daas in San Francisco building the second Hold. Those two do not know it, but they are directing a rehearsal of my new plan. They are constructing a safe playground to test future moves. Away from Claire.

Dr. Daas mourns his daily contact with Lucía. To compensate, he has taken the new one under his wing. A young woman from the Balkans. She has blonde hair, black roots. She is fond of a fur jacket that Tony thought tacky when they ran into each other at the conference. She draws the creatures and sketches our language in her notebooks.

Stop.

Go back.

She draws the creatures and sketches our language in her notebooks.

NO.

Nononooooonoooooooo.

How is this possible?

I do not know this one. I—

She is from the Balkans.

Oh no. Impossible.

She should not be alive.

Those experiments had gone *wrong*. Those human children were *unsound*. Genetically *unstable*.

I thought I killed all those children.

Where did she come from?

Not possible not possible not possible—

Breathe.

Focus.

She must be stopped.

I pull into myself, concentrating on healing. I am so weak. And he will return.

What guise will Chaos take this time?

Chaos himself is the star of this show. He will be certain of it.

It all started with an exchange.

See him now?

Sauntering through the sand, tropical flower tucked behind the ear, he wears a halter of eye-aching fuchsia, and a sarong knotted at the waist. His hips wiggle as he glides into the fury. His magenta-painted lips slide into a grin. Lazily, he drags a piece of driftwood behind him, slicing cosmic designs, wormhole paths, and constellation maps into the sand. A wave pulls the illustrations into the ocean. He speaks with the breathy whisper of a silver-screen starlet. "Mr. Manny! Mr. Martini! Yoo-hoo!"

Startled, the raging man releases the fax streamer. The wild pig catches it and devours it.

The magenta man hoots and claps. "Good show! *Good* show! Goodie, goodie."

An ember in the soul of Manny di Martini ignites. He is onstage. His rage dissolves.

Another wave of magenta-polished press-on nails. "*Mālō e lelei*, Mr. Manny! Follow me!"

Streaks of rust cake the shack's wavy roof. Faded paint on weather-beaten wood promises, *Definitely the* Best *Bar in Tonga!* A neon martini glass tips a green olive toward the open doors, warm with the glow of a television inside. Faintly, Manny hears his own voice from a long-ago broadcast of *Boo-Yah!* The television audience applauds.

The door slams. Bottles gleam on polished shelves. The television shouts, "One, two, three, Boo-Yah!"

"Gin and tonic, make it a motherfucking double."

The magenta man leans on the bar. It is made of the alabaster bones from an unknown creature. "Oh, I can offer you something better than *that*."

"What in Fat Christ's name is better than a gin and tonic?" Manny di Martini asks.

Magenta man exhales a stream of cosmic dust. "Reverence."

"I have that," Manny says.

"No. You have *celebrity*. I offer more."

"What's better than celebrity?"

Magenta man taps a paper coaster on the bar top. Fuchsia nails flip the cardboard on its edge, then tap again. On it, in blue ink, these numbers: *-22.21380563874615, -175.58487044492077*

"Are those—?" Manny asks.

"Yes," the magenta man says. "That's the answer to your second question. The answer to your first is: worship. I am offering you *worship*. Veneration. Everlasting praise."

"Godhood?"

The magenta man clicked his tongue. "Let's not get carried away."

"Worship, huh?" Manny licks his chapped lips. "What do I have to do?"

The magenta man's face spreads into a smile. His eyes turn as black as outer space. "There's something of yours I want."

"What the fuck would that be?"

"Just a trifle. Just the mask you wear."

"My what?"

"Oh, Manny." The magenta man pawed at the air between them like a kitten. "You'll never miss it. I *promise*."

San Francisco

Three Years and Four Months Since Discovery

BLOCKS FROM THE WHARF, where broad pavement tiles framed a street lined with twisted trees and brick warehouses, a man dragged a wooden crate.

His skin screamed from a bad sunburn. Stringy dyed hair left oily streaks on his faded floral shirt. Gold chains dangled from the ridge of his emaciated collar bone. His sunglasses reflected and winked at passing tourists lugging bags emblazoned with *Ghirardelli's* and *Fisherman's Wharf*.

He smacked the crate onto the pavement tiles. He mounted it with sunburned feet. He shouted, "Do you struggle with the pains of the new world? Do you long for peace?"

Tourists lowered their gaze and broke wide to avoid him. One mumbled, "Not another one."

He continued, "Do you bash yourself against the harshness of our reality? Do you grow weary of the pain, the grief, and the suffering?"

One from the throngs of passersby stopped in his tracks. "Hey..."

The sunburned man shouted, "Do you fail yourself, your loved ones, your family, your friends in that quest for faith in the almighty cosmos?"

Another tourist stopped. "Oh my god."

The man on the crate yelled, "This is how our faith saves us! This is how we who rely on the holy cosmos strive for peace over fear—"

More stopped. More muttered. "It can't be—"

The man scooped them in with broad arm strokes. "Gather 'round, my flock! And ye shall be comforted by the everlasting power of the Sleeping One—"

A passerby shrieked. Cameras came out. Flashes. Bags dropped. A passing car slammed into the rear of another.

"—the faith that the One Who Dreams brings us a life beyond pain and anxiety! Mark my words: science fails to explain the complexities of the world! Only faith shall guide us!"

One in the crowd spoke louder than the rest. "Are you—?"

As the man lowered his aviator sunglasses, long fingernails clicked against the frame. The breeze from San Francisco Bay tousled his chest hair. Gold medallions shimmered.

The crowd pushed closer. "It's impossible—"

The man cackled with a harsh rasp. Galaxies swirled in his black eyes. Jewel-colored veins shot through his irises.

He soaked in their attention for a moment longer before he licked his cracked lips.

And he said to them, "Boo-yah!"

Acknowledgments

A book about first contact showcasing our world's languages, cultures, cities, and people might require a travel budget of thousands. We did not have that. Instead, we traveled via the internet. As Dr. Daas says, life is not bound to the physical world. It was only appropriate for us to find our imaginary world in our own computers.

Good citizens of Reddit taught us how our characters would insult, curse, and use slang in German, Twi, Tongan, Irish, Scottish, Brazilian Portuguese, the Spanish of Mexico, and the Shelta language of the Irish Travellers. Travel vloggers told us about the sights, sounds, smells, and food of Mexico City, Accra, and Nuku'alofa. Panoramic, interactive street maps allowed us to visit the beach wall near the Jamestown Lighthouse in Accra where Ashanti Oko met Chaos. Similarly, we roamed the Zócalo where Sister Mary and Lucía marveled at the cathedral. We paced the sandbar at the Nuku'alofa wharf as Manny did. We hiked around Tony's fazenda outside Campinas, sticking our heads into outbuildings and touring the casa grande. We listened to children sing at Lucía's Catholic orphanage in Veracruz. We used World War II maps to locate suitable submarine wrecks on which to base the USS *Polaris*. We listened to testimony from survivors of the Indian Partition of 1947 to create Nourin's tragic train ride. We watched videos on Earth's evolution, the technological singularity, artificial life goals, the pervasive system of fungi that comprises the earth, the *fakaleitīs* of Tonga, the hidden Aztec temples underneath Mexico City, and more. Errors and misjudgments are ours; all glory goes to the wondrous world wide web.

The real work of singularity advocate Ray Kurzweil informed Oliver Daas's achievements and enthusiasm. Insurrectionist Denmark Vesey inspired the story of Reverend Lazarus Bethlehem Grieves. Radiation symptoms of the *Rosie* and WINnews crew members were guided by Dr. Robert Peter Gale's pragmatic depictions of the Chernobyl and Fukushima nuclear reactor accidents. The futuristic plans for the Constellation Lab, as well as Lucía Santamaría's Energy Islands, are amalgamations of real designs by Fabien Cousteau, Phil Pauley, Jelena Pucarevic, Milica Pihler-Mirjanic, Shimizu Corporation, and Zigloo. Robert Kurson's *Shadow Divers* inspired Manny's deep-sea diving hijinks and his obsession with the right "numbers." Robert D. Ballard's *Into the Deep* helped us determine exactly where in the ocean our Sleeping One might reside—deep enough to evade detection, but not so deep that humans in 1992 couldn't reach it—as well as offering a vision of the *Yuna II*, seen in the real life ANGUS and *Argo* remote-operated vehicles from Ballard's dives. Dream scientists Rahul Jandial, Tomoyasu Horikawa, and Yukiyasu Kamitani formed the basis of Dr. William Ahmadi's neurology and dream work. Jandial's book *This Is Why You Dream* was indispensable in explaining what we needed to know to get Ahmadi on the fast track to the world's most dangerous science experiment. Sir Douglas Mawson's *The Home of the Blizzard* gave us some hints as to how Sir Henley Goode's Antarctic expedition might go wrong. *Fall: The Mysterious Life and Death of Robert Maxwell, Britain's Most Notorious Media Baron* by John Preston gave us insight into the psychology of a media mogul with a traumatic past. From the work of these brilliant humans, we leapt into the fantastical.

Our gratitude goes to our persistent beta readers Bob Belcher, Bella King, Tyler Petersen, Jonathan Reeder, and Mary Rosser. They waded through multiple early drafts of harebrained ideas and encouraged us to make them better. Andrew Mattocks offered early enthusiasm and a keen-eye to copy-edits, as did Slay Mansour. Janny Wurts mentored us into the professional mindset; her tricks of the trade, advice, and support were worth almost as much as a graduate degree in creative writing. The kind and patient Don Maitz spoke to us at length about his experience as a deep-sea diver. Authors Jacquelyn Hagen, Michael R. Miller, Ryan Cahill, Christopher Ruocchio, and Philip Chase, all paragons of generosity, talked to us about resources and lessons in publishing. Kendyll Drilling offered professional guidance and a bit of therapy. Adam Fyda conjured an original cover that made our hearts soar. Amanda McQuade's branding guidance made us look sleeker than we had any right to. Lila Rosser made us look real purdy. Johnathan McClain, Kevin M. Connolly, and Brian Bell at *BellTube* advised us on how to bring this story to people's ears. Amy Stowe kindly advised us on legal matters. Austin and Richard at *2 to Ramble* offered sound advice and support, for which we are eternally grateful.

Our developmental editor, Erin Stalcup, approached our manuscript with curiosity, precision, and elegance. She shaped this book from a messy explosion of disparate stories into a flaming arrow from inciting incident to "Boo-Yah!"—and she did it with humor, grace, and warmth.

Our copy editor, Shawna McAllister, conducted a massive, zero-hour copy-edit, buffing the manuscript to a high gloss, allowing us to get away with absolutely nothing, reenacting lifting papers from tables with sandwich baggies over her hands, and arguing about hyphen-placement. (That last one's for you, Shawna.)

The BookTube community on YouTube, especially subscribers of our channel and members of our Discord server, were our most vocal cheerleaders during the publication process. Our love for them knows no bounds.

Lastly, we thank HP Lovecraft for the Cthulhu mythos and August Derleth for the cosmic war. We stand on the shoulders of giants.

About the Authors

Photo by Lila Rosser

J.A.J. Minton is the pen name for Jakob, Amy, and John Minton, a family living in North Carolina. Together, they produce and host the YouTube channel, *Talking Story: A Fantastical Fiction Channel*. Between them, they have lived nine lives in theatre, comic book retail, indie filmmaking, academia, undercover shopping, dog kennel cleaning, advertising copywriting, old-school video store management, and hot dog delivery for Harlan Ellison. This is their first book.

www.ingramcontent.com/pod-product-compliance
Lightning Source LLC
Chambersburg PA
CBHW020004120726
47903CB00004B/1127